A BOAT
IN OUR
BAGGAGE

A BOAT IN OUR BAGGAGE

Around the World with a Kayak

Maria Coffey

Photographs by
Dag Goering

For Bee and Justina

An *Abacus* Book

First published in Great Britain in 1994 by Little, Brown
This edition published by Abacus in 1995

Copyright © 1994 by Maria Coffey

The moral right of the author has been asserted.

A CIP catalogue for this book
is available from the British Library

ISBN 0 349 10631 2

Typeset by M Rules
Printed in England by Clays Ltd, St Ives plc.

Abacus
A division of
Little, Brown and Company (UK)
Brettenham House
Lancaster Place
London WC2E 7EN

Contents

Acknowledgements

Our venture was greatly helped by the companies who so generously sponsored us, and we wish to thank:

Feathercraft Products Ltd. for the boat in our baggage; Qantas Airlines for transporting the baggage free of charge; Dermtek Pharmaceuticals for the Ombrelle sun lotion and the unexpected financial gift; The New Delhi Maurya Sheraton Hotel for its supreme comfort and its unsurpassable chocolate mousse; Lisle Kelco Ltd. for the tough cases which not only protected Dag's cameras but also served as chopping boards and seats; Cascade Designs Inc. for the waterproof Great Barrier bags; Mustang Manufacturing for the Meta Inflatable Collars; Tilley Endurables Inc. for the hats and clothes; Berghaus for the rucksacks and sweaters; ACR Electronics Inc. for the emergency locator unit and Firefly strobes which thankfully we never had to use; Moss Tents for our Deltoid tent; Teva and Nike Inc. for our footwear; Powerfood Inc, for the delicious Powerbars; Georgia Bay Kayak Ltd for the sea anchor; Parlour Products Plc. for the Mosquito Milk; Dr Stan Eng, Ciba Vision and Alcon Canada Inc. for my contact lenses and solutions; Geodicke und Co for the Ewa Marine chart covers which kept our maps dry.

Just as it has been impossible for me to record in one book all we experienced during our journey, so I am unable to list everyone who helped us and offered us hospitality along the way. Many of these people are mentioned in the text; in the chapters on Malawi, I have changed most of their names. Our heartfelt thanks go to them all – they left us with a renewed faith in the essential goodness of mankind.

We especially wish to thank Jurgen Goering for looking after our affairs in Canada, Bapi Sarkar for his songs, laughter and enthusiasm, and Lord and Lady Wilson, Maria Osmon, Shona Adhikari, Olaf Fiegel, Sabine Zuschrott and my family for their warm welcomes and the much appreciated homes away from home they provided.

For their practical help and advice we are grateful to: The South Pacific Peoples Foundation of Canada, the members of CUSO we met on Saltspring Island, Clark Stede and Michelle Poncini, Gord Hartman, Tony Gibb and Connie McCann, John Dowd, Avinash Koli, Colonel Kumar, Sudhi Sahi, Tejbir and Mala Singh, Tarana Maya Das, Mr J D Gupta, Reg Noble, Cindy Pilskaln, Sharon and Dennis Tweddle.

For their part in the creation of this book, I am indebted to my agent, Vivienne Schuster, Hilary Foakes of Little, Brown and Company and my computer guardian angel, Liz Hammond – Kaarremaa.

Most of all, my love and thanks to Dag, for having the idea in the first place, and for his indefatigable sense of humour that kept me laughing all the way around the world.

A BOAT
IN OUR
BAGGAGE

Route by air
★ Kayaking destinations

Fiji
Solomon Islands
Hong Kong
Australia
India, River Ganges
Afric, Lake Malawi
Europe, River Danube
Ireland, Beara Peninsula
Canada, Protection Island

1

A Daunting Prospect

Fine red desert dust streamed through holes in the floor of the taxi. Every warning light was on, and where once had been seat-belt mountings were two large stereo speakers blasting out Mexican pop music. The driver's head bobbed about in time with the songs, and as he took a corner on two wheels, a statuette of the Virgin Mary hanging from the rear-view mirror swung crazily from side to side.

Next to me on the back seat, Dag was staring out of the window with a glazed expression on his face, as if he wasn't seeing the scrub desert landscape flying by. I, however, was gripped with ter-ror. When the Virgin Mary started to pirouette, I could stand no more. 'Slow down!' I yelled at the driver, who obediently reached for a knob on the radio, dropping the music level enough for us to hear the squealing of the tyres.

'OK, Señora, OK, I turn it down,' he said, grinning devilishly at me in the mirror. 'You no like Mexican songs?'

Sitting back, I resigned myself to my fate. It was at least six more miles to Loreto, from where we were to catch a plane that afternoon.

'I hated packing up the boat,' sighed Dag.

He was referring to the folding kayak which we had just taken apart and stuffed into the boot of the taxi. It was an ingenious, seaworthy craft, big enough for us, our camping gear and a good supply of food and water. We had spent the last three weeks pad-dling it on Mexico's Sea of Cortez, where we'd faced stiff winds and steep seas, but nothing as alarming as this taxi ride.

'I felt as if I was just getting into my stride,' he said. 'I could have carried on for months.'

We were now on a long, straight and narrow stretch of road. On one side of us was a sheer sandstone cliff, on the other a rutted and cactus-covered plain. Ahead, through a cloud of dust, a local bus was approaching. As it drew nearer, I realized we were on a collision course. Both drivers were hunched over their steering wheels, with no obvious intention of giving way, or even slowing down. A game of chicken was being enacted, with us and a full contingent of bus passengers its hapless victims.

'I've just had an idea!' cried Dag.

The bus was now so close that I could see the alarmed expressions of its passengers.

'Let's quit work for a year,' he continued, apparently oblivious to our imminent deaths, 'and go kayaking all over the world!'

Moments before impact, the two drivers swung their respective steering wheels – luckily in opposite directions. We scraped along the side of the cliff while the bus careered across ruts and between cactus trees before regaining the road. The sudden movement threw me heavily against Dag, who took this to be a sign of agreement and gleefully hugged me. 'We'll start planning as soon as we get home!' he announced.

An exact definition of 'home' was tricky for us, as our roots were widely spread. For the last few years, its nearest approximation had been the west coast of Canada. We met there in 1986, when I was over from England to work as an exchange teacher and Dag had come from Germany to do his PhD research. At the end of that year, I should have been back in Manchester, and Dag in Munich. Instead, we were living together on tiny Protection Island, a mile and a half from the far bigger Vancouver Island. I was writing a book, and Dag was trying to boost his dwindling research fund by working part-time in a friend's fibreglass shop. It was there that Dag got one of his ideas: to build two kayaks so that we could cheaply commute between Protection Island and Nanaimo, the nearest town. I wasn't exactly enthusiastic about this plan. I barely knew what a kayak looked like, but had vague memories from school geography lessons of fur-wrapped Eskimos in flimsy seal-skin boats. The prospect of paddling my groceries home wasn't an

appealing one, and I railed against it until the day Dag introduced
me to the new kayaks. They bore no resemblance to the ones I'd
seen in school geography books. They were 14ft long, pointed at
either end and fat in the middle. Each had a cockpit fitted with a
comfortable bucket seat and foot pedals to work the rudder.
Awkwardly, I clambered into mine and tentatively paddled along
Protection Island's rocky shoreline. A great blue heron hunkered
on the beach, undisturbed by my quiet progress, and a curious
seal surfaced so close to me that I could almost touch its nose. As
I paddled away from the shelter of the shore, a wave rushed
towards me, its top curling into a white crest. I stiffened, but the
wave passed beneath the kayak and I was lifted and set down again
like a piece of driftwood. Eagerly I paddled on, enjoying the wind
on my face, the rhythmic movement, the sense of being part of the
ocean. I didn't know it then, but I was hooked.

From the beginning, kayaking for us was more a means of
transportation than a sport. Initially it was how we got ourselves
and our shopping between town and home, then it became a
way of exploring the world around us. We went off for weeks on
end, meandering up and down the coastline of British Columbia.
Our boats drew only a few inches of water, and we were therefore
able to access beaches and bays unsuitable for most other craft.
We could carry enough gear, food and water to be totally self-
sufficient. As it was impossible for us to do more than a few knots
an hour, we had lots of time to see clouds form and dissolve, to
watch the patterns made when wind meets water, to observe animals and birds. The more we paddled, the further we wanted to
go. When we got married, my parents wrote us out a hefty cheque
and told us to use it for something that would make us happy. We
bought a double folding kayak, and headed down to Mexico . . .

During that dreadful taxi ride, the idea of a year-long, world wide
kayak trip had seemed quite feasible. Back in our cosy home,
however, it was a daunting prospect. Night after night, Dag pored
over the atlas, muttering ominous place names. 'The Zaire
River . . . The Andaman Islands . . . Mongolia . . .'

He wanted, he told me, to go to some remote corners of the
world, places that weren't easy to reach. The more I thought
about the logistics of this proposed trip, the more disquieting
they became.

'What if one of us gets sick?' I nervously enquired, imagining tropical terrors like worms crawling across my eyeballs and larvae burrowing into my skin. 'What about wild animals?' I continued. 'And bandits and rip tides and storms?'

But Dag was born with a sunny optimism which his thirty-six years have left untainted. 'Remember that taxi ride in Mexico?' he asked. 'And how dangerous it was?'

I certainly did.

'We'll avoid taxis!' he pronounced, and returned to the atlas.

There was, I had to admit, a growing sense of inevitability about this venture. During the previous four years we had established careers, bought land on Protection Island, built a house and planted a garden. The next logical step, so the people around us intimated, was to start a family and prepare for a comfortable, secure middle age. But our restless spirits weren't having any of this. They began tugging at our roots, whispering to us to glance up from our safe little world and out to the much bigger and uncertain one beyond. Dag was easily convinced, but I equivocated. The coward in me argued with the restless spirit, and came up with all sorts of excuses for staying put. 'That house you've built isn't finished,' the coward insisted. 'Look, it hasn't even got any drain pipes from the gutters yet.'

'Drain pipes!' snorted Dag, when I relayed this to him one night. 'Who cares about *drain pipes?*'

His roots were already out of the ground and trailing along behind him. I had the options of yanking mine up as well, or staying at home and worrying about drain pipes. In the end, it wasn't a difficult decision.

Dag arranged for a year's leave of absence from his college job, and I found myself discussing 'our trip', and the book I'd write about it, with everyone I met. Unconsciously, I was using a ploy, a type of self-daring, that I had developed long ago: talking so freely about my ambitions that eventually I felt duty-bound to turn them into reality. At the New Year's Eve party we threw to herald 1991, at least half of our guests asked us when we were leaving on 'our trip'. When the first hangovers of the year had subsided, we began serious planning.

For months we discussed, researched and argued over the itinerary, then made our final decisions in a capricious fashion. We read up on the South Pacific and found tourist information on everywhere except the Solomon Islands, so decided that was the place for us. Inspired by Eric Newby's *Slowly Down The Ganges*, I suggested we kayak along India's holiest river. At a conference, Dag met an Englishman who worked in Malawi and who fired him with tales of the country's marvellous lake. Wanting to visit friends and family in Europe, we slotted a trip along the River Danube into the grand plan, and to round things off we decided on a final jaunt in Alaska. We sat back and congratulated each other for a job well done. Then the nasty subject of money cropped up.

One evening in February 1991, we realized that our finances and the estimated cost of our trip were two sides of an unbalanced equation. As well as travel and living expenses, we were going to need a new boat and equipment of high enough quality to sustain months of continuous hard wear in a variety of climates and conditions. Quite simply, we didn't have enough money for everything. As this unpleasant fact sank in, we sat in glum silence. I don't know what Dag's thoughts were, but I was casting my mind back to my life in England, which for ten years had been linked through friendships and romance to the British mountaineering scene. I'd witnessed the preparations for numerous climbing expeditions to the Himalayas, I'd listened to phone calls to arrange last-minute monetary and product sponsorship, and I'd seen mounds of new, donated gear grow on living-room floors. 'Let's go for sponsorship,' I suggested to Dag.

He gave me a blank look. 'Why would anyone sponsor us?'

'Why wouldn't they? How many people have spent a year kayaking in different parts of the world? We'll call ourselves an expedition . . .' My voice trailed off as I realized that, yet again, I was dragging out the old self-daring ploy.

'It's a brilliant idea,' he said, in an awestruck tone. 'You're in charge. You tell me what to do.'

At the time, I was teaching English as a Second Language to recent immigrants to Canada. One day, a guest speaker came to give my class a talk entitled Starting a New Business. Ann, a buxom woman in her early thirties, spent most of her allotted hour discussing different ways of raising capital. Over coffee, I told her of our impending trip and my sponsorship idea.

'Companies will be lining up to back you!' she cried. 'They'll pay for everything, they'll even give you a salary on top of expenses. Why don't you let me help you? I'd love to be involved.'

I rushed home to share the good news with Dag, who was immediately infected by my enthusiasm. The next afternoon, we met Ann in a wine bar. Between conversations on her cellular phone, she managed to convince us that we should target North America's top companies. As chance would have it, she had a list of these companies, with stockmarket reports on each, in her briefcase. First, with her help, we would put together a proposal to send to chief executive officers. 'Make it glossy and sensational,' she advised. 'Photos, maps, information about the countries you're going to and the dangers you'll face. We'll meet again on Monday. Have a first draft ready to show me.'

Her phone rang again, and the person on the line summoned her to another meeting. 'Most consultants charge at least two hundred and fifty dollars a day,' she said as she was leaving. 'But I like you guys, I'm inspired by what you're doing. I'll settle on ten per cent of whatever sponsorship you get.'

After a few more drinks, we weaved our way back to the kayaks. 'I don't know about all this,' muttered Dag, as we paddled home. 'It's not our style.'

I thought back to Britain, and how the climbers I knew there had raised money. I couldn't recall any snappy, sensational proposals. 'This is North America,' I said lamely. 'It's how things are done here.'

The proposal took weeks to prepare. I produced draft after draft to show to Ann. 'Not positive enough!' she would say.

She insisted on writing one section, which began: 'Ms Coffey and Dr Goering represent an ideal couple in that they are young, professional, athletic, attractive and have a real sense of *joie de vivre*.'

'Young?' I asked her. 'I'll be turning forty next year.'

'Keep the lid on that,' she said.

Eventually, we had the finished product. Bound in shiny, laminated plastic, it announced our 'Jungle to Ice Expedition' and had an executive overview, chapters on marketing, advertising and promotional strategies, information about our destinations, a detailed budget, and colour photographs of us looking like the 'ideal couple'.

'I don't feel comfortable about all this,' I told Dag.

'I said that weeks ago,' he replied.

Next, we began contacting companies. The first was American Express.

'I can see it now,' said Ann. 'A full-page magazine ad of you paddling through shark-infested waters with your credit cards between your teeth.'

She gave me the name and number of a top executive. Before I made the phone call, I did deep breathing for ten minutes. Then the number was busy for half an hour. Finally, I got through to the executive's secretary, who demanded to know the nature of my business.

'You need to talk to the director of usage and retention, ma'am,' she told me.

'I do?'

'I'll put you through.'

The usage and retention man was called Bill, and he was disarmingly self-effacing. 'Sounds like I run an incontinence clinic, doesn't it?' he said.

Haltingly, I explained that we were seeking sponsorship for a year-long, world wide kayaking expedition.

'Fascinating, Maria. Send me a proposal.'

The phone went dead. I dialled Ann's number. 'I talked to someone at American Express,' I told her. 'He wants to see a proposal.'

'Fantastic!' she screeched. 'I knew they'd go for it!'

'He didn't agree to anything . . .'

'Once he sees what you guys have got to offer, he'll go nuts. Now, tell me who he was and *exactly* what you said to him and what he said to you.'

She listened. She wasn't pleased.

'You've got to be more assertive than that. You need a conversation flow chart in front of you when you make these calls. You've got to push all the right buttons as soon as you get through.'

Before long, our kitchen table was awash with flow charts. By six o'clock each morning we were on the phone to CEOs all over North America. But the more adept we became at pushing buttons, the more we realized that we didn't really want corporate sponsorship. What we did want, what we'd wanted all along before we'd been infected by this profit ethic, was an unfettered, independent adventure.

One day, I was speaking to a promotions officer in New York. 'On my desk right now,' he said, 'I have a request for funding by a guy who intends to snowboard down Mount Kilimanjaro, another from someone who's going to walk across Australia and back again, and this proposal from you two crazies wanting to drag a kayak round the world. That's just this week's batch and it's only Tuesday! How did people like you manage before the multinationals came along?'

'Listen,' I told him. 'Take that proposal of ours and throw it in the paper shredder.'

He roared with laughter. 'That's the spirit. Have a great trip.'

'You want to borrow money for *what?*'

The loans officer of our bank was a small woman with huge shoulder pads, lots of costume jewellery and long red fingernails. Predictably enough, she was unimpressed by our forthcoming adventure, and her only suggestion was that we request to make a loan against our mortgage, effectively doubling it, with an interest rate that made us shudder. We retreated to a nearby café to confer.

'It's an awful lot of money,' I mused, as cups of coffee were set down in front of us.

In the long silence that ensued, we both stirred our coffee. 'We could forget the whole idea,' said Dag.

I nodded. 'That's one possibility.' There was another silence while we drank the coffee.

'Ready?' he asked.

I was. Without further discussion, we returned to the bank and arranged for a loan.

It was now April, four months before we were due to leave. We were still on the phone at six o'clock each morning, but now with the purpose of arranging product sponsorship. Most of the companies we contacted were small, specialized and eager to be involved with our venture, and we were offered more than we could accept. Several times a week we paddled into Nanaimo to collect our parcels. Clothes arrived, a tent, flashlights, energy bars, contact lens solution, sun block, life jackets, pocket knives, flares, and much more. With a strange sense of the past echoing through the present, I watched a heap of donated gear grow on our living-room floor.

The most important piece of our equipment was, of course, a kayak. We decided on a Feathercraft K2, a sophisticated boat with an aluminium frame and a nylon and synthetic rubber hull, which folds up into a bag measuring four feet by two. The Feathercraft company operates from Granville Island, a trendy section of Vancouver's waterfront. We rang the owners, Doug and Larry, and arranged to meet them to discuss the possibility of sponsorship.

Although we both hated dressing like hardy, outdoor types, commuting by kayak had forced us into it. So a trip to Vancouver always gave us the chance to happily swap our practical waterproof jackets and fibre-pile sweaters for some fashionable city clothes, and we turned up at the Feathercraft workshop looking the antithesis of a couple about to embark on a year-long kayaking expedition. Doug and Larry, who were wearing fibre-pile sweaters, regarded us with mild suspicion. I handed them copies of our new expedition proposal (honed down, rewritten and excluding the 'ideal couple' photos), my book and an article of mine just printed in the *Guardian*. They both skimmed through the newspaper article.

'You can obviously write . . .' said Doug. His voice trailed off. As he stood there, lost for words, I saw us through his eyes: a couple of neophytes wearing clothes that would curl up at the sight of salt water.

I finished his thought for him. '. . . but you're wondering if we can kayak.'

Our K2 Feathercraft was delivered to Protection Island a month before we were due to leave. While being filmed for a local television station, we assembled it for the first time. Back in their workshop, Doug and Larry had made it look easy. Now, I frantically paged through the instruction manual while Dag wrestled with aluminium tubing and plastic crossribs. Finally, we stood back and admired the finished product: a 19ft-long, bright red, brand-new kayak. The cameraman patted its hull. 'You're going a long way, baby,' he told it. Then he turned to us. 'When are you flying out?'

'We're not sure of the exact date,' I said. 'We haven't booked our tickets yet.'

The look on his face told us it was time we did.

We'd left this 'minor' detail to the last minute, thinking it

would be a simple, straightforward matter. It wasn't. The travel
agents we spoke to were all terse, overworked and infuriated by
us. 'Round the world,' they'd begin. 'No problem. Northern or
southern hemisphere?'

'Both.'

'Ah. More complicated. What are your proposed destinations?'
I'd begin to reel them off: the Solomon Islands, India, Malawi—

'That's not just around the world,' said one. 'That's up, down
and all over the place.'

Put more precisely, our route was a gigantic W which would
take us, and our boat, into five continents and across the equator
four times. Each of the travel agents claimed that working out a
price for such a complicated itinerary took hours.

'I'll do it,' said the most enterprising, 'if you promise to buy the
ticket from me.'

'How can I promise if I don't know what it will cost?'

'That's your problem,' she haughtily responded.

Impressed by such audacity, I told her to go ahead. Her price
was the best, so we booked and paid for the tickets there and
then, over the phone.

'Now this kayak you mentioned,' she said. 'How much does it
weigh?'

Her simple question heralded one of those awful moments
when you know that you're about to hear bad news.

'Because once you've flown out of North America,' she continued, 'your weight limit is usually around twenty kilograms per
person, and the excess baggage charge is one per cent of the first-
class fare, per kilo, per flight.'

It didn't take a mathematical genius to work out that this
meant an awful lot of money . . .

'It's impossible! We'll be carrying a hundred and twenty kilos!'
One of our cats fearfully peered from beneath the sofa as Dag
paced our living-room floor, loudly ranting. 'On every flight, the
excess will cost us the same as the first-class fare! Do you know
how much first-class fares are? We can't do it!'

Once again, I cast my mind back a decade. I remembered all
the times I'd said goodbye to my mountaineering boyfriend at
Heathrow Airport. He always seemed to be on good terms with
some official who would smooth out any problems concerning
the heaps of excess baggage. If he could do it, I thought, so can

I. Picking up the phone, I began contacting the airlines.

If I could chose someone for beatification, it would be Bill Duplak, the Western Canada manager of Qantas. He thought our forthcoming trip was a splendid idea. He arranged for our luggage to be transported free of charge on all our Qantas flights. This would take us as far as Hong Kong, where we would transfer to British Airways.

'I don't mean to be unprofessional,' advised Bill, 'but the Brits might be a bit sticky.'

The Brits, in a word, said no. In vain, I begged, pleaded and cajoled.

'You may wish,' said one particularly snooty woman, her plummy English tones only slightly tinged with a Toronto accent, 'to negotiate this matter with airport managers en route. But I can't imagine you'll have much success.'

With only weeks to go, our 'to do' lists were reaching mammoth proportions. We sent off parcels around the world: supplies of contact lens solutions, suntan cream, mosquito repellent, spare parts for the boat, and clothes and a sleeping bag for the colder areas. We made a will and took out life insurance. We found tenants for our house and started packing away our belongings. Dag, who trained as a vet, put together a large, comprehensive medical kit. At a tropical health clinic, we loaded up on anti-malarial pills and were given a battery of injections by a nurse who insisted we didn't need to be inoculated against cholera.

'But we're going to kayak down the Ganges,' I told her.

'In that case you'll definitely need cholera injections!' she cried.

Friends constantly invited us for dinner, and one honest soul admitted, 'I felt I had to cook for you, because I might never see you again.'

She wasn't the only one who was worried. Despite all the furious pre-planning, at this point neither of us could see beyond flying to the Solomon Islands, assembling the kayak and paddling off – into what? The bald truth was that we were heading for the tropics, of which we had no previous experience, and to a country about which we'd been able to glean precious little information. Even people who had worked in the South Pacific – and this also went for our destinations in India and Africa – were of little help. Because of our mode of travel, they said, we would be reaching areas that few outsiders ever got to. They could advise us on cultural mores and on what medicines to take, but they couldn't tell us what to expect.

Finally, eighteen months after that taxi ride in Mexico, we were as ready as we'd ever be to set off around the world with our kayak. It was the perfect excuse for a party . . .

Our friends presented us with a book entitled *Shark Attack*, and a card depicting two corpulent crocodiles lying on a beach surrounded by remnants of a canoe, paddles and life jackets. As the evening wore on, we were nudged and winked at about the stunning sex life we'd enjoy on those balmy tropical nights, and advice was offered to us on what to do if we were disturbed in the act by a croc.

'Run around in circles!'

'Poke it in the eyes!'

'Don't even consider climbing a tree,' said one friend cheerfully. 'Crocs can stand on their tails, you know.'

Of course, everyone wanted to see the boat. We assembled it watched by a crowd of people, little knowing that this was something to which we would soon become very accustomed. And then various friends asked to be taken out for a spin. Eventually, we laid the kayak on the deck of the house, and the party simply raged on around it. The last guests left around 4 am. I promptly went to bed, but Dag said he wanted to stay up to watch the dawn. At eight o'clock, I woke with a start, realizing he wasn't in bed with me. It didn't take me long to find him. He was outside, fast asleep in the back cockpit of our brand new kayak, with a blissful expression on his face and the sea breeze ruffling his hair.

It seemed like the best of omens.

2

Unexpected Luxury

The air smelled of sandalwood and exhaust fumes, and the piercing screeches and whistles of birds vied with the revving of jet engines. Porters with yellow flowers tucked behind their ears wheeled handcarts heaped with luggage across the tarmac towards Nandi Airport's tiny terminal. 'Welcome to Fiji! Nice rooms in Nandi Motel! Very cheap! I take you there!'

A squat man with a shock of frizzy hair tugged at my sleeve. 'Best taxi price! No tip!'

Fiji was as close to the Solomon Islands that our round-the-world air tickets could get us. From here we had to buy our own connecting flights, which left from Suva, half a day's drive from Nandi.

'How much to Suva?' I asked the taxi driver.

'Cheap! Best price, no tip! I help you with your baggage! Where is your baggage?'

I pointed over to where Dag was standing next to our two large red sacks. The driver picked up the end of the one containing the kayak, which weighed over 100lbs, and promptly dropped it again.

'What's inside?' he demanded.

'A boat,' Dag told him.

'Boats cost extra.'

'How much?'

'Ten dollars,' said the driver.

'Too much,' said Dag.

'How much you say?' asked the driver.

'Five dollars.'

'Hah!' snorted the driver. 'You think I am a crazy man!'

Dag relishes the cut and thrust of bargaining, but it always make me feel like a heartless profiteer. The driver obviously sensed this. 'Madam,' he pleaded, 'I have a wife and five children! They must eat!'

'I'm terribly sorry,' I remonstrated with him.

He kicked one of the bags. 'These are so heavy, they ruin my car. I take these, then I need new tyres, new suspension, new everything.'

'I'll meet you halfway,' said Dag. 'Seven dollars, or I'll find another taxi.'

'You try find one, you go!'

'Look after the bags, Maria,' said Dag, and he strode off towards a group of parked taxis.

'Come back!' the driver cried, and set off in pursuit of him. I gazed at the bulging sacks, and glumly wondered why we'd ever imagined we could drag this lot around the world. Suddenly, amid much hand-shaking and guffawing, Dag and the driver were back. Within minutes, the taxi was stuffed with our baggage and we were on our way to Suva.

We drove across the island of Vita Levu, through a landscape of sun-browned hills and lush sugar cane fields. Lines of washing hung outside shacks built of branches and corrugated iron. Men walked under the shade of brightly striped umbrellas, women carried bundles of firewood on their heads. We stopped at a road-side stall and bought green coconuts from a barefoot boy. With a huge machete, he chopped off the tops so we could drink the sweet, refreshing milk, then fashioned little spoons from the shell for us to scoop out the gelatinous flesh.

'I could live on this,' I enthused.

'You'll probably have to,' said Dag.

It took us over an hour to walk the mile from Suva's South Seas Hotel to the airline office in the centre of town. This was our first time in the tropics, and we were like a pair of three-year-olds, wide-eyed with wonder and stopping every few minutes to minutely examine new discoveries: huge purple banana pods drooping on fruit-laden stalks, trees heavy with papayas, streets littered with frangipani and hibiscus blossoms. The soil was dark red and moist, the air rich with strange scents, the vegetation lush, voluptuous and blatantly fertile. Little wonder, we decided, that the tropics have a sexy image – although we were soon to be dissuaded from any carnal pleasure by the heat and humidity of our cell-like hotel room, which we shared with a resident family of shiny brown cockroaches.

We did however, manage to eat, and had a late lunch at Jake Tulele's Drop-in Lovo Caravan. Jake had nut-brown skin, broad bare feet and a cultured British accent. Although born and raised in Fiji, he had lived in England for fourteen years, served in the Royal Air Force and studied at the South-west London School of Business. His converted caravan was garishly painted with pictures of taro leaves, parachutes and nautilus shells, and emblazoned with slogans such as 'We serve with speed for your delicate taste. To the caravan with haste!' The fried fish he served us was delicious, but the baked taro root was as cloying and unpalatable as wallpaper paste.

'I can't eat this,' I whispered to Dag, slipping the taro to the skinny cats that skulked around our feet.

'You'll probably have to live off it,' he teased.

We told Jake of our plans to kayak in the Solomon Islands.

'What a super adventure,' he said. 'I hear it's a trifle backward, though. Hardly anyone ever goes there.'

His sentiment was echoed by the airline official we met later that day.

'Few tourists go to Solomon Islands,' she told us, 'which is why the flights are so expensive.'

The price she quoted made us gulp: it was way above our budget. Despondently, we returned to the South Seas Hotel. Lounging in rattan chairs on its veranda were two young Englishmen. One sported ripped shorts and blond dreadlocks, the other had a shaved head and a ring through his nose.

'I tried to get to the Solomons last week,' commiserated the one with the nose ring. 'I applied for a job crewing on a yacht, but the rich bastards who owned it wouldn't take me on.'

Dag and I exchanged a glance. 'Where was this yacht?' we asked him.

'Lautoka Marina, close to Nandi,' he said, wiping his nose with the back of his hand. 'It's probably still there. They seemed pretty choosy about who they'd take on board.'

*

Twenty-four hours later we were in Lautoka, a rather grim sugar mill town, and on our way to the marina. Before we got there, however, a tropical rainstorm struck and within minutes the main street was awash with mud and hopping with frogs. Not wanting to turn up at the marina looking like a pair of drowned rats, we scurried for shelter.

'Come and have some tea!' called a woman from a doorway. She was resplendent in a scarlet silk sari, and her grey hair was pulled tightly back into a bun. Above her, a sign was suspended from a bamboo pole. In child-like red lettering it announced:

S.S. MUDALIER'S

WESTERN COFFIN DEALER AND REFRESHMENT BAR.

We stepped into a narrow, gloomy room with red brick walls and a creaking ceiling fan. A table and three chairs were arranged next to the door. At the back of the room, on rough wooden frames, several coffins were stacked up. Painted a matt black, with dull metal handles, they looked light and insubstantial, like stage props.

'Welcome!' cried Mrs Mudalier, her smile flashing with gold. 'I make you hot tea with bread and butter, very nice!'

While she fired up a kerosene stove, she told us she'd been born in Fiji, a descendent of indentured labourers brought from India to work in the sugar cane fields. The coffin business had been in her husband's family for years, and she'd recently branched out into refreshments.

'Do you sell many coffins?' I asked.

'Yes! Yes! People are always dying and it is good for us!' She handed us cups of sweet, milky tea and a plate of buttered white buns. While we ate, she paced up and down, fiddling with her sari and plying us with questions. Where were we from? What were our professions? Why were we in Lautoka?

'We're on our way to the marina,' Dag told her. 'We're trying to get a ride to the Solomon Islands.'

I could tell she wasn't listening. 'Do you have any unmarried brothers?' she asked.

'Dag has one,' I replied.

'Very hard to find a good husband for my daughter,' she confided. 'She is twenty-six and very short. But she is a good girl. Is your brother tall? What is his profession?'

'He builds pianos,' Dag answered, mischievously adding, 'but I'm sure he could turn his hand to coffins.'

'Very good! Very good! My husband is getting old, he needs help! Do you have a photograph of your brother?'

Realizing how serious she was, I began casting about for a tactful excuse. 'He has a girlfriend—' I began.

'I know, I know,' said Mrs Mudaliar sadly. 'In Canada all nice tall boys have girls already. They are not interested in my poor short daughter. You like more tea?'

After our fifth round of tea, the rain eased off and we continued on our way to the marina. About thirty yachts were anchored there. A tall blond man was scanning the billboard and when we stuck up our notice, 'Two cooks and their kayak seek passage to the Solomons,' he read it, looked carefully at us, but said nothing.

'So what do we do?' I asked Dag.

'Come back tomorrow, I suppose,' he answered.

The blond man cleared his throat. 'I'm Soren, skipper of *Swedish Caprice*,' he said, holding out his hand. 'We're going to the Solomons and our cook is on holiday. Can you come aboard now for an interview?'

Early next morning, the red bag containing our folded boat disappeared into one of the *Swedish Caprice*'s voluminous holds. As Soren steered us out of Lautoka Harbour, Ole and Gael, the other crew members, showed us around our new home.

It was 80ft long and had teak decks, an interior lined with highly polished mahogany, a computerized navigational system, electronically controlled sails, a fax machine, a dive compressor, a water desalinator, two fridges, two freezers, a washing machine and dryer, a VCR and a compact disc player with speakers all over the boat.

'It belongs to a Swedish businessman,' explained Gael. 'We're sailing it around the world for him. He only comes aboard once every few months.'

She opened a door on to a cabin with a double bunk. 'You'll sleep here.'

'Ooh, look, it's got an en-suite bathroom,' I enthused, gazing at the marble wash stand and its bright brass taps.

'It's called a head, Maria,' said Dag from the side of his mouth.

Ole smiled at me. 'I take it you haven't sailed much.'

'Only in a kayak,' I admitted.

'You'll find this much easier,' he said.

Up on deck, another surprise awaited us. We were cruising past tiny islets covered with palm trees and ringed with dazzling white sand. Where the encircling reefs appeared, the water changed from aquamarine to a translucent, glacial green, and appeared to be lit from beneath. Our mouths fell open at the scene. 'It's astonishing!' I cried.

'What is?' asked Soren.

'This,' I said, waving my hands to encompass the panoramic view. 'It's exactly how the South Seas are supposed to look—'

'It's a cliché!' Dag chipped in.

'—just like a tourist poster!'

Thoughtfully, Soren scratched his head. 'I've been here too long,' he said. 'It all looks normal to me.'

Soon there was no land in sight and nothing to see except for an occasional school of flying fish. The trade winds filled the sails and pushed us along at a steady 12 knots. Soren, Ole and Gael took turns on watch, and Dag and I prepared three meals a day. We adopted our usual cooking roles: I did the peeling, chopping and washing up, and he took over the creative work. A superb chef, he's able to whip up delicious meals from basic ingredients in adverse conditions, a skill honed by many kayak trips. On *Swedish Caprice*, he had a wealth of food to choose from – the freezers were stuffed with meats, fish and vegetables, the cupboard with dry and tinned foods, the fridge with fine French wines.

'Let's stick to something simple,' he said, when it was time for us to prepare the first night's dinner. Coq au vin may be simple to prepare in a kitchen on land, but in the galley of a yacht under sail it's quite another matter. Neither of us had yet developed the 'lean', a technique for staying upright when the ship is keeling over, so we staggered about, Dag trying to dismember the chicken and me attempting to slice onions. The Pacific Ocean pressed and swirled at the porthole above the stove, and soon we both began to feel a little nauseous.

'How are things going?' asked Soren as he walked past the galley, perfectly balanced.

'Fine, fine!' we chorused.

Seconds later, hit by a rogue wave, *Swedish Caprice* pitched wildly. The chicken pieces took flight, the cupboard door I'd forgotten to clip shut spewed out spice jars, sauce bottles and a bag of flour which hit Dag squarely in the back and burst open, and I was catapulted into the arms of Soren, who narrowly missed being stabbed in the neck with the sharp vegetable knife I was still clutching.

Miraculously, however, the crew seemed happy with our food and our company. Soren even intimated that as extra deckhands were always welcome, maybe we should consider staying on the boat beyond the Solomons and up to the Philippines, where the owner was due to join it. The offer was tempting, especially during the balmy evenings on deck when we sat sipping wine and listening to the creaking of the rigging, the soothing rush of water against the hull, and the stories of our fellow crew members. They had all stumbled by accident into this lifestyle. Gael had been invited by a friend to help deliver a newly built boat to its final destination.

'We spent five months sailing it from France to Mauritius,' she said. 'As soon as I got there, I was offered another crewing job. It took me two years to get back to France.' This was her second jaunt at sea. Again, she'd been away from home for two years, 'but this time I don't know when I'll return'.

Soren had trained as an architect in Sweden, and before settling down to his career he decided to do a spot of sailing. He crewed on an Atlantic crossing and, ten years later, had still not got around to designing houses. And Ole was supposed to be taking over his father's car business in Denmark, 'but I keep putting it off – I can't imagine going from this to selling cars'.

And we couldn't imagine leaving such luxury for months of rough travelling. But the folded kayak in the hold of *Swedish Caprice* kept tapping at our consciences. We pulled it out; we assembled it and lashed it to the railings on deck. I took to leaning against it while I was making notes; I fancied I could sense its disappointment in me.

After five days at sea we reached the island of Efate, in Vanuatu. Port Vila's marina was bristling with yacht masts flying Australian, New Zealand, British, French and American flags. And its thatched, open-walled clubhouse was packed with the yachts' owners – or 'yachties' as they called themselves. They emanated a carefree sense of wellbeing that bordered on smugness. They all seemed to know each other, and there was a lot of loud greeting and back-slapping going on. And as it was 'Happy Hour' they were drinking with a vengeance. Within minutes of a local band starting to belt out Western pop songs, the small dance floor was heaving, and Ole had dragged me into its midst.

'Have you tried *kava*?' he yelled, as we hopped about in time to the music.

'Once, in Fiji,' I yelled back. 'It didn't have much effect.'

Kava was a mildly narcotic drink, made from the roots of pepper shrubs. 'The stuff here is the strongest in the South Pacific,' he told me. 'They get virgin boys to chew the roots!'

One of the yachties had joined the band on the stage. 'I wanna sing "Rawhide"!' he bawled into the microphone.

The crowd whistled its approval.

'Bring me a whip!' he commanded. 'And buzzards!'

It seemed a good time to go and find some *kava*.

A taxi took Dag, Ole and me out of Port Vila and past fields of sugar cane and bananas. After a fifteen-minute drive we turned on to a dirt track and parked by a shed with a corrugated iron roof. Inside, a man stood behind a table set with a large kettle, a pile of half coconut shells and a cash box. A couple of hurricane lamps hung from the ceiling, but the few customers were slumped on benches in dark corners.

'*Kava* makes you sensitive to light and noise,' whispered Ole.

One of the customers lurched over to the table, gulped down a half shell of *kava* then staggered back to his corner. There was no conversation, only the wet sounds of hawking and spitting. No one seemed to have noticed our presence. I sat on a bench while Dag and Ole went up to the table. In the dim light, beneath the low roof and next to the small ni-Vanuatu who served them, they looked ridiculously tall, like elongated shadows. They returned with three brimming coconut shells. I looked suspiciously at mine, and took a hesitant sip. It was thick with sediment and, unlike the refreshing Fijian *kava*, it had an unpleasantly sour taste.

'What about hepatitis?' I whispered to Dag.

'You don't really think they've got virgins chewing roots in the back room, do you?' he replied, but I noticed that he hesitated before swallowing his portion. Before long, my lips and the inside of my mouth began to feel numb. Then my eyelids and legs became heavy. I decided against a refill, but my companions were soon on to their third round. When Ole went up for a fourth, he staggered slightly, and had to lean on the table while the barman poured the *kava*. Beside me, Dag had begun to hawk and spit, and he was slouched over, resting his elbows on his knees. 'I think we should go,' I whispered to him.

'This stuff's great,' he mumbled back.

Thankfully, the barman waved the kettle about to show it was empty, and I led the shuffling men to the waiting taxi.

Back at the bar things were winding up. The band had left, and the Rawhide man was playing a mouth organ for the few couples still jigging around the dance floor. The rest of our crew was nowhere in sight. To get from the dock to *Swedish Caprice* we had to walk along a length of planking ten feet above the water. Crossing it during the day was bad enough, but at night, under the influence of alcohol and *kava*, it was nerve-racking. Despite a few wobbly moments, we all made it. Someone else hadn't. Below deck, all the lights were on, and the stereo was playing full blast. A trail of puddles and wet footprints led to the door of our cabin. Inside, soaking wet clothes lay in a heap on the floor, and two crew members from another boat were curled up together on our bunk. Gael was nowhere to be found, and Soren's cabin door was firmly shut. Dag and Ole promptly passed out on sofas in the saloon, and lay snoring with their mouths wide open.

I got a bottle of wine from the fridge, poured myself a drink, and went up on deck. Just beyond the marina grounds there was an open-air market. People came from surrounding islands to sell produce there; those who couldn't afford to rent a room for the night slept on sacks next to their bundles of fruit and vegetables. From where I sat I could see a couple of women wearing cotton dresses, lying side by side on the ground, their arms over their eyes to block out the glare from streetlamps. A cat rubbed itself against their bare feet and ignored the long-tailed rats scuttling about. For a while I pondered the incongruity of it all: returning from a sleazy bar to a yacht worth several million pounds, where I could sit, drink French wine and look at women too poor to afford a roof over their heads. A sense of unease settled over me. I went below, found an empty bunk and escaped into sleep.

The next day began slowly on *Swedish Caprice*, with people who didn't belong on board leaving and those who did returning. We ate a late breakfast on deck, bantering with the people on the boats moored either side of us. One was owned by a Californian who had made his fortune on stocks and bonds, the other by an Australian couple who had saved for ten years to buy a yacht and sail it around the world. They advised us on the best shops in town to buy imported foods, and grumbled that there were no well-stocked, air-conditioned supermarkets like those in Lautoka or Honiara. Meanwhile, at the open-air market, women padded along on broad, bare feet, balancing baskets of pineapples and papayas on their heads, or sat on the hard baked mud with piles of taro neatly arranged on huge banana leaves. Chickens languished inside bamboo cages, next to stalls selling tourist souvenirs – *sulus* and carvings and 'grass' skirts made of recycled plastic.

'That's a swell kayak you have there,' the Californian called over to me as I cleared away the dishes. 'How many miles have you put on her?'

'About five,' I told him. He thought I was joking.

From Port Vila we sailed to Espirito Santo, the biggest island in Vanuatu, and moored in a bay wrapped around with dense jungle. It was an ominous, brooding place, and oppressively hot. The sky was heavy with cumulus clouds, and during periodic showers, fat raindrops bounced off a flat, grey, silky sea. For the first time in years, Dag was ill. He had developed a nasty chest cold, and lay snivelling and wheezing in our cabin while the rest of us dined on deck. As we were finishing dessert, two men came alongside in a dugout. Both wore only ragged shorts. Lying at their feet were a few parrot fish. We called out greetings but they simply stared up at us, their blank expressions giving no clue to their thoughts. Watching them paddle away, my feelings of unease crystallized into a realization. I wanted to be camping on beaches and cooking over a fire instead of sleeping between linen sheets and eating off china plates. I felt that *Swedish Caprice*, because of its size, its luxury and the wealth it represented, was putting an impenetrable barrier between me and the country I was travelling through. In bed, I shared these feelings with Dag.

'Our fancy kayak will seem just as alien to local people,' he said.

'Yes, but I won't feel so bad,' I feebly replied.

Illness had sapped Dag of his usual optimism. 'It's not going to be easy. We'll be exposed to the elements and totally reliant on peoples' good natures. You might end up wishing you were back on *Swedish Caprice*.'

That night, I dreamed we were paddling our kayak through waters infested with sharks and crocodiles, that we both had malaria, and that insects were crawling all over my body. Just before dawn, I awoke with the unmistakable signs of a bladder infection. Beside me, Dag was sweating with a fever.

During the five-day crossing to the Solomons, Dag's temperature steadily rose, and as well as a bladder infection I also got motion sickness. Gael took over in the kitchen whilst I alternated between resolutely staring at the horizon from the deck and dashing to the toilet. By the third day at sea, unable to keep down any antibiotics, I had started to pass blood in my urine. Dag was becoming increasingly feverish and had a racking cough. On the morning of the fourth day, we looked out of our cabin porthole to see the southernmost tip of the Solomon Islands slipping by. For months we had stared at maps of this 900-mile long archipelago, and tried to imagine how it looked. At first sight, it was even more exotic than we'd expected. Lush jungle cloaked steep mountain ridges, clouds of mist hung in the valleys, and along the yellow beaches leaf houses stood on stilts over the water. A pod of pilot dolphins surfaced and birdwing butterflies as big as our hands flapped by. We stared out of the porthole for almost an hour, then lay back, ruefully smiling at the irony of the situation. Here we were, at the first destination of our great adventure, and barely able to climb down from our bunk.

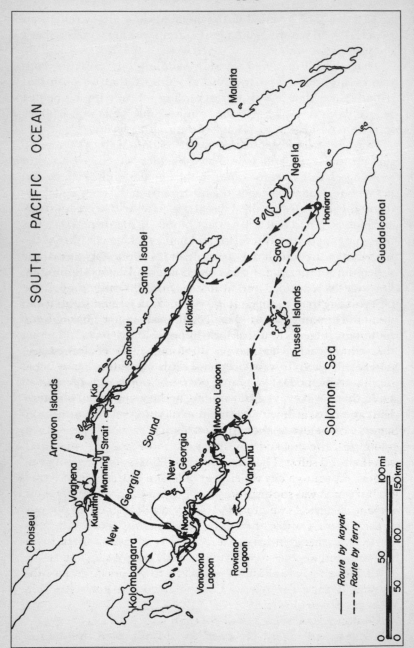

3

Hospital Horrors

'Your bodies are very hot' pronounced Dr Pimbo Ogatuti. After feeling our foreheads and listening to our litany of symptoms, he disentangled a stethoscope from the three hanging around his neck and began to examine Dag's chest. 'How much time will you spend in Honiara?' he asked us. The answer to that, although we tried to say it tactfully, was as little as possible.

From what we'd seen so far of Honiara, the capital of the Solomon Islands, it wasn't a particularly appealing place. The main street was stiflingly hot and humid, and lined with dismal stores. Crowds of wild-looking young men hung about. They were small and muscular, with bare feet and bushy hair. Their cheeks bulged with betel nut, their lips and teeth were a nasty rust-brown colour and the cracked pavement around them was splattered with their red saliva. They were some of Honiara's transient population, drawn to a city which had only one traffic light and one lift, but which was sophisticated beyond belief compared to their outlying villages. As we stumbled along past these men on our way to the doctor's office they gave us suspicious looks. This was hardly surprising: tourists were a fairly uncommon sight in Honiara, and we were a particularly sickly pair of specimens.

We told Dr Ogatuti about our plans to spend three months kayaking in the Solomons, and that we needed to get well and fit again as soon as possible.

'Could we have some tests—?' began Dag.

'Oh tests, silly tests! No need for those!' cried the doctor, scribbling out two prescriptions. 'Soon you will be paddling your boat.' Which was, of course, exactly what we wanted to hear.

Outside the Mendana Kitano Hotel, minibuses disgorged groups of elderly Japanese and American men, veterans of the Second World War who were revisiting the sites they once fought fierce battles over. In the open-walled lobby, lily-white Australian businessmen in shorts and long white socks sat drinking beer and reading week-old copies of the *Sydney Herald*. 'It's expensive to stay here,' one advised us. 'But all the other places in town are shit pits.'

A quick tour by taxi around Honiara's handful of hotels had revealed that his assessment was not far off the mark. Reassuring ourselves that it would only be for a few days, we checked into the Mendana Kitano. From the balcony of our room, we sadly waved goodbye to our friends on *Swedish Caprice* as they pulled up the anchor, motored out of Honiara harbour and headed north towards the Philippines.

'Listen to this,' said Dag, reading from the local newspaper. 'The Honiara Kilu'ufi Hospital authorities have confirmed that an amputated leg was found in a garden close to the hospital grounds. A principal nursing officer said that a dog must have stolen the leg from the incinerator before anyone had a chance to dispose of it.'

We shuddered and laughed and said that we'd never put ourselves at the mercy of such a place. Two days later, with Dag's temperature at a steady 40 degrees and me with such pain in my kidneys that I could no longer stand up straight, we had no choice in the matter.

A morose receptionist sat behind a glass slatted window with names written into the thick dust. 'You need Dr O'Brien in the Guadacanal Referral Clinic,' she informed us. 'Go through the emergency ward and around the corner.'

The ward had about ten beds covered with rumpled grey sheets. A man was doubled in pain, three small children huddled together, and several women lay with babies at their breasts. At a table, a teenager sat clutching his arm and groaning loudly. There wasn't a doctor or nurse in sight.

In blinding sunshine, we sat on a bench waiting our turn to see Dr O'Brien. Next to us was a young mother and her two children.

They had coarse, straw-blond hair and the scars of ritual cuts on their brown cheeks. All three of them gave us sympathetic looks.

'Youpelas sick?' asked the woman shyly.

'Yes,' I told her. 'Fever.'

'Fevi?' she nodded wisely. 'Youpelas plenti sick.'

Dr O'Brien was a brisk man from Northern Ireland. He prescribed a different drug for me and, brushing aside Dag's requests for sputum tests and an X-ray, sent him off to the laboratory for a blood test. As we climbed the stairs to the lab, a white-coated woman came past us carrying a cardboard box filled with blood samples. One of the phials had fallen over, and blood was running over her hands and dripping through the bottom of the box.

Dag was instructed to take his blood sample to the Malaria Lab – 'Follow the arrows,' he was told. The arrows led back down the blood-spotted stairs, and along a grimy wall to a boarded-up window with a sign that said, 'Knock and Wait'.

We did. The board slid back, and from a dark interior a hand reached out and grabbed the phial from Dag. 'Fifteen minutes!' announced a disembodied voice.

Gingerly, we stepped across an open drain filled with purple water, slime and bits of cardboard, and entered the 'waiting-room', which was a piece of corrugated iron balanced on concrete posts. Around it, tall irises were in full bloom, their yellow flowers shaking in the breeze.

'Mr Goning!'

A hand thrust a white piece of paper from the dark window.

'That must be you,' I said.

Dag recrossed the drain and took the paper.

'The test was positive!' he said in dismay.

We scrutinized the result slip. Dat Goning, Canadian, Positive—

'Mr Goning!'

This time, a head poked through the window. 'Give me your result, please!'

The paper was snatched back inside, then thrust out again moments later. The 'Positive' stamp had been scratched out and 'Negative' hand-written beneath it.

'Mistake!' cried the disembodied voice.

*

'I'm sure it's nothing serious,' said Dr O'Brien. 'The climate here always gets to tourists when they first arrive. Finish off the course of drugs that Dr Ogatuti prescribed. That should sort you out.'
On our way back to the Mendana Hotel, we stopped off at the shipping office and booked tickets for the following Sunday's sailing to New Georgia Province, where we planned to do the first part of out kayak trip. That gave us six days – ample time, we thought – to recuperate.

The week passed in a haze of pain and fever. We rarely left our hotel room. By day, we listened to the clinking and chattering from the open-air bar below us, and at night the tinny recorded music of the hotel's Gilbertese dance troupe pounded through our walls. When the maids came to clean the room, we sat on the balcony and looked longingly at the ocean. Gradually, my infection began to retreat, but Dag showed no sign of improvement. He had eaten little for two weeks, and he was exhausted by coughing and delirium. A day after our ship sailed, we were back at the hospital. After sitting in the sun outside the doctor's office, Dag passed out.

'Good God,' said O'Brien. 'How did he get into this state?'

An X-ray showed up a shadow on Dag's lung. Pneumonia and pleurisy were diagnosed and a suitable drug prescribed. Within forty-eight hours, his temperature was down, his appetite had began to return, and we'd rebooked out tickets to New Georgia Province.

It didn't take us long to provision for our trip, because there was little to choose from. From the Chinese-owned supermarkets we bought rice, tinned fish, sugar, milk powder, tea, and, after a long, hard search, some garlic. Honiara's market was a sad affair: beneath black umbrellas set up on sun-baked mud were pathetic little piles of peanuts, withered bundles of green onions and stalks of overripe bananas. To supplement the trade items we had brought from Canada – fishing lures and line, needles, thread, balloons – we purchased some of the tobacco that was coiled up like thick rope. Then we had lunch at one of the food stalls on the edge of the market. Posted next to the counter was a large, formidable notice:

TO ALL CUSTOMERS

– Do not sit down and tell stories
– Do not eat food from other snack bars here
– Do not move the chairs from one table to another
– Do not chew betel nut and spit around here
– If you have no business to conduct here
GET LOST!

Quickly, we ate our chicken and rice and left.

That night, we spread the parts of our kayak over the hotel patio to check that nothing had been damaged during the journey from Canada. One of the lily-white Australians wandered over to us, clutching his beer can inside a polystyrene holder. 'What's all this about?' he asked.

We told him of our plan to go to New Georgia Province and kayak through Marovo Lagoon, reputed to be the largest island-bound lagoon in the world, and on to the smaller Roviana and Vonavona Lagoons. And then, to travel to Isabel Province, where we would kayak the length of Santa Isabel Island and cross the Manning Strait to Vaghena Island.

'Christ, that sounds like a lot of bloody hard work,' he commented. 'Especially for a pair of saplings like you!'

'You can hardly blame him,' said Dag later, as we were preparing for bed. 'Just look at us!' Side by side, we surveyed our reflections in the full length mirror. After weeks of illness, Dag's once muscular legs now looked like they belonged to a chicken, while my skinny frame and scrawny neck made me resemble a praying mantis.

'Five years of kayaking,' I said, quoting from our original sponsorship proposal, 'have honed this couple's survival skills and developed their stamina!'

'Don't make me laugh!' Dag protested. 'It hurts my chest!' Stifling our mirth, we fell into bed. Ready or not, we were setting off in the morning.

4

Drawbacks of Paradise

The *Iuminau* sat by Honiara's wharf, puffing smoke from its funnels like a contented old man with a pipe. Three hours before it sailed, this rusty ferry boat seemed full to capacity. The toilets were already overflowing and the air-conditioned first-class lounge smelled of vomit. We heaved our baggage up a narrow stairway to the top deck, where there was what appeared to be a convention of representatives from every corner of Melanesia. Among the solid mass of people were skin colours ranging from pale brown to ebony, and hair from black and tightly frizzed to straw yellow and straight. Men reclined on mats, chewing sticks of sugar cane. Women leaned against sacks of betel and coconuts. Around them were heaped stalks of bananas, and live pigs lay trussed and wrapped in bright cloth. When we appeared there was a flurry of goodnatured shuffling and rearranging, hands reached up to help us with our baggage and soon we were comfortably settled down. As yet more passengers came aboard, the goodnatured shuffling continued, until I was practically sitting on top of a small child, who regarded me with an unblinking stare while her father picked through her hair for nits.

When the *Iuminau* was an hour out into New Georgia Sound, an elderly man clad only in shorts began weaving his way through the crowd towards where we sat. 'Where are your children?' asked Jim Kolikeda, when he reached us.

On hearing we had none, his face fell.

'I am so sorry. I will pray that God sends you a son.'

Jim was a retired schoolteacher from the village of Mbili, where, in thirteen hours' time, we were planning to disembark and begin our journey by kayak through Marovo Lagoon. He was also an active member of the Seventh Day Adventist Church, and as the only white people on deck he'd targeted us for a donation.

'Who has invited you to stay at Mbili?' he asked, as he wrote out a receipt for the money we'd given him.

We admitted to knowing no one there.

'The people believe the night is full of spirits,' he said. 'They will be afraid when they see two white people appear from the darkness. I will tell them that you are my *wantoks* from overseas, and that you have come to stay in my house.' '*Wantoks*' was a loose term referring to relatives and close friends. Custom demanded that Solomon Islanders always helped their *wantoks*, even if they turned up uninvited and unannounced. Jim assured us that his explanation of our sudden appearance would perfectly satisfy his neighbours.

We met the only other tourist on board when he emerged from the first-class lounge and came up on deck to get warm. He was a small, handsome Austrian with a walrus moustache, wearing the sort of clothes a mercenary might favour, with lots of pockets for bullets and guns. He told us that he worked as a receptionist at one of Salzburg's top hotels, and during his annual holiday he always headed off to some far-flung place. But the Solomons, it appeared, had been flung a bit too far for his taste.

'In first class, it is like the Arctic,' he complained, 'and one woman is vomiting. Out here,' he swept his arm around to encompass sacks and baskets and grunting, wet-nosed pigs, 'it is hell. If I brought my mother here from Vienna, she would have a heart attack and die.'

When he had returned to first class, a man who had watched our exchange curiously leaned forward and asked if we lived in the same village as the man we'd been speaking to. 'Em *wantok* bilong yu?' he asked. 'Is he your relation?' No amount of explanation could persuade him that we'd never met the Austrian before.

Towards midnight the *Iuminau's* engines slowed and an anchor was dropped.

'Here is Mbili,' said Jim.

Beyond the ferry there was only utter blackness, without even a twinkle of light to signal a village or a harbour. From the dark, two motorized dugouts materialized. We were instructed to get into one of them, and our baggage was perched precariously atop sacks and cloth-wrapped bundles in the other canoe, which slid away into the night.

Ten minutes later, our dugout ran on to a beach. Fireflies twinkled between trees, and the air was damp and sweetly scented. Our bags lay on the sand a few yards away; with impressive ease, Jim hoisted the one containing the kayak on to his shoulder, and padded off along a path through the trees, while we struggled along behind him with the rest of our belongings. His house stood on stilts, and had an iron roof, plywood walls and thatched window shutters propped open with twigs. From a back room came the snuffling and crying of children. Jim's wife, Linethy, greeted us. She was a rotund woman, with a direct manner.

'You want the toilet?' she asked, and led me back along the path to a rocky section of beach, where she turned away to give me privacy.

That first night in Mbili, sleep was impossible. Our bed was a mat in a corner of the main room. Above us the tin roof seemed to steadily release all the heat it had stored up during the day. We lay as far away from each other as our sheet sleeping bag would allow, sweating profusely and panting like dogs on a summer's day. Mosquitos whined around our ears. Cats fought beneath the house and a neighbour's baby wailed unremittingly. While it was still dark, roosters began warming up their vocal cords. As light seeped through the windows, chickens squawked, dogs barked and someone revved up an outboard engine. Then one of Jim's children came out of her bedroom, took one look at us and burst into terrified screeching.

With Jim and Linethy we shared a breakfast of pawpaw, coconut biscuits we'd bought in Honiara and water from the rain catchment tank. As Mbili was a Seventh Day Adventist village, its inhabitants were forbidden tea, coffee or alcohol.

'Sometimes your *wantoks* come in their yachts,' said Jim, 'and they bring us many problems. They trade beer and whisky for carvings, they give our young men bad ideas. And then they go with spears on to our reefs and they catch our fish without permission, without compensation! You must tell your *wantoks* not to do such things!'

Almost every inch of land in the Solomons is privately owned under a complicated system of customary tenure. Primary landowners, like Jim, have the final say over what happens to the land, while secondary owners have the right to live and grow food on the land and fish off the surrounding reefs. As 90 per cent of Solomon Islanders live from subsistence fishing and farming, these rights are jealously guarded, and the subject of much legal wrangling. We got the impression that if we camped or fished without permission, it would be comparable to us discovering that a total stranger had spent the night in our spare bedroom and helped himself to the contents of our fridge. When we took out our map of Marovo Lagoon to show Jim our intended route, he swept a finger across its bottom end, encompassing islets, reefs and ocean.

'This is all my land,' he told us, grinning broadly. 'I give you permission to stay there. You have been very generous to our church, there will be no charge.'

It took us an hour to put the kayak together, and almost as long to pack it. From beneath the shade of an enormous banyan tree, a crowd of villagers watched mesmerized as we fiddled about with waterproof bags and camera boxes, arguing over what should go where. Their curiosity turned to pure astonishment when we set about protecting ourselves from the sun. We donned sunglasses and canvas hats, and smeared every inch of exposed flesh with sun block cream.

'They want to know why you are doing these strange things,' said Jim.

We explained that without the glasses we would be blinded by the dazzling light, and without the hats and cream the sun would turn our skins the colour of a red hibiscus blossom. The villagers gave us pitying looks, and we paddled away feeling rather foolish.

The lagoon stretched away before us for over sixty miles. It was sprinkled with jungle-clad islets, as if New Georgia Island had once shaken itself in a fit of fury and tossed fragments of its mountainous spine into the sea. Paddling towards their shores, we were met by wafts of warm, fragrant air, and sometimes a large fruit bat languorously flapped out from the trees to circle us, as if sent by some unseen but watchful presence deep in the forest. This was the jungle of my childhood fantasies, inhabited by huge, strangely shaped trees draped with hanging vines, the day shut out by a dense canopy of leaves, the darkness pierced by shafts of light in which insects danced and weaved. There was no disputing the beauty of the place, but paradise has its drawbacks, especially when you're not acclimatized to it. The temperature was around 32 degrees, and humidity was almost 100 per cent. Sweat streamed off my face, my sunglasses slid down my nose, my wide-brimmed hat became unbearably heavy and I was convinced I was paddling through treacle. After two hours we had covered only three miles, and we were exhausted. There were no beaches in sight, only islets ringed by mangrove swamps. In one of these swamps we found some shade beneath the spiky leaves of a gigantic succulent plant.

'Do you think I can get out to pee?' I asked Dag. 'What about crocs?'

'Jim told me that crocodiles have been hunted to extinction in Marovo Lagoon,' he said.

'How does Jim know?'

'Because he lives here.'

'Marovo Lagoon's a big place.'

'Local knowledge is always the most reliable source of information, Maria,' said Dag archly.

Only partially reassured, I hopped out of the boat and balanced on a thick root.

Since leaving Mbili we'd not seen a soul, but as soon as I pulled down my shorts a man in a dugout suddenly appeared from the mangrove thickets. Luckily any prurient interest he may have had in a debagged white woman was diverted by the kayak. Like most Solomon Islanders, he'd learned how to paddle a dugout almost before he could walk, but this was the first time he'd seen a canoe such as ours. He leaned over it, stroked the hull, put his head right inside the front cockpit to examine the construction of this strange and wonderful boat. Dag explained how it could be folded up and stored in a bag.

'Really, you break it up?' he asked. 'You put it in a basket?'

His name was Montgomery, and he was returning home to his village some miles away after working in his garden on this islet.

He showed us the way to Njapuana, one of the lagoon's bound-

ary islands, which had the only sand beach for miles and where
Jim had given us permission to camp. From a distance it looked
ideal, shaded by leaning coconut palms. As we glided towards
shore, one of the coconuts plummeted down and splashed into
the water. Another hurtled itself at us while we were dragging the
kayak up the beach and made a sizeable crater in the sand a few
feet away. By the time we'd found a missile-free spot and established camp I was dribbling with sweat. Longingly, I gazed out at
the lagoon. 'Mi suim long hia?' I asked Montgomery, who was
now engrossed in a thorough examination of our tent. 'Can I
swim here?'

'Yesss,' he replied.

Dag pointed beyond the turquoise shallows to the deeper
emerald water where the coral reef ended in a steep drop-off.
'Gat bigfela sharks long hia?' he asked. 'Are there sharks here?'

'Yesss.'

'Oh well,' said Dag. 'There are sharks all over the Solomons.
We can't spend the next few months worrying about them.'

Donning our snorkels, we went in. Dag headed for the drop-off
but I decided to stay in the shallows. Minutes later, I saw a baby
shark. It was about ten inches long, with a large head, a pudgy
body and fat fins. It looked so like a stuffed toy that I gazed at it
without fear. But then another shark, too big to be a toy,
appeared. It was 5ft long, with a sleek white body tipped with
black. It came up from behind me, and seemed to turn its head
to look in my direction before it swam away. Splashing and splut-
tering, I headed for the beach and hit the sand on all fours.

Dag, who had heard the commotion I made, followed me in
and stood waist-deep in water, sternly lecturing me. 'That was
only a harmless reef shark! But if you act like a wounded fish
you'll attract every dangerous shark for miles around!'

Obviously, I already had, because minutes later it was his turn
to scramble ashore. 'I just came face to face with a hammerhead!
At least 12ft long! It swam right by me, just beyond the drop-off,
it was moving like a train!'

'Bigfela shark,' I told Montgomery. 'Hammerhead.'

He shrugged. 'Hammerhead im no gat tis,' he said nonchalantly.

'No teeth?' I repeated incredulously.

'Im tru,' he insisted. 'It's true.'

My faith in local knowledge crumbled.

We were woken at dawn by something pattering on the dome roof of our tent. Scattered over the beach were fist-sized blossoms with pinky-white petals cradling long scarlet stamens. They were dropping from the trees above us, and on impact with our tent and the sand they released a sweet, heady scent. The lagoon was still as glass; a shimmering lizard darted over my feet; a white cockatoo with lemon tail-feathers flashed past; parrots chattered in the branches above my head. It was November, a month I usually spent wrapped in bulky sweaters and socks, yet here I was, before sun-up, clad only in a *sulu*, a light cotton wrap.

'This' I wrote in my notes, 'feels like nothing short of a miracle.'

For several days we wandered amid the lagoon's myriad islets. The ocean was calm and lambent. The only sounds we heard were the natural ones of wind, water and birds, and the night skies were undimmed by any electric glow. Gradually, we established the rhythms and routines necessary for us to survive months sharing a small boat and a small tent. We divided up the work involved in packing and unpacking the kayak, in breaking and setting up camp. We created individual personal space: the left of the tent next to the sleeping mat was mine, the right was Dag's. Quickly, life was whittled down to a simple, satisfying core. We had one change of clothes each, and ate mostly fish, rice and coconuts. Our decisions concerned how many miles to cover each day and where to spend each night. Our worries were about finding drinking water and staying healthy. This last consideration, because of our isolation and vulnerability, was a fairly weighty one. We religiously took our malaria medication. To prevent small skin cuts or scrapes festering we immediately treated them with tincture of iodine. Fungal infections flourished on us: Dag developed something which he referred to as 'crotch rot', I got vaginal thrush and we both had athlete's foot. Every night, smothered in various powders and creams, and sprayed with a noxious mosquito repellent, we lay sweating in the tent, wondering what had happened to the stunning sex life our friends had forecast for us.

Those same friends had filled me with dread about sharks and crocodiles, but we quickly realized that we were in far more danger from the tiny malarial mosquito. One afternoon, after paddling past endless mangrove swamps and despairing of finding a campsite, we came across a clearing in the jungle a few feet from shore. Wild orchids grew waist-high around a patch of ground covered by dried palm leaves. Gratefully, we set up our tent then went snorkeling over the reef. Rainbow-hued parrot fish munched noisily on purple coral heads as big as tabletops, a small iridescent squid moved in a pulsing rhythm: so engrossed were we by this marine world that we failed to realize what was happening above water. A cloud of mosquitos had risen from our delightful orchid garden and was homing in on the two floating hunks of pink flesh. Too late, we made a dash for cover, hotly pursued by the cloud, some bits of which ended up zipped into the tent with us. After a frantic half-hour of exterminating the mosquitoes, we had no choice but to settle in for the night, even though it was barely past four o'clock and unmercifully hot. Trying not to scratch our bites, we watched and listened as the whining beasties outside worked themselves into a frenzy. They covered the tent, swarming over the insect screens and poking their proboscises through the tiny holes. Dag took my eyebrow tweezers and began exacting his revenge, but it was a fruitless task: there were thousands more for every mosquito he managed to put out of action. Dinner was a dispiriting affair: a tin of second-grade Solomon Blue tuna fish which resembled cat food in texture and taste, and a packet of Hard Navy biscuits, which were stale and soggy. Then we lay, and sweated, and listened to the surrounding jungle. Something crashed through branches, piercing screams echoed around, water dripped from foliage, insects whirred, frogs croaked, and land crabs rustled across the dried palm leaves. Inadvertently, we'd pitched our tent over the hole of a crab, which spent much of the night tirelessly trying to scrabble its way though our groundsheet.

Sleeping in the leaf huts of villages was infinitely more pleasurable. In Chubikopi, on Vangunu Island, we were invited to stay with the family of David Livingstone Nonga. The houses of Chubikopi stood on stilts over the water. Behind them was a steep forested hillside with areas cleared for gardens. As we'd paddled towards the village, children ran along the shore, whooping in excitement, and adults gathered on verandas to watch our approach. Their shyness had been quickly overcome by curiosity.

'What happens to this boat in big seas?' the men asked as we tied it to one of the house stilts. 'Why do the paddles have two blades? What is the purpose of this journey?'

While Dag talked to the men, the women beckoned me up to a veranda. Gratefully, I stepped into a cool, airy house. The floor was made of bamboo and mangrove wood slats, the walls and roof of dried pandanus leaves, and everything was sewed or tied with vine. I removed my sunglasses and hat, and my hair fell around my face in lank, sweat-soaked strands. The women giggled, and whispered to each other in a soft language that sounded like Italian. Children peered at me from behind the safety of their mothers; one reached out and tentatively touched the hairs on my arm, another peered suspiciously at my sandals.

David took us on a tour of the village, along a path made of coconut husks. Around each house, the dirt had been meticulously swept, and there were flowerbeds full of exotic irises. We stopped briefly at the village store. It was an ugly structure of wood and iron, inside as hot as an oven and with little for sale, but David was inordinately proud of it. 'It is a permanent building,' he boasted. 'Everyone in the village wants a house like this, with an iron roof and a rain tank to collect water, but few can afford it.'

The other permanent building in Chubikopi was the elementary school. It had two rooms and crushed coral floors. There were no desks or benches, no furniture of any kind except a couple of ancient blackboards. One hundred and twenty pupils studied there, and only a fraction of these would go on to one of the country's handful of secondary schools. 'When a pupil wins a scholarship to secondary school,' David told us, 'everyone in the village helps his family to buy his clothes and books.'

In a smoky cooking hut I helped David's wife Merver prepare dinner. While she wrapped taro and cassava roots in banana leaves and laid them on hot stones, I worked on the slippery cabbage, discarding each stem and shredding the leaves. Outside the hut, her eldest son sat astride a log, vigorously grating the innards of coconut shells. He heaped the flesh into a bowl and squeezed out its thick, white juice. Merver stirred this into some warm water, added the cabbage and the contents of a tin of tuna we'd brought, and let the lot simmer gently over the fire. 'When

I saw you in your canoe I wanted to laugh,' she said. 'White people paddling! It is our custom to paddle, not yours!'

She was surprised to learn that Dag and I were married. 'I heard that white people do not do this. How much did he pay for you?'

'Nothing,' I told her.

'Nothing!' Her eyes widened. 'No bride price? For me, David had to give many pigs, yams and mats!'

I asked how she had met David.

'My parents told me I had to marry him. They said he was a good man and would look after me.'

'Were you happy?'

'I was very cross!'

'Could you have refused to marry him?'

'No. Too much trouble.'

'Were your parents right? Is he a good man?'

'He is not lazy. Some people here have not one cent to buy kerosene or soap, but they can grow food to eat and cut down sago palm to make their house. But some people are too lazy to make a garden or a house, so they go to their *wantoks* and depend on them.'

All afternoon, two of David's *wantoks* had been lying on the veranda, chewing betel and resting their heads on empty Coca-Cola tins. When we carried the food to the house they were still there, and they sat up to eat. Everything had a strong smoky taste, and I found the taro cloying and difficult to swallow. Merver was closely watching me, and she hurried off to fetch a jug of water, and two brand-new glasses that still had labels stuck to them. 'We hear that foreigners drink water with their food,' she said.

After a brief, spectacular sunset, darkness fell like a curtain. Beyond the veranda, frogs croaked and fruit bats squabbled in the trees. Huge bugs dived at the kerosene lamp, and four children lay around it on their stomachs, paging through a twenty-year-old copy of *National Geographic*. When I asked Merver the ages of her children, she looked vague. 'This one was born in the season of the ngali nut,' she said, pointing to the biggest. 'And that one in the season of the pineapple.'

We slept out on the veranda. Towards dawn, I was woken by an archer fish which missed its insect prey and squirted me through

the split bamboo floor. For a few minutes I lay listening to the slap
of the ocean against the stilts of the house, the regular breathing
of the family in the rooms inside, a gecko rustling in the leaf
thatch above my head, the pops and trills of birds in the jungle.
Opening my eyes, I peered down through the floor slats: our
kayak bobbed peacefully about next to David's dugout canoe.
The sky was streaked with pink and violet, and there was an
orange glow on the horizon. I crept down the steps of the
veranda and over to the outhouse. It was also built of thatch, and
stood on stilts over the water. In the pig pen standing next to it,
a large sow snuffled and snorted at me through the bars of its
pen.

When I returned to the veranda, David was up.

'Will you drink tea with us?' he asked.

He was horrified to learn that I had presumed Chubikopi to be
a Seventh Day Adventist Village. 'We are in the United Missionary
Church! The SDAs are bad people, they come from America with
much money, they preach damnation, they forbid people to
dance, they steal our congregations. When you were at Mbili, I
hope you did not give money to the SDA church!'

Before leaving Chubikopi, we gave David some fishing hooks
and line, balloons for his children and a donation for the school.
In the Solomons, receiving a gift is akin to going into debt, as
whatever is accepted must in due course be paid back, and David
looked nervous as he accepted our offerings. 'Repayment for
your hospitality,' we assured him.

'It is too much,' he said. 'Now we must feel obliged to give you
something more.'

We paddled away with his gift of cassava and coconut strapped
on to the deck of the kayak.

5

Hunted Heads

'Will there be another war?' cried Chief Nathan, peering at us through grease smeared spectacles.

After ten days in Marovo Lagoon, we'd surfed across its outer reef at a spot called Hele Bar, then headed along the exposed south-west coast of New Georgia Island. It was late afternoon by the time we slipped between two offshore islands and into the shelter of Roviana Lagoon. About a mile along it we came across a permanent house on stilts close to the water, and Chief Nathan had anxiously hurried out and beckoned us ashore.

'In 1941,' he told us, 'a Japanese man came here in a boat like yours. One year later, the Second World War began. I remember watching the tops of palm trees being shot off. There was such noise, such suffering. The war ended, the trees grew over the crashed planes, once more we had peace and quiet. Today, when I looked through my window and saw you in your boat, I was much afraid. I said to my wife that another war is coming to Roviana Lagoon.'

A rainstorm had followed us across the lagoon, and Nathan hurried us inside his house. He told us he was eighty-two years old, the custom owner of five villages, and was in the midst of a legal wrangle over land rights. He seemed to positively relish the thought of going to court.

'I will win!' he said gleefully. 'I always win because for years I have written down every fact of my life!'

Before we left, he took out a grease-stained exercise book and wrote down our names, ages, the fact that we had no children and our assurances that we were not another harbinger of war.

As we paddled to an islet owned by Chief Nathan, we met a man fishing from a dugout canoe. He was using a twig, a piece of string and a scrap of cloth for bait.

'Yu laikim yangfela coconuts?' he asked, and passed us two green coconuts from the bottom of his boat.

We drank the juice and ate the flesh of the coconuts as an appetizer to our dinner of boiled rice and fried green onions. We'd traded for the onions in Marovo Lagoon the previous day, and now they were crawling with large ants which we carefully blew out of the stalks before chopping the onions up. The man reappeared, and proudly presented us with a small parrot fish.

'I bet it's his only catch of the day,' said Dag, but we couldn't refuse. In thanks, we gave him some nylon fishing line and a brightly coloured lure. At first he was speechless, then he insisted he was going to paddle five miles to his village and back again to bring us potatoes. We managed to persuade him to stay with us and share our meal instead. While the fish cooked, I asked him if there were any crocodiles in Roviana Lagoon.

'Plenti pukpuk!' he replied. 'Tumora, you twofelas kam long ples bilong me, and lukluk long pukpuk.'

'He wants us to visit his village tomorrow and see the crocodiles,' said Dag, interpreting my blank look as incomprehension of the man's pidgin. In fact I had understood, but wished I hadn't.

A baby saltwater crocodile lay panting in the bottom of a Second World War petrol tank. Adolescent crocs stared at us from inside bamboo cages with banana leaf roofs. The grown-ups, a male and a female, were in separate enclosures made of split logs driven into the ground and lashed together with vine. I peered over the logs at the female. She appeared to be sleeping in the sun, her mouth wide open.

'Don't get too close!' cried Likey, the English-speaking son of the man who had invited us to Nusa Hope.

The crocodile's legs seemed to suddenly grow and lengthen beneath her, and with her jaws snapping she made a furious dash at me across the enclosure and threw herself against the logs. They quivered, and held.

'She thinks you want her eggs,' Likey explained, referring to the contents of the large mound of earth in the middle of the enclosure.

'Tell her I don't,' I said, rapidly retreating from the rather insubstantial barrier that separated me from six feet of deadly reptile. 'Most definitely not.'

Silas, the old man who kept the crocodiles as mascots, came out to meet us. He was adorned with a shell necklace and a wreath of frangipani blossom. His wife hovered in the shadows of their hut, trying to get a peek of me while I tried to get a peek of her. Her bare chest was intricately tattooed, and her long earlobes sported huge holes, stretched by years of wearing heavy clam shell earrings. Silas talked non-stop in Roviana, a dialect of which we understood not one word.

'He says he feeds the crocodiles on chickens, pigs and dogs,' Likey told us.

'Live ones?' I asked.

'They are live until he puts them in the pen. Then they die of fright.'

Our appearance in the village had emptied the school of its pupils. A teacher was running around with a bamboo stick, vainly trying to round up his flock and herd it back to the classrooms. Finally, he started furiously ringing the bell. This had an instantaneous effect on the children, who took to their heels and raced away amid a cloud of dust.

'Where do the crocodiles come from?' I asked Likey.

He stared at me as if I'd gone mad. 'From here,' he replied, waving his arms around to indicate the lagoon and its mangrove-lined shores. After a last, rather nervous look at the crocodiles, we carried on with our journey.

Tacked on to one of the leaf walls of Chief Gideon Buka's house was a picture torn out of a magazine showing Chris Evert playing tennis at Wimbledon. Gideon's wife scurried around, shooing out the hens and berating the villagers who peered at us through the doorways and windows of the house. 'You must not mind these people,' said Gideon. 'It is not often that white people come to Baraula. But next month, ten Peace Corps workers will come here to learn pidgin and custom cooking. We are digging a latrine for them, a place where they can sit down. I am sorry that it is not ready for you.'

The subject of toilet arrangements in villages had become rather a tricky one to broach, because there were so many different systems. United Mission villages had tiny leaf outhouses built on stilts over the water. SDA villages had separate beaches for men and women. In an Anglican village I'd been told to 'use any rock'. Now, in Baraula village, for the first time we'd encountered the Christian Fellowship Church and, perhaps, a different set of lavatorial rules. Gideon's wife Mary accompanied me to the 'custom toilet'. We walked for ten minutes, past rows of pigs snuffling inside bamboo cages, to an area planted with bananas. Mary pointed along a narrow path that wound through the large green leaves and towards the lagoon. It led me to a long, exposed beach where, at any minute, a fisherman could paddle by in his dugout and find me with my pants down. Glumly, I returned to Mary, who looked surprised to see me back so soon.

We set up our tent under the shelter of a half-built house in the centre of the village. From the rafters above us, shark fins were hung up to dry. Three rows of children sat silently watching us, as if we were on a stage, until it grew dark and houses began to glow with the soft light of kerosene lamps. Like the surrounding jungle, Baraula was far from quiet at night. Babies wailed themselves to sleep. Adults snored. Western pop music crackled from someone's radio. Around 3.00 am, I crept out of the tent and made my way by flashlight to the 'custom toilet'. On the path through the banana leaves, I narrowly avoided stepping on an eight-inch long centipede. The thought of these fearsome-looking creatures, and the fever induced by their painful bite, threatened to thwart my needs yet again. Trying not to think about crocodiles, I waded into the ocean and did what had to be done as fast as possible.

Turquoise water faded to glacial blue around islands ringed with bright white sand and shaded with palms: Vonavona was the smallest of the three lagoons and the most idyllic. It was only a few hours paddle from there to Munda where we were due to catch the *Iuminau* back to Honiara. We deliberately missed one sailing of the ferry, and spent several days exploring the lagoon. News of our presence quickly spread, and men paddled to our campsites to trade with us for fish hooks. They brought lobsters with pink and green carapaces, shimmering reef fish, juicy watermelons, coconuts. One evening, a fisherman called Charlie stayed with us to share our feast. He carefully sucked the flesh off every fishbone, and opted for the head of the lobster, considering it most odd that we should prefer the tail. While we ate, he told us of a place in the lagoon where the remains of former chiefs and the spoils of head-hunting days were kept. Intrigued, we asked him how to get there, but he shook his head.

'Skull Island is a *tambu* place,' he warned. 'If you go alone you will fall sick and die. The Chief of Mandou Island must take you.'

Charlie relayed the news of our interest in Skull Island to the Chief, who sent his eldest son Pinto to accompany us there. After agreeing on a custom fee of $20 Solomon, we set off with him across the lagoon. Pinto's dugout was extremely leaky, and he baled it with his feet while paddling at a furious rate, his arms working like a pair of pistons. Struggling to keep up, we followed him to a tiny, windswept outcrop of volcanic rock on the edge of the outer reef. On its far side, crashing waves sent spray high into the air. Anchoring on the lee side, we took a few steps to the heart of the island, where the undergrowth had been cleared away and a cairn built. I'd expected to see, at most, perhaps a dozen skulls. But there were scores of them, scattered over the cairn, tucked into its crevices, lying around it on the ground. Their crania were veined with fine moss and lichen, their eye sockets spun with spiders' webs and crawling with plant roots. With them lay arm bones, leg bones, ribs, an old clay pipe, a shark's tooth. Some of the skulls were disquietingly small, some had the lower jaw missing. All of them appeared to look back at us with steady, quizzical gazes. Pinto picked up one of the skulls on the ground and shoved it between two rocks.

'I can touch, but not you,' he warned. 'Once, a white man came here, put his cigarette between the jaws of a skull and took a photo. Soon after, he died of the three-day malaria.' Cerebral malaria – the deadliest kind. With renewed respect, I peered at the carved wooden chest on the top of the cairn. It was overgrown with pink and grey lichen and inside it were a dozen more skulls lying on a pile of clam shells, the traditional currency of the Solomons.

'Before the missionaries came, this is where we put our chiefs' heads,' said Pinto. 'My great grandfather is in here. My grandfather is over there.'

He pointed through the scrub vegetation to a gravestone and cross roughly engraved with the inscription: 'Devito Vino. December 23 1986.' Standing on it was a grimy glass jar containing a few plastic flowers, while all around colourful blossoms grew on trees and bushes.

'Whose – how – I mean – these skulls –' Pinto waited patiently as I struggled to form my question. 'Where did they come from?' I finally managed.

'Mostly from Isabel Province,' he said. 'Our people took the men's heads and brought back the fair-haired women as slaves.'

'We're going to Isabel Province,' I told him.

'Not many people left there,' he said.

As the return journey to Honiara was by night, and rain was forecast, we decided to treat ourselves to one of the *Iuminau*'s two cabins. In relation to elsewhere on the boat, at first glance it appeared rather luxurious, with large windows, two single beds, a writing desk and a bathroom. On closer inspection it was less appealing. Brown cockroaches clung to the yellow walls, the sheets were stained and the bathroom was grimy and festooned with pubic hair. At least, we thought, we could both sleep without worrying about the safety of our boat and baggage and we stretched out on one of the beds. Half an hour later, the first intercom announcement woke us. From the speaker above our heads a strident voice yelled that as the weather was rough and we were heading into open ocean, we should secure all our goods on deck and take particular care to not let our 'pikininies rollem off'. Soon the boat was pitching about, and the bathroom door was repeatedly swinging open and banging shut. Cockroaches began dropping on us from the ceiling, and a crunching, rustling noise started up in one corner of the room. The noise came closer, moved past the bed and over to another corner. Flicking on the light, we saw that a plastic bag and some paper had been removed from the wastepaper bin by the door and stuffed into a hole in the wall.

'It's only a rat,' mumbled Dag, switching off the light and pulling the sheet over our heads.

Throughout the night the rat busied itself around us. We woke to discover it had stuffed several pieces of paper into its nest, chewed on one of my notebooks, munched through a waterproof bag, and snacked on Dag's T-shirt, leaving it with seven holes, each with distinctive teeth marks.

As we approached the island of Guadalcanal, and Honiara, I sat in bed and watched Dag getting dressed. He sported a patchy tan and a scruffy beard, and three weeks of fish and coconuts had helped replace much of the weight he'd lost during his illness. As he shook his sun-bleached mop of hair to dislodge any errant cockroaches, and pulled on a pair of grimy shorts and a rat-chewed shirt, it struck me that he looked happier than he had for ages.

6

Island Life

'I didn't recognize you!' cried the clerk at Honiara's shipping office. 'You look so healthy!'

When we told him of our plan to go to Isabel Province, his face fell. 'No tourists go there! There are no roads, no hotels! You will be bored.'

We assured him we needed neither roads nor hotels. In our kayak, we planned to explore the entire south-west coast of Santa Isabel, the longest of all the Solomon Islands, wend our way through the archipelago of islets at its western end, and cross the Manning Strait to Choiseul Province.

'There's a boat scheduled to sail for Santa Isabel in two days,' he told us. 'But departure time could be brought forward from anything between one to thirty-six hours.'

'How will we know?' we asked.

He shrugged. 'Listen to the radio. Or keep an eye on the boat. When smoke comes from the funnels, go aboard.'

The yellow funnels of *Ligomo V* belched out black smoke at nine that night, twenty-four hours ahead of schedule. A small wooden cargo boat with a 10-degree list, it was half the size of the *Iuminau*, and twice as basic. After we had spent a sleepless night steaming across a mercifully calm Solomon Sea, a lifeboat took us ashore at the south end of Santa Isabel Island. As the *Ligomo V* chugged away, we assembled the kayak feeling hot, tired and very alone. All day, we paddled north-west along a rugged, exposed coastline. White sandy bays alternated with black beaches and jungle-covered cliffs. The kayak creaked and bent in the steady swell, and Dag chose this time to tell me that he'd left our emergency locator unit and VHF radio in Honiara.

'I figured,' he said blithely, 'that there would be no one out here to rescue us, so it wasn't worth taking them along.'

During the morning, huge grey clouds glowered at us, then around noon deluged us with torrential rain. As we passed a rocky, offshore islet, hundreds of frigate birds rose up in a huge, wheeling spiral. Blue kingfishers flashed past us, and enormous butterflies with wings brown on one side and brilliant blue on the other flapped lazily by. In mid-afternoon we rounded a steep headland, where the water was made sloppy by rebounding waves. Beyond it, dwarfed by the steep mountainsides rising above it, was a village.

A crowd gathered on the beach and several people splashed into the water and pulled the boat ashore with us still sitting in it. A grey-haired, bare-breasted woman smoking a pipe reached into my cockpit and began pulling out bags and passing them to children.

'Where are they going?' I nervously muttered to Dag as the children, with his camera cases balanced on their heads, disappeared behind leaf houses. I needn't have worried. The people of Santa Isabel are renowned for their hospitality, and in every village there is a leaf hut which is left empty and ready for any dignitaries who may pass through. Waiting for us on the steps of Kilokaka's guest hut, with all our baggage neatly piled behind them, were the village organizer, James, and his small grandson. James told us that over the past few months only two people had stayed in the hut. 'A government official,' he said. 'And a health worker.'

'Any white people in kayaks?' I asked.

'No white people,' he replied. 'Not since three years.'

Solemnly, he accepted the tobacco and fish hooks we gave him, and encouraged his grandson to take the balloon we held out.

'I will bring you taro to eat,' he said.

'We have our own food,' I quickly told him. 'But if anyone has fruit, we have things to trade for it.'

First a woman arrived with an armful of papayas. When we

offered sewing needles in return, she shook her head. 'Balloon,' she insisted.

Next came a spindly old man holding a huge machete in one hand and in the other a thick stalk heavy with green, hard bananas.

'We can't take those along,' I muttered to Dag.

'We have to,' he muttered back. 'The poor fellow just cut them down from his garden.' He handed the old man some stainless steel fish hooks, which were scrutinized then handed back. 'Balloons,' he said.

Another woman brought pineapples, a man came with coconuts, children rolled oranges across the floor, someone offered eggs, and soon there was a noisy crowd of people around the door and a pile of food that was already too much for us to carry in the kayak. And everyone wanted balloons.

When darkness came, the women and children hurried home, but a group of men stayed to 'story', and questioned us about life in Canada and England until past midnight. After what seemed like minutes of sleep, we were startled awake by loud drumming a few feet away from our heads. The hut next door was the church, and outside it, in the pre-dawn light, the pastor was summoning the faithful to prayer by furiously banging two wooden sticks on a slit drum. Dag immediately got up, but I stayed under our bedsheet, sure that the noise would stop at any second. It went on for half an hour. At six o'clock, I was about to drift off to sleep again when I had the strong sense of being watched. Opening one eye, I saw three blond heads sticking through a hole in the bamboo floor. Directly beneath me, a dozen more small bodies were sitting cross-legged on the sand, staring up through the slats.

'Wefelas go lukim haus bilong yu?' asked the bravest of the three heads. 'Can we visit your house?'

Taking my groan as an assent, within seconds the children had swarmed around me. While I faked sleep, they examined my scalp for lice. Presently they grew bored; I sat up, rummaged through our bag of trade items and found a balloon for them. They solemnly passed it around, then handed it back. I blew it up.

'Yu ple olgeta long balloon,' I told them, 'Play together with the balloon,' and gave a quick demonstration of patting it to keep it in the air.

They filed out in silence, then erupted into delighted yelps, and I was able to dress in privacy while balloon game went around the house. Inevitably, there was a loud pop! followed by a long, tense silence. A child appeared in the doorway. 'Balloon gud no more,' he told me in a small, frightened voice.

'No problem,' I said.

'No problem?'

'No problem.'

For the rest of the day the village echoed with the children's repeated cries of 'No problem! No problem!'

I found Dag outside the church, admiring a man's pet baby opossum.

'Im bite?' he was asking.

'Im no bite,' its owner assured him, and, as if to prove him wrong, the opossum promptly sunk its teeth into Dag's index finger. Another man appeared pulling a tiny wild pig on a vine lead. He thrust the loudly squealing animal into Dag's arms.

'What's going on?' I asked.

'I told them I trained as a vet,' he explained. The next exhibit was a baby flying fox. It was hanging upside down from a length of bamboo, its face hidden beneath the soft, velvety skin that was strung between its long fingers and wrapped like wings around its body.

'Im *kaikai*,' said its owner, poking it awake. 'It's food.' The wings unfolded to reveal a furry black body with a pointed face, devilish ears and popping brown eyes. The bat yawned, opening wide a pink mouth lined with tiny, sharp teeth. Then it stretched out its 'wings' and had a good scratch with the hooked end of an index finger.

'He's just like you in the mornings,' I told Dag.

'I've got an idea,' he said.

I didn't have to ask what it was. 'It's not possible—' I began.

'He could hang from the mast!' Dag said. 'Look, he's already tame . . .'

'Yufelas laikim?' asked the bat's owner. 'Do you like him?'

'Wefelas laikim tumas!' enthused Dag.

'Yufelas taikim!' the owner offered.

'We can't take him,' I said firmly.

'But he's so sweet,' coaxed Dag, and he lifted the bat from the bamboo and attached it to my arm. Placing one claw over another, it started to make its way towards my armpit.

'Dag, please get it off.'

'We could take him back to Canada! We've got a perfect house for him. He'd be a wonderful pet.'

'Don't be ridiculous, we can't drag this thing around with us.'

The bat, having discovered that my armpit wasn't a cave, had stretched up one long finger and hooked its claw into my hair.

'*Get it off!*'

'All right, all right,' grumbled Dag, disentangling the baby bat.

'Sori tumas,' he regretfully told its amused owner. 'Misis bilong mi no laikim.'

Although villages along the coast were few and far between, and without road or telephone connection, news of our journey travelled up the coast ahead of us. Some days later, when we arrived at Samasodu, the village organizer was waiting for us on the beach. 'We are expecting you,' John Selwyn said. 'Your house is ready. Tonight there is a nativity play and you will be our special guests.'

In the village meeting hall, banana leaf streamers hung from the tin roof, and patched sheets and *sulus* were pegged on to a rope to act as stage curtains. The audience sprawled over mats, babies slept on their mothers' backs, toddlers staggered around and tripped over sleeping dogs. Outside, the sky was star-filled, palms rustled in the warm breeze and the sound of breaking waves drifted over from the shore. Beneath the curtains, which didn't manage to reach the ground, a dozen pairs of bare black feet were hurrying about. The headmaster appeared, set two kerosene lamps at either side of the stage, then stood between them, wringing his hands.

'Mi sori long disfela drama,' he began. 'I'm sorry about this play.'

Unctuously, he explained that he'd had to go to Honiara for a meeting, his return had been delayed and so he'd had little time to write and direct the play, or supervise the making of the costumes. The curtains were pulled back to reveal a girl and boy dressed in white sheets. Both looked uneasy. The boy had a pair of cardboard wings tacked to his back and he clutched a piece of paper.

'Angel Gabriel is come to Mary as a messenger from God!' announced the headmaster.

Gabriel began reading in a monotone from his notes. 'Do not be afraid. Mary you have found favour. With the Lord you will be with child. And give birth to a son. And you are to give him the name Jesus.'

Mary stared ahead, unblinking. 'How will this be. Since I am a virgin,' she said.

The headmaster paced up and down in front of the stage, wringing his hands. Gabriel cleared his throat, and continued. 'Even Elizabeth your relative. Is going to have a child in her old age. And she who was said to be barren. Is in her sixth month for nothing is impossible with God.'

A long silence ensued, while Gabriel and the Virgin Mary looked increasingly panic-stricken.

'Curtains!' hissed the headmaster, and the *sulus* and bedsheets were jerked shut. Gabriel, minus his wings, and the Virgin came and stood in front of the stage.

'Joseph and Mary!' announced the headmaster. 'No room at the inn!'

The solemn couple walked up and down in front of the curtains, while behind it ten pairs of feet belonging to the choir huddled together. 'Silen nie, holy nie,' the choir began singing, in soft uncertain voices, 'all is cam, all is brie . . .'

On reaching the familiar chorus, the voices let rip. 'SLEEEEP in HE-venly PEAS!' they screeched. 'SLEEE-EEEP IN HE-VENLY PEAS.'

When the carol was over, Mary and Joseph ducked behind the curtain. There was some angry muttering, the feet shuffled back and forth, then the curtain was yanked back to reveal a puzzled choir, Mary and Joseph kneeling either side of an empty box and three boys wearing cardboard crowns standing uncertainly at the side of the stage.

'Because I was in Honiara,' the headmaster explained to the audience, 'I had no time to teach the words of "These Three Kings", or to make a baby Jesus.'

Someone at the front of the audience volunteered their baby, but the frazzled headmaster rejected it. 'Come on, kings!' he said crossly, and in silence they shuffled over to the empty box and stared reverently down into it. The curtains closed for the last time.

'The drama is over,' said the headmaster. 'Sorry that we didn't have time to prepare more, but I was in Honiara.'

Samasodu was the first village we'd visited that had running water. Down at the stand-pipe next morning, I washed our breakfast pots alongside a group of women who were scrubbing their already shining saucepans with sand. One of them grabbed my small, sooty kettle and set about it with a vengeance, while her friend went my for my frying pan. Fearing for its non-stick lining, I tried to tactfully dissuade her, but she carried on, tut-tutting about what she presumed to be stubborn stains.

'What is the purpose of your journey?' she enquired.

We'd been asked this question a hundred times already, and I still hadn't found a satisfactory answer. The concept of seeking adventure, and of taking time off work to do so, was alien in a place where people's lives revolved around the basics of survival. While I was still casting around for an explanation, she fired another question at me.

'And is it true that you left all your children at home?'

'I have no children,' I told her.

She was stunned by this news, and I took the chance to gently prise the frying pan from her fingers. To cheer her up, I asked, 'How many children do you have?'

'Five,' she said. 'But only three are with me. My sister is barren so I gave her my two youngest.'

She thought for a moment. 'You must ask your *wantoks* for some of their children!' she pronounced.

I tried to imagine how my brothers and sisters-in-law would react to such a demand, or how Dag would feel about one of my boisterous nephews and nieces moving in with us. I was about to explain that adoption in my part of the world was far less casual than in hers, but she was so obviously satisfied with the solution she'd found to my dilemma that I thought better of it.

After Samasodu there were fifty miles of uninhabited coast-line to the next village, Kia, on the northern tip of Santa Isabel. We paddled beyond the outer reefs, crossing them when neces-sary with a wish and a prayer that a rogue wave wouldn't decide to dump us on to the coral and wreck the kayak. And we kept our fingers crossed that the clement weather we were enjoying would stay with us. Through calm, crystal clear water, sharks cruised by us, curious but unobtrusive. Dolphins leaped up into the sunlight, or swam on their backs right next to the boat, showing us their bright white bellies. And turtles popped their heads up, taking in gulps of air.

One evening, we camped on a black sand beach which appeared to have been chewed by an earth mover. These were the tracks of giant leatherback turtles: at this time of year they came ashore at night to lay their eggs in the sand. After dark, we walked along the beach, straining our eyes and ears. Soon, we heard a deep grunting. We crept forward, Dag turned on the flashlight, and we jumped back in alarm at what its beam picked out. The turtle was at least half a ton in weight; the top of her ridged shell stood four feet from the ground and her splayed front flippers, tip to tip, were eight feet across. But there was nothing to fear from her: she was so engrossed in her egg-laying preparations that I doubt she even noticed our presence.

Using her back flippers like scoops, she spent an hour digging a narrow hole in the sand. When the hole was two feet deep, she began to lay her eggs. They were surprisingly small, like soft golf balls. As they fell out of her, her grunts changed to long groans, and big gelatinous tears oozed from her eyes. It took her half an hour to lay about a hundred eggs. She rested for a while, panting as if trying to regain some strength. Then, with the utmost tenderness, she gently patted sand over the eggs and began filling in the hole. By now, her groans must have been those of pure exhaustion, but her work wasn't over yet. Shuffling sideways, she dug two more holes and filled them in as decoys for the predatory lizards. Finally, her work completed, she turned and lumbered back to the water. The waves broke over her shell, and she was gone. All night, turtles emerged from the surf like huge mythical creatures, and all night we stayed up and watched them. The last ones retreated to their own element just before dawn broke. We managed an hour of sleep before the sun rose and started beating into the tent. When we crawled outside, it was to discover four feet long monitor lizards up and down the beach, busily digging for their breakfast.

The lack of sleep made us grumpy for the rest of the day. We

paddled past long stretches of inhospitable swamp and mangroves, and through a muddle of steep, rocky islets where the air
was still and unbearably hot. I constantly had to shift around in
my seat to ease the discomfort of a fungal infection and a few saltwater sores. I remembered the advice of a friend in Canada, who
had said that when the going got rough I should try creative visu-
alization techniques.

Dutifully, I imagined myself as a hermit crab, curled up in my
cool, dark shell. It didn't work. Then I imagined myself lying
between crisp linen sheets in a shuttered room. That didn't work
either.

'Let's stop soon,' I suggested.

'Good idea, can you suggest somewhere?' Dag snapped.

'You've got the map, doesn't it show any beaches?'

'I've been looking at this map all day, why don't you take over
that side of things?'

By now, we'd perfected the art of paddling and squabbling at
the same time. Dag hurled his wrath at my back; I hurled mine at
the ocean. 'For heaven's sake, just tell me if there are any beaches
about!'

'No, there aren't.'

'What are we going to do?'

'I don't know, why don't you make a suggestion for a change?'

'What's the point, we always do what you want anyway!'

The row was interrupted by a piercing whistle. We turned to
see a man waving to us from one of the rocky islets. 'Hello!
Helloooo! Over here!' he called, and guided us into a small bay,
concealed by mangroves, where an open fronted house stood on
stilts over the water.

Kora Islet was very different to the pristine Melanesian villages
we'd visited so far. Plastic kerosene bottles floated among the
mangrove roots. Beneath a washing line, clothes were trampled
into the mud. Pieces of corrugated iron and firewood lay around.
A path of coconut husks had been partly built and then abandoned. Next to a ramshackle kitchen hut, smoked sea slugs, or
bêche-de-mer, lay scattered over the ground and scruffy chickens
scratched in the dirt. But Victor Thagramana warmly welcomed
us, pushing aside heaps of clothing and bedding, and laying a
mat for us to sit on by the open doorway of the tiny house. He
told us that he was a police bandmaster in Honiara, and that

Kora Islet was his custom land. He, his Polynesian wife Christina and their daughter Jemima were here for the Christmas holidays, visiting Christine's mother Rhonda who lived in this, the only settlement on Kora.

'In Honiara, I work hard, earn money, spend it all on food and rent,' said Victor. 'Here, I live freely. I eat cassava from the garden and fish from the sea. If I need money I sell a little bêche-de-mer or copra. I enjoy island life. I forget about work!'

While Victor rejoiced over forgetting about work, the women of his family were out catching dinner. Towards late afternoon they paddled their dugout back from the reef, singing Polynesian songs in three-part harmony. Victor's wife and mother-in-law were portly women with halos of frizzy hair. His nineteen-year-old daughter Jemima had a lithe body, the colour of nutmeg, covered only by a casually knotted *sulu* which kept slipping from her breasts. Straight black hair framed her face and cascaded to her waist. Around her forehead was a garland of fresh turmeric, and in one hand she held the afternoon's catch of several large trevally.

After a dinner of fish and rice, Dag presented Victor with some tobacco. 'We have had no tobacco for one week!' Victor cried. 'Now there are smiles everywhere!'

Using school exercise-book paper, he rolled up several fat cigarettes, handing the first to his mother-in-law. Then he produced a large battered kettle filled with *kalevi*, a strong grog made from fermented coconut palm sap. 'It has to be finished tonight!' he announced gleefully, passing me a half coconut shell brimming with the opaque, slightly fizzy liquid. 'Otherwise it burns holes in the kettle!'

It was pleasant stuff, but strong, and after two shellfuls I was yawning. Leaving Dag and Victor to work their way through the kettle, I helped the women to hang up mosquito nets from the ceiling of the house and to lay out mats and sheets beneath them. Soon I was drifting off to sleep. Rhonda and Christina snored wheezily, a bêche-de-mer exploded on the smoking rack in the cook house, and, below me, water slapped around the mangrove roots.

'This is island life!' I heard Victor cry. 'You drink, fall down, sleep, get up, fish!'

At dawn, a hand lifted a corner of our mosquito net and slid in a glass jar containing several freshly picked wild orchids. Minutes later the net was lifted again and a thermos flask and two plastic cups were pushed beneath it. Inside the flask was a hot drink made from lemon grass, water and sugar.

'We're in heaven,' said Dag.

By the time we had dismantled the mosquito net and rolled up the mat, Jemima had arrived with our breakfast: Hard Navy biscuits, home-made coconut jam liberally peppered with ants, and three boiled eggs. Dag peeled off one of the egg shells, releasing a powerful, sulphurous smell and revealing a well developed embryo.

'I can't eat that!' I whispered to Dag.

He, however, can eat almost anything. He rummaged around in our food bag for a bottle of soy sauce, and tipped it liberally over the peeled egg.

'Don't!' I said, watching in horror as he put the whole egg into his mouth and, with a grim expression on his face, began determinedly chewing. He swallowed, reached for the water bottle and drank steadily from it for half a minute. Then he slipped the remaining eggs into the pockets of his shorts.

'I'll be back soon,' he said, and sauntered off towards the mangroves.

A little later, Jemima sidled over to me. 'You want a swim?' she asked me, meaning did I want to wash. Hitching her *sulu* over her breasts, she led me along the coconut path. It turned into a muddy trail, and wound through huge ferns to where a stream trickled out of the rock and formed a small, murky pool. Scattered around it were broken plastic bowls, bits of laundry soap, and more trodden-in washing. Jemima squatted down by the pool, and trailed her long fingers across the surface of the water. I hunkered down next to her, uncertain of what I was supposed to do. She looked from side to side, her dark eyes searching the dense foliage around us. Then she put her head close to mine.

'Your husband went to mangroves,' she whispered. 'I saw.'

'Yes,' I whispered back, casting around for an explanation of the egg disposal.

'He makes his toilet on land?' she asked. 'Or sea?'

'Sometimes in the sea,' I told her. 'Sometimes on land.'

'Land is dangerous!' she hissed. 'There are *velas* around here!'

We'd heard a lot about *velas*, the magicians said to get their power by murdering the person they love the most. I'd been warned that a local girl could make Dag fall in love with her by stealing a hair from his head and taking it to *vela*. We'd heard of *velas* with crooked fingers who could kill us by putting our spirits in a basket, and *velas* who could steal our footprints and possess us. Now, Jemima had news of a different type.

'If you make your toilet on land, the *vela* can take a piece of it and use it to put bad magic on you. But the sea has a good spirit and if your toilet is in it the *velas* cannot touch it.'

'Where are these *velas*?' I asked.

Her eyes skittered about. 'Everywhere! Some places are not blessed and evil spirits live in the trees.'

Above us, the leaves rustled, and I looked up and met the gaze of a large, green monitor lizard clinging to a branch.

'We'll make our toilet in the sea,' I promised her, and we hurried back down the path towards the sunlight.

Days slid lazily by. Each afternoon we paddled with the women to the reef to fish and to dive for bêche-de-mer. On the way home we stopped at mangrove swamps to collect firewood. Once, we snorkelled around the submerged remains of a Second World War fighter plane. It was surprisingly intact, and lay on one wing in twenty feet of sun-dappled water. I tried to imagine the gunfire, the flames, the pilot's fear as the plane went down. But staghorn coral grew from the rudder, angel fish fluttered through the port-holes, a moray eel curled around a machine gun mounting and all echoes of violence seemed long, long gone.

In the evenings we sat under the stars, drinking *kalevi* and swapping stories, then retired to the house to sleep with the mosquito nets billowing around us in the warm breeze.

'Stay for Christmas!' said Victor one night. 'Stay longer! We'll build you a house!'

It was perfectly possible to imagine cancelling the rest of our trip around the world and spending months on Kora Islet. One morning, we realized that if we didn't leave right away, we never would. After a last breakfast, Jemima slipped frangipani garlands over our heads, and presented us with a jar of her ant-peppered jam. We gave the family fishing lures and line, the rest of the tobacco, a hat, and a T-shirt. They squeezed into their dugout canoe and paddled with us to the outer reef, singing Polynesian songs of farewell. By the time we crossed the reef, I was so awash with tears that the open ocean ahead was a blur. Behind us, the Thagramanas floated in their canoe, singing until we were out of sight. Their sweet harmonies gradually faded away, but once Victor's shout rang out, loud and clear. 'Remember island life! Come back to us one day!'

7

A Reward

After Kora, the large village of Kia seemed almost urban. Leaf houses crowded the narrow shoreline, and outside its several well-stocked stores groups of young men, heavily stoned on betel, hung around with ghetto-blasters glued to their ears.

'Oh mi Anita!' went the popular song of the time. 'Mi bilong yu! Yu breakin' heart bilong mi! Mi kam back again, mi hope yu wait mi!'

In one of the stores, where we replenished our dwindling food supplies, we met a woman called Edith who had lived in Ottawa for one year, and was soon to leave for Melbourne to complete her BSc in nursing.

'I go to foreign countries to learn the latest methods,' she told us, 'then I come back here to a ward full of patients who think they are bewitched. Sometimes I wonder if my training was a waste of time.'

She invited us into her parents' house, where her father was boiling fish heads over a kerosene stove while his wife grated coconut.

'I came to check on my customary land and my parents,' said Edith. 'I will go back to Honiara tonight or tomorrow, whenever the boat comes, so they make food for my journey. See how hard the island life is? No electricity, no running water. Working in the garden all day, then spending hours preparing food.'

I asked her how she had felt when she first arrived in Canada.

'I was amazed! Like the people from Kia when they first go to

Honiara, like you when you came here. But then I got used to it. That is the problem, you get used to one thing then you must change. Sometimes I think it would be better if I had stayed at home, and not gone to secondary school and to college. My life is too confusing, I don't know where I belong.'

The fish heads were left to boil over while Edith's father scrutinized our map. We told him of our plan to find a channel through the maze of islands north of Santa Isabel, then cross the Manning Strait, notorious for its currents and rip tides.

'Should we go through the channel when tide is high or low?' Dag asked.

'Yesss,' answered Edith's father.

Dag tried again. 'When is the best time to go through the channel?'

Edith's father scratched his head. 'Tomorrow,' he said.

Erratic currents led us astray, islets and bays not shown on our map appeared, and soon we were lost. Steep slopes towered above us, and the jungle pressed in, steamy and oppressive. As we searched for the channel, a series of alarming twists and turns took us into dead ends where huge tree roots grew from the water and vines hung in such tangles that we had to haul the boat through them. Thick prickly leaves ripped our skin and grabbed at our hair. The thought of crocodiles was never far away. Once, we got stuck among low overhanging branches, floating in shallow water infested by large stingrays with black tails and speckled backs that zoomed around the boat. It took hours of this torture before we found the channel, and by then our drinking water was worryingly low. Finally, towards evening, the steep jungle walls eased back, and we spied the open ocean. We were through. Just before the end of the channel we found a protected bay with a small beach, a rock bluff – and a stream! Unable to believe our good fortune we pulled ashore. As the day drew to a close, and tiny bats started flitting around our heads, Dag fried cassava slices over a small fire, while I washed myself in the stream. Our relief was too great for us to be concerned about the rushing sounds of the tide rips, out in the Manning Strait.

Four hours of fighting hard against strong currents and steep waves had their reward: the Arnavon Islands, a few uninhabited scraps of land, sculpted by wind and waves, in the middle of the Manning Strait. The island we chose as our home for a few days had a long, wedge-shaped beach, tapering to a point with the luminous blue sea curling around it on both sides. It was an impossibly pretty, romantic place, the desert isle of everyone's dreams. We stripped off our clothes, which were so stiff with salt they could practically stand up by themselves. There was no fear of causing offence with our nakedness – as far as the eye could see there was no sign of human life, not even a boat on the horizon or the tail of a jet in the sky.

Surrounding the island was a coral reef made intriguing by exposure to currents, and untouched by humans. At the edge of the reef there was a dizzying drop-off, a sheer cliff where the shafts of sunlight were swallowed up by the shadowy depths, and where parrot and grouper fish of an immense size advanced curiously upon these two strange creatures invading their domain. I only peeked over the edge of the cliff, preferring to snorkel in the security of the shallows and their pretty coral gardens. But Dag spent hours exploring it, using a weight belt, flippers and great lungfuls of air to dive deep. Spooked by the size of the fish, however, he never bothered to take out his spear gun.

'I'm worried,' he said, 'that *they* might decide to take *me* home to their wives for supper.'

When I wasn't snorkelling, I did little but move from one shady spot to another. Scattered over the sand around me were weathered, grey coconuts, some sprouting fresh green shoots topped with tender ribbed leaves. Hermit crabs busily crawled about, and through the bushes I could see gawky megapode birds, which laid their large eggs in the warm sand and then abandoned them to incubate on their own. The branches above me swayed as red parrots hopped about them, pecking at flowers and scolding each other. Kingfishers dive-bombed into the water, white cockatoos swooped by. Large bugs, like deer flies, constantly hovered around me, attracted by my sticky skin. It was too hot to do much but lie back and think. Often, my thoughts would concern Dag, swimming off the reef. I'd consider the possibility of him being attacked by a shark. What if he came back with some terrible gaping wound? We had suture materials with us, but he was the one with a medical background. What if he simply didn't come back? Through binoculars I scanned a distant reef, where perfectly sculpted waves seemed to pause and show off their smooth green bellies before breaking in a surge of white foam. And beyond, the currents of the Manning Strait met with wind and kicked up waves that made the horizon look bumpy and blurred. Where, in this expanse of sea and sky, would I go for help? Just as panic would begin to creep up on me, I'd see Dag's head as he came up for air, the sunlight glinting on his body as it curved through the water and finally his flippers sliding beneath the surface.

Our food supplies were so low that they rattled around in the bottom of the once bulging waterproof bag. One night we cooked up some taro leaves that we'd brought from Kia. Although they were horribly wilted, we steamed them along with some grated coconut, and the result was quite tasty. 'They're very tender,' commented Dag after his first bite. 'I wonder why local people always cook them for so long.' As we each had a second bite, I suddenly remembered what I'd seen in the village cook houses.

'They boil—' I began, but Dag was already clutching at his neck, with his eyes a pair of bulging question-marks.

'What's going on?' he croaked.

'They boil them—' I managed, before my throat seemed to close up and speaking became impossible. It was as if my oesophagus had suddenly sprouted hundreds of burning, itching barbs. Terrifying thoughts flashed through my mind – of our windpipes being cut off, of us staggering around and slowly choking to death, of our bodies lying undiscovered for months. Gradually, I realized that, while not going away, the effects weren't getting any worse, and that we were both still breathing.

'You have to boil taro leaves twice,' I finally managed to hoarsely whisper.

'Thanks for the tip,' Dag rasped back.

Repairing our throats accounted for a good deal of our water supply; soon, we realized, we would have to get across the Manning Strait and over to the villages on Vaghena Island. 'We shouldn't linger here, anyway, because bad weather could move in fast,' said Dag. 'Besides, we've got to find out about a ship from Vaghena back to Honiara. Our flight to Australia leaves in just over a week, you know.'

I knew, but I didn't want to think about it.

8

Ships That Have Sailed

By noon next day we'd completed the crossing of the Manning Strait and arrived in Kukutin, on the south-west side of Vaghena Island. Here, we learned that the last ship before Christmas to Honiara had already sailed. In two days' time another ship was scheduled to leave for the capital from the port of Noro, on New Georgia Island, seventy miles across New Georgia Sound.

'Let's paddle to Noro,' I suggested.

Dag looked at me in horror. 'Are you kidding?'

'We can set out before dawn,' I insisted.

'What if bad weather moves in? We'd be on open ocean for forty miles. Do you realize how committing such a long crossing is? Have you gone nuts?'

Obviously I had.

'We're fit and acclimatized,' I said breezily. 'It will nicely round off our time in the Solomons.'

'It might round us off as well,' said Dag sardonically, but I could tell he was pleased that, for a change, it was me taking the initiative, me pushing for challenge, me coming up with a crazy idea.

Vaghena Island's original Melanesian population was wiped out last century by disease and head-hunting. Thirty years ago, Micronesians began moving from the overpopulated Gilbert Islands to Vaghena, where they established three villages, of which Kukutin is the largest. Unlike Melanesians, the Gilbertese people don't have a tradition of self-sufficient gardening, so on

Vaghena their main livelihood comes from the abundance of seafood in the surrounding waters. Recently, a Taiwanese company had made some investments in Vaghena Island. It equipped fishermen with engines for their canoes, it installed generator-run freezers in the village and it made contracts to buy up the harvests of giant clams and crayfish which it regularly collects in high-speed boats. Vaghena, a remote island with no roads, telephones, electricity or running water, suddenly became a consumer society.

In Kuktutin's narrow river mouth, we'd nosed the boat through slimy water strewn with floating litter and fish carcasses. Tied up next to a small bridge was a large and modern motor boat with the name 'Mr Muscle' crudely stencilled on its prow. Lounging on deck, chewing gum and listening to a pop version of 'Jingle Bells' on a ghetto-blaster was a Taiwanese fish trader in blue jeans and a tight T-shirt. When he told us that we'd missed the ferry to Honiara, we asked about the possibility of camping in the village. 'You must talk to Henry,' he said.

On a mat spread over the crushed coral floor of his kitchen hut, Henry sat cross-legged and contemplative. He was a squarely built man, with sad, almond-shaped eyes and thick grey hair combed back from a wide forehead. He wore only a towel, wrapped *sulu*-style around his waist, and a large digital wristwatch. Scrawny chickens pecked among the coral, searching for crumbs, and if one came too close to Henry he swatted it with the palm leaf he was using as a fan. His wife, June, who was also big, wide-faced and towel-wrapped, was busily feeding wood into the oil drum cooking stove, and heaping food from blackened pots on to metal plates. Soon, the mat was covered with dishes: sweet potato, rice, corned beef with onion, lobster, fresh bread and margarine. One of the chickens managed a few brave pecks at the rice before Henry's wrath descended on it, and it ran, squawking loudly, right through the plate of corned beef and out of the door.

'Eat,' commanded Henry. He was terribly concerned about our plans to cross to Noro, and from time to time he rubbed his eyes with the back of his hand and gave a deep sigh. 'Please do not leave on this terrible journey,' he said.

In Kukutin, Henry was a man of influence. He owned a general store, he had a house with a corrugated iron roof and a generator, and he ran the village cinema. After lunch, we went to his store and bought packets of a savoury snack called Cheese Twisties, tubes of frozen fruit cordial called Ice Blocks and tickets for the afternoon video show. A video! After two months spent on isolated beaches and in traditional villages, with our only power sources a flashlight, a kerosene lamp and the fuel for our cooking stove, this seemed sophistication beyond belief. We followed Henry into the back room of the store. Its concrete floor was spread with cracked linoleum and the windows were covered with sheets of corrugated iron. Henry insisted we sit on the only two chairs, amidst a jumble of old oil cans, sacks of rice, coils of ropes and empty cardboard boxes. The audience – men leaning against the walls, teenagers and small children sprawling on the floor – was focused on a large television screen, across which Cher was dancing about in a black leotard with strategically placed holes. 'If I could turn back time!' she sang, thrusting out her pelvis.

On broad, bare feet, Henry plodded up to the VCR and pressed a button, causing Cher to instantly disappear. In the sudden hush, we could hear the steady thumping of the generator. He slotted a cartridge into the machine and the afternoon feature began. It was a Chinese film, its plot made incomprehensible by the lack of dubbing or subtitles. Nonetheless, the crowd was agog, and roared its approval of the sword fights, gory stabbings and decapitations.

'Let's go,' I whispered to Dag, but he was working his way through a packet of Cheese Twisties without taking his eyes off the screen. He didn't seem to notice when I crept away through a side door.

Outside, a sour smell rose from the river. It was mid-afternoon, the hottest part of the day, and men lay about in the shade of houses raised several feet off the ground on stilts. On the grey sand, a group of women sat weaving bright green sago palm leaves into sections for a thatched roof. Two girls walked by carrying between them a bamboo pole with a bucket of water suspended from it. Naked children played in the dust, flicking rubber bands to see who could get them to go furthest. A hen and several chicks wandered into the store, and were shooed out, clucking and flapping. The peaceful scene was broken when a motorized canoe roared into the mouth of the river. Its driver cut the engine and began yelling, causing a general rousing among the sleeping men.

'What's happening?' I asked one of the women.

'They have caught big turtles,' she answered.

It took two men to slaughter a turtle. Together, they heaved the creature out of the canoe and on to its back. One man stood on the turtle's front flippers to immobilize it. The other used a long, sharp knife to cut around the edge of the shell. Thick blood oozed and then flowed freely, turning the water bright red. The man slid the knife beneath the skin of the belly and lifted it clean away, revealing pulsating innards. The turtle was still alive. Helplessly, it raised its head and waved its back flippers. The man put down his knife, plunged his hands inside the turtle and began disembowelling it. I closed my eyes, and thought of the sleeping turtles we'd seen while snorkelling, the small turtles that often surfaced for air in front of the kayak, the giant leatherback turtles we'd watched laying their eggs. When I reopened my eyes, one man was wrenching off the turtle's flippers, and the other was scraping out its shell.

As soon as the afternoon video finished, Henry helped us unpack our boat, standing with us in the filthy river water. Then he and June carried our gear to their house and insisted we share their upstairs living area. Flimsy walls separated the space into four rooms furnished with mats and cardboard boxes. From one of these rooms some children, of which Henry seemed to have an indeterminate number, were cleared out to make way for us. We were shown the outside latrine and bath house, an impressive arrangement with a cement plinth for squatting on and a large tin bath filled with fresh water for washing. And, for the evening video show, in my honour Henry chose an English B movie about gang warfare in London.

The night-time crowd was bigger than during the afternoon and included women, teenage girls and small babies. They watched white men chase around in cars, blow up safes, rob banks and shoot each other. It was such a bad copy that Dag and I could barely understand the dialogue; to everyone else in the room it must have been as incomprehensible and alien as the Chinese film earlier that day. When it was over and the lights went up, Henry padded over to us.

'There is a dancing practice in the village. The people are preparing for Christmas. Would you like to see? My daughter Agatha will take you there.'

In seconds, we were transported from London's underworld to a tropical island, where fruit bats squabbled in the papaya trees and a balmy wind blew in from the sea. We followed Agatha along paths between thatch houses to the far end of the village, where an open-sided meeting house was packed with people. In the centre, a group of ten men sat on the floor, drumming on upturned wooden boxes and leading the crowd in songs about village affairs, fishing and Jesus. At one end of the house, women were dancing. They wore T-shirts with slogans like 'Surf City' or 'Rock 'n' Roll', grass skirts and frangipani garlands. In contrast to the exuberant singing, they danced with precise, perfectly timed movements of head, hands, arms and feet. Agatha was too busy questioning me to join them.

'Why don't you have any children? How long have you been married? What is your religion? Does it rain like this in your country?'

A sudden, tropical storm had hit. Rain hammered on the corrugated iron roof and bounced off the ground outside. Shuffling inwards, away from the open sides of the house, the crowd sang louder than ever. It was after ten o'clock when we returned to Henry's house, where the generator still thumped and electric lights blazed.

'Do not go on this journey,' Henry pleaded over breakfast. 'Stay here for Christmas.'

We assured him it was something we were choosing to do, but he wouldn't be convinced. 'You are like my son and daughter. I am worried about you in your little boat.'

All day, the generator thumped while we sat in Henry's house sorting through our gear. As we were shortly to fly out of the Solomon Islands, we wanted to lighten our luggage as much as possible. We heaped Henry with gifts: a weight belt for diving, fishing tackle, a fish grill and the rest of our trade items.

'It's not enough to repay your kindness,' we insisted, but he accepted the gifts with a mixture of gratitude and profound concern. That night, he showed what he considered to be his best video, featuring a young Steve McQueen playing a half-Indian. It was a favourite of the audience, which cheered at the scene where McQueen paddles a dugout canoe through a Louisiana swamp. As soon as the film finished, we went to bed, needing a good rest before the long ocean crossing. We set our alarm for four o'clock, then settled down, expecting the lights and the noisy generator to go off at eleven, as they had the night before. But they stayed on, and on, and on. The thump of the generator reverberated through the floor of our room and rattled the walls. At 2.00 am, Dag got up to use the latrine. He found Henry sitting Buddha-like and surrounded by white feathers outside the kitchen hut, while his wife busied around inside it.

'Why are you up so late?' Dag asked him.

'We are cooking a chicken,' said Henry.

For us, of course. With all our gifts, we had tipped the delicate balance of generosity, and now Henry felt in our debt and was anxious to repay us. 'Sleep now,' he insisted. 'Rest for your journey.'

This was easier said than done. We dozed fitfully, and just before the alarm went off, we woke and sat bolt upright, convinced that the sun had risen and that we'd overslept. But then we heard the beat of the generator, and realized the light came from electric bulbs. Loud snoring told us that the whole family was now asleep. Stepping over the children on the veranda, we crept downstairs and over to where the boat was anchored. Minutes later we were joined by Henry, June and Agatha, who held our flashlights while we packed the boat.

'You do not have to go on this journey,' said Henry. 'You can stay with us for Christmas.'

Repeating our gratitude, we said goodbye, and June handed us the chicken and warm, freshly baked bread.

The moon was already down, the night inky black and the sea so flat calm that it mirrored the stars, and we seemed to be paddling off into the sky itself. After ten minutes I turned around; the lights at Henry's house had finally been turned off, and it was as if Vaghena Island had never existed and our time there had been an illusion.

With dawn came a cloud cover that kept the morning cool and helped us to establish a steady paddling rhythm. Around eight o'clock huge cumulus clouds moved towards us, trailing veils of rain. But within minutes the sun came out, the clouds burned off and our shirts steamed dry. We stopped for breakfast: peanuts, June's bread and the ant and coconut jam we'd saved from Kora Island. Behind us, Vaghena was a faint line on the horizon. Far ahead, across an eerily calm expanse of cobalt water, we could see the peak of the volcanic island of Kolombangara. There were no birds in sight, no boats. Once again we were utterly alone, out in the Solomon Sea, this time not on a tiny island, but in a kayak.

It's one thing to paddle a few miles offshore – although being in striking distance of land is not necessarily a guarantee of safety, psychologically it has a most reassuring effect. But an open ocean crossing is quite another matter, especially when you reach the halfway point, and turning back is no longer an option. By then, you are committed whether or not you like it, and you simply have to keep an eye on the compass, make one paddle stroke after the other and, if you're lucky enough to have good conditions, hope that they hold.

We had no storms to contend with, no cresting waves, no strong currents, no headwind. Unfortunately, there was no wind at all. The air was so still that it seemed as if the day was holding its breath, and heat seemed to hang from the sky like a heavy, damp curtain. At eleven we stopped for a lunch break, and pulled out the unfortunate chicken which had been responsible for our lack of sleep the night before. Despite its unappetizing pale grey colour, it was surprisingly tasty. We ate it with the salty Hard Navy biscuits we'd bought in Henry's store, and tossed the remains overboard. Then we considered a swim. We were paddling across a stretch of water where shark fishermen make big catches. They go out with rattles made of giant clam and half coconut shells strung on to thick vine, and shake these just below the surface of the water to summon up the sharks. 'Out there,' Henry had warned us, 'Sharks are always watching and listening, and many things attract them.'

Many things? Fingers, toes, legs, feet, chicken carcasses? All morning, such considerations had prevented me plopping into the water to cool down. When I'd needed to pee, I hung over the side of the kayak. But now, the urge to swim was becoming irresistible.

'Are sharks attracted to chicken bones?' I asked Dag, as casually as I could.

'No, but they are to pink shorts,' he teased.

In we went. Although the water temperature was probably around 28 degrees, compared to an air temperature in the thirties and a humidity approaching 100 per cent it felt refreshingly cool. We swam around and under the boat. Suddenly, from the corner of my eyes, I saw a flash of something long and white. Part of my brain instantly reminded me that the worst thing to do in the vicinity of sharks is to splash about. But another, more dominant part overrode this sensible advice and propelled me to the boat and into the cockpit in a mad frenzy of flailing limbs.

'There's something in the water!' I yelled at Dag.

He was the picture of relaxation, floating on his back, his arms behind his head, his chest puffed out to give him buoyancy.

'I saw it,' he laconically replied. 'It's a length of toilet paper. It floated out of your shorts pocket.'

At midday, when our skins were parched and encrusted with salt, the sun began its serious torment. It bounced off the water and on to my face and neck, making my hat and sunglasses practically redundant. The heat became a physical entity. It lowered itself on to us, it beat down on our heads and sucked the moisture from our bodies. Wearing shirts became unbearable, so we took them off, soaked our *sulus* in the ocean and draped them around our shoulders. The gaps between our breaks became shorter. We went into the water every hour, and then every forty-five minutes. We stopped eating, and just drank litre after litre of water, grateful that we'd decided to carry so much with us. The colour of the sea and sky bleached out until the horizon was hard to distinguish, and seemed to dance about before our eyes. My arms felt as if they were no longer part of my body but some piece of machinery which had been attached to me and programmed to paddle and paddle and paddle . . .

During the afternoon, the islands of Kolombangara and New Georgia gradually eased up from the horizon, and began to loom to the west and south. By six o'clock we could make out individual trees on the slopes of New Georgia, and it seemed we would be there in minutes. We planned to find a beach, camp overnight and set off at dawn for the last stretch to Noro. Now that the end of the day was in sight, my arms became reattached to my torso and my brain told me how very tired they were. The water seemed to have become thick and viscous, and pushing a paddle through it was a terrible effort. The sun slipped away in a blaze of colour, turning the clouds shrouding the summit of Kolombangara a vivid orange. A school of dolphins surfaced and frolicked around us. Apart from a few flying fish, they were the only other living creatures we'd seen all day. Darkness began to settle, and still we hadn't reached our goal.

'I've heard of receding hairlines,' Dag groaned. 'But never of receding coastlines!'

Slowly, slowly, we drew closer. The moon came up, but played peek-a-boo behind a thin cloud cover forming across the sky. Ahead of us, the jungle-clad slopes of New Georgia Island were a dark, dense wall, eerily echoing with screams, whistles, pops and trills. A warm wind blew offshore, bringing with it the heavy scents of tropical flowers and damp earth. And the sound of breaking waves told us we were approaching a coral reef. We inched along, listening, peering through the darkness at the white foam of waves where we knew couldn't cross the reef, and hoping to see dark patches of deeper water where perhaps we could. There were no dark patches. Behind me, Dag cursed.

'It's December twentieth,' he said. 'Tomorrow is summer solstice. We're arriving here at one of the lowest tides of the year.'

'What shall we do?' I asked.

We both knew there was only one answer to that question, but neither of us wanted to voice it. The tide was dropping, we couldn't cross the reef, so we simply had to carry on.

Around ten o'clock, a new smell drifted to us from shore: burning wood. We saw a soft glow swinging through the darkness. Someone was walking along carrying a kerosene lamp. Listening keenly, we heard voices, and a dog barking. The proximity of somewhere to stop and rest was an unbearable thought.

'We couldn't go ashore there anyway,' said Dag reassuringly. 'The people would think we were ghosts. We'd scare them silly.'

My vision was playing tricks. Kolombangara Island reared up from the sea like a gargantuan tidal wave. Lightening storms hurled dazzling, writhing snakes across the sky. Just before midnight, we decided that we were too tired to continue. Dropping a sea anchor to prevent the boat drifting, we wriggled down and folded our legs around all the bags of gear stowed beneath the deck. Although far from comfortable, we both fell instantly asleep. It was a short respite: three hours later we were awake again, feeling damp and shivery. But now there were two incentives to keep paddling: ahead was a faint glow of light which we presumed to be the port of Noro, and to the east, stars were beginning to fade from the sky.

Dawn was slow and unspectacular, just a grey light pushing away the last vestiges of the night. It found us paddling through a stretch of protected water between Kolombangara and New Georgia Islands, and fantasizing about soft white beaches. Alas, there were none in sight. As soon as the reef was safe to cross we headed over to New Georgia, where, between thick jungle and the water, there was a narrow coastal strip of sharp volcanic rock. I knew from experience that, in terms of somewhere to rest, this would be the equivalent of a bed of nails. But we were desperate to get out of the boat, even it was only to stand and stretch. As we came close to the shore, I thought my eyes were starting to play tricks again. The rocks appeared to be undulating. They were also making strange clicking sounds. Abruptly, Dag stopped paddling. 'No way,' he said quietly, 'am I getting out here.'

Stretching from the shoreline to the forest wall was a deep, writhing layer of land crabs. There were thousands upon thousands of them, clambering and scuttling all over each other, four and five deep in places. Horrified and fascinated, we watched from a few yards offshore. Each crab had an egg sack on its lower abdomen, and when it scrambled down to the edge of the rocks, it raised its pincers and wriggled its body in a comical hula dance, releasing a cloud of eggs into the water. Then it turned and fought its way back through the tide of oncoming crabs. The water was murky with eggs, and colourful fish were milling about, enjoying the feast. Once again, not wanting to voice the inevitable, I asked an unnecessary question.

'What shall we do?'

'Keep paddling,' said Dag.

After a few miles, the crab layer thinned out, and eventually disappeared. We anchored the boat and waded to shore, stepping gingerly over sharp rocks. We'd been at sea for twenty-five hours; our limbs were tired and stiff, our backsides raw and aching. Finding a patch of jungle that had been cleared and planted with taro and cassava, I lay down on a fallen log while Dag opened up our last can of tuna and spread it on to biscuits.

'We've got company,' he said, and I looked up to see two small boys pulling a dugout canoe on to the shore. On bare feet, they walked across the sharp rock and sat down a short distance away, staring at us with wide eyes.

'How far is it to Noro?' we asked them.

'Two hours,' they said

'That means four,' I predicted, and I was right.

When we clambered back into the boat I felt as cold as I had been during the night, and I longed for the sun to climb up into the sky and warm me. Which it soon did, and with a vengeance. Once again the day was totally still, without even the slightest breeze. The heat felt like a solid wall, pressing against us from all sides. We began going into the water every forty minutes, then every half-hour.

Just before we took our last dip, I saw a large grey fin slicing through the water. It was portside, perhaps thirty yards away. For a couple of seconds it veered towards us, and then disappeared below the surface. Calmly, I thought: that was a shark.

I turned to Dag. 'Did you just see something in the water?'

'No,' he answered.

He was easing himself out of his cockpit.

'One more swim,' he said. 'And then we'll make a final push for Noro.'

He sat on the side of the boat and, with a loud splash, fell backwards into the water. I thought: perhaps it's not a good idea.

But my body was so assaulted by heat that it wasn't interested in common sense, or in entertaining any of my usual fears and paranoias. Seconds later, I had joined Dag.

When we finally rounded a point and saw a beacon marking the opening of the harbour, we cheered. A breeze came up, so we raised our sail and cruised slowly along towards the smoking chimneys of Noro's fish processing plant. On one side of the harbour, company houses crawled up the hillside. They were ugly, dilapidated structures with plywood walls and iron roofs. On the other side, the leaf houses of a traditional village stood on stilts over the water.

After thirty hours of paddling across an empty ocean and along uninhabited jungle coastlines, we arrived at the Japanese owned Tai-Yo factory, the place from where all the tins of tuna fish we had consumed during the past months had originated. As we came alongside a wharf, some workers ran down to greet us. They were astounded to hear that we had paddled from Vaghena; we were astounded to learn that one of them, Peter, was related to Henry. 'He's my cousin brother,' he said.

Peter took us under his wing. First, he led us to where a

skipload of tuna was being hosed down with fresh water. He handed us the hose pipe, and we took turns underneath its strong gush, washing the salt out of our hair, skin and clothes. Dripping wet, we followed Peter through the factory site. After the peace and solitude of the ocean, this seemed like a bizarre dream: the clanging of skips being loaded on to cargo boats, machines pounding inside concrete buildings, radios blaring out rock music, trucks revving their engines. Japanese supervisors in pristine white shorts and shirts jumped out of brand-new jeeps and purposefully scribbled on clipboards. The heat bounced off tarmac, metal and concrete, and the still air was saturated with the smell of rancid fish.

'What time does the *Iuminau* leave?' we asked Peter, referring to the ferry, our old rat-infested friend, that was scheduled to call at Noro that night.

'The *Iuminau?*'

We nodded. 'We have to get to Honiara to catch a plane.'

'I take you where you can buy cold drinks!' he cried, and the subject of the *Iuminau* was dropped.

At the gates of the factory compound, Peter hailed down a passing truck and we climbed in the back. Half a mile down the road, it dropped us off at the company store. Behind the counter, a heavily sweating Japanese man was in charge of the cash register, while several local teenagers ran around collecting customers' orders from the well-stocked shelves and fridges. We bought three cold beers, and sat outside in the shade of a corrugated iron shelter to drink them. When we handed a can to Peter he checked that no one was watching, then hid it inside his shirt.

'If I drink this in public, I will lose my job,' he explained.

'What time is the *Iuminau* coming?' Dag asked him again.

'Why don't you come to my village?' he said, pointing across the harbour. 'You can stay in my house.'

If it hadn't been for our alcohol-induced feelings of wellbeing, we might have remembered that Solomon Islanders will go to great lengths to avoid passing on bad news or giving a negative answer; we might have realized what it was Peter was trying his hardest not to tell us.

We got another lift back to the factory, where I went to use the women's washrooms. Inside, I found a girl dressed in white rubber boots, lab coat and cap, stretched out for a rest in one of the trough-like sinks. On the opposite wall were several cubicles, each with a handwritten sign stuck on the door. One read 'Noro', another 'Marovo', another 'Munda'.

'Where you from?' the girl asked.

'England,' I told her. 'Which toilet should I use?'

Laughing heartily, she got out of the sink, walked over to the 'Noro' cubicle, ripped off the sign and ushered me inside.

When I re-emerged, she was back in the sink, but sitting upright. 'Where you go?' she asked.

'Honiara,' I told her. 'We're catching the *Iuminau* tonight.'

She frowned.

'*Iuminau* no coming,' she said.

'It's not coming?' I repeated in alarm.

'Yesss.'

'Is it coming?'

'Yesss.'

I tried a new tack. 'When is the *Iuminau* coming?'

She thought for a moment. 'Six o'clock,' she said.

Relieved, I thanked her and headed for the door. '*Iuminau* coming no more!' she called after me.

I turned back. 'No?'

'Yesss,' she said.

Outside, Dag was talking to a Japanese man who clutched his clipboard to his chest and bowed to me.

'I've got bad news,' said Dag.

'I think I know what it is,' I told him.

For reasons no one could explain to us, the *Iuminau* had sailed from Noro at six o'clock that morning, twelve hours before schedule. The next boat to Honiara wasn't due until the New Year, several days after our flight left for Australia.

In a whirl of efficiency, the Japanese man came up with solutions. There was a new road which ran through the jungle and connected Noro to the small town of Munda. At Munda there was an airstrip, and bush planes that flew to Honiara. He phoned, booked a flight, arranged for a truck. The truck came. We must hurry! he said. No time to take the boat apart now! Do it on the way to Munda! Eight burly Melanesian men lifted the fully laden boat on to their shoulders and jogged with it right through the factory compound and to the road. The truck was parked beyond a tree that had many low hanging branches. The men were heading for the tree at a steady jog.

'The mast!' cried Dag in warning. '*The maaast!*'

Too late. The aluminium pole met a low branch. The men kept jogging, their sheer strength making them unaware of the resistance. With a sickening *crack*! the central section of our mast broke in two and hit one of the men on the head. They stopped, and put the boat on the ground. Catching up them, we looked at the mast in dismay.

'Him gud no more?' asked one man.

'Problem?' enquired another.

The mast certainly was 'gud no more', but there was no point worrying these kind men about it. Besides which, we were on our way to Australia, where such problems could be easily solved.

'Im gud,' Dag reassured them. 'No problem.'

'The men's faces brightened. 'No problem!' they cried, and stood waving us goodbye as our truck rumbled towards the jungle.

9

Hiatus in Hong Kong

'I hungry!' cried the taxi driver, stuffing his mouth with biscuits. 'No time for eating, I work velly hard, but I fliddle tax man, too, ha ha!'

Trams rattled past, and above us towered Hong Kong's sheer cliff faces of glass and steel. 'OK, you tell me, where you want go really?' he asked.

'Government House,' I said.

The first two taxi drivers had refused point-blank to take us there. Now it seemed that this man had agreed only because he thought we were joking.

'Government House, ha! ha! You know David Wilson? Velly funny!' he chortled.

As it happened, I did know David Wilson. In 1981, I'd met him through my boyfriend, Joe Tasker, when they'd both been part of the first British mountaineering expedition to China. Joe was one of the climbers and David, who at that time was political adviser to the Governor of Hong Kong, had gone along as interpreter. The last contact I'd had with David and his wife Natasha was in 1982, when they sent their condolences after Joe's death on Everest. Weeks of living in the bush must have affected my sense of propriety: during our stopover in Australia I'd faxed David, who was now Governor of Hong Kong, without a second thought. 'You may not remember me . . .' I began the fax.

A reply came straight back. 'Of course we remember you! Do get in touch as soon as you arrive in Hong Kong.'

My sense of propriety was still amiss when from Kai Tak Airport
I phoned Government House and asked to speak to David or
Natasha. 'I presume,' said the voice on the other end, 'that you're
referring to Sir and Lady Wilson.'

Natasha, when she came on the line, was effusively friendly.
'Maria! We must see you! The problem is that we're awfully busy
this week, and we're leaving for Bonn on Saturday, but could
come for dinner on Friday? Yes? How lovely! Where are you staying?'

'Well, we're um – . . .' A sudden wave of snobbery prevented
me from admitting that we'd booked into the Hong Kong YMCA.
'We're going to find a hotel now,' I lied.

'Oh, dear! We can't have you running around the city at this
time of night! Look, why don't you come here? I'll have to see
what I can sort out room-wise—'

'We have a tent with us—'

The words were out before I realized how stupid they were, but
Natasha didn't miss a beat. 'That won't be necessary, but would
you mind awfully getting a taxi here? It's rather difficult to
arrange for an official car at this time of night.'

It wasn't until we were outside Government House, and guards
had stopped the traffic in both directions to let us drive through
the gates, that the taxi driver believed me. 'You really know David
Wilson!' he shouted incredulously. 'He a velly nice man, give
him my regards, don't tell him what I said about my taxes, OK?'

Dag and I were too dumbstruck to reply. We had expected
something fairly grand, but nothing like this expansive, floodlit
palace. Through its porticos and down its wide steps swarmed a
clutch of men in white jackets with red epaulettes. Some of
them heaved our dusty baggage out of the trunk, others held
open the doors of the taxi for us. As we clambered out, a uni-
formed official standing at the foot of the steps saluted, and a
young woman ran down to greet us. She introduced herself as
'Elspeth the housekeeper' but looked as if she belonged in the
pages of *Tatler* magazine. As I shook her hand, I was horribly
aware of my faded *sulu* and Dag's stained shorts and rat-chewed
shirt.

'Sir David and Lady Wilson regret that they will not be able to
meet you tonight,' she said. 'They've asked me to take you to your
suite and make sure everything is comfortable for you.' Numbly,

we followed her through a huge foyer, up a winding marble staircase and into the cavernous Tennis Court Suite. Sumptuously draped windows reached from the deeply carpeted floor to the high ceilings and opened on to a vast balcony. After months of sharing a small tent, we now had at our disposal two sitting-rooms, two bedrooms, two bathrooms, a dressing-room, a safe and a well-stocked bar. Not to mention a servant each. Ah Hon and Janet had slipped silently into the main sitting-room, and stood waiting for us.

'If you have any laundry,' said Ah Hon quietly, 'we will take it now and return in the morning.'

'We'll – er – have to change out of it first,' I stammered.

'Could we take your order for breakfast?' asked Hon.

'Breakfast? Oh, breakfast! I really don't know – I mean I – well . . .'

'Perhaps an English breakfast, madam?' Ah Hon kindly suggested. 'With grapefruit, tea, coffee?

'Yes, of course, whatever you think . . .'

Ah Hon and Janet slid out of the room.

As soon as we were alone, I filled one of the huge baths with steaming hot water and gratefully sank into it. After the Solomon Islands and Australia, Hong Kong in January was decidedly chilly. Dag, meanwhile, headed for the bar. He brought me a gin and tonic, and then wandered off clutching a glass filled with twenty-five-year-old, single malt whisky. I could hear him in the bedroom, chuckling and talking to himself.

'I don't believe this! They've got to be kidding! I don't believe it!'

His voice faded away, and I sank up to my chin into the hot water. Suddenly, Dag was back.

'They're here!' he gasped.

'Who?'

'The Wilsons! There was a knock on the door, I thought it was Ah Hon or Janet, and in they walked, and me with these filthy clothes and a bucketful of whisky in my hand! Come on, they're waiting to see you!'

He grabbed one of the long, fluffy bathrobes hanging on the wall, and thrust it at me. I had a brief glance at myself in the dressing-room mirror as I hurried out, and saw tousled, wet hair framing a lobster-like face.

As the Wilsons greeted me with hugs and kisses I held my breath, fearful of overpowering them with gin fumes. They were exactly as I remembered them: David tall and distinguished, with sharp yet kindly features; and Natasha with black hair framing a pale complexion and a ready smile.

'We're on our way out, but we thought we'd pop by first to say hello,' said Natasha.

They perched on chair arms, quite relaxed, while Dag stood shifting uncomfortably from one foot to the other. Amid the luxurious furnishing of the sitting-room, and next to David and Natasha, who were suitably dressed for the function they were about to attend, he looked impossibly dishevelled.

'One of our sons sometimes turns up from his travels looking just like you,' Natasha reassured him. 'We find it rather refreshing.'

The starched linen sheets we slept between had crown insignia embroidered on them, and when I woke up thirsty during the night, I reached for the silver flask next to my bed, and poured water from it into a crystal glass. At 7.30 we heard faint clinking sounds from the sitting-room. I opened the adjoining door a crack and peeked in. A table had been brought into the room and was being laid by Ah Hon and Janet, who were moving around as if on wheels. On the dot of 8.00 we were summoned for breakfast. The table was set with fine china and silver. The eggs were perfectly cooked, the tea piping hot, and there were newspapers from Hong Kong, Britain and America.

After breakfast, Ah Hon and Janet slipped past us to deliver two pathetically small piles of laundry to our bedroom. In what was nothing short of a miracle, someone had removed most of the stains from Dag's shorts and rat-chewed shirt, and then meticulously ironed the tattered garments. My faded *sulu*, T-shirt and underwear had been similarly treated.

'Do have any laundry for this morning?' asked Janet.

'Well – er – no, not yet, we'll have to change out of it . . .'

Despite our scruffy appearance, everyone in Government House made us feel at home. Elsewhere, however, we were subjected to puzzled scrutiny.

'Where are you staying in Hong Kong?' asked the bank clerk who was filling in a form to arrange a cash advance on our credit card. When we told him, his pen froze in mid air and he gave us a long, withering look before writing 'In Transit' on the form. A similar incredulity met us at the British Airways office, where we went to broach the subject of excess baggage on our forthcoming flight to New Delhi. The official who phoned me to further discuss the matter was stunned into silence to find that the unsophisticated creature she'd met the previous day was, in fact, a guest of the Governor.

For two days we rushed around Hong Kong, dazzled by its pace and its mind-boggling contrasts. After a morning spent sorting out our affairs in the business district, where immaculately dressed men and women bustled along talking into cellular phones, we turned a corner and found ourselves outside the Central Market. A dank stairwell led up to a first floor which was wall to wall with chickens. There were live chickens crammed into bamboo cages and stacked eight high, dead chickens hanging in rows from meat hooks, dismembered chickens arranged on stone counters into neat piles of livers, hearts, wings, heads and feet. Incongruous among them all was one lonely heron, magnificently feathered, hunched up and peering with beady eyes through the bars of its cage.

'Will you eat him?' I hesitantly asked a woman who was washing a chicken carcass in a vat of bloody water. She promptly dropped the bird, which sank from sight, grabbed a cleaver and headed for the heron. Hurriedly, we sorted out the misunderstanding and escaped to the vegetable market on the floor above.

In the evenings we sought out alleyway Chinese restaurants, tiny places where no one spoke English and we rarely knew what we were ordering. But on Friday night we had dinner with the Wilsons in a blue and white room hung with signed portraits of visiting royals. Servants hovered at a discreet distance, watching carefully to ascertain when they were needed. Each time they came to set down a plate or pick up a glass, Natasha thanked them by name. I was impressed by her faultless courtesy, and told her so.

'Oh, I couldn't be any other way, the staff here are wonderful, they're like family. We shall miss them dreadfully.'

David, who was casually dressed in white pants, a red sweater and bright red socks, had a preoccupied air. Two weeks before, he had been informed by the British Prime Minister that he was to retire after just over five years, and that a new Governor would oversee Hong Kong's transition from British sovereignty to

Chinese control. Despite this, he found time to be worried about us, and the way we were haphazardly lurching around the world.

'How are you getting your kayak to India?' he asked. 'Isn't it costing a fortune to fly it there?'

'British Airways has agreed to waive excess baggage charges,' I told him.

His eyebrows rose. 'Well done. They're usually pretty sticky about that sort of thing. How did you manage it?'

A blush spread upwards from my neck. 'I – sort of – well – mentioned – ah – that I was staying here.'

'How enterprising of you,' he said, and the conversation switched to the Peking Duck we were eating.

Our flight to New Delhi left the following evening, and the Wilsons insisted that first we should go on a tour around some of the beauty spots of the New Territories. At noon, our driver Raymond held open the doors of a shiny black limousine which had gold crown insignia instead of number plates. We slid through the streets of the city, and when we stopped at traffic lights curious pedestrians gathered to peer at the two unlikely characters inside one of the Governor's cars. We were beyond the city limits, and on our way to Lion Rock Park when I leaned back and said, 'Funny to think that tonight we'll be in New Delhi.'

'No kidding,' said Dag. 'How come we don't need visas for India?'

My stomach lurched, then went into a tight knot. Arranging visas for India had been my job, one I was supposed to do in Australia. One I had totally forgotten about.

There was a phone in the back seat. I called Elspeth and asked her for advice. 'All the consulates are closed now,' she told me, 'but I'll track down the private numbers of consulate staff and get back to you.'

'Please,' I said, 'don't tell Sir David and Lady Wilson about this.'

'I wouldn't dream of it.'

While Raymond cruised us around Lion Rock Park, I gabbled down the phone to a series of Indian officials. They told me that visas took between one and four weeks to come through, and that I should have thought about them sooner. Abject apologies, self-recrimination and some furious name-dropping seemed to soften the rules. By the time the limousine slid to the main entrance of

Government House, I'd arranged for a meeting with a high-ranking official of the Indian consulate early on Monday morning. I'd also rescheduled our flights to Monday night and booked a room at the YMCA. As if he hadn't heard a word of the conversations on the back seat, Raymond turned and said, 'I will be collecting you at seven to take you to the airport.'

'We won't be going there, we'll be going to—' began Dag, but I silenced him with a sharp poke in the ribs.

'We can't turn up at the YMCA in a Government House limousine,' I hissed.

'Why not? God, you and your inverted snobbery,' he said, and leaned forward to Raymond.

'You'll be taking us to the YMCA instead,' he told him.

Once again, I was in the bathroom when David and Natasha called into our suite. They were on their way to Bonn, and they wanted to say goodbye. By the time I emerged Dag had already spilled the beans and Natasha was sitting on a chair arm next to our heap of baggage, wringing her hands.

'Oh Maria, I'm so sorry, how absolutely dreadful for you to spend all afternoon worrying. You should have let us know, I'm sure we could have helped.'

'It's all my fault anyway,' I explained. 'A stupid mistake, I just forgot—'

'But that's so easy to do! It happens to all of us!'

'You did awfully well, arranging a visa for Monday,' said David, looking a trifle uneasy. 'How did you manage it?' Natasha suppressed a smile as I blundered through an explanation.

'I mean, I didn't use your name exactly,' I said eventually, 'but I sort of mentioned that we were staying here.'

'Well done,' he said.

'Now about this idea of yours to move to an hotel,' said Natasha.

I gave Dag a grateful glance. 'You've been so kind already and really it's no trouble for us to—'

'We won't hear of it!' she cried. 'You *must* stay here until Monday. We'll be gone and there will only be a skeleton staff, but I'm sure Ah Hon and Janet will come in to make your breakfast and see to your laundry.'

Monday was Dag's birthday, and I gave him a small brass monkey with lucky coins on its back, a little talisman I'd picked up the day before on one of the stalls along Ladder Street. As this was the Year of the Monkey, his sign in the Chinese horoscope, it seemed an apt gift.

'I hope it brings us luck today,' he said.

The Indian Consulate was in the business sector of the city, a brave new world of glass-covered walkways that spanned roads and connected high-rises. On the sixteenth floor of the United Centre, we were ushered into the high-ranking official's office. From behind his vast, polished desk, he slowly looked us up and down.

'Let us sit together on the sofa,' he said, gesturing towards acres of upholstered leather. 'May I offer you coffee?'

A button was pressed, coffee was brought and poured from a silver pot. I tried to stop my hand from trembling as I lifted the cup to my lips. The high-ranking official, by contrast, was supremely composed. 'How unfortunate that you have no visas. How did this come to be?'

I decided on honesty. 'It's my fault. I simply forgot. I know this is terribly inconvenient, but we are on a tight schedule and it's very important for us to get to India by tonight.'

Turning one of his gold cuff links, he considered this for a few seconds. My coffee cup rattled as I set it down on the saucer.

'I believe you are guests of the Governor? How very nice. What is the purpose of your visit to India?'

'We're going to kayak down the Ganges,' I told him, adding what I thought might be helpful information, 'and collect material for a book.'

'So you are writers?'

'Yes.'

'No,' said Dag, pressing his foot hard against mine.

'That's right,' I said. 'Not really, I mean it was only an idea, there's nothing arranged, we don't have a contract or anything—'

As the pressure of Dag's foot increased, I realized it was time to shut up.

'It is possible for us, in special circumstances, to arrange tourist visas at short notice,' said the high-ranking official. 'But visas for the purpose of business are a very different matter. A very different matter indeed. And far more expensive. Perhaps I should pose the question once more. What is the purpose of your visit to India?'

'A holiday,' answered Dag.

'Absolutely,' I added.

The high-ranking official gave us the ghost of a smile. 'Very good. Your visas will be ready by four o'clock.'

The plane banked steeply; below us, the anchor lights of hundreds of boats hovered like fireflies in the harbour, and along neon-red roads cutting through the forest of glittering high rises, car head lamps streamed and flashed and searched. A cloud engulfed us; Hong Kong, with all its glamour and excitement, was suddenly gone. We sat back, and began to nervously consider the next part of our journey.

10

A Holy River

'Kayaking along the Ganges!' cried Mr Gupta, a government official in New Delhi. 'You must be potty!'

Long before we arrived in India, Dag and I had become inured to such comments. They had followed us from Canada halfway across the world in letters, in phone calls, in chance conversations. We'd been urged to drop our plan and opt for something safer and more sanitary. Once we were in India, however, we had hoped to find some encouragement: after all, Hindus believe that the river embodies the Goddess Ganga, that its waters have the power of physical and spiritual purification, and of releasing a soul from the painful cycle of rebirth. If only a little of the river's holiness rubbed off on us along the way, surely we'd be all right? Mr Gupta didn't think so.

'I am a devout Hindu,' he said, 'but when it comes to bathing in the Ganges I struggle between my faith and my knowledge of bacteriology. I beg you to reconsider this journey.'

At two minutes past midnight on a January night, we'd dragged our baggage past sleepy customs and passport control officials and out into the forecourt of New Delhi Airport. The air was cool, and so polluted with exhaust fumes, grit and smoke that it stung the backs of our throats. A taxi driver wearing a lumpy hand-knitted sweater and an old tweed jacket led us to his Hindustani Ambassador, a copy of the British 1950s Morris Oxford. He carefully steered the vehicle around a cow that sat ruminating in the airport driveway, then barrelled along a wide boulevard beneath dim, yellowish street lights. Apart from a few scooters, there was little other traffic about. On either side of the boulevard, old trees grew behind high stone walls, suggesting the unseen presence of imposing residences. In front of them were stalls covered with tarpaulins, huddles of shacks, and men sleeping on handcarts.

'Welcome to the Maurya Sheraton,' said a smiling young woman attired in a gorgeous green and gold silk sari. 'We are greatly pleased to be hosting you.'

From Canada I had contacted the Maurya Sheraton, one of New Delhi's most exclusive hotels, suggesting that in return for hospitality we could offer some useful promotion. It seemed like a long shot, but a positive and enthusiastic reply had come by return of post.

'The yacht, Government House and now this,' muttered Dag, as a gold-mirrored lift smoothly whisked us up to the deeply carpeted Executive Suite. 'And I thought we were supposed to be the adventurous types!'

'We'll be sleeping in the mud soon enough,' I assured him.

Early next morning, we gazed over a scene made silent by the triple-glazed windows of our room. A large brown garuda bird flapped by, like some prehistoric creature. On the boulevard, traffic was snarled by up a train of fifty camels ridden by straight-backed soldiers. Beyond it, miles of parkland stretched away, and the only sign of the city was a dense grey-blue haze that hung over the treetops.

A concierge in red livery and turban saluted us and held the door open as we left the hotel. The morning was warm and muggy. Waiting at the end of the hotel driveway was a line of autorickshaws, yellow and black vehicles that were little more than three-wheeled scooters with double passenger seats and canopies. Their drivers leaned against them, smoking small, pungent cigarettes called *bidis*.

'Where to, sir?' cried one.

'Connaught Place.'

'I have no knowledge of this place, sir.'

Connaught Place, which we tried pronouncing in every conceivable way, is the commercial heart of New Delhi. Yet none of the drivers who had gathered around to listen to our verbal acro-

batics appeared to have heard of it An elderly man walking out of
the hotel grounds stopped to see what was going on. He carried
a briefcase and wore a sports jacket and a *dhoti*, fifteen feet of cotton tied around his waist and looped between his legs.

'May I be of assistance to you?' he asked.

We explained our dilemma.

'Connaught Place!' he told the autorickshaw driver, who immediately understood him. 'And don't charge an anna more than
twenty-five rupees!'

It was rather like some terrifying fairground ride, where you
pay to be scared witless. Traffic rules, if any existed, were ignored,
especially on the large roundabouts, where cars cut across us
with inches to spare, buses loomed up and veered away, and we
swerved around scooters on which women rode side-saddle, their
shawls and saris fluttering behind them like flags. There was a
cacophony of ringing bells, honking horns and squealing brakes,
and vivid images flashed by: men lathered themselves at stand-
pipes, or sat on wooden chairs having their faces shaved, their
heads massaged, their nose and ear hairs clipped. Shutters
banged open to reveal the interiors of bike repair shops, shops
selling ropes and brass pots, shops filled with baskets of roses
and marigolds. At a construction site, women in saris and heavy
pewter anklets carried piles of bricks on their heads. Cows, pigs
and goats foraged amid rubbish swept into piles at the side of the
road. School children with satchels slung over immaculate uniforms picked their way around the rubbish and the dung. At
traffic lights, beneath a sign exhorting drivers to PLEASE STOP
WHEN LIGHT IS RED, we came to a halt. Beggars ran up and
extended skinny arms and upturned palms into the autorickshaw. Around them, pale sunlight shafted through dusty air, air
which smelled of exhaust fumes, flowers, roasting peanuts and
urine.

In Connaught Place roads radiated from a bustling circle like
wheel spokes, and torrents of cars, autorickshaws and scooters
poured along them, horns honking and bells ringing, hell bent,
it seemed, on exterminating pedestrians.

'Fifty-five rupees, please sir,' shouted the driver.

'That gentleman at the hotel said you should charge no more
than twenty-five'

'*Fifty*-five rupees the gentleman was saying, *fifty*-five!' Grateful to have survived the ride, we couldn't be bothered to argue. And now, to get to Mr Gupta's office, we had to cross the road. As we stood up on the kerb, plucking up enough courage to face the onslaught of traffic and merciless drivers, it occurred to me that gathering information on the Ganges could be far more danger-ous than paddling along it.

Our plan was to transport the kayak to Hardwar, where the Ganges leaves the Himalayas and enters the great northern plains. From there we hoped to paddle to the holy city of Varanasi, thus travelling along the most revered part of the river, and across the huge state of Uttar Pradesh. In search of maps and pertinent information, we climbed one dank stairwell after another, and sat in the gloomy offices of government officials amid desks and shelves piled high with tattered papers. The dark-suited men we met told us how much waste water gets pumped each day into the Ganges, or Ganga as it is more commonly known in India, and how many sewage plants and electric cre-matoria are being built along its banks. They also warned us of its bandits and the unsanitary living conditions of its villages. But they couldn't provide us with a detailed map of the river, or advise of its pre-monsoon water levels, or even agree on the distance by river between Hardwar and Varanasi.

'It's six hundred and fifty miles,' said Colonel Kumar, of the Indian Mountaineering Association.

Having given up on government officials, we were now explor-ing other channels of information. We met with the colonel in the Gymkhana Club, a crumbling monument to bygone colonial days, where we sat on vinyl-covered sofas beneath high, arched ceilings, while waiters pushed trolleys over creaking wooden floors and served us with china cups of lukewarm tea.

'Don't worry about maps!' Colonel Kumar assured us. 'You won't be needing them.'

Some years before he had stage-managed Sir Edmund Hillary's expedition by high-powered speedboat up the Ganga, and he seemed to have similar ideas for us. 'For twenty thousand rupees I can provide for three weeks a land support crew of jeep, driver and guide,' he told us. 'This crew will meet you each day at pre-arranged spots along the river, set up your camp, cordon it off to keep away the locals, and cook for you.'

We explained that our idea was to meander along the Ganges

as whim and fortune took us, and to learn about local life without having to worry unduly about schedules or time pressures. Singularly unimpressed by this, the Colonel quickly lost interest in us, and advised us to contact a Mr Koli, who ran the Wild Life Adventure Tours.

'I estimate the distance you will have to travel is at least nine hundred and fifty miles,' said Avinash Koli, sensibly adding, 'but Mother Ganga is flooding her banks and changing her course every year, so really she is the one you should ask.'

Unlike most people we'd met in New Delhi, he regarded our plan with open enthusiasm. 'The journey will spiritually uplift you,' he promised. 'And it will be a great adventure – I know of no one who has kayaked on this part of the Ganga. But you will have problems with bandits, and the people there speak only Hindi. You must take a guide. I will send you my best man. He is an experienced kayaker and his English is faultless.'

Silently, I wondered how we could be guided along a river which no one had kayaked on before. But after our few days in India we'd already grown used to such illogicalities; we struck a deal with Koli and arranged to meet up with his man in Hardwar.

In Old Delhi Bus Station, stunned by the hubbub of whistles, shouts, revving engines, honking horns and shrill, incomprehensible announcements, we watched two porters hoist our red bags on to their heads and promptly disappear behind a muddle of buses. It took half an hour of frantic chasing about before we relocated the bags, which were in fact strapped on to the roof of the Hardwar bus. The 120-mile journey took ten bone-rattling hours, and included innumerable stops at squalid towns along the way. The bus was packed: between our second-row seat and the driver's cabin I counted seventeen adults, four children, six sacks, three bedrolls, four suitcases and eight boxes. A baby in the seat in front of us threw up every half-hour or so; each time he erupted his mother cupped her hand to catch the vomit, and smeared it on the side of the bus. We arrived in Hardwar after dark, amid a blustery rainstorm. The bus station was on a narrow street of shuttered and heavily padlocked shop fronts. A large billboard advertised 'Orbit TV – The Divine Choice', a few scrawny cows loafed about, and a man who had just finished defecating in the gutter squatted by a puddle to wash himself.

The Tourist Bungalow was cold and bleak and we were the

only guests in its restaurant. Our waiter was bundled up in an old jacket and a thick woollen scarf, and the index finger of his right hand was wrapped in a thick wad of dirty bandage. Before setting our plates down before us, he breathed hard on them and wiped them with a grey rag. The meal, however, was delicious: flat, pan-fried bread called *roti*, and *paneer bhuji*, a delicious mixture of scrambled milk curds and chopped vegetables. We ate quickly then went to our room. In the adjoining latrine I had a strip wash in a bucket of lukewarm water, and tried to banish from my mind thoughts of the Maurya Sheraton's luxurious bathrooms. Dag was already fast asleep when I joined him beneath the heavy cotton quilt. All night, a cold wind blew down from the Himalayan foothills and whistled through the broken window and under the ill-fitting door of our room.

Koli's 'best man', Bapi Sakar, had already arrived from New Delhi by deluxe bus, and we met him in the guest house over a breakfast of milk porridge and *chapatis*. A Bengali in his early twenties, he was small and wiry, with a dazzling smile and mop of black curls. Dressed in an oversized woollen sweater, baggy knee-length shorts and baseball boots, he looked like an Indian caricature of an American teenager, and exuded a self-confidence to match.

'I've done a Wilderness Survival Course,' he told us, reeling off an unrequested curriculum vitae. 'I can catch fish and turtles and make a shelter in the woods. I've studied under India's most famous ornithologist, I've guided white-water kayak tours in Canada and the States, I've led treks in the Garwal Himalayas, I can identify flowers and wildlife, and once an elephant charged me and I was almost killed!' He had with him a map of Uttar Pradesh, a plastic white-water kayak without a rudder, a leaky tent and an ample supply of *bidis*. But he had no food, stove or cooking equipment. His first job, we decided, would be to guide us to Hardwar market, and help us buy provisions for the trip along the Ganga.

From an open-fronted grocery, where goods were displayed in sacks on the wooden floor and weighed out on brass scales, we bought rice, lentils, milk powder, biscuits, tea and sugar. From a murky back room with grease-smeared walls we bought ghee, or clarified butter. From vendors who couldn't understand why foreign tourists should want such things, we bought a kerosene lamp, paraffin and rough woollen blankets for the cold nights. And from a canopied road stall we bought onions, carrots, ginger and garlic. The stall was hemmed in between a wall and a tight knot of people, scooters and cows. While we were stuffing the vegetables into our bags, a funeral procession came by. A body covered by a thin white sheet and strewn with marigolds was carried on a rough stretcher by eight men. They weaved their way through the crowd, and to get past the dense section where we stood, they lifted the stretcher above their heads. The body shifted, and for one horrible moment I thought it was about to tumble off and land on our shoulders.

The river below Hardwar was in an alarmingly shrunken state as much of it had been diverted into the Upper Ganges Canal, and the rest was at its pre-monsoon level. We assembled our kayak on some steps, or *ghats*, leading down to a narrow channel of grey-green water. Opposite us was a row of temples and ashrams; ahead, the flood plain rolled away, dry and dusty, towards the Chandi Hills. A little way downstream, a line of *dhobi wallahs* – laundry men – were standing ankle deep in the river, ferociously beating rocks with articles of clothing. 'Swack! Hah! Swack! Hah! Swack! Hah!'

The men whipped the garments into the air and brought them down hard – Swack! – on the rock, with an accompanying shout of 'Hah!' Our arrival gave the clothes a temporary reprieve, because as soon as we started to assemble our boat, the *dhobi wallahs* abandoned their work and crowded around us.

Half an hour later, our kayak had begun to take shape. I was on my haunches, fitting a plastic combing around the back cockpit, while Dag, with his head, shoulders and arms inside the front cockpit, was struggling with a piece of the aluminum frame. The laundry men had been joined by some friends; knees pressed against my back as I crouched over the kayak, eyes stared into mine from inches away, and I suddenly realized that I couldn't see the bag containing the rest of our gear – our camping equipment, stove, food and clothes. All the warnings we'd received about theft along the Ganges had convinced us that if we didn't constantly keep an eye on our belongings we'd be left with only the clothes on our backs. I struggled to my feet, the men stepped back to form a corridor for me, and there was the bag, lying undisturbed behind them. I dragged it forward and sat on it, and the men rearranged themselves around me. One of them, a hollow-cheeked old man with enormous ears leaned forward. 'What is the nature of your business here?' he shouted.

'We will travel in this boat to Varanasi,' I told him.

When the old man translated this news for our audience, there was a murmur of approval. 'A *yatra*, madam,' he said. 'A pilgrimage.'

'No—'

'Excuse me, madam, but yes. You are travelling from one holy place to another along Mother Ganga. This is a pilgrimage, and it will purify you of all sin.'

According to Hindu lore, any journey along the Ganges must begin with a *puja*, or act or worship, and I was far too superstitious to eschew this tradition. From one of the temples, Bapi summoned a *pujari*, a Hindu priest who arrived holding a stainless steel tray heaped with marigolds, a coconut, banana leaves and an assortment of small brass pots. When the kayaks were ready and packed, we climbed into them, and the *pujari* crouched down next to us. After wedging burning incense sticks between the stone slabs of the *ghats*, he rang a small bell and the *puja* began. Murmuring prayers, he tied red strings to our wrists and kayaks, and smudged our foreheads with *tikkas* of sandalwood paste. I lowered on to the river an offering of a tiny banana-leaf boat filled with marigolds, sweets and burning camphor. A coconut was cracked open, and its milk sprinkled over us and the kayaks. The flesh was broken into pieces and passed around; eagerly the *dhobi wallahs* reached for this *prasad* or blessed food, and touched it to their foreheads before eating it. Finally, the *pujari* bade us drink three times from the river. With deep misgivings about the effect of Ganges water on my system, I scooped some up in my palm and took a tentative sip.

'You must drink three times!' Bapi reminded me. The *puja* completed, I placed 100 rupees on to the tray.

'Give one more,' whispered Bapi. 'Even numbers are unlucky.'

The *pujari* took the money in his right palm, counted it, then lifted it to his forehead.

'Ganga ma ki jai!' yelled Bapi. 'We salute you, Mother Ganga!'

The watching crowd took up the cry – 'Ganga ma ki jai!' – but their words were whipped away by the wind, and lost somewhere in the vast expanse of sky and space that lay ahead of us.

11

Arduous Days

Although our kayak floats in a few inches of water, it got barely 200 yards down the Ganga before running aground on a gravel shoal. As we pushed the boat free, we cracked jokes about being stuck so soon after embarking on so long a journey. Four hours and fifteen gravel shoals later, the jokes had worn thin. The channel was winding languidly across the plain, and dividing up into a tangled skein of shallow waterways. By the time we stopped for the day, we estimated that after paddling a total of eight miles we were a mile and a half from where we'd started. We had six weeks to reach Varanasi. If, as Mr Koli had insisted, it was 950 miles away, to get there we would have to achieve a daily average of twenty-three miles – which meant that already we were behind schedule.

'We'll never make it,' I whined, as we unpacked the kayak.

'Don't worry!' said Dag, as sanguine as ever. 'Things can only get better!'

Considering how disheartened I felt, it's fortunate that I had no idea of how wrong he was.

We camped that first night on an large arrow-shaped sand island that stood high between two channels. For safety's sake, we erected the tents facing each other with the kayaks between them. Crows and mynah birds hopped about the patches of scrubby grass, doubtless surprised to see humans on this desolate and transitory scrap of land. I was on my way down the bank to fill our kettle when I saw two strange creatures silently sliding across the surface of the water. They appeared to have misshapen heads and truncated torsos, and it was only as my eyes adjusted to the fading light, and as the creatures drew closer, that I recognized them as men. Wrapped in shawls, they were sitting on bamboo slats laid across inflated inner tubes which they propelled with small, spoon-shaped wooden paddles. I stared wonderingly at them: they stared wonderingly back. Dag and Bapi appeared beside me, and Bapi began talking to the men in an exchange so shrill and high-pitched that it sounded argumentative, but which I soon came to recognize as the tone of almost every conversation in Hindi, how-ever mild and uncontroversial the subject being discussed.

'They are fishermen,' Bapi told us. 'They are coming to put down their nets. They are saying that there are dacoits around here, that it is not safe for us to camp alone. They are wanting us to go with them to their village of Agitpur.' The thought of dacoits was unappealing, but so was the prospect of taking down the tents, packing up the boats, paddling across the river, unpack-ing the boats and hauling them for over a kilometre. We decided to stay put and take our chances. The men set their nets, turned and silently slid across the surface of the river, disappearing into the deepening gloom. The sun slipped away, leaving an eerie orange glow and a sickle moon in its wake. While I made notes by the kerosene lamp, Dag and Bapi fired up our tiny stove and cooked *kedgeree*, a mess of rice and curried vegetables. From somewhere beyond our small circle of light, a jackal began to bark and laugh. Another joined in, then several more, and soon the air was filled by the mad frenzy of their calls.

At first light, we were woken by the sound of revving engines. The rocks and gravel we had cursed the afternoon before were obviously valued here: men were throwing boulders into the back of the trucks and sieving gravel through baskets woven from branches. With dismay, we watched a fully laden truck ford the river downstream of our campsite, the water barely covering the bottom of its tyres.

'I never expected to get run over on the Ganges,' sighed Dag. Beyond the trucks, a herd of wild blue buffalo ambled along, touched by the glow of the rising sun. Away on the horizon, mist rose from the a blur of trees marking the far side of the flood plain, the Chandi Hills were softly etched against the sky and a glistening snow-capped mountain peeped above them.

As I dipped our tea kettle into the river, the remnant of a marigold garland twirled by in an eddy and caught in the spout. Carried downstream from Hardwar, the debris of *pujas* was strewn all along the banks: flowers and coconuts and scraps of red cloth. Doubtfully, I peered into the brimming kettle. The water was grey, and thick with sediment. I emptied it out, waded into the river and refilled the kettle from a faster current. I was about to turn back to the shore when I noticed three men on the opposite bank. They were hunkered down, completely covered by blankets and as motionless as statues. They were still there an hour later when, after a quick breakfast of tea and biscuits, I was back at the water's edge with my toothbrush and toothpaste. I had rather hoped to get around cleaning my teeth in the river, but our ceramic filter was struggling with the amount of silt it had to deal with, and was only producing enough water for drinking purposes. I gave my teeth a cursory scrub, and spat out as much of the river water as I possibly could. The statues gazed at me, unnerving in their stillness. When we paddled off, their heads very slowly turned to watch our progress downstream.

Although the river was soon boosted by a couple of tributaries, it continued to spread out and sub-divide. Each time it branched we had to make a decision about which channel to take. Sometimes, choosing wrongly, we paddled into dead ends and had to haul the boats across gravel banks back to the main channel. This was exhausting work, but at least we had a remarkable array of birds to distract us. There were sandpipers, egrets, cranes, mergansers, eagles, kingfishers and many more we couldn't identify.

'What's that bird, Bapi?' I once asked him.

'Which bird?'

'There – it's black with a white belly and an iridescent green neck.'

There was a long silence, a sign that I was soon to realize meant he didn't know the answer to a question, so was busily making one up. 'It's called a Black Indian Bastard!' he finally pronounced.

Twice, while we were hauling the boat, I slipped on the smooth stones and managed to get thoroughly wet in three inches of water. I flung imprecations at the gravel banks, but by mid-afternoon I was longing for their return. The river seemed to be progressively wearing down the land it travelled over. Boulders became rocks, rocks became gravel, gravel became sand and the sand itself was sifted down to a state so fine that, although well nigh invisible, it could be borne on the breeze and deposited in our ears, noses and eyes. And worse, it could mingle with water to form nightmarish traps.

The sand bank that snared us was concealed just below the surface of the turbid water. With resigned sighs, Dag and I climbed out of the kayak to push it free. Something sucked at my feet, cold mud closed around my ankles, and I realized I was sinking into the river bed.

'Quicksand!' cried Dag.

Before either of us had time to react, we were up to our knees in the evil stuff. We threw ourselves over the cockpits, hauled ourselves free and awkwardly tumbled back into our seats.

Eight more patches of quicksand awaited us. By the end of our second day on the river, we and the inside of the kayak were smeared with a layer of Ganges mud.

The river swung away from the Chandi Hills, the plain widened to nine miles across, and the horizon became as flat as if we were at sea. We were travelling through one of the most densely populated parts of India, along a river that was a lifeline to millions, yet there was no one and nothing in sight, only an arching, empty sky and an immense expanse of silver-grey desert. As we wormed our way across it, I sometimes imagined how we must have looked from high above. I fancied someone peering down from a plane and picking out two tiny dots, one red and one blue, unrecognizable as boats. It was a humbling thought. During those arduous days, I felt myself shrinking away in the midst of this solitary wasteland until I was a mere speck, almost swallowed up by space, light and silence.

Each night's campsite was more desolate than the last. There was a day of rain, when the sand flats were transmuted to a muddy moonscape and honking geese flew furiously above us, as if heading to a warmer place. Cold, damp and miserable, I kept asking myself why we'd come here and how we'd survive weeks of this numbing desolation.

And then, after days of nothingness, people appeared. Standing on the white sand, etched against the empty sky, men swathed in brown blankets with mattocks slung over their shoulders, women in bright cotton saris carrying shiny brass bowls on their heads. With them, a buffalo pulling a wooden wheeled cart. This was time rolled back, a scene unchanged for hundreds of years. At first, the people were rendered mute with astonishment at the sight of us. But when we pressed our palms together and called out greetings they rushed down the bank and bombarded Bapi with questions about where we'd come from, where we were going. '*Hardwar sey, Varanasi tak? Yatra!*' 'Hardwar to Varanasi? A pilgrimage!'

They told us they were walking to their fields from their village, and pointed back across the empty plain. 'How much longer must you walk?' we asked them.

'Two hours,' they replied, 'maybe three, maybe four.'

There was the same vagueness when we asked about distances.

'How far to the Bijnor barrage?'

'Thirty-five kilometres,' they said.

The next people we met told us it was fifty kilometres away, the next said seventy-five. As Bapi had left the map of Uttar Pradesh in his hotel room in Hardwar, he was trying to navigate with our map of the subcontinent of India, constantly poring over it, measuring distances with string and coming up with estimates as wildly varying as the ones the farmers were giving us.

On our fourth day, we rounded a bend in the river and saw the outline of the Bijnor Barrage, a kilometre or so away. Pulling into a back eddy, we waited for Bapi to catch up with us. On the bank, a dead cow was being picked over by some enormous brown-black vultures which hopped around in an ungainly way, sticking their heads and hideous necks right inside the cow's gaping chest cavity. A little further along, some men were reinforcing a section of the river bank, piling up bags of stone behind a retaining wall, built of branches, that looked as if it would be whisked away by the first hint of the monsoon. The men waved at us, shouting and pointing towards the barrage.

'They are saying we can paddle through the barrage,' said Bapi, when he arrived.

'*Through the barrage?*'

'They are saying a channel is there and we can follow it.'

'Yes, and it probably drops fifty feet on the other side of the barrage.'

He thought for a moment. 'Perhaps it is nonsense for us to be going to the trouble of a portage when we could be paddling through the barrage.'

Bapi was overruled and we pulled out of the river a hundred yards away from the barrage. It was a huge structure of concrete and blue metal that doubled as a road bridge. From the girders, black-faced monkeys swung above the trucks that rumbled to and from the nearby town of Bijnor. At river level, only one of the barrage's iron gates was open; a torrent of water funnelled through it and became a crashing waterfall on the other side.

While we began to unpack our kayak, Bapi went to hire some men as porters. After half an hour he returned with a father and son. The father was old, half blind and wafer thin, while his son had a heavily bandaged left hand and a vacant expression on his face.

'They want twenty-five rupees each,' said Bapi.

By our standards this was a pittance, the equivalent of a dollar each, but by theirs it was a handsome fee, a day's wages for carrying some heavy bags for 200 yards. Bapi relayed to them our acceptance of this price, but by now they were staring intently at the boats and bags. The old man looked up at Dag and served him a volley of rapid Hindi.

'He is saying,' Bapi translated, 'that this is too much for them. He is saying that for one hundred rupees extra they will walk back to their village and bring a bullock cart here.'

'And how long will that take?' asked Dag. 'It's not far across the barrage. Tell them we'll all help with the portage.'

Bapi looked alarmed. 'Really, I am thinking that the bullock cart is a good idea. And anyway, they are insisting on it.'

'Tell them we'll find someone else,' said Dag.

This incensed the porters, who claimed we could not break the verbal contract we'd made with them. We countered by saying that the contract had not included a bullock cart. There was a lengthy discussion, involving much head-waggling and repetitions of '*Acchha*' which can mean, according to context, 'OK', or 'I see', or 'Oh, really?' or 'Very good'. Finally, a compromise was reached and a plan agreed upon. Dag, Bapi and the porters would carry as much gear as they could across the bridge while I stayed to guard the rest. Then Bapi would remain on the far side of the bridge while Dag and the porters returned for a second carry. It didn't work out like that. We divided the contents of our

kayak between the two red sacks. Dag lifted one sack on to his
shoulder and set off across the bridge, the porters carried the
kayak behind him; I sat on the other sack and Bapi started to
unpack his boat. He was still unpacking it when the two porters
sauntered back. I stood up and indicated to the sack. The old
man shook his head and shot off down the embankment towards
Bapi. The younger man picked up the sack, staggered a few steps,
dropped it in the middle of the road and went to join his father.
Ten minutes later they reappeared, one carrying Bapi's light plastic boat and the other his bags, while Bapi walked behind them,
empty-handed and with a regal air.

'You'll have to help me with this bag,' I hissed at him, in a tone
so icy he obviously thought better of demurring.

A half-hour's paddle from the barrage, we camped in the
shade of a grassy sand dune. A farmer was there, preparing a
field to plant pumpkins and watermelons. He was heaping sand
into long mounds to demarcate the field, sticking sheaves of
dried grass into the mounds to act as windbreaks, digging hollows
and filling them with soil and seedlings he'd brought by bullock
cart from his village. Each day, he said, he would return here to
water the crop, which he would harvest before the monsoon,
when his painstakingly created field would disappear beneath
the river. And for this he would receive fifty paise – half a rupee –
for each kilo of watermelons and pumpkins, which would then
sold in the market for 10 rupees a kilo. Why, I asked, didn't he
sell the produce himself?

'I am not of the market seller caste,' he answered.

Bathed in evening light, the sand was golden, the sky a delicate
blue and the grasses a soft yellow. Geese wandered up and down
the shoreline, and as darkness fell their honking mingled with the
barking of jackals and the hum of distant traffic. The lights of the
barrage were faulty and throughout the night they blinked on and
off in an unintentional and disconcerting *son et lumière*. Around
2.00 am, I crawled out of the tent to pee. The lights snapped on
and illuminated two figures paddling on inner tubes across the
river towards our campsite. I shook Dag awake, but by the time
he'd poked his head out of the tent door the lights were off.

'I can't see anyone,' he said.

The lights snapped on again, outlining the two figures about to
reach the shore, not twenty yards away.

'*Hey! You!*' he shouted. 'What do you think you're up to?'

The figures froze. The barrage lights snapped off. When they came on again, two minutes later, the inner tube people were heading back across the river, in the direction from which they'd come.

We slept fitfully, and at 5.30 decided we might as well get up. The river was shrouded in a cold mist, which swallowed up the blinking lights of the barrage and intensified the sense of desolation. The quick wash I had in the river froze me to the core, and I piled on every article of clothing I had and paddled off with my teeth chattering. We hadn't gone far before we saw a human skull amid the dry yellow grass on the bank. A little further along, a full skeleton lay on its back with its knees askew. The river continued to wind and divide; it seemed that another arduous, monotonous day lay ahead. But then, from behind the curtain of mist, we heard tinkling cowbells and a herdsman singing a lilting melody. The sun began to break through the mist, which lifted like a curtain. Swallows swooped around our heads, a tiny brown dolphin surfaced close to the kayak and water hyacinths twirled in the eddies made by our paddles. Buffalos pulling carts loaded with whole families forded the river ahead of us, fishermen cast nets from the bank, women walked along with bundles of fodder on their heads. The sky was bright blue, the sun warm, and it was as if we'd emerged from one world into another.

Around midday, we stopped to wait for Bapi. His rudderless boat was hopelessly slow on flat water, and he was forever struggling along behind us. Despite this, he continued to cheerfully refer to himself as our 'guide', something I was finding increasingly irritating.

'At this rate, we'll never get to Varanasi,' I said peevishly. 'Maybe it's not such a good idea having Bapi along.'

'Don't be such a grouch!' retorted Dag. 'He's great company, and he's not slowing us down that much. What's your problem?'

The problem was that I was jealous. For months now Dag and I had been travelling as a tight, self-contained unit, each of us the other's chief point of reference amidst a flurry of new experiences. But the dynamics of our relationship had been instantly changed by the presence of a third person. Dag was thrilled to have some male company, and an easy cameraderie had quickly developed between him and Bapi. At our campsites they prepared meals together, joked around, smoked *bidis* and swapped stories. To me, Bapi was courteous and considerate, and always insisted on relieving me of my washing up duties.

'I know you are busy with your note writing, Maria!' he would say, cheerfully trudging off to scrub our pots in the cold river water.

But even such kind gestures failed to soften my resentment at how much of Dag's attention he was diverting from me, and I was often supercilious towards him.

'You're making a mistake by treating Bapi so harshly,' Dag remonstrated. 'He's more important to the success of this trip that you give him credit for.'

As we talked we were drifting along beneath one of the river's 'permanent' banks. Houses peeped between the trees on top of the 20ft high bluff, and in front of it, rising up from the sand, was a skinny brick tower. Soon, children came careering down the bank. They were barefooted little ragamuffins with snotty noses and infected eyes, who splashed into the river then screeched to a halt a few feet away from us, huddling together and giggling into their hands. From the bluff, adults beckoned to us. Anchoring the boat, and clutching our Hindi phrasebooks, we went up to their village.

The houses were built of mud and dung, and had pumpkins growing on the straw roofs. A *charpoi* – a wooden bed base with a woven rope mattress – was pulled out into the sunshine for us to sit on. Villagers pressed around: handsome, sharp-featured old men with leathery skin, young men holding babies and smoking *bidis*, women hiding their faces behind the ends of their saris. One of these women dunked a couple of stainless steel beakers into a clay pot filled with black, greasy water. She dried the beakers on her sari, then filled them with milky tea that she poured from a brass jug. '*Bahut acchha*,' we said, sipping the tea. 'Very good.'

In Hindi, we asked some of our onlookers their names and the name of their village. Spurred on by success, Dag asked a man called Antram if he could tell us the purpose of the brick tower. There was a puzzled silence, then some whispered conferring. The men holding babies slid away and the children around our feet were yanked out of sight, but the remaining villagers pressed tightly around us. And the mood had changed; there was tension in the air. 'I think we'd better go,' I whispered to Dag. We stood up.

'*Sit down sir!*' commanded Antram.

He produced a school exercise book and a pencil, and on the back page he wrote: 'What is your name? Where are you coming from? What are you doing here?', then thrust the book and pencil at Dag. The first two questions were simple to answer. The third was rather more problematic. What, after all, *were* we doing there? Antram seemed to read our thoughts. '*What are you doing here, sir?*' he yelled at Dag.

Before he could reply, a familiar voice rang out.

'Hey, Dag!'

The crowd parted to reveal Bapi striding up the bank, his shorts flapping against his legs. 'What's going on?'

'We're not sure,' said Dag.

In the midst of my relief at seeing Bapi, I was struck by the fact that he was, indeed, our guide. Not in a physical sense, perhaps, but in situations like these, when he could help us bridge huge gulfs of language and culture. After a short conversation with Antram, he turned to us with a questioning look.

'These people are worried. They say you have been asking them about their children. They are thinking you want to take one of them with you.'

Amid much relieved laughter, the misunderstanding was cleared up, we were brought more tea, and Antram explained about the tower. It was a well, and until a few years ago it had been in the centre of the village. During each monsoon, part of Sherpur was swept away. Within a few months, the house we sat outside would probably be gone.

'That's terrible,' I said. When Bapi translated this, Antram smiled. 'Not terrible. Holy Mother Ganga takes away, but she gives us fertile soil and good water. She is our life.'

12

Centre of Attention

Crows squabbled over the remains of our milk rice breakfast as we broke camp. It was now eight days since we'd left Hardwar, and our progress had been pitifully slow. One consolation was that the early mornings were losing their chilliness. By nine o'clock, the sun had already begun to bleach the sky of its blue, and along the banks of the river, small turtles lay sunbathing on clods of earth. As we approached them, most plopped into the water, but some, perhaps fast asleep, stayed as they were with their necks outstretched and their back flippers at right angles to their bodies. We were so engrossed in these creatures that at first we didn't notice the black smoke drifting towards us. Then we registered its acrid smell, its disquieting overtones of fat left sizzling too long in the pan. Coming around a bend in the river, we saw a burning pile of wood and dung. Inside it lay a body. Two men tended to the blaze with bamboo poles; about fifteen others stood to one side. On noticing our approach, they abandoned the pyre and ran to the water's edge, shouting and waving. They were wrapped up in *dhotis* and blankets, with only their faces and stick-thin legs showing. Some were very old, with wizened skin and eyes like birds. I turned around and called to Bapi, who was busily trying to catch a turtle on the end of his paddle, but he was out of earshot.

'*Namaste*,' I said, pressing my hands together and raising them to my forehead.

'*Namaste!*' they all delightedly chorused.

There was a soft thump as the bow of our kayak ran on to a submerged sandbank. The current pushed us sideways, and in seconds we were firmly aground. Behind the men something on the fire cracked and popped. The wind shifted, and smoke began drifting and curling around us. As we struggled to push the boat off the sandbank with our paddles, ashes pattered against my face and caught in my eyelashes.

'We must join these people,' said Bapi, as he caught up with us.

'What?'

'They are requesting this.'

A young man named Danbir spoke for the whole group. He was tall, rangy and rather dashing. He wore his blanket over one shoulder, like a toga, and he had a haughty way of holding up his long nose, as if sniffing the air. He invited us to sit with the men, and spread out a white cloth next to the tractor trailer that had brought the body, the mourners and the fuel down to the river bank. Lumps of *gur*, crude cane sugar, were passed around. We were given the largest lumps, and mine was as big as a tennis ball. One of the old men sat very close to me, fixing me with his twinkling eyes as I began gnawing at the sweet, sticky stuff. Each time I took a break, he nodded vigorously, as if urging me on.

The body on the pyre, we learned, was that of Rishpal Singh. He had died only hours before, aged eighty-five. His eldest son, Sidraj, a man with a long, elegant face framed by a white cotton shawl, sat quietly talking to Bapi.

'Sidraj is requesting that we go back with him to his village,' said Bapi. 'He is saying that we have been sent to him as a blessing.'

The village of Gessapur was five kilometres away from the river bank. Going there would mean we'd lose a day, maybe more, putting us even further behind schedule. But Sidraj fixed us with a clear, steady gaze.

'He is saying that God took his father from him, and sent us as a blessing to comfort him in his grief,' Bapi told us, and we found we couldn't refuse.

After two hours, the pyre was almost burned down, but a piece of backbone with something fleshy attached to it still lay among the coals. The mourners swept the lot into river, and went in themselves for a ritual bath, holding their noses and immersing themselves three times. Then our boats were loaded on to the

tractor trailer, and everyone squeezed around them. We drove
along a bumpy track, between fields of mustard, chilli peppers,
fennel, aubergine and wheat that were dazzlingly colourful after
the pale vistas of the flood plain. The men laughed and chattered, as if returning from a party rather than a funeral.

Gessapur was a large village of over 800 people. Its houses were
tightly packed along lanes of deeply rutted mud, and as we rumbled by we caught glimpses of buffalo tethered in courtyards and
munching from mangers built into the walls, of old men sitting
on *charpois* smoking hookahs, of women covering their faces with
the ends of their saris and scuttling into dark, windowless rooms.
Sidraj's house was on the edge of the village, next to fields spread
with drying dung patties. Off its courtyard were a tiny kitchen
with a dung-fired stove and two small rooms. Our boats and
belongings were carried into one of the rooms; Bapi's kayak fitted
inside, but the back half of the double kayak stuck out of the
doorway. Sidraj led a buffalo into the courtyard, milked it, and
presented us with beakers brimming with the warm, white liquid.
I've never been partial to milk, even when it comes in sterilized
bottles; the thought of drinking it straight from the udder turned
my stomach. Watched by Sidraj's entire family and assorted
neighbours, however, I had no option but to gulp it down and
bravely smile.

Danbir decided that Dag and Bapi needed a shave, and took
them off to find a barber. I was left in Sidraj's courtyard, surrounded by women. I sat on the *charpoi*, and they squatted on the
ground around me, giggling at my sturdy sandals and my odd
assortment of crumpled, dusty clothes. Over my thermal leggings
and vest I was wearing a *kurta*, shorts and, for modesty's sake, my
faded South Pacific *sulu*. The women had a long discussion, then
one slipped away and returned a few minutes later with her arms
full of magenta silk. I was led into a bedroom off the courtyard, a
cool, dark place with mud walls. Six women crowded around me.
Their glass bracelets tinkled as they deftly removed my clothes,
and their fingers felt like cold marble against my skin. They first
dressed me in a bodice that left my midriff bare – several bodices
had to be rejected before one small enough was found, and this
provoked a great deal of amusement. After tying a long cotton
petticoat around my waist, they wrapped me in yard after yard of
fine, rustling silk, which they expertly folded and tucked into a

sari. My hair was combed and oiled, and a small round of red plastic, a *bindi*, stuck on to my forehead to indicate my marital status. The three women stepped back to admire their handiwork, clapped their hands in delight, then led me off to be reunited with Dag.

Getting from one place to another in Gessapur proved to be a protracted affair. We usually managed only a few steps along one of the narrow streets before someone came flying out of a wooden door set into an ochre mud wall, dragged us into a courtyard and served us with sweet, milky tea and bowl after bowl of food. Everyone was curious about us, and anxious to invite us to their homes where we could properly be examined. But there was no such thing as privacy in Gessapur, as its flat roofs gave a grandstand view into neighbouring courtyards. If one family treated us to potato *pakora*, the next-door family would immediately find out and feel prevailed upon to be seen offering us potato and onion *pakora*, and perhaps some milk curds as well. There was also the matter of *darshan*: as our journey was seen as holy and our arrival at the cremation far from coincidental, our presence was believed to be highly auspicious. We, in turn, felt duty-bound to force down the great quantities of food and drink offered to us, as any refusal was met with open dismay.

Back at Sidraj's house, I sat on the mud floor of the kitchen, watching his wife Durta prepare mustard leaf curry and maize *roti*, a meal traditional to this area. From my afternoon in the village I'd gleaned something of the average daily workload of women like Durta. I'd seen how they meticulously swept mud floors and fireplaces, how they washed clothes by hand and pressed them with coal-filled irons, how they milked buffalo and churned the butter, how they collected dung and made it into fuel patties or mixed it with water to smear on the walls and floors of houses, how they spun and carded wool, how they winnowed lentil seeds and chopped up the fodder for the animals; all this as well as rearing children and catering to demanding husbands. And now, after such a day, pale scrawny Durta, who had four living children and one on the way, was cooking, hunkered over a fire, feeding it with twigs and dung and constantly blowing it to keep a strong enough flame burning. At the same time, she mixed maize flour and water, kneaded the dough and rolled small balls of it into flat rounds on a stone slab. She cooked these *rotis* one at a time over a dry pan, transferring them to the hot coals and leaving them there just long enough to puff out without burning. It was an operation I would have balked at in my high-tech kitchen, never mind this smoky little hut.

We ate in the courtyard, sitting on the *charpois*. Sidraj kept calling to his wife to bring us more *rotis* and to replenish our curry.

'Why doesn't Durta eat with us?' I asked Bapi.

'In the villages,' he told me, 'the women must wait until the men of the family have finished their food, and then they can eat what is left.'

I'd just scooped up some curry with a piece of *roti;* it froze midway to my mouth.

'This is the tradition,' he continued. 'The women are treating their husbands like gods.'

I began to protest, then stopped. Durta's life was regulated by age-old rules and rituals. For all I knew she might have been well aware of the iniquity of her situation, and of her powerlessness to change it, so who was I to breeze in, throw challenges around on her behalf, and then breeze out again? Without questioning Bapi further, I quietly finished my bowl of curry and refused the offer of more, hoping there would be some left for Durta.

'I am so tired,' sighed Bapi, as we settled into our sleeping bags, 'my eyelids are collapsing automatically.'

We were in the same windowless room as the kayaks, squashed up against piles of dried dung patties. This had been where Sidraj's father had lived; Dag and I shared the *charpoi* on which he'd died the night before. A small oil lamp set in a wall niche threw weird shadows over the thatched ceiling. Outside, a mercury lamp hissed and spluttered, and Sidraj, who had insisted as acting as our nightwatchman, intoned a mantra. Despite its morbid associations, the room was cosy and snug, and we all quickly fell asleep.

'*Chai! Chai!*' yelled Sidraj, shaking our *charpoi*.

'What time is it?' I mumbled. It was pitch dark. Our little oil lamp had burned down, but outside the mercury lamp still hissed.

'Four-thirty,' Dag told me.

'*Chai! Chai!*'

Sidraj was now at work on Bapi, who moaned and slid further

down inside his sleeping bag. We staggered to our feet, and Dag bent over Bapi and shook his shoulders.

'*Chai! Chai!*' he called into his ear. 'Get up, we need an interpreter!'

'Really, I think you are learning Hindi very well,' came his muffled reply.

Outside, we joined two men who were sitting on Sidraj's *charpoi* watching him wrestle with a temperamental kerosene stove. Like them, we were wrapped in blankets, but they insisted that we snuggle beneath the heavy quilts that Sidraj had slept under, and one of them obligingly sat on my feet to warm them up. Once Sidraj had the stove going, he prepared a *chillum*, a cone-shaped marijuana pipe. From a pink plastic bag he took a handful of dried leaves and flower heads, poured a little water on to them, squeezed them between his palms then stuffed them into the *chillum*. On top of the pipe he laid some glowing dung coals from a small fire close by which seemed to have been made specifically for this purpose. With a damp cloth around the end of the *chillum*, he put it to his lips, inhaled, then passed it on. Mercifully, being female excluded me from this ritual. But it was a strong drug: the second-hand smoke, or perhaps just the soporific atmosphere that quickly developed, made the already strange situation seem quite bizarre. Dag, meanwhile, seemed to have suddenly mastered the basics of Hindi, and he happily chatted with the men and interpreted the conversation for me.

'Sidraj wants to know if we slept well. I told him it was the best sleep we'd had in ages.'

'I wish it had been longer. When did you learn all that Hindi vocabulary?'

'I dunno. I can just tell what he's saying.'

We drank cup after cup of sweet milky *chai* while two more *chillums* went round and a sepia dawn crept over us. From time to time, Sidraj yelled into the hut, but got only groans in reply. At 6.30, a bleary-eyed Bapi finally emerged.

'You know what Sidraj was shouting?' he asked Dag.

'He was telling you to get up,' Dag confidently answered.

'No! He was asking why you got up so early! It was not necessary, he only came to ask if you wanted bed tea!'

The problem with drinking so much tea was that I soon needed to dispose of it, and Sidraj's house didn't have a latrine.

The night before, under cover of darkness, I'd slipped away beyond a field of drying dung and into a thicket of bamboo. But now I couldn't reach the end of the field unobserved, and once I practically stumbled over a man who was squatting down next to his *chembu*, a brass pot filled with water he would clean himself with after defecating. Despondently, I wandered along a lane, listening to noses and throats being vigorously cleared behind courtyard walls. Some women overtook me, carrying on their heads baskets filled with steaming dung. One of them yelled what sounded like an oath at a house, and seconds later the gate opened and a head popped around it.

'*Garam chai!*' the head cried. 'Hot tea!'

A hand shot out and I was whisked inside.

As this was one of the wealthier houses of the village, it had two courtyards, three rooms for living and sleeping in, a bath house and, to my great relief, a latrine. Although it was merely a hole in the ground behind a low mud-brick wall, to me, at that moment, it was utterly luxurious. Yet even here I wasn't totally alone – a tethered buffalo with pieces of grass stuck to its wet nose peered over the wall to watch what I was doing.

It proved impossible to leave Gessapur that day, as Danbir had organized a tractor to take us and his extended family to a religious festival that was being held some miles away. He'd also arranged that we should move to the house of some of his richer relatives where, he said, we would be more comfortable. I was relieved, as much for my own sake as for that of Sidraj's wife, for whom we were undoubtedly adding to an already gargantuan workload. Dag, however, was crestfallen. He had loved sleeping by the dung pile and chatting with the boys at 4.30 am. Sidraj was as gracious as ever, insisting that as we were now part of his family we could wander where we wished, but his house would always be our home. Leaving our boats in his care, we followed Danbir to our new abode, which we finally reached after six stops on the way and innumerable cups of *chai*.

Rahul Choudhary met us at the gate of his family's outer courtyard. For our benefit he'd got dressed up in his best clothes: tight-fitting polyester trousers, a sports jacket and blue plastic shoes.

'This is machines,' he said, pointing to the Enfield motorbike and tractor, both covered by muddy tarpaulins, that were parked next to the cow and buffalo mangers. Rahul was twenty-two, and unmarried. His elder brother, Shiv Kumar, was traditionally dressed, and more concerned with showing off his one-year-old daughter, who had eyes ringed with kohl to ward off evil spirits, and silver bells hanging from chains around her plump ankles and wrists.

'This is baby,' said Rahul, pointing to his niece. 'This is arm. This is leg.'

Since their father had died three years before, Shiv Kumar and Rahul had run the household. Their 150 acres of farmland were worked by labourers; they had two house servants and they were cooked for and cosseted by Ewartidevi, their mother, and Rita, Shiv Kumar's wife.

In the inner courtyard, an old servant in a thin cotton sari used ash to scrub brass pots to a high shine. Next to her, Rita filled buckets with water from a hand pump. In the kitchen Ewartidevi was stoking up a fire to warm the water so we could wash in the bath house, a small room with a drain hole in the floor. My offers of help were rebuffed: like the men, I was to sit and be waited on hand and foot.

Some bricks had fallen from the wall on one side of the courtyard, and several of the neighbours' faces were pressed close to this makeshift window. Their eyes followed me as I was led off by Rita to be dressed in a pink sari. For a time, their interest switched to Rita, who washed my clothes in a bucket and held up each dripping garment for general inspection. The sight of my knickers provoked much ribald cackling, but I managed to regain the audience's attention by inserting my contact lenses. The family crowded around to watch this operation, and the neighbours, no longer able to contain themselves, raced up their stairs, across the roof and down into the Choudhary's courtyard. By the time they arrived, both lenses were in place. I was persuaded to repeat the procedure, and it was only after I had removed and reinserted my lenses a total of six times that we were allowed to set off for the religious fair.

This was the women's big day, the chance for them to escape from the courtyards and the smoky kitchens and do a spot of socializing. As the tractor bounced through the narrow streets of the village, more and more women climbed aboard until, by the time we were out on the plain, rumbling across a brick road, I was well protected from the chilling wind by a solid press of laughing, singing bodies.

For most of the seven-mile journey the road followed the Ganges Canal, an uninspiring stretch of green, slimy water with concrete embankments. From half a mile away we could see a bridge which led across it to the site of the festival. As we approached, traffic from surrounding villages built up until the road was a muddled, noisy confusion of tractor trailers, buffalo carts, bicycles, scooters and thousands of people. We parked at the side of the road, and as I awkwardly clambered down from the trailer, Ewartidevi took hold of a corner of my sari. Pulling me firmly along behind her, she launched into the human tide heading across the bridge.

The fair was an annual celebration of Kali, the goddess of destruction, who is usually depicted garlanded with skulls. Despite her fearsome reputation, Kali's temple was an innocuous pink building atop a small hill. Beneath it was the fair, row after row of stalls selling sweets, fried vegetables, betel leaves and nuts, and an astonishing array of gaudy trivia: plastic bangles, combs, mirrors, hairpieces, lacy padded bras, cheap make-up and plastic potted plants. There were snake charmers, holy men giving blessings in return for alms and a greasily handsome singer belting out religious songs. Bapi ran excitedly among the stalls, buying gifts for all the members of the Choudhary family. 'Maria, stop, let me buy you something, too!' he cried. But Ewartidevi still had me in tow and, tripping on the hem of my sari, I stumbled through the mêlée with her as we made our way to the temple.

On the steps an excited crowd was jostling its way towards the double doors of Kali's shrine. Everyone carried offerings: *chapatis*, bowls of milk, bottles of *ghee*, sweets. Close to the doors, the excitement mounted to near hysteria and some people began throwing their offerings on to the flat temple roof, where two *pujaris* dressed in pink and splattered with food fielded the solid offerings like *chapatis* and dodged the wetter missiles like milk and curds. From inside the temple came a deafening clamour of bells, gongs and shouting. By standing on tiptoe and peering over heads, I could see to the far door, from where worshippers were emerging with their hair plastered in *ghee* and curds. My feet, I realized, were sinking into a sticky goo, and when the man in front of me was doused in milk I decided it was time to retreat.

Ewartidevi had the same idea. With an impressive backhand she flung her *rotis* at the roof, then elbowed a passageway for us back down the steps.

The true goal of the day was the picnic lunch on the tractor trailer. Women shared out *rotis* and vegetable *sabzee*, or stew, and gossiped with people from other villages. All the men, including Dag and Bapi, had their cheeks stuffed with *paan*, leaf-wrapped bundles of betel nut, spices, lime and opium which were causing their eyes to glaze and their teeth to turn a nasty shade of rust-red. Rahul was in his element, cheerfully answering an onslaught of questions about his Western guests. He already knew the answers to queries on our origins, our professions and our journey. But when it came to how old we were and how many children we had, he first had to check with us.

'I'm thirty-five and Maria's thirty-nine,' Dag told him. 'And we have no children.'

Rahul's face was a picture of horrified disbelief. He turned to Bapi for affirmation of this untenable information. Bapi, however, was equally flabbergasted.

'Maria, you are thirty-nine? How can this be? My mother is not so old as that!'

My age and my childlessness were the subjects of furious debate all the way back to Gessapur. The women around me yelled the news to the occupants of other tractor trailers and bullock carts. I was pointed at and given long, sympathetic looks. I sat, draped in a sari and wrapped in a blanket, feeling thoroughly confused. In comparison to these women, I was rich, privileged and with freedoms beyond their wildest dreams: I'd chosen my husband, I could earn my own living, direct my own destiny, control my fertility. And yet they felt desperately sorry for me, because I lacked the one thing that gave their life some purpose and meaning – a child. Whatever successes I had were negated by the tragic fact that I was barren. I could, I suppose, have tried to explain to them that in my culture it was possible to find other means of status and fulfilment, other insurances against old age. I could have admitted that I had chosen to be childless. And yet I said none of these things. I watched Ewartidevi comforting her granddaughter with a nipple, contentedly cooing at the baby and tickling it under the chin, and I wondered what in fact I was doing, at almost forty, dragging a boat around the world instead of being at home and raising children. Unable to answer this to myself, it was hopeless trying to communicate it to the women, so I simply nodded when they told me to that I should pray to Goddess Ganga for a child, and return next year to Gessapur with a baby in my arms.

Back at the Choudharys' house, we ate dinner sitting on the mud floor of the kitchen, while Ewartidevi and Rita flipped *rotis* straight from the fire into our bowls of *dhal.* At seven o'clock, Dag and Bapi went to visit Sidraj, but I was exhausted and started getting ready for bed. My hopes for sleep were dashed by the arrival of Mr Succha Singh, the local vet. He had heard that Dag was also a vet, and had come to discuss with him the matter of a sick buffalo. Dag was sent for, and in the meantime I was asked to entertain Mr Singh. We sat in the bedroom that Dag, Bapi and I were sharing with Rahul. Mr Singh comfortably sprawled out on one of the four beds, smoking pungent tobacco from an enormous hookah. I sat opposite him, and the family and neighbours gathered around to watch our exchange. For a few minutes, the vet simply puffed on his gurgling hookah, fixing me with an intense stare through the billowing clouds of smoke. Then, in a loud, barking voice, he announced, 'Economics is the science of wealth!' I blinked at him.

'*Economics is the science of wealth!*' he yelled.

'Oh,' I said. 'Yes.'

'Philosophy,' he said, as if this was a statement in itself.

'Yes.'

'Sociopoligy.'

'You mean sociology? I asked.

He glowered at me.

'*Yes!*' There followed a long, pregnant pause, during which he drew deeply on his hookah. 'You have lallergy from the government?' he finally asked.

'Pardon?'

'The Indian government!' he shouted. 'The service civil!'

'The civil service?'

'*Yes! Do you have lallergy?*' The crowd tightened around us, bristling with tension.

'I don't know,' I said.

By now Mr Singh appeared quite exasperated. 'Lallergy service civil the Indian government! Your boat the Ganga! Lallergy!'

Inspiration struck. 'Permission?' I hesitantly enquired.

'*Yyyyesss!*' he shrieked, showering me with spit.

'We have a letter of permission,' I told him, 'from the Ministry of Tourism.'

'Very good!'

The crowd sighed with relief, and Mr Singh grinned triumphantly.

Shortly afterwards, Dag arrived back from his session with Sidraj. Despite his rather glazed state, he listened carefully to Mr Singh, who didn't actually want his opinion, but rather wished to be seen and heard discussing the matter with him.

'And I am thinking,' the vet loudly concluded, 'that this buffalo is having foot and mouth disease!'

Only the bubbling of Mr Singh's hookah broke the long silence, while Dag cast around for something tactful to say about this wildly inaccurate diagnosis.

'I'm not sure if . . .' he began.

Mr Singh's eyes narrowed dangerously. Dag stopped, and reformulated his sentence. 'I have no experience of buffalo,' he said. 'But Mr Singh has much experience.'

'This is right!' shrieked Singh. 'Exactly right!'

And what will you prescribe?' Dag asked him.

'*Vitamins!*' he shouted.

Two more days passed before we managed to leave Gessapur. While Dag and Bapi went off wild boar hunting and visiting other villages with the men of the family, I stayed in the courtyard with the women. It was a fly-ridden place, and in the summer months must have been unbearably hot, but it was where Ewartidevi and Rita spent most of their lives. Keeping their women closeted at home while servants shopped and labourers worked the fields was how families like the Choudharys showed off their wealth. My presence was a welcome diversion from this monotonous existence, and women from other courtyards also flocked to see me, arriving via the system of interlocking roofs and stairways. For almost every minute of every day I was surrounded by curious onlookers with a very different sense of personal space to mine. This was particularly the case with the older women; they blithely felt my breasts or lifted up my sari to have a good look at my body, they picked through the contents of my clothes and toiletry bags, they paged through my notebooks. While I endeavoured to graciously submit myself to such intense scrutiny, I began to look forward to the relative privacy we would enjoy back on the river. And while I was reluctant to leave the company of the women and to exchange this pampering and relative comfort for slogging through sand banks and camping in mud, I was becoming increasingly anxious about the fact that we should really be continuing with our journey.

Dag, however, was in his element and in no hurry to leave Gessapur. He was adopting the characteristics of a rural Indian, wearing a *kurta*, smoking *bidis*, peppering his conversation with '*Acchha*' while waggling his head from side to side, spitting on the ground and blowing his nose into his fingers. Bapi, too, was happily settled in. Considering that he was a thoroughly urbanized, Westernized and secularized Indian, he had a unusually strong affection for rural life, and his empathy with village people opened doors and hearts to us everywhere we went with him. The downside of this was that he was forever in league with the villagers, trying to entice us to stop, to accept tea, to rest, to stay another night. All of which was delightful, but at this rate it was looking increasingly unlikely that we'd ever get to Varanasi. On our fourth evening in Gessapur I put my foot down and said quite firmly that we had to leave the following morning.

News of this decision quickly spread, and within the hour we received a visit from the school committee. This formidable posse of elderly men in *dhotis* and plastic slip-on shoes marched into the Choudharys' courtyard and sat facing us on a *charpoi*. We'd met them once before, on our first day in Gessapur, when we'd made a donation to the school of 41 rupees.

'You are a rich family,' said the leader, a stern man in a white Nehru cap.

The Choudharys watched and listened carefully. As tradition demanded, both Rita and Ewartidevi had covered the bottom half of their faces, but above the silk their eyes were blazing with fury.

'Our school is poor,' continued the man. 'You must be giving more money – at least one thousand rupees!'

There was a moment of shocked silence. A thousand rupees! By local standards it was an exorbitant amount. We had to consider village politics, for by being particularly generous to one family or faction, we would arouse considerable jealousies. What we didn't know at this point, but should have guessed by the Choudharys' glowering faces, was that the school committee was widely renowned for its venality. Quickly, Bapi stepped in as interpreter and mediator. He explained that because of the vulnerability of our mode of transport we were not carrying a lot of cash.

'Tell him,' said Dag, 'that we will donate another hundred rupees.'

'That's too much,' Bapi replied. 'If you want to give more, make it sixty rupees so that the total amount is one hundred and one rupees.'

The stern man, understanding the gist of this conversation, yelled in fury at Bapi, remonstrating with him for trying to per-suade us to donate less. At this, Ewartidevi could no longer contain herself, and she launched into an attack, first at the com-mittee for marching uninvited into her house, and then at us for being foolish enough to consider giving these criminals a single rupee more. Bapi talked and soothed and translated until an agreement was reached. Sixty rupees were handed over, another receipt was written out, and Dag shook hands with the five men.

'Very good, very kind,' said the man in the Nehru cap. 'Now, tell me, sir, is it true that in North America sex is free?'

We left Gessapur at dawn. Ewartidevi and Rita looked stricken as we gave them gifts and made our farewells, and I had to blink back my tears.

'Maria, no cry!' insisted Rahul. 'Cry bad luck!'

At Sidraj's house, after more *chai* and a final *chillum*, we loaded our boats and baggage on to Danbir's buffalo cart. As it rumbled along the village lanes, people ran from their courtyards, heaping us with their blessings and exhorting us to return. With a strong sense of loss, we slowly made our way through the fertile fields and back to the empty expanse of the flood plain.

13

Full Immersion

We lay in some long grass on a ledge halfway up a clay bluff. A pale, hazy sun warmed us and a breeze rippled the surface of the river murmuring thirty feet below.

'What's the date?' I asked Dag. He checked his watch. 'Valentine's Day!'

Our eyes met as we shared the same thought. Bapi was about forty-five minutes behind us. Dare we take advantage of this, the most private moment we'd had in two weeks? Before we could even reach for each other, however, the peace of the morning was rent by a burst of shouting. Peering over the ledge we saw three men hurrying towards our beached kayak. Half a mile back, we'd paddled past some large, cone-shaped heaps of dung patties, stacked right on the edge of the high embankment and covered with straw to protect them from rain. Although this was the sign of a village close by, we'd decided to carry on for fear of being waylaid by Indian hospitality so soon after leaving Gessapur.

By the time we reached the kayak, the three men were hopping about in excitement. '*Baba!*' they cried, pointing to the path they had just run down. '*Baba!*'

Baba is the familiar name given to *saddhus*, or mendicant holy men. Along the river we'd encountered several of them, in orange robes and wooden sandals, their hair wild and their fore-heads marked with sandalwood paste according to which Hindu god they worshipped. The *saddhu* these men took us to had fore-head markings in the shape of a trident, Shiva's symbol. His hair,

like Lord Shiva's, from which the Ganges is said to have originated, was matted into waist-length dreadlocks. He had a long
straggly beard and he was wrapped in saffron cloth and a biscuit-
coloured shawl. In front of him, a tomato held open the pages of
a holy book, and he was reading in a sing-song voice to a rapt
audience of men from the nearby village. Our arrival did not
seem to surprise him in the least; he motioned for us to sit down,
and called to a young man who sat tending a cook fire outside a
brick hut to make *chai*. Beyond the hut, and surrounded by tulsi
and neem trees, was a small Shiva temple with pink walls and
turrets and heavy wooden doors. The *saddhu*, whose name was
Baba Amardas, had apparently found a temporary resting place,
and it was soon obvious that he was inviting us to share it with him
for the night.

'What do you think?' asked Dag, looking hopefully at me. I
gazed around. From our high vantage-point we could see the
Ganga looping across the flood plain, and the splashes of green
and yellow fields around the ochre tones of the nearby village.
After days spent inside walled courtyards, it was good to be out in
the open, and with such a view. And then there was Bapi to consider, no doubt weary after four hours of hard paddling. Baba
Amardas was smiling, showing off even white teeth, and waggling
his head from side to side.

'*Acchha? Acchha?*'

By the time Bapi arrived, our kayak had being carried up the
steep bank, and set on the holy ground by the temple.

Before long, Baba Armardas produced a *chillum*. According to
Hindu mythology, Shiva spent a lot of time smoking marijuana,
and the Shivite *saddhus* we met all seemed to be striving to follow
their lord's example. While the *chillum* went around, through
Bapi I asked the *baba* to tell us about himself. He was from Assam,
but he couldn't say when he'd left there or at what age, as when
he became a *saddhu* he'd renounced and 'forgotten' everything
of his former life, including his name. He had been at this spot
for some weeks, and complained that the villagers were looking
after him too well, bringing him too much food, and that he
could pray better when he was hungry. By this time the *chillum*
had gone round several times, and the *baba* was in full flow, without any need of my prompts.

'Oh God, I don't believe it,' said Bapi. 'He is talking now in rhyme, and he is saying that the *chillum* is his rifle, and he is load-ing it with ganja and aiming it to heaven in a salute!'

Baba Armardas broke wind, then turned and made a com-ment to Bapi, who went into convulsions of laughter, clutching his sides and rolling on the ground. The villagers, who had not been partaking of the *chillum*, looked rather alarmed by this irrev-erent behaviour.

'Oh God! *No!* I don't believe it!' gasped Bapi. 'He's a crazy *baba!*'

'What, Bapi? What did he say?'

'He said sometimes when he lights his weapon it fires out of the wrong end!'

And that, for a while, was the end of Bapi as a useful translator, as he spent much of the next eighteen hours either laughing or asleep.

Leaving Bapi with Baba Armardas, Dag and I walked into the village. The winding path took us through a hummocky land-scape, and past gnarled trees with parrots squawking and fluttering in the branches. Shinkiteela village was half the size of Gessapur, and its houses had a fairytale quality about them, with rounded steps and lopsided doorways, blue and white friezes painted on to dung and mud walls and iridescent peacock feath-ers hanging in windows. But the people who gathered around us were pitifully poor. Children with ragged clothes, mud-caked feet and tousled hair peeked out from behind their parents, and one of the mothers, still in her teens, held on her hip a small child with horrifying burns. Three days before, we ascertained, the girl had fallen into a cooking fire, and now her leg was covered with blackened crusts, some of which had rubbed off, exposing raw flesh that oozed thick yellow pus.

To the dismay of the villagers, who obviously thought we were fleeing from the sight of this dreadful wound, we hurried back to the kayak to collect some first-aid supplies. Baba Armardas was now singing, one of the village men was playing a small harmo-nium which he pumped with his left hand while working the keyboard with his right, and Bapi was doing some impressive tabla-like drumming on a metal plate. His conversation, however, had become inane. 'I asked the *baba* for this plate and he was thinking I was wanting his food! It is so funny!

'Bapi, come with us, we need you to translate.'

'Oh God!' It is not possible! I cannot walk!'

Flies crawled around the child's eyes as she stared unflinchingly at Dag while he cleaned and dressed her wound. By now we were surrounded by aspiring patients, most of them elderly men with no obvious afflictions. They coughed theatrically, or grimaced and patted their stomachs, or hobbled to and fro with pronounced limps.

'The old buggers,' said Dag. 'They're put out because two females got all the attention.'

Inside Baba Amardas's hut Dag cooked a *sabzee* over our kerosene stove, and the villagers bought us *rotis* and milk curds. The *baba* blessed all the food by sprinkling it with Ganges water that he'd carried from the river in a brass pot. He ate voraciously and messily, with many appreciative burps.

'The *baba* says the day after tomorrow is an inauspicious day to travel,' Bapi told me.

'Why?'

There was a brief and giggly exchange between them. 'He is saying this is a holy place, and if you are staying here you must tolerate all sorts of holy shit.'

'Bapi, he didn't say that!'

'He did! I swear!'

After dinner I left the three men and crawled into our tent, which we'd erected a little distance from the hut. I drifted in and out of sleep, only dimly conscious of the raucous laughter and singing that went on far into the night.

At first light, the *baba* started moving around, muttering his mantras, burping and farting. He emerged from the hut wearing only a *dhoti* and carrying a brass bucket, and set off towards the river. I followed at a discreet distance. His *puja* was a simple one: he scooped up water in his palms, let it slowly trickle through his fingers, and held his upturned face and hands to the rising sun. Praying aloud, he filled the bucket and returned to the temple, which was now a glowing violet colour. Three times he walked around it, sprinkling water on the holy ground, on the revered tulsi trees, on our kayak. Swinging open the heavy doors, he stepped inside and began to sing, his voice reverberating around the domed ceiling. Over the lingam, a phallic stone symbolizing the creative aspect of Shiva, he poured water, scattered marigolds and wafted burning incense sticks. Still muttering prayers, he backed out of the temple and pulled the heavy doors so that they banged shut with a sepulchral boom. Turning to face the Ganga, he blew on a conch, three long blasts which resonated across the flood plain, made the hair on my neck stand on end and managed to wake even Bapi and Dag.

Stripes of vivid red and yellow sandalwood paste were freshly daubed on Baba Armardas's forehead, and his dreadlocks were piled on top of his head and wrapped in orange cloth. Squinting against the bright morning sunshine, he bent to touch and bless our boats before we carried on with our journey.

'He is saying,' said Bapi blearily, 'that our pilgrimage is cleansing our hands, our food and our water. He is saying also that ahead there are bandits and we must take care.'

I handed him a donation inside one of the plastic ziplock bags that he had so admired the day before. His eyes registered surprise, his head waggled from side to side, and he smiled. And then, to my own considerable surprise, I knelt and placed my forehead on his feet to receive his blessing.

Towards late afternoon of our twelfth day on the Ganga, we reached the town of Anupshahr. According to Bapi's estimates, we were about a third of the way to Varanasi. The last section of the river had been delightful, with deep water, strong currents, warm sun and the wind at our backs. We'd sped by constantly changing scenes, each one a cameo in itself: a lush green village with young palms and ancient peepul trees; a temple that was literally crumbling into the river; buffalo contentedly lolling in the water while children scrubbed them down; fishermen casting nets from wooden boats; a sweep of sculpted dunes where three women stood holding up freshly washed saris to dry in the wind, so that yards and yards of emerald, azure and scarlet silk flapped like giant flags against the silvery sand.

Temples lined the bank at the town of Anupshahr, and on one of the *ghats*, the steps leading down to the river, a *pujari* sat and watched our approach as if it was the most normal thing in the world.

'If you are wanting to buy toilet paper,' he told us, 'I am sorry but you will not be finding it in Anupshahr.'

There was a pause while we considered this information.

'We are looking for a safe place to spend the night,' said Dag.

The *pujari* waggled his head. '*Acchha*. You will be finding it here, sir.'

He told us we could store our boats in the *ashram* next to the temple, and that there was a room on the roof where we could sleep. The room was a bare cell, with a glassless window. Stuck on to a nail between two bricks was a garishly coloured picture of the boy Krishna with his hand in a bowl of milk curds. Outside, on the parapet, monkeys with black faces and white ruffs tugged at the zip of our red sack, and one of them bared its yellow fangs at me when I tried to shoo it away.

'These are holy monkeys,' Bapi remonstrated. 'You must be respectful of them.'

Beyond the *ashram*, pigs snuffled in the open drain that ran down the middle of Anupshahr's main street. At a *chai* stall, we sat on a plank propped between two oil cans and drank tea from small terracotta beakers. It was customary to use these beakers only once, and around our feet the discarded ones lay broken and crumbling into the mud. The stall's owner squatted on top of his adobe oven, fanning the fire inside and adding more milk, tea, water and *gur* to a smoke-blackened pot. Before long, a crowd had formed around us, and soon the narrow street was congested with people, scooters, rickshaws and pigs. Two gun-toting policemen came wading through to see what was causing such a commotion. After shooing away the onlookers to a reasonable distance, they joined us on the plank.

'When you reach Narora,' one of them told us, 'you must be stopping for a picnic. It is not far and indeed a beautiful place, the biggest hydro-electricity dam in Asia!'

'Madam,' the other asked me, curiously eyeing my kayak jacket. 'Why is it that foreigners always are having so many pockets?'

Later that night, I crept down from the roof, hoping to find a private spot that I could use as a toilet. I was loath to follow Bapi's suggestion to 'Do it into the river' or the *pujari*'s vague instructions to use a nearby alleyway, 'Women on left and men on right!' From one of the temples came frenzied chanting: '*Hare Ram Hare Ram Ram Ram Hare Hare! Hare Krishna Hare Krishna Krishna Krishna Hare Hare!*' I considered going in there and asking about a latrine, then thought better of it. It was after midnight, and the sight of a western woman in pink longjohns might not be a welcome one. Finding a place to pee and shit, at home a simple, straightforward matter, had for months now presented me with a daily dilemma. It had been bad enough in the Solomon Islands, where there were crocodiles, centipedes and snakes to worry about, but at that moment I would have happily waded into a mangrove swamp instead of skulking around these shadowy streets, hoping in vain to come across a few bushes. Finally, I ventured into the alleyway, only to be chased out by a pack of snarling dogs. I gave up, and went back to bed in a foul humour.

But at dawn, when I stepped out of our tiny room, my bad mood evaporated. The plain stretched away, awash with an amber light. Music blared from the temples, incense drifted up from the *pujas* taking place on the *ghats*. A woman stood praying in the river, her maroon sari floating on its bronze surface. A barber tonsured a three-year-old Brahmin boy, carefully leaving one long strand of hair on his crown. The boy's mother placed some of the shorn hair on a banana leaf and offered it to the river. Men wearing *dhotis* and the sacred thread of Brahmins across their bare chests sat meditating in perfect lotus positions. A cow wandered about the *ghat*, and people pressed their foreheads between its horns to receive its blessing. Also in progress were secular affairs. Women rinsed out basketfuls of lentils, washed cooking pots and clothes, or squatted on the *ghats*, rubbing their heels against the rough stone to remove hard skin. Men lathered themselves from head to foot with soap and cleaned their teeth with twigs.

Presently, over all this activity a new light was cast, as the red orb of the sun peeped over the horizon. The bathers turned their faces to it, and held their palms upwards. Quickly, before I had time to reconsider, I wrapped myself in my *sulu* and hurried down to the women's *ghat*. A woman in a wet sari that clung to her body as revealingly as if she were naked reached out her hand to me. She drew me into the cold water until I was chest deep, and my bare feet had left the steps and were sinking into mud. With her free hand she held her nose and nodded at me to do the same. Shutting my eyes and holding my breath, I ducked my head beneath the surface for the ritual three immersions.

Our *pujari* friend smeared my forehead with sandalwood paste and gave me a *prasad* of blessed sweets. Sitting cross-legged on a wooden table, he recorded in a large ledger my name, my act of worship and the merit I had accrued towards gaining a place in heaven. Around him were *puja* items for sale: camphor, marigolds, coconuts and red cloths, as well as combs and mirrors that he rented out to worshippers so they could tidy up their hair after bathing. He offered me one of the greasy combs, but I couldn't face using it. My first full immersion in the Ganga had been experience enough for one day.

By noon we'd reached Rajghat, a muddy pilgrimage site where hundreds of red and yellow flags fluttered above temporary straw shacks. A railway bridge spanned the river and beneath it men stood neck-deep in water, their heads moving almost impercept-ibly from side to side. It wasn't, as I first thought, some form of devotion we had not yet encountered. 'People throw money offerings to Ganga from the train windows,' explained Bapi. 'And these men are making a living by looking for the money with their toes.'

To get past the huge, hulking structure of Narora Barrage, we employed the services of a man and his handcart. The cart was a hopelessly rickety affair made of a few short planks tacked on to a scrap metal frame and resting on four flat bicycle tyres. We loaded the boats and baggage on top of it and set off on the long portage, with Dag holding one end of the double kayak and Bapi the other, the cart groaning and jolting beneath the weight and all four wheels wobbling around in different directions.

Narora, as the policeman in Anupshahr had intimated, was indeed a popular picnic site. There were lawns and flower beds, swings and roundabouts for children and a 3-D ceramic display of the course of the Ganges from source to sea, with Narora Barrage and power station prominently displayed. And there were scores of well-dressed Indian tourists who looked up from their picnics on the parched grass to watch in amazement the uncertain progress of our cart. A group of urbane youths in Western clothes latched on to us.

'Excuse me, what is the exact height of your husband?' one asked me.

'Six feet two inches.'

'That is the exact height of Amitabh Bachchan, India's famous movie star. Are you knowing this man? His attempts to enter political life ended in the most terrible scandal.'

Walking towards us from the opposite direction was a frail old pilgrim. He was wrapped in jute sacking, carried a staff, and looked for all the world like some ancient prophet. At the sight of us he opened wide his toothless mouth, and hooted with loud, merry laughter.

We made it through the park, past all the picnickers, across a busy road, over a bridge and to the far side of the barrage. Where, to our collective dismay, we saw trucks bowling over a wide plain, raising clouds of white dust and easily fording a shallow, shrunken river.

14

The Bouncing Baba

Once more blighted by low water and submerged sand banks, for the next three days we pushed and poled our way downstream more than we paddled. As if taunting us with the ridiculousness of our situation, men crossed the river ahead of us on bicycles, and the *saddhus* walking along the bank easily overtook us. I tried to block out the discomfort and the frustration by turning my thoughts to home. I wondered how our cats were, if our fruit trees had survived the frost. I pictured our house, lashed by winter winds and rain – and suddenly the drain pipes, or rather the lack of them, popped into my head. 'When we get back to Canada,' I told Dag, 'let's get all the jobs on the house done straight away.'

'Jobs?'

'Yes, you know, like the drain pipes, and the—'

'*Drain pipes?* Is this a joke?'

'No! Look, if we don't get on with things like the drain pipes, the house will be falling down around our heads before it's even finished.'

'Why the hell are you worrying about drain pipes when we're in the middle of—'

He was interrupted by a soft thump as a submerged sand bank snared us.

'Instead of coming on this trip,' said Dag through gritted teeth, as we struggled to push the boat free, 'we could have spent a year finishing the house and inviting all the neighbours over to admire our nice new drain pipes.'

At that precise moment, standing knee-deep in mud and with the wind filling my ears with sand, it didn't seem such a bad option.

'And maybe,' he continued sarcastically, 'we could have mowed the lawn every Sunday and bought plastic garden furniture and one of those lovely striped umbrellas—'

'Actually,' I interrupted, as I heaved at the boat, 'I'd like to buy a lawn mower.'

'*A lawn mower?*' he spluttered.

At Dag's insistence, we'd left our field-sized lawn in its natural state.

'Last summer I had to hack my way through the long grass to get to the vegetable patch.'

'And I suppose you'll want to put weed killer down as well?' he cried, glaring at me across the cockpit. 'And how about a few garden gnomes while you're at it?'

'*I just want to mow the bloody thing!*' I yelled back.

'What's the matter?' cried Bapi, who was stuck behind us.

'Oh, nothing,' I replied. 'We're just having a domestic squabble.'

'I'm about to murder my wife,' Dag told him. 'And then I'm going to cremate her on the river bank.'

'I am very sorry about this, Maria!' said Bapi. 'But at least you will be going straight to heaven.'

The river got wider and deeper but, as if reminding itself not to hurry, it snaked about the plain in dramatic loops and bends, so that often we found ourselves paddling back in the direction from which we'd just come. At the end of the third day, we were reconciling ourselves to yet another desolate campsite when, beyond the grey-green water, and over the shoals of silvery sand, people appeared as if in a mirage. First just a handful of them, running towards us, their saris and striped *lungis* fluttering against the white sand and the sapphire sky. Then more and more sprang up, until a big crowd was bearing down on us. An evil-looking man with bloodshot protruding eyes and stubby black teeth reached us first. He grabbed our kayak by the rudder and began dragging us to shore. Dag jumped out of his cockpit to fend off this unwanted attention, but within seconds the man was just one of over a hundred people, pressing in from all sides, yelling at us in Hindi, wildly gesticulating, pushing and shoving us in their excitement. Bapi and his boat were out of sight, lost somewhere in the mêlée, and I was hit by a flash of panic: we were hopelessly outnumbered and at the mercy of this near hysterical throng. Suddenly heads turned away from us and bodies moved back, and a tall, strongly built *saddhu* with fierce eyes and a black beard appeared, beating people away with a bamboo pole and hurling handfuls of sand into their faces.

'My God!' cried Bapi, appearing at our side. 'I believed I was about to suffocate!'

The *saddhu* promptly began berating Bapi. He was with a theatre group that for the holy month of Magh was travelling along the Ganges giving four-day long performances of the *Ramayana*, one of the Hindus' epic poems. Much to his chagrin, we had ruined that day's performance, which was taking place on a high bank beyond the shoal. A rumour of foreigners on the river in a strange boat had spread like wildfire and the audience had abandoned the play to seek us out. Nonetheless, he invited us to come and spend the night at the troupe's encampment. He turned to the crowd, now shaking sand out of hair and *lungis* a safe distance away, and marshalled it into carrying our boats up the embankment.

The stage was a free-standing, rickety affair, constructed from rough planks and bamboo and festooned with ropes and pulleys to raise and lower six hand-painted backdrops. To one side was a row of temporary straw huts. We were given one of these to sleep in, and our kayaks and belongings were laid down outside it. *Sabzee* and *rotis* were brought for us, and ginger-flavoured tea. While we ate and drank, our *saddhu*, whom Bapi nicknamed the Bouncing Baba, tirelessly ran about. He chased curious children away, thwacked the dogs that mooched around, ordered food to be brought to us and supervised the lighting of a fire fuelled with straw pulled from the roofs of the huts. The actors, musicians and *saddhus* gathered to stare at us, and eventually the Bouncing Baba settled down to join them.

After three days of struggling with sand banks, we were worn out, and retired early to our shelter. Unfortunately, it was open-fronted, so our audience simply shifted position to continue watching us. Rather pointedly, Dag hung up one of our blankets, but the men simply craned their necks to see around it. Minutes after we'd settled down, a PA system crackled to life – from where it was powered we never discovered – and strident religious music blasted across the camp. It went on for a couple of hours, until it was replaced by the more humdrum sounds of chanting, talking, snoring and dog fights. A rat nosed about the hut, and once ran across our legs. An hour or so before dawn there was a new and haunting disturbance. It started in the distance and got steadily closer and louder: female voices, flat and childishly high, singing the same refrain over and over again. I lay in my sleeping bag, imagining a line of women with brass bowls on their heads, walking through the fields. The voices grew closer. I got up, slipped into my clothes and stepped out into the cool, damp air. The women passed by the camp unseen, cloaked in darkness. Wrapping myself in a blanket, I walked down to the river bank. The moon was still up but a golden glow was spreading across the horizon. From the nearby village a lone dog howled. At the edge of the river, *saddhus* were doing *puja*, fashioning lingams from the muddy sand and anointing them with water. I sat down to watch another sunrise over the Ganga. Despite having spent an uncomfortable night in a straw hut, I felt immensely calm and ridiculously happy.

My good mood was soon taxed, however, by the overbearing scrutiny that dawn brought. A group of men sat around the doorway of our shelter, watching me thrash around under my blanket, trying to divest some of the warm clothing I'd earlier piled on. Soon they were joined by three village women who followed me to the river, chattering like birds, and squatted on their haunches to peer at me washing my face and cleaning my teeth. They were quickly dispersed by the Bouncing Baba, who descended on them with wildly flapping hands, like some exotic bird. This was a Tuesday, his weekly day of silence, but he was managing to be as bossy as the night before. Through a combination of grunting and gesticulation, he led me to the camp kitchen, where he bade me sit on the sandy ground and thrust a lump of *gur* into my hand. Tackling this sweet, cloying stuff at seven in the morning was bad enough, but worse was to come. Over by the cooking fire, an old *saddhu* was peeling a heap of freshly boiled potatoes, while another was mashing them with his hands. The *baba* grabbed a peeled potato and gave it to me. At first I was relieved to exchange my *gur* for something more palatable, but I'd barely finished the first potato when another was passed over, and a pair of blazing eyes commanded me to eat it. Three potatoes later, in an attempt to fend off the tuber attack without upsetting anyone, I retrieved my lump of *gur* from the ground, picked off as much sand as I could and began nibbling on it. By now one of the old *saddhus* was bent over a large pot on the fire, stirring up a mixture of mashed potatoes and water and adding various brightly coloured spices. Issuing thanks all around, I sidled over towards the door of the hut, but before I could reach it the *baba* handed me a bowl heaped with the potato *sabzee* and sprinkled with cardamom seeds. Then he dipped a metal beaker into a pail of water that had just been carried up from the river, handed it to me and, with his face six inches from mine, glared at me until I drank it all.

By eight the camp was bustling with activity. A line of singing women, perhaps the ones I'd heard hours before, marched through the camp carrying on their heads bundles of sugar cane and coconuts. Bejewelled ankles and toes flashed from beneath their saris, and glass bracelets jangled on their wrists. This was the day of the full moon, and they were on their way to the river to make a special *puja* to ask for the protection of their newly sown crops. Actors just up from bathing in the Ganga shivered around straw fires, putting their bare feet right into the flames and holding up sodden undershorts to dry. Musicians began warming up on their tablas and harmoniums. Villagers were setting up refreshment stalls selling *bidis*, sweets, *pakora* and guavas. Dag, Bapi and I had a quick conference. Staying to watch the play, which would doubtless be a protracted affair, would cause us to lose yet another day of paddling. We were about to reach a consensus decision to pack up and leave when the Bouncing Baba joined us and began scrawling Hindi words in the sand with his finger.

'He says we must stay until tomorrow,' Bapi translated.

Regretfully, we told him this wasn't possible.

The *baba*'s eyes blazed as he dashed off his next message.

'He says he will start the play immediately and that we can leave by noon.'

Rather reluctantly, we settled down in front of the stage. For the next hour, however, we were the main entertainment, watched by an appreciative and ever-swelling audience. The actors and musicians busied about to no obvious effect, and the

Above: Curious children surround Maria and the kayak in Vonavona Lagoon.

Right: Remains of former chiefs on Skull Island, Vonavona Lagoon.

Below: Dag befriends a baby fruit bat in Samosodu, Santa Isabel Island.

Stoking the cooking fire on a campsite on Santa Isabel Island.

Planning the next day's journey in a leaf hut in Kia, Santa Isabel Island.

Maria and Bapi drink water from the Ganga during a puja in Hardwar.

In Gessapur, a neighbour comes to watch Maria insert her contact lenses.

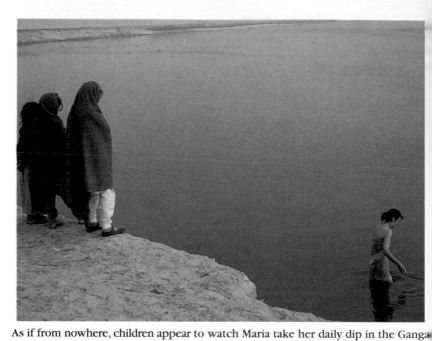

As if from nowhere, children appear to watch Maria take her daily dip in the Ganga

A view across the Gangetic plain from the temple of Sultanpur.

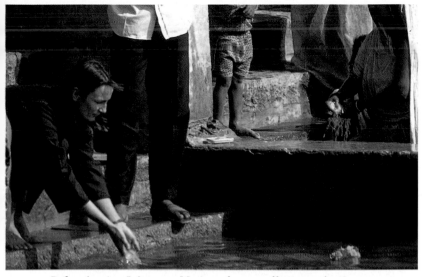

Before leaving Sultanpur, Maria makes an offering to the Ganga.

Below Left: Blowing on a conch shell, a saddhu greets the rising sun.
Below Right: At Varanasi, the boat is folded up and packed into its bag.

Fishermen launch a dugout as dawn breaks over Lake Malawi.

The kayak is dwarfed by a giant baobab tree on Likomo Island.

Sunrise on the shores of
Lake Malawi.

Washing up while keeping an eye out for
crocodiles, Likomo Island.

A cloud of flies rises up from Lake Malawi.

Children play in a waterfall near Chisanga.

saddhus sat around our kayaks firing up one *chillum* after another. Sensing our restlessness, the Bouncing Baba set upon the troupe with a bamboo cane, thwacking its members into action. Eventually, eight men stood on stage, in front of a backdrop depicting a room with an arched pink and green ceiling, orange and yellow striped pillars and a golden chandelier. Five of the men were dressed as women, but the effect of their make-up, jewellery and the false breasts straining at their saris was rather spoiled by their heavy wristwatches and their heels poking out of well-worn nylon socks. They launched into a sinuous dance which, after half an hour, proved to be only a preamble to the play. A new backdrop came down, and now the scene was of the Ganga flowing out of the Himalayas alongside a four-lane highway. Three of the actors came centre stage and began to sing. 'This is Rama, his wife Sita and his brother Lakshmana,' explained Bapi. 'They are going into exile in the jungle, where Lakshmana will be cutting off the ears of the sister of Ravana, who in revenge for this will be carrying off Sita, so that Rama will be making an alliance with Sugriva, king of the monkeys, who will be sending Hanuman to help him, and Hanuman will be building a dam across the straits—'

'Stop!' I implored him. 'You're going too fast, I'm lost. How do you know all this?'

'I learned the story when I was a child. And now it is a soap opera on the television.'

By noon, the wind was blowing sand around the camp and whipping up lengths of orange cloth from the straw roofs where they'd been left to dry. Bapi had wandered off to share a *chillum* with the *saddhus*, and the play had ground to a halt. All the actors were now on stage, huddled behind a man in a *dhoti* and a jacket who was hectoring the audience to make donations to the theatre troupe. As rupees were passed up, he announced the names of the donors and the exact amount of their donations. An hour later, with the play still no further forward and a sandstorm threatening, we decided that we would leave after all. Our announcement to this effect caused the *baba* to fly into a temper, and he scribbled furious messages into the sand: that our departure would once again disrupt the entire proceedings, that we should stay another night, and the next day as well. When we were adamant, he demanded that Dag and Bapi go on to the stage and explain to the crowd why we were leaving. Dag said a few words in English about our reasons for having to press on to Varanasi, then Bapi took the microphone to translate and launched into a long, rambling, marijuana-inspired speech. When the time came for us to say goodbye to the *baba*, he sat with his arm over his eyes, literally refusing to see us.

The scene of our departure was even more chaotic than our arrival the day before. The entire audience, the actors, the musicians and most of the *saddhus* came to see us off. Dag left me and Bapi standing knee-deep in the river, hanging on to our boats and submerged by people, while he sprinted up the hill to take a photo of the scene. Even when we paddled off, the crowd stayed with us, running along the banks and only gradually falling back and returning to the play.

Despite a stiff wind that whipped up clouds of stinging sand, it was a relief to be back on the Ganga and alone once more. Flocks of cranes and cormorants flapped up from the river, bright white and deep black against a grey landscape and sky. Sometimes people emerged from the sand clouds, like ghosts in a dream: a lunatic sitting on the bank gabbling to himself, a bare-chested Brahmin wearing the sacred thread across his torso, doing *puja* in celebration of the full moon. The sounds of drumming and singing drifted from nearby villages, but we paddled on until we were bathed in moonlight, and camped alone and undisturbed on a muddy bank.

15

Blessings and Bodies

While Dag still slept, I crawled out of the tent. In the dawn light, the river looked like dull pewter, and tendrils of mist crept along its surface. Quickly, I undressed, and despite my only companions being two red-legged storks delicately stepping across a nearby sandbar, I wrapped myself in a length of cloth. I'd learned that in India people can materialize from nowhere, and to be found bathing naked in the Ganga would be an untenable transgression of holy law. As I waded into the sluggish water, the storks flapped their wings and skimmed away with long legs trailing behind them. Holding my nose, I immersed myself for three quick, cold dips, then struggled back to the bank. Bending to my small pile of clothes, I realized I was standing among cinders and brittle bone fragments. Nearby, a makeshift stretcher and a muddy shroud lay discarded.

After three weeks on the river, we'd grown used to seeing cremations in all their various stages. We'd seen naked corpses being ceremonially smeared with ghee, we'd seen a man carrying a lighted torch five times around the pyre on which his dead father lay, we'd seen people too poor to afford enough fuel simply pushing a half-burned body into the water. Later that day, as we paddled by the third cremation in as many hours, Dag and Bapi lapsed into black humour.

'Smells like chicken – must have been a skinny one.'

'No, no, you are quite wrong, it is smelling exactly like roast beef. This was a fatter person!'

As always, the mourners always ran to the water's edge, beckoning to us. We didn't intend to stop. We wanted to reach Fatehgarh that day, and we had no clear idea of the distance we had to cover.

'You will get there by nightfall,' a *saddhu* we'd met earlier had predicted.

'It's fifty kilometres away,' a fisherman standing waist-deep in the river had told us. Now, the mourners had yet another estimate.

'*Do sau kilomitar!*' they cried. 'Two hundred kilometres! Come and rest!'

We put our palms together in *namaskar*, and carried on. After a few paddle strokes, I turned to wave at the men. They were shading their eyes with their hands to watch our departure. Seen through the flame-heated air, they appeared to shimmer, like ghostly creatures. The river took a wide bend, and suddenly, the men were out of sight.

The next section of the river had a forsaken feeling to it. It made tortuous loops, a hot searing wind swept across the plain and the sky glared down. There was nothing to distract us from the monotony save sand banks and skeletons. Once, we became stranded on a bank in the company of a full human skeleton, picked clean of flesh but with cloth still wrapped around its torso.

We'd already given up the idea of trying to reach Fatehgarh that day when we saw a red flag fluttering from a long pole, the sign of an encampment of *saddhus*. Drifting towards us on the wind were the rhythmic beating of a gong and the droning of a mantra: '*Sita Ram Sita Ram Sita Ram Sita Ram . . .*' A crowd of *saddhus* ran down to the river bank and pulled our boats ashore. They had long matted hair and were ash-smeared and naked except for loincloths. Around their feet, scabby, dun-coloured dogs barked, leaped and fought, raising clouds of sand. The *saddhus* told us they were camped here for the month of Magh with their 111-year-old guru, Moni Baba. Chattering excitedly, they led us to a large tent made of ragged canvas thrown over bamboo poles. Next to it, some women from the nearby village of Kadarga were sitting in the dirt making *rotis* and potato *sabzee*. They stopped working to stare at us, and the cloud of flies buzzing around them settled on to the dough, changing its pasty grey colour to black.

Inside the tent, the ground was spread with dusty straw and the air was thick with flies, but it was a welcome respite from the wind and the blinding light outside. We were brought mugs of lukewarm tea that was the same muddy colour as the river. Several *saddhus* crouched around to watch us drink it. Others peered around the tent flap and through holes in the canvas. Despite my strong suspicion that the water hadn't been boiled, I gulped it down. The *saddhus* grinned in delight. The tent flap was thrown back and a young *saddhu* came in with two plates heaped with *sabzee* and *rotis*. Fleetingly, I remembered the fly-covered dough outside, and then I pushed the thought aside.

'They are asking us to sleep tonight in this tent,' said Bapi. I looked doubtfully at the thick cloud of flies circling our heads. The *saddhus*' eyes followed mine.

'They are telling,' said Bapi, 'that you must not worry about these flies, because when darkness comes they will go home.'

Bowls of warm buffalo milk and lumps of *gur* followed next. To allay the arrival of yet more food, we requested an audience with Moni Baba.

We were ushered to the doorway of a tiny tent. Two *saddhus* knelt either side of a heap of blankets and began singing to it. The heap stirred. A hand emerged. The blankets were thrown back and a wizened old man sat up. His rheumy eyes were heavily-lidded and his head was totally bald except for a few long strands of fine hair sprouting from the crown. He was instantly alert and listened carefully to the *saddhus*' explanation of who we were and what we were doing. Then, as this was his weekly day of silence, he reached for a chalkboard. While he scrawled some Hindi script, I noticed how remarkably young his hands looked. Bapi translated what he wrote.

'Moni Baba says that our *yatra* purifies the food we eat and the water we drink.'

With a measure of relief, I thought of the meal we'd just consumed.

'He says that we will reach Varanasi in safety, but the hardest part of the journey is ahead. He says that we should sing *Rama Sita*.'

The guru began clapping his hands together. Feeling rather self-conscious, we chanted the mantra in time with him. The *saddhus* pressing around the tent joined in, the man beating the gong fell into our rhythm, conches were blown, cymbals clashed, and soon the entire camp echoed with fervent singing. Despite the heat inside the tent, and the flies crawling over my face and arms, I felt myself slipping into a strange, hypnotic state, and gazed in homage at the old man before me. Abruptly, he held up his hands for silence. All around the camp, the singing and music faded away. He closed his eyes, and his lips moved as if in prayer. There was a pregnant hush in and around the tent. Then the guru's heavy lids snapped open, and his eyes twinkled at Dag. 'Good day, sir!' he cried, and dissolved into helpless chuckling.

The *saddhus* gasped in alarm: the guru had broken his day of silence!

Moni Baba composed himself. 'Today I go to Varanasi,' he solemnly pronounced. 'Yesterday, I went to Varanasi. Tomorrow I shall go to Varanasi.'

'He is practising his English!' cried Bapi. The guru sneezed.

'*Rama!*' yelled the *saddhus* in unison. '*Sita Ram!*' and a fresh round of chanting and clapping ensued.

When darkness came, the flies did go home, forming a dense coating on the inside walls and ceiling of the tent. I lay in our sleeping bag, listening to the muttering of mantras all around the camp, and wondering if Moni Baba had been right about the purification of our food. Since leaving Hardwar, every night I'd expected to wake up with the gut-wrenching pains that presage an attack of gastro-enteritis. So far, though, I'd had the opposite problem: whether it was because of the starchy diet, or as a result of my inhibitions due to the lack of privacy and toilet paper, I was suffering, on the Ganges of all places, from constipation.

At six o'clock the flies woke and descended upon us, forcing us to flee the tent. All around the camp, *saddhus* were meditating, or doing *puja* at the water's edge, or hunkered around small fires. Moni Baba's appearance at eight drew them all together, and they greeted him with fervent delight, blowing on conches, banging on cymbals, gongs, drums and tin plates, and shouting out mantras. He shuffled along to a small platform shaded with yellow cloth, where he was lifted up to sit amid heaps of flowers, tin boxes filled with blessed sweets, pictures of Rama and holy books bound in red cloth. One by one the *saddhus* knelt before him to receive his blessing and accept a *prasad* of sweets. Then it was our turn. We strewed marigolds over his head and touched our foreheads to his feet. As he gave us *prasad*, he spoke in a childish, sing-song voice.

Bapi's face broke into a huge grin. 'Moni Baba is wanting to see your kayak!'

Helped by the *saddhus*, the guru inched his way to the river bank. For several minutes he stood in silence, staring down at the red boat. When he finally spoke his words were greeted with gasps and squeals of surprise.

'He is wanting to ride in the boat!' cried Bapi.

'*Rama Sita!*' the *saddhus* shouted. '*Sita Ram!*'

I held the boat steady as the old man was lowered into the front cockpit. He pulled his shawl tightly around his shoulders, and held out one hand for his staff, which he laid across the deck. Dag got into the back of the kayak, tentatively pushed off from the bank and paddled the frail guru around in circles.

'*Sita Ram, Sita Ram!*' sang the *saddhus*, leaping about in pure joy, and showering the boat with marigold heads.

'If you insist on these tearful leave-takings, you'd better learn how to blow your nose the Indian way,' said Dag, as we paddled away from the camp.

Overcome by the exuberant faith of the *saddhus*, and by their open-hearted acceptance of us, I was openly weeping. By the time I managed to stop the flood of tears, their chanting had faded out of earshot, and the marigold heads on the kayak deck were withering in the sun.

The river still lazily wound about, and despite long days of paddling we seemed to get no closer to Fatehgarh. But there was a change of atmosphere along the river banks. The curiosity of the farmers we met along the way was tinged with suspicion and resentment, and the warnings of dacoits steadily increased.

'There are *jungli* people around here,' the farmers said. 'You must not camp alone.'

We finally reached the outskirts of Fatehgarh on a bright and sunny morning. Women in vivid saris worked in fields of pumpkins and mustard, and *dhobi wallahs* stood in the river, wrestling with huge lengths of material which stained the water with red and purple dyes. All over the bank, shirts, saris and bolts of cotton were spread out to dry in the afternoon sun. Burros lay in the dirt, curled up and sleeping like dogs.

'To your left,' said Dag.

I looked, and wished I hadn't. A few feet away from us, the corpse of a young man floated on its side in a foetal position. The bloated skin was a sickly yellow colour, and part of the face was eaten away. During four weeks on the Ganges, my stomach had hardened up enough to withstand fly-infested food and water straight from the river, but this was simply too much for it.

'Are you OK?' asked Dag, when I stopped retching. 'Because there's another one up ahead.'

During the next twenty minutes, we paddled past a dozen more bodies. The fresher ones were still wrapped in cloth which ballooned up above the surface of the water. From a distance, they could have been mistaken for discarded pillowcases, were it not for the crows and vultures which flapped down to peck at them, and the dogs which swam out for a meal. One of the bodies was tragically comical, floating face down with only the buttocks showing above the water. Another lay trapped on a sand bank, its ribcage exposed and pieces of its flesh fluttering in the current. But worse of all was the corpse which had become completely submerged save for the feet: toes splayed, skin mottled and shrunken, and murky water concealing the horror below. This was the stuff of nightmares.

It was enough for one day. We went ashore at the *ghats* of a small temple, and the *pujari* hurried down to meet us.

'You are making a thesis about this river?' he shouted, standing a mere two feet away.

'Yes, we're collecting material for a book,' I replied.

'Very good! Very good! You are a poet?'

I told him I wasn't, and he shook his head as if in consolation. 'Oh dear. I am very sorry. Here in India, we like poets very much. What is the difference between India and your country?'

A corpse floated by; downstream, dogs fought over another that lay rotting on the bank.

'India is spiritual,' I said. 'My country is materialistic.'

'Ah, yes,' he responded. 'I have been hearing this before. Where is God?'

'God is everywhere,' I replied.

'It is true!' he cried, clapping his hands. 'Perhaps your husband is Lord Rama and you are his wife, Sita! So we treat you as our gods! You must sleep here tonight! There are many robbers close by but have no fear, we will be guarding you.'

Leaving the kayaks in his care, we walked into Fatehgarh. As we stopped off at street stalls to buy fruit, tea and rice, people pressed in at our backs and elbows, making it difficult for us to move. By the time we arrived at the post office, from where I wanted to place a call to my mother, the crowd had grown, and practically filled the small room where an ill-tempered clerk sat behind a desk.

'What is the code number for England?' I asked him.

Impatiently, he paged through a battered, torn telephone directory.

'You've gone past it,' I told him.

He slammed the book shut. 'The international section is missing!' he shouted. 'You must call from Varanasi!'

'I won't be there for two weeks,' I protested. 'Can't you call the operator?'

'The operator has gone!' he shouted.

'It's very important that I talk to my mother,' I coaxed. 'Please show me the directory.'

Reluctantly, he handed it over. Within seconds, I had located the international section and the country code for England. The clerk passed me an ancient black telephone, and I dialled my mother's number. There were whooshing and fizzing noises on the line, as if I was trying to connect with outer space, then a clear ringing began. On either side of me were men with their faces about three inches away from mine, and their eyes popping with curiosity.

'Hello, Mum,' I said, when she answered. 'I'm calling from a small town along the Ganges.'

'She is calling her mother,' announced the clerk to the crowd. 'Her mother is living in England. She is happy to be hearing from her daughter.'

'How are you?' asked my mother. 'What on earth is it like over there?'

'We're both really healthy,' I said. 'And it's incredible here, it's heartbreaking, inspiring, everything you can and can't imagine.'

Frowning, the clerk scratched his head. 'She is telling her mother how is the weather!' he triumphantly announced to the expectant crowd.

'What *are* you laughing about?' asked my mother.

16

A Change in Atmosphere

According to the *pujari* in Fatehgarh, the corpses in the river were the remains of people stricken by infectious disease, or whose families could not afford the fuel for a pyre, or who had died unmarried. This last fact upset Bapi, and he fretted about it all day.

'I must discuss it with my parents!' he repeatedly cried. 'I do not want to be ending up in the river!'

Neither did we. Travelling so slowly and so visibly, with only nylon walls to protect us at night, we were feeling increasingly vulnerable. The closer we got to the industrial city of Kanpur, the dirtier the river became and the more disquieting the atmosphere along its banks. At Singrampurghat, the faded paintings of peacocks and snakes on the arches of an old temple had Hindi graffiti scrawled over them, and there were little piles of human faeces up and down the stone steps. A few yards from where a corpse floated on its back, several men were standing on the shore, drying themselves after a ritual bath. Their rifles lay around their feet, and as we paddled by one man reached for his weapon and sprinkled it with a libation of river water.

As the afternoon wore on we began moving through a predominantly Muslim area. People stared suspiciously at us from villages cut into the steep rock escarpments on the permanent bank. When we asked if they knew where we could find shelter for the night they shrugged and shook their heads. We paddled close to Bapi, who was visibly tense. The river looped away from the permanent bank and out into the plain, where once more it began dividing up into a maze of small channels. There was no way of knowing which one carried the main flow, so we chose at random. Half a mile on, the water in our channel petered out, and we were stuck. Children from the last village had followed us thus far, and now, as the sun slipped down behind the horizon, they ran back home.

'No doubt,' commented Dag, 'to tell their fathers about the three sitting ducks on the river.'

'I am not feeling at all happy about camping here,' said Bapi. 'Perhaps we will be waking up with our throats slit.'

For half an hour we heaved our boats through the trickle of water, until finally we met up again with the main channel. A short distance downstream, on the far bank, we saw the glow of a fire.

'These people could be fishermen or dacoits,' said Bapi. 'I will go ahead and talk to them.'

Slowly, we paddled behind him, straining our eyes to see through the fast-descending gloom to the small encampment. There was one large shelter set up, made from a tarpaulin slung across bamboo poles sticking out of the sand. Large, flat baskets were scattered over the shore, and as we drew nearer we passed a man standing waist-deep in water and using one of these baskets to scoop up tiny silvery fish.

'Come on, come on!' shouted Bapi. 'It is safe!'

Twenty-five fishermen were camped at that desolate spot, waiting for a contractor to arrive and collect their catch. They were all armed with large rifles which they casually slung over their shoulders. They told us we were lucky to have come across this encampment, as there were many dacoits about.

'At first they were thinking we were dacoits,' said Bapi. 'They could not understand what it is we are doing here, so I told them Maria is a writer with a special interest in Hindustani fishermen.'

Twenty-five pairs of eyes watched us unpack and set up our tent. When I lifted Dag's telescopic camera tripod from the kayak, the eyes narrowed.

'They are asking if it is a gun,' said Bapi. 'So I am telling them, "What do you think? These people are well prepared." '

They must also have wondered why the writer with a special interested in Hindustani fishermen crawled away into her tent without asking anyone a single question. I was too exhausted to eat, and rather than sit around the fire considering our situation – out in the middle of the Gangetic Plain with twenty-five heavily armed strangers – I preferred to escape into sleep.

When I unzipped the tent door at six o'clock next morning, twenty-five pairs of eyes were still focused on me. Most of the fishermen lay under the tarpaulin, wrapped in dirty blankets and cotton quilts and with their guns at their sides. Some of them were already up, and were sitting round the fire sharing a *chillum*. I walked away from the camp to find a private spot for my morning ablutions. But the river was so slimy, and so stinking of rotting fish, that I couldn't face washing in it. I felt absolutely wretched. My hair, skin and nails were grimy, I had fungus growing on various parts of my body, and my few articles of clothing, which I was thoroughly sick of wearing, were in dire need of a wash. I'd just spent the night in bandit country, and, to cap it all, in two days time I was going to turn forty. Glumly I returned to the tent. Bapi was sitting outside it and he made a valiant attempt to cheer me up. 'Maria, it is a great achievement,' he said, in the respectful tone he'd adopted since discovering my age, 'for a woman as old as you to go on such a journey!'

'And just think,' added Dag, 'you can claim to be the first woman to turn forty while kayaking down the Ganges!'

It was little consolation. Over the next few hours of paddling I hardly noticed a pale golden light spreading across the plain, the sky fading from grey into blue, the vultures fighting over a washed-up corpse. I'd escaped to London, where, after having my hair washed and cut, and spending a considerable amount of money on clothes, I was walking through pale winter sunshine towards a Covent Garden restaurant, on my way to a long, leisurely and utterly civilized birthday lunch.

'Ana! Ana! Come! Come!'

The shouts interrupted me just as I was about to look over the wine list.

'*Ana!*'

We had taken the left channel around a large sand island, and were paddling quite close to the far river bank. The man shouting to us was striding along the shore of the island, a hundred yards away, and clutching a rifle. Sensing that this was no friendly farmer wanting us to stop for a chat, without a word to each other Dag and I picked up speed until water flew from the end of our paddles.

'Ana!' yelled the man. '*Ana!*'

He lifted his rifle and levelled it at us.

'Jesus!'

'Move it!' barked Dag, and I paddled as if my life depended on it, which it probably did. The man broke into a run, shouting and waving his gun. At the end of the sand island he gave up the chase, but we maintained our speed up for another half a mile, until we saw a temple on the shore and a red flag fluttering from a pole. When we pulled ashore, I began trembling uncontrollably.

'I'm pretty sure we were out of his accurate range,' said Dag tersely. 'but I hope Bapi's OK.'

Ten minutes later, we saw the flash of Bapi's paddles in the sunlight. 'Did that bloody madman chase you, too?' he cried, as the prow of his boat hit the shore.

A *saddhu* wearing a large digital wristwatch had come down from the temple to greet us, and now he turned to Bapi with a torrent of Hindi. Bapi listened seriously, waggling his head and assenting with '*Acchha, acchha.*'

'He is insisting we must not carry on with our journey. He is saying that between here and Allahabad is a most dangerous place, the dacoits have rifles and hand grenades. He is telling us it is not safe for us to camp by this temple, but that a little way down the river there is a house where we can rest in peace.'

Dilip Saxena's house stood on a high bank overlooking the Ganges. It was an old colonial building, once owned by the British Army and now falling into disrepair amid dusty, windswept gardens. The rooms were cool and shuttered, with thick stone walls, flagged floors and an odd assortment of Indian and British furniture. Dilip received us with a disinterested air, but was kind nonetheless, offering us shelter for the night and, if we wished it, transportation by pony trap to the bus station the next day. Sitting in the sunshine on a *charpoi*, Dag, Bapi and I discussed what to do. The two men agreed that we should avoid the stretch of river infamous for dacoits, and go by road to Allahabad. I, surprising even myself, argued vehemently for carrying on by kayak. I felt inextricably linked to the Ganga, as if I'd made her a promise that I could not break. Despite its hardships, and now its dangers, the river gave me a sense of contentment and peace which I couldn't bear to be dragged. away from.

'We must carry on,' I said. 'We're on a pilgrimage, a stream of grace.'

Dag rolled his eyes. 'Tell that to the dacoits when they're at the other end of a gun.'

'We can stick close to Bapi,' I insisted, 'and we can make sure we're off the river and in a village each day by early afternoon.'

'Maria, what if we are finding no village?' asked Bapi. 'Really, I do not want us to be camping alone in this area. There are too many terrible stories about.'

'By road it's about a hundred and twenty-five miles from here to Allahabad,' added Dag, 'and two, maybe three times as much by river. If we only paddled in the mornings, it would take us a week to cover that distance, and that wouldn't give us time to reach Varanasi by the second week of March.'

I was outvoted: we were to go by bus to Allahabad. While Dag and Bapi took our kayak apart, I sulkily went for a wash. Dilip's wife carried a bucket of warm water into a room off the court-yard. In one corner there was a small drain, and in the other a manger filled with straw. While I gave myself a much-needed scrub, a cow wearing a red scarf round its neck plaintively mooed outside the door, obviously put out that I had disrupted its feed-ing time.

That night, as if he'd decided that the journey was practically over, Bapi began reminiscing about the experiences we'd shared. 'When we arrived in Gessapur,' he said, 'some of the villagers were opposed to us staying there.'

Shocked, Dag and I stared at him. 'Really, Bapi? Why?'

'They said it was because you were foreigners, and also so untidy.'

I thought back to the women peeling off my dusty clothes, and my toes curled with embarrassment. 'Why didn't you tell us?'

'There was no point. It was sorted out.'

I thought for a moment. 'What else didn't you tell us, Bapi?'

'Oh, this and that,' he said. 'Always the people were telling me what their caste was and asking me about yours.'

'Why didn't you translate this?'

'Caste is a bad system. I didn't wish to speak of it, it was too embarrassing.'

Anger bubbled up inside me. 'What do you mean, you didn't wish to speak of it? You were supposed to be interpreting, but you were censoring what was being said!'

'Maria, that's not fair,' interjected Dag. 'You don't speak a second language, so you've no idea of how difficult translation is. This is Bapi's first shot at it and he's been doing well.'

'Really, Maria, I have been trying my best,' said Bapi, his face a picture of hurt. 'I have been telling you what I thought was useful.'

Although remorseful, I was still smarting about the decision to pull off the river, and I went to sleep without apologizing.

For once, Bapi was the first up next morning.

'You hurt his feelings,' Dag told me, as we stepped from the dark room into warm sunshine.

Dilip's servant, an old man with bandy legs, fussed around us, bringing *chai* and biscuits, and then watched awestruck as I prepared to insert my contact lenses. It occurred to me, as I set out the bottles of solution and washed my hands in a small bowl of water, that to him this must have seemed like some Westernized form of *puja*.

'*Bapi kahan hai*?' I asked him. 'Where's Bapi?'

He pointed towards the river. '*Ghat*,' he said.

'Let's go and find him,' I suggested to Dag. He picked up his yellow camera case and followed me down the bank.

The *ghat* was a small sandy beach, not more than fifty feet long. At one end a *pujari* sat next to a tray of offerings to sell to people who came from the nearby village for morning *puja*. At the other end Bapi stood stock still, facing the river. I walked over to him, and was about to touch his arm and offer my apologies when I saw what he gazing at. At the water's edge was the body of a young girl, maybe five years old. Her black, shoulder-length hair was caked with mud. She lay on her back, with one arm thrown over her face as if to shield her eyes from the sun, or from the horror that had befallen her. A dog was chewing on one of her legs; it had already consumed her foot and was halfway up her calf. I froze, and the sounds of the sun-dappled morning seemed to sharpen – the cat-like cries of a peacock, the chirping of sparrows, the tearing of flesh, the crunching of bone. Shaking its head hard, the dog flipped the girl over, and she landed on the sand with a dull thump. I turned away and put hands over my ears, but the sight and sounds were imprinted on my memory.

'She was thrown in the river last night,' said Bapi quietly. 'The *pujari* pulled her out an hour ago.'

'Why didn't he leave her in there?' I whispered.

'The river is so low and sluggish, she would pollute this place where people are bathing. Really, it is better that the dogs are getting her.'

It was an inauspicious start to the day, which an eight-hour bus journey along the Grand Trunk Road did little to improve. The bus careered through small towns, constantly swerving around cows and out of the path of oncoming traffic. Within the first half-hour we drove past the smouldering remains of two grisly vehicle crashes, making me consider that perhaps we would have been safer on the river after all.

Two brave tricycle *wallahs* insisted they could transport us and our boats on their gaudily painted vehicles from the bus station in Allahabad's old town to a hotel called the Tourist Bungalow. We sat atop our two bags, while Bapi perched on the back of the other tiny carrier, clinging to his boat which stuck nine feet into the air like a giant arrow.

As we approached the Tourist Bungalow, Dag nudged me. 'Over there!' he shouted, pointing to a man and woman walking along the road. Blond, dressed in scarlet and carrying rucksacks, they were the first Westerners we'd seen for over a month.

'Aren't they strange?' he mused, craning his neck for a better view. 'No wonder everyone's staring at them.'

As this was the eve of my birthday, Dag decided to treat me to a posh meal, and the receptionist of the Tourist Bungalow recommended the Tandoor Restaurant. On the way there we passed a row of food stalls illuminated by mercury lamps, where local people sat on wooden benches eating simple curries with *rotis* straight from clay ovens.

'Let's go to one of these instead,' I suggested.

I was still attached to the simplicity of our life on the river, and not really ready to face a sophisticated restaurant. But Dag insisted that I deserved something special. The Tandoor was full of wealthy Indians, the men in well-tailored suits, the women garbed in gorgeous silk saris and lots of gold jewellery. Since leaving Hardwar, we'd eaten only vegetarian food. Not wanting to break this aspect of our 'stream of grace', I ordered a humble dish of *dhal* and peas. Dag, however, opted for lamb curry and Bapi for chicken. The *rotis* were served in filigree silver baskets and we toasted my birthday with ice cold Guru beer.

'Wouldn't it be a joke if we got sick in a place like this?' quipped Dag.

'You deserve to,' I teased him, 'for eating meat along the holy river.'

In the middle of the night he woke up groaning and clutching his stomach. Early on the morning of my fortieth birthday I lay in bed helplessly listening to him in the adjoining bathroom, suffering a violent attack of gastro-enteritis.

For the next twenty-four hours Dag's temperature steadily rose, and when he wasn't uttering wretched sounds in the bathroom he was pacing around, breathing through his pain like a woman in labour. It was obvious that we wouldn't be leaving Allahabad in a hurry, and that evening the decision was made that Bapi should return to New Delhi. He was anxious about some pressing work and family commitments, while Dag and I had begun to feel that we should experience this last part of our trip along the Ganga without Bapi as a buffer. We knew we were going to miss him, though, and we sadly waved goodbye as a rickshaw *wallah* pedalled him out of the Tourist Bungalow compound and back to the bus station.

Two days later we set off early in the morning to rejoin the river, looking far more respectable than when we'd left it. I'd given our clothes to the hotel's *dhobi wallah*, apologizing for their appalling state. They were returned missing several buttons and, in the case of our socks and thermal underwear, several sizes bigger than before, but startlingly clean.

There are seven sacred rivers in India, and Allahabad is situated at the convergence of three of them, the Ganga, the Yamuna and the invisible Saraswati. We launched the kayak on the Yamuna, and floated towards the *sangam*, the meeting-point of the three rivers. The morning was warm, and in the bright sunlight the deep, slow-moving waters of the Yamuna were a sparkling greeny-blue. Wooden pilgrim boats rowed by us, going upstream from the *sangam*, their canopies spread with the drying clothes of the bathers inside. We passed beneath the massive sixteenth-century fort of Akbar, built of roughly cut stones which,

from our perspective, each looked to be the size of a house.
Beyond the fort, on the same side of the river, was a large
promontory of sand almost obscured by the colourful throng of
people swarming across it. Winding through the crowds were
long processions led by men beating on drums, blowing on dis-
cordant pipes and holding aloft yellow and orange flags. Had it
not been for the bicycles and the tour buses inching through the
confusion, it could have been a mediaeval scene. Everyone was
focused on a point where hundreds of stalls were set up on the
shore, where the water was erupting with the splashing of innumerable bathers, where a thick swarm of boats bobbed about,
where incense hung thickly in the air and where we finally put
down our paddles and simply floated: the point where the clear
Yamuna met and was swallowed up by the muddy Ganga. The
actual confluence was surprisingly obvious, like an undulating
line drawn between the two rivers. We turned the boat so that our
bow faced along it. For several seconds we were held in limbo,
gazing at the garlands of marigolds strewn across the water.
Suddenly, the Ganga drew us to her, and a pod of dolphins surfaced around us as if in welcome. It was with a strong sense of
homecoming that we turned the kayak and headed downstream.

On the edge of Manaiya village, we cooked *dhal* over our stove,
and ate it watching a hazy, mauve sunset beyond the deep golds
and greens of the wheat fields. Crickets whirred, toads croaked,
jackals yelped and fruit bats rustled in the branches above us.
Music and singing drifted from the temple, growing louder and
softer as the wind shifted. A man called Dukhi, who was most dis-
tressed by us preparing our own food, insisted that we visit his
home. Although Manaiya had only 300 inhabitants and no running water, it was serviced by electricity. In a house built of mud
bricks with a terracotta tiled roof, we watched a cricket match
played in Australia between India and Pakistan, and ate rice
sweetened with coconut chips and raisins.

'We are poor,' said Dukhi. 'You are rich. We are happy that you
accept our simple food.'

One of the neighbours murmured something to Dukhi. 'He is
asking what is your caste,' he translated.

'What is yours?' we enquired.

'We are Sudras, of the boatman caste.'

'We are also boatman caste,' said Dag, and this was greeted with delight.

Someone had strung a lightbulb from the nearest house and attached it to a bamboo pole next to our tent. As we prepared for bed, elongated shadows of the people hanging around outside were thrown across the nylon walls. At first these people were quiet, listening to the alien sounds emanating from inside the tent – zips closing, an air mattress inflating, velcro strips coming apart, nylon rustling. Once we'd settled down, it was our turn to listen – to hawking and spitting, to puzzled conversations in Hindi about our water filter hanging from the tent door, to yelping dogs being thwacked. Then we heard something heavy being dragged towards us, and Dukhi shooing everyone away.

'Mr Dag!' he called. 'Do not be fearing! I will be guarding you!'

With that, he stretched out on the *charpoi* he'd brought from his house, fell asleep and kept us awake all night with his snoring.

At dawn I crept past him and went down to the field. From the private place I found, behind a row of corn that shivered in the breeze, I watched an old man coming up from the river bank. He wore a *dhoti* and *kurta*, a pink scarf wrapped around his bald head and a blanket. He was carrying a staff and a canister of water, and he prayed aloud as he walked up through the fields. Beyond him, the flood plain was bathed in an amber light, and bronze rays were fanning across the sky. The path took the man close by my hiding place. His mumbling faded away, but I stayed where I was, staring at the space he had passed through, not wanting to disturb the dream-like quality of these moments, suddenly aware that our time on the Ganga was soon to be over.

Fed by tributaries, the river became deep and fast-flowing. It was also busier. Camel trains plodded along the banks, carrying sand being dredged up with buckets from the river bed. Fishermen plodded upstream like Volga slaves, hauling their boats by long ropes attached to the masts. Others relaxed on bedrolls inside the domed canopies of boats, while their cantilevered nets hung in the water. We passed electricity pylons, fort-like pump houses, and newly built *ghats* with concrete steps, and I began to long for the isolation of the upper part of the river, and the sense of timelessness we'd experienced there.

Laxagir village, set on a high cliff above the flood plain, had
brick houses with television aerials on the tiled roofs and shiny
tractors parked on the dirt road. We were invited to spend the
night at Baba Ram Das's small *ashram*, a dusty, untidy place with
a jumble of bikes leaning against the temple wall. Baba Ram Das
was an obese, fierce-looking character with grey matted hair
falling to his waist. When we were ushered through a rusty iron
gate into the leaf-strewn courtyard, he was lying on a *charpoi*
beneath a veranda, having his feet massaged by a young *san-
nyasin*. Propping himself on one elbow, the *baba* told us we could
stay, then ordered his followers to clean the place up. His followers didn't take kindly to this, or to us. They scurried around,
sweeping the floor, shouting at the children hanging around the
gate and giving us resentful glances. We were shown into our
room for the night. It had a door made of corrugated iron, sacking spread over the floor, a wooden table, and a few bricks
knocked out of one wall to form a window. I peered outside. The
sun was a pale, yellowish white dish, almost indistinguishable in a
sky and above a landscape of identical hues.

At 5.00 am the sounds of morning *puja* blared out from the
speakers hanging up close to our cell. I had just scrambled out of
bed and was half dressed when the door was flung open, and
one of the bad-tempered *sannysins* marched in and set down two
beakers of tea on the table. I sat in the doorway to drink mine. A
small village girl crept up to me, stared for a long time at my bare
feet and then, mistaking my sunburn lines for dirt, began vigorously rubbing them with a moistened finger. Taking the hint, I
persuaded Dag to come down to the river with me to wash. We'd
already waded in up to our waists by the time we noticed a pair of
buttocks floating nearby.

'That one followed us from Fatehgarh,' joked Dag.

Beating a fast retreat, we adjourned to one of the village *chai*
stalls, and sat in the warm morning sunshine, contentedly chatting to the villagers who gathered around. A policeman joined us,
carelessly laying his rifle on the wooden bench.

'What is in the yellow box?' he asked.

'Cameras,' Dag replied.

'Show me.' It was more of an order than a request. People
pressed around as Dag opened the box, and sharp intakes of
breath greeted the sight of a camera body and three lenses. I felt

horribly embarrassed by this blatant show of our wealth, and the policeman's resentful expression unnerved me. Suddenly, I was anxious to get away from Laxagir, to be back on the Ganga and simply moving along with its flow.

'Let's make a move,' I said to Dag, 'before it gets too hot.' In the *ashram*, we hurriedly packed up. While Dag and a couple of *sannyasins* carried the boat to the water, I sorted out the rest of our gear. Catching sight of the *baba* in the courtyard, I popped out to give him a donation for the *ashram*. I was away from the room for perhaps three minutes, and returned to it at the same time as Dag.

'The door's closed,' I said.

'So?'

'I'm sure I left it open.'

We were gathering up the last of our belongings when Dag noticed a pair of white, upturned soles beneath the bed. 'There's a kid in here!' he cried, hauling out a small, skinny boy dressed in ripped shorts and shirt. 'What the hell are you doing? Get lost!'

The boy was about to flee when the policemen we'd had tea with appeared in the doorway. He pushed the cowering boy into the corner and began poking him hard in the chest.

'What have you got?' he demanded. 'Show me!'

It was only then that we realized the boy was clutching something in his trembling arms. '*Amrud, amrud,*' he whimpered. '*Guavas, guavas.*'

'Show me!' the policeman shouted, but the boy held the bundle still tighter to his bony frame.

Still we didn't suspect the child of anything, not until the policeman yanked the bundle from him and unwrapped the filthy rags to reveal one of Dag's cameras.

'Holy *smokes!*' cried Dag, whirling round to the camera case he'd left lying on the table, and which the child had carefully closed up again to cover the traces of his theft. The policeman laid into the boy, slapping him hard on the head. When Dag tried to intervene, he grabbed the child by the hair and forced him to his knees. 'Beat him, sir! Beat him!'

There was nothing to be done but leave quickly. We hurried down the bank, away from the thumps and yowls, sharing the same suspicious thought about the policeman.

The river was now a quarter of a mile wide, and we had a wind from behind that filled our sail and pushed us along at a fast clip. The banks rose into fluted sandstone cliffs with dramatic rock pillars and steep man-made stairways zigzagging down to the water. Ferries were being rowed across the river, and their passengers waved to us, once laughing uproariously when a gust of wind caught our sail and nearly tipped us. In terms of speed and distance covered, this was the most successful day we'd had during our five weeks on the river. Towards late afternoon we arrived at Mirzapur, a city literally crumbling into the Ganges. For two kilometres, the bank was lined with once grand temples and *ashrams* which were now dank and decaying. We pulled up at a *ghat*, and while Dag went to see if we could find accommodation in the *ashram* above it, I held on to the kayak, trying to ignore the raw, stinking sewage pouring from a pipe a few feet away. A wretched, filthy *saddhu* shuffled up to me, babbling and staring into my face. Teenage boys jeered at me, women collecting water not two feet from the sewer pipe gave me spiteful looks. Dag returned from the *ashram*, pursued by a raving mad man in thick make-up who grabbed at his thighs and tried to pull down his shorts. We hurried on, but each place we stopped at was worse than the last: a *ghat* covered with mud and excrement, a dilapidated temple infested with rats, streets that were even dirtier and more foreboding than the river front. As the evening closed in, we paddled for a mile beyond the outskirts of the town. Seeing a fisherman casting his net, we headed over to him to ask advice. When he looked up, his face filled with terror and he scuttled fearfully to the far end of his boat.

'*Jana! Jana!*' he shouted. 'Go away!'

Shortly afterwards, and to our great relief, a house with a red flag fluttering from it came into sight. We pulled ashore at the landing-point for a ferry, where a crowd of people were waiting for a ride across to the opposite bank. One of them ran up to the house for us, and returned with a young, stern-faced Brahmin.

'We are seeking a safe place to spend the night,' we told him.

'You cannot stay here,' he said.

'May we ask the *baba?*'

'It is not possible. You are not welcome. You must go away.'

By now the ferry had arrived, and people were clambering aboard. The ferryman, who looked a fairly decent sort, called out '*Tahum jao sakte ho mera gaon!*' 'You can go to my village!'

We looked to where he was pointing. Although there were no houses in sight, smoke and the glow of electric light rose above the trees. We thanked him, but a woman leaned down from the ferry, hanging over the side so far that her face almost touched mine. '*Khatara!*' she hissed. '*Khatara!*' Danger.

By now it was past six o' clock and almost dark. There was only one option left: to spend the night in the kayak, out on the river, and to paddle until dawn.

Luckily, the moon was waning and we were cloaked in darkness. From the villages along the shore we heard coughing, chanting, drumming, the wailing of babies – sounds once comfortingly familiar, now made sinister by the night and our vulnerability. Lights twinkled through trees, and sometimes there was the silhouette of a person, standing and perhaps wondering what the dogs had sensed to make them bark so furiously. We crept along like thieves, whispering to each other. Our quiet progress startled birds, which flapped up from the surface of the water right in front of the kayak, startling us in turn. Once we heard the mumbling of a mantra; a man was on the bank, hauling upstream a boat that came so close to us we could reach out and touch its gunnels. Sometimes, when the river divided around sand islands, we found ourselves in narrow channels, only feet away from camps of fishermen who huddled by fires, laughing coarsely. Fearing they might hear us, mistake us for dacoits and take a pot shot, we floated by with our breath held and our paddles out of the water. My other fear, irrational though it was, concerned the corpses. I dreaded bumping into one, and when we ran aground, as we did several times during that long night, before pushing off I tentatively poked around with my paddle, hoping that it wouldn't hit a rib cage or a face.

The tension was constant, it stiffened our necks and backs, it exhausted us to the point where we were wondered if the dolphins blowing around us were real or a hallucination. By 4.00 am our nerves were frayed, we were cold and wretched, and fed up with this river, with India, with kayaking. At 4.30, the lights of Chunar Fort appeared, glimmering like a spectre, almost 200 feet above the river. Floating in a back eddy, we waited for dawn, then went ashore on a sand bank below the impressive walls of the ancient fort. Wrapped in our blankets, we hunkered down by the water's edge. A lone fisherman poled by in his boat, looking as tired as we felt, but full of merry greetings. Like us, he seemed relieved that the long night was over.

Varanasi, our final destination, was now about thirty miles away. As we sat below Chunar Fort, breakfasting on water and raisins, Dag suggested doing one final push, and ending the journey by nightfall. This filled me with conflicting feelings. Five weeks on the Ganga had left me physically, mentally and emotionally exhausted; my mind was crammed with its images and confusions, and the idea of any more floating corpses, muddy campsites or curious crowds of onlookers was simply unbearable. And yet, increasingly I was filled with dread at the thought of leaving the river. For years I had wanted to see the ancient city of Varanasi: now it was a place I was loath to reach.

17

Light Years Away

For two hours we drifted downstream. Ahead, the patchwork sails of fishing boats billowed in the wind, and, on the left bank, a host of red flags fluttered from a sandstone bluff.

'I don't want to stop,' warned Dag.

Beneath the flags the shore was awash with colour, as if a carpet of butterflies had settled upon it. As we drew closer we saw a narrow *ghat*, packed with people who were spilling over into the river. Above them, on the steep bank, rows of pilgrims' huts were hung with lengths of brilliantly coloured material, and flower-sellers' baskets were heaped with red and orange blooms. The flags were flying from a yellow temple on the top of the bluff, and mud-coloured buildings huddled at its base.

'Let's go and have a look,' I coaxed.

'I can't stand another village,' Dag insisted. 'No more questions, no more staring, I've absolutely had it.'

'Just for a minute,' I persisted. 'You stay in the boat, I'll go and buy some *chai* and *samosas*.'

His resolve softened by the idea of hot tea and fresh food, Dag turned the rudder and we paddled up to the shore, a little way from the *ghat*. As I hopped out of the boat, a diminutive young man hurried over to me. 'What do you want?' he shouted. 'How can I help you?'

'I want to buy some food,' I told him.

'Come with me! I am Sudraj! This village is Sultanpur! What is your name? Maureeya? Nice name! Come on!'

I followed him up the steps and into a winding, bricked lane. Red dust motes danced in the sunlight shafting between softly contoured buildings. Long-eared goats wandered about, women carrying baskets of steaming dung on their heads sashayed by, pilgrims made their way to the river, singing as they went. Vendors called cheerfully to me from behind their stalls, where the red and orange sindoor powder used for *tikkas* had been heaped into perfect little pyramids.

'Here, Maureeya!' cried Sudraj. '*Chai! Chai!*'

The owner of the *chai* shop was hunkered on top of his adobe oven, frying *pakora* over the open fire and swatting away flies. He had a bull-like neck, a downturned betel-stained mouth and wild, staring eyes. Brusquely, he thrust a beaker of tea into my hands, then wrapped up several *pakoras* in a banana leaf for me. When I tried to pay him he waved away the money.

'He says it is a gift,' said Sudraj.

On the river bank, Dag was surrounded by men who were incredulous to hear that not only had we come all the way from Hardwar, but that we'd just paddled through the night from Mirzapur.

'Go and have a quick look around the village,' I urged him.

He returned elated. 'I take everything back,' he said.

We asked the men if there was a place in Sultanpur where we could camp for the night.

'*Acchha! Acchha!*' they cried delightedly, and pointed up to where the red flags fluttered against the solid blue of the sky.

Thinking back to my Catholic days, I tried to imagine how I would have reacted to a pair scruffy foreigners camped in the church vestibule. It's doubtful that I'd have been quite as magnanimous as the pilgrims who arrived to worship Goddess Sitala, and found our kayak and tent parked in a corner of the temple courtyard. They came all day in a steady stream, laden with offerings. They rang a brass bell hanging from the door of the shrine to announce their presence to the goddess, touched blessed sweets to her mouth, lay money at her feet, garlanded her and sprinkled her with coconut milk. Meanwhile, their children played in the courtyard, wriggling over the dusty stone slabs in a game of 'snake', or chasing each other round and round our tent. Things got rather hectic during the noon-time *puja*. Clamorous bells were rung and the little courtyard heaved with people pushing and shoving to get close to the shrine. The *pujaris* waved lights and incense around Sitala's small, gold-plated face, and when one of them emerged holding a bowl of burning camphor, there was a mad scramble as everyone reached forward to run their hands through the anointing flame. Another scrum ensued when the second *pujari* began handing out a *prasad* of blessed sweets. In the midst of this frenzy was the temple goat, happily gobbling up dropped sweets and tearing chunks off   peoples' marigold garlands when they weren't looking.

The goat was a large bearded male, Billy Goat Gruff in the flesh, but Indianized with sandalwood paste smeared on to his forehead. The pilgrims thoroughly spoiled him, reverently feeding him with coconuts, sweets and flowers. Our arrival left him deeply disgruntled. As soon as the kayak was set down, the prow sticking into what we later discovered was one of his favourite sleeping corners, he began determinedly nibbling on it. And to show his disgust of our tent, he repeatedly headbutted it and left liberal amounts of his droppings around the door.

When the noon *puja* was over and things quietened down, I leaned on the wall of the small courtyard and gazed over the Gangetic Plain. After weeks on the river, it was dizzying to suddenly be high above it and have a bird's-eye view of the land we had journeyed across. Water and sand merged into each other, grey on white, to form an empty landscape that teemed with vivid life. I thought about all the paradoxes: the monsoons which swept away homes and laid down fertile soil, the compelling beauty of the poorest villages, the rotting corpses in a river said to have the power of physical and spiritual purification. I remembered the ministry official in New Delhi who had declared us potty for wanting to embark on this journey. I was glad we'd ignored his advice to reconsider our plans. It was a journey that had turned me inside out, challenged every one of my values, and made me question how, or why, I would ever return to the safe world, so bland and pale in comparison to this one, that I'd so long and so smugly inhabited.

My thoughts were abruptly interrupted by Sudraj.

'Maureeya, I see you are now wearing our traditional dress!' he cried, surveying the long loose pants and tunic I'd bought in Allahabad, and changed into inside the tent. 'Your husband must wear a *dhoti*! He would look in the mirror and instantly be restored in his self-esteem! The *dhoti* is suiting tall men like your husband. Even I, a dwarf, am feeling so happy when I see myself in a *dhoti*.'

He took us a small, gloomy shop owned by one of his friends, where he selected a length of fine white cotton, and showed Dag how to wrap it around his waist and loop it between his legs.

'Mr Dag and Maureeya, now you are a fine couple!' he pronounced. 'And please tell me: is your marriage love marriage?'

We spent most of the afternoon in Tilak's *chai* shop. Squatting on his oven, he watched us like a hawk, descending upon us to refill our tea cups and our banana leaf plates, crying 'Eat! Eat!' and standing over us with a maniacal expression on his face until we passed verdict on the food. When we insisted on paying for all we had, he took the money in a growling fashion.

We were joined in the *chai* shop by a varied array of fellow customers. Three *saddhus* came in first, and paid homage to the framed pictures of Hindu gods on the roughly plastered wall, hanging garlands around them and flicking them with Ganga water. Settling down on the long, wooden bench beneath the pictures, they accepted Tilak's food and drink offerings and then turned to the serious business of smoking ganja. A toothless old village man arrived next, followed by a local dairy farmer with milk for sale in the two buckets suspended from a plank across his shoulders. Finally a suave young man called Pradip came in. He wore Western clothes, said he was from Varanasi and claimed to be India's break-dancing champion.

'Michael Jackson is my guru,' he told me. 'He had operation to make him white. Very beautiful now.'

Dag was attempting a conversation in Hindi with the old man and the dairy farmer. '*Janver doktar*,' he was saying, 'Animal doctor.'

The dairy farmer was excitedly waggling his head, while the old man pulled at Dag's *dhoti*, asking '*Kitna? Kitna?*' 'How much?'

'*Ek sau rupees*,' Dag told him. 'One hundred rupees.' This information stopped the conversation. Tilak descended from his perch on the oven, the *saddhus* laid down their *chillums* and everyone gathered around to examine Dag's *dhoti*. 'Bahut mehenga!' 'Too much!' cried the old man, and hurried out of the *chai* shop.

Tilak remounted his perch looking intensely worried, no

doubt anticipating the storm about to break. 'Your husband was cheated,' explained Pradip with a bored sigh. 'This *dhoti* is farmer standard, worth no more than fifty rupees.'

When the old man reappeared with Sudraj in tow, everyone jumped to their feet and chaos ensued. One of the *saddhus* declared Sudraj to be an honest man, another accused him of being in league with the *dhoti*-seller, the old man shook his staff in Sudraj's face, Sudraj imploringly bleated, 'Mr Dag, Maureeya, I am not a cheating man!', the *saddhus* began arguing with each other, the dairy farmer tried to soothe them, and Tilak squatted up on the counter, scratching his belly and giving passers-by the 'tension' signal, wrapping his second finger over his index finger. After half an hour of this, with no apparent resolution, Sudraj slunk out of the *chai* shop and everyone else calmed down.

'It has been agree,' said Pradip.

'What has been agree?' we asked.

'The problem is over,' he insisted, wafting his hand about as if to remove a bad smell. 'Now, please be telling me, is it true, as I see on the television, that in America some people are starving themselves to death while others are eating themselves to death?'

'Quite true,' I told him.

'And this dairy farmer wishes you to tell him if it is true that in America people are eating cows?'

'I'm afraid so.'

He relayed this fact to the dairy farmer, who shook his head in dismay.

After evening *puja*, Dag set up our camp stove on top of the courtyard wall and began preparing *dhal*. The villagers who gathered to watch were at first relieved to learn that we were not eating meat, like our friends in America, then horrified to realize that Dag was cooking while his wife relaxed. Enjoying the attention, Dag put on quite a show, giving the men an impromptu cookery lesson and sharing with them his secret ingredient of a spot of sugar added to the lentils. We'd now been awake for over forty hours, so as soon as we'd eaten I went straight to bed. When I was in my sleeping bag, I unzipped the tent window. Through the screen I could see our kayak, and the goat curled up against it, scratching its head on the prow. Some musicians had joined Dag on the temple steps. They played haunting rhythms on tabla, harmonium and hand bells, and sang slow, sad songs. Pleasantly lulled, I drifted off towards sleep.

But not for long. A dazzling light shone full on my face, then traced around the inside of the tent. Shielding my eyes, I peered out to see Tilak hunkered down by the tent door, and four or five men bending down to peer in at me over his shoulder.

'English,' one of them said. 'Plastic.'

Tilak grinned at me, and again shone the light into my face. '*Nind!*' I said firmly – Sleep! – and to clarify the point I zipped up the window.

The men had a brief conference and left, but minutes later I heard approaching footsteps, and the tent began shaking violently. 'Maureeya? Maureeya?'

'Sudraj,' I hissed. 'Please go away, I am very tired.' Another flashlight beamed through the nylon walls. 'Maureeya! Hello! Come on! Music! Tabla!'

It carried on – footsteps, shaking, flashlights, insistent voices – until, in desperation, I took a sleeping tablet and finally escaped into sleep.

At 4.00 am, the goat got up and peed against the side of our tent. Then someone began noisily sweeping up the courtyard, including right around the base of the tent. The clanking, squeaking and muttering that started up next turned out to be people stopping to fill up their *chembus* from the temple pump before heading to the toilet areas along the river bank. Still bleary from the sleeping tablet, I forced myself out of bed and down the hill towards the women's toilet area, anxious to take advantage of the privacy of darkness. When I returned to bed I fell into a deep, blissful sleep – until 6.00 am, when a deafening clanging of bells announced the beginning of morning *puja*.

During the next three days, the temple steps became a village clinic as news of Dag's first-aid skills spread. He treated burns and ulcerated wounds, and gave away most of our medicines to remedy anything he could diagnose. On our last afternoon, the clinic was joined by a wedding party. We offered to move our campsite for the occasion, but no one would hear of it. Sackcloth was spread over the stone flags of the courtyard for the guests to sit on, and the ceremony went on around our tent and kayak. The bride was completely wrapped up in a golden cloth, so that even her face was hidden. A *pujari* with a dramatic Salvador Dali moustache led her and the groom through a series of *pujas*. Coconuts were broken, rice scattered, sandalwood smeared, incense burned. The groom tied a cloth to the bride's sari, slung the cloth over his shoulder and walked several times around the temple while she stumbled along behind him, loudly weeping and supported by her female relatives. The couple were then knotted together with the cloth and taken over to pray by a sacred fire burning in a corner of the courtyard. By now several of the guests had lost interest in the wedding. Some were clustered around our kayak, minutely examining it; others had joined me on the steps and were peering over my shoulder at the notes I was taking. Dogs were lolling about, the goat was chomping its way through one corner of the sackcloth, and pilgrims arriving at the temple were getting muddled up with the wedding party. Wanting to escape the heat of the afternoon, we wandered off to Tilak's *chai* shop for tea and a chat. As we left, the bride was being led into the Sitala shrine, and the weary groom was sitting next to our tent, surrounded by women who were smearing his face with milk curds.

An hour or so later, shouts, screams and wails coming from the direction of the temple brought us to our feet. '*Aram, aram,*' said Tilak. 'Relax'. He flapped his hands to gesture that we should sit down. A huddle of people hurried past, clutching in its midst a gold-wrapped figure. Some wedding guests ran by next, shouting news of the scandal to Tilak as they went. Down at the temple, the groom's family had complained that the bride's dowry was too meagre, and had demanded an extra 4,000 rupees. When this wasn't forthcoming, a fight had broken out and the couple had been separated and dragged off in opposite directions by their respective families. 'It happens every time,' Tilak told us as he nonchalantly stoked the fire in his oven. 'By nightfall,' he said, 'it will all be settled.'

That evening we were invited to eat with a hollow-faced man called Ramcharan, who was a poor Brahmin and a *pujari*. We sat cross-legged with him on a wooden table in his courtyard. The place was spotlessly clean, and Ramcharan was dressed in bright white *kurta* and pants. Food was served to us by his eldest son on stainless steel trays. The spinach and potato *sabzee* was delicious, but the *dhal* was strangely sweet – news of Dag's recipe had obviously spread and been exaggerated. At the end of the meal, we were served with bowls of warm buffalo milk, and a dish containing some sugar. There was no spoon to add the sugar – as usual we'd eaten with our hands. Ramcharan came to the rescue: looking me straight in the eye, with his right hand he scooped up some sugar and dropped it into my bowl, then stuck his fingers in the warm milk and waggled them around until the sugar dissolved. Graciously, I thanked him and lifted the bowl to my lips, while next to me Dag suffered a sudden, and unconvincing, fit of coughing.

Because this was a Brahmin family, the kitchen was at the back of the house, safely out of sight of the defiling eyes of lower-caste visitors. I'd only once got a glimpse of Ramcharan's wife when she peeked around a door, her face covered by her sari. But after the meal I was taken into the kitchen to meet her. I went through a small room filled with three *charpois*, ducked under a low doorway, and stepped into the kitchen. It had a ceiling of split bamboo, and in one corner mud steps led up to the attic where wood was stored for fuel. Bala Devi sat behind a low mud wall, next to an adobe oven and a neat array of brass pots and spoons. She was dressed in a simple cotton sari, and had buck teeth and a betel-stained smile. She laid down some sack cloth for me to sit on, fetched a bowl of oil and began massaging my feet and calves. The plastic bangles around her wrists rattled as she forcefully kneaded my muscles. This was an honour usually accorded to elderly women. News of my age and childlessness had spread like wildfire around the village, and before we left their house, Ramcharan and Bala Devi made a *puja* to the statue of Goddess Sitala in one of their wall niches, asking that I should be granted a son.

After four days, we had to tear ourselves away from Sultanpur. It took hours to say goodbye to everyone. Our parting with Tilak was typically brusque. 'In Varanasi,' he yelled, poking Dag in the chest, 'no ganja! Poison! No *chai*! Poison! No guide! Robber!'

Assuring Tilak that we would remember this advice, and thanking him for his kindness, we headed to the *ghats* for our last bathe in the Ganga.

As I stood waist-deep in water, a woman teasingly splashed me like a buffalo. The debris of *pujas* littered the surface, and a little upstream of me a man cleared his throat and spat out the contents. Impassively, I watched the glob of green sputum float by. Then I held my nose and ducked beneath the water.

We sat in the kayak while Ramcharan did a final *puja* with us. He tied new strings around our wrists, rubbed our forehead with sandalwood paste, sprinkled us with coconut milk. Six weeks ago, in Hardwar, I'd participated in the same ritual with a cool detachment. Now, as I watched our banana-leaf boats bob away downstream, their little camphor flames brightly burning, I found myself silently thanking Holy Mother Ganga for our safe passage along her.

Field after field of orange marigolds slipped by. Ahead, tiers of curlicued *ashrams*, temples and palaces rose up, stretching away for miles and fading into a brown-gold haze. We were approaching Varanasi, the City of Light, the holiest place along the Ganga, the most auspicious place for a Hindu to die. We pulled down our sail, put our paddles away, and let the current take us. The *ghats* seemed to go on forever: *ghats* where *pujaris* sat beneath large sun umbrellas, *ghats* where bathers undressed in open-fronted wooden cubicles, burning *ghats* where buffalo chewed on piles of wood fifteen feet high and where assembly lines of funeral pyres crackled side by side; submerged *ghats* where the onion domes of collapsed temples emerged from the water, *ghats* where Western *sannyasins* bathed, *ghats* from where Japanese tourists videoed us. We drifted by them all, until the stone *ghats* ended and were replaced by muddy banks leading up to dilapidated buildings, four storeys high, with narrow, dank lanes running between them. Just before a railway bridge, we pulled ashore, and were quickly surrounded by a group of louche characters in ragged *lungis* and shirts, who greedily eyed our boat and its contents. We took out the *prasad* we'd brought from our *puja* in Sultanpur – sweets and pieces of coconut – and handed it around. Instantly, the mood changed. The men touched the *prasad* to their foreheads, smiled at us with blackened, broken teeth, and then helped Dag take the boat apart.

Two days later, in our air-conditioned room in the New Delhi Maurya Sheraton's Executive Suite, I unpacked the bag containing our grubby clothes and blankets. Fine sand, flecked with glittering mica chips, showered on to the thick carpet, and then some small, hard, black balls rolled out. I called Dag over, and we knelt down to peer at the holy goat's droppings. There was a knock at the door, the room service boy came in and stepped carefully around us, bearing a tray with a silver teapot and china cups. As I stood to sign the bill, I thought of Tilak brewing up *chai* over his adobe oven, of Bala Devi smearing dung over her kitchen floor, and of Ramcharan, walking along the lanes of Sultanpur on his way to the temple – 400 miles and several light years away.

Route by kayak
Route by ferry

18

Into a Storm

'Who are all those young men in green overalls and helmets?' I innocently asked.

If we hadn't just flown directly from India to Malawi, if in my head I hadn't still been somewhere along the Ganges, perhaps I would have understood more quickly the implications of the truncheons and loutish looks of those men all over the streets of Lilongwe; perhaps I would have sensed the tension in the air and never asked the question at all.

The Malawian man sitting opposite us in the dingy restaurant stiffened. Half an hour before, he had slipped us a note that read, 'Please forgive me. I am interested in US dollars. Can you help me?' He was an office clerk, shabbily dressed in a worn suit. His short, tightly curled hair had a line shaved into it from forehead to crown to resemble a parting.

'If you want to enjoy your time here,' he said in a quiet voice, 'zip up about politics.'

To cover our confusion, we scanned the menu, which was handwritten on a thin sheet of paper. 'Nsima with Meat,' it offered, 'Nsima with Chicken, Nsima with Fish, Nsima with Cabbage, Storked Sandwich.'

'Storked?' I said out loud.

'With margarine,' our new friend explained.

The people at the next table were eating *nsima* with meat. They broke off little pieces of the doughy maize porridge, kneaded them into balls and used them to scoop up the lumps of gristly beef. Their eyes shifted about, watching us without meeting our gaze. From the green-painted wall, a portrait of His Excellency the Life President Ngawazi Dr Kamazu Banda benignly smiled down. The country's diminutive dictator was said to be in his nineties, though it was against the law to make any public reference to his age. The man opposite asked what we were doing in Malawi. We explained about our kayak, and our plan to paddle the length of Lake Malawi.

'What is the purpose of your journey?' he enquired.

'Oh, I intend to write a book,' I blithely told him.

Without a word, the man slid away through the door of the restaurant and into the darkness of the back street. The people at the next table had finished eating, and they concentrated on washing their hands in a plastic bowl the waiter had set before them. We decided against ordering a meal, and left.

'You're lucky there weren't any Special Branch spies hanging around in the restaurant,' said Reg Noble a few days later. Reg was the man who Dag had met at a conference two years previously, and who had inspired us to chose Malawi as one of our destinations. We'd travelled from Lilongwe to visit him in Zomba, where he was working on an aid project. 'Foreign journalists are banned,' he continued. 'You could have been arrested and deported; the man talking to you would probably have ended up in leg irons.'

We had some excuses for our ignorance. For much of the past eight months we'd been cut off from news of the outside world. Besides which, during almost three decades of dictatorship, Dr Banda had made sure that little news about Malawi ever got beyond the borders. And so we'd arrived knowing only what most tourists to this tiny, landlocked country know: that it lies in the southern part of the Great African Rift Valley, that its lake is the third largest in Africa, that compared to surrounding countries Malawi is a considered a haven of law and order. We didn't know that its one-party state had maintained control by appalling violations of human rights and by suppression of free speech and the press. We didn't know that the boys in green overalls were part of an effective network of spies, informers and paramilitary used to stifle opposition.

'Most tourists who come here see the infrastructure – the good roads, the efficient bus service, the new vehicles, and they think all is well,' said Reg. 'They don't realize the infrastructure exists to create money that goes out of the country or straight into the presidential coffers. They don't see the hospitals without doctors or the prisons full of political detainees.'

Reg was an ecologist, working on a scheme to develop the culture of talapia fish in village ponds. 'It's been successful at a grass-roots level,' he said wearily, 'but my funding is always being threatened because the fish produced is for local consumption. It doesn't generate any export dollars. It would be a different story if I was building a bridge, bringing over contractors from Europe and producing an end product that looked good in a glossy brochure to be shown around EC boardrooms.'

We were having drinks on the porch of his bungalow, set high on a hillside. The light was incredibly clear, allowing us to see further than seemed humanly possible. Red roads cut across a green plain and around the steep outcrops of volcanic rock that popped up from it. It looked such a verdant place – but this was a sad illusion belied by the endless fields of dried-up maize that we'd driven past on our way to Zomba. This year, the rains hadn't come, the staple crop had failed and starvation was encroaching.

'The political situation is just as paradoxical,' said Reg. 'Up to now, everything has seemed calm on the surface, but underneath it's been seething.'

Our arrival had coincided with the breaking of a political storm. The country's Catholic bishops had published a pastoral letter, read out in every Catholic church in the country, which mildly but firmly criticized the dictatorship. 'Nobody should ever have to suffer reprisals for honestly expressing and living up to their convictions,' the bishops had stated. 'We can only regret that this is not always the case in our country.'

The reaction to this, the first dissenting public voice heard for years, was instantaneous. There were countrywide riots and arrests. Exiled pro-democracy leaders began making contingency plans. It was declared an offence to have a copy of the bishops' letter. 'You must buy a radio to listen to the BBC World Service News,' Reg advised us. 'It's everyone's lifeline here, the only way we find out about what's going on in the country.'

'If there are no foreign journalists,' I asked, 'how does the information get out?'

He took a swig of his gin and tonic. He was a tall, gangly man with reddish hair and freckles, a man who looked as if he'd spent most of his life in libraries.

'It's sent out by people with access to a fax machine.'

'Do you have a fax machine?'

'Of course.'

We were staying at Zomba's Government Rest House, a sprawling single-storey building next to the bus station. In the adjacent street, South African reggae music boomed out of bars and restaurants, and men selling grilled chicken danced around their barbecues. We had a beer in the Hot Spot Bottle Shop, which had a large sign announcing it to be 'Probably The Best Drinking Joint In Town'. It was a one-roomed box, with a bar at one end and wooden benches running around the walls. There was Malawian gin for sale, and two brands of beer, Brown and Green, named after the colour of their bottles. A boy walking past the bar stared in at us. He had a stick over one shoulder, and hanging on to the end of it was a blind man, very old and frail.

'I am hungry,' said the boy. 'Give me money to buy a banana.'

Polio victims went by, hobbling along in callipers, or sitting on home-made skateboards and propelling themselves with their hands, or simply dragging themselves along the uneven street. Some of them stopped, looked into the bar and extended a hand. 'Sir, how can you help me?' they asked Dag.

We were joined by a small, fidgety man called Elias, a journalist with the Malawi News Agency. He was in Zomba, which was Malawi's seat of government, to cover the opening of parliament. I felt as if everything he said was in code. 'My agency is part of the Ministry of Information. Do you understand? We send information about our internal affairs to foreign publications, but we must edit this information. We had a Reuters man in the agency but, well, he had to leave. You know how it is.'

A pro-government demonstration went by; there were about thirty women, each wrapped in cloth printed with a photograph of Banda. They held placards on which different slogans had been scrawled in the same handwriting: 'Don't Confuse the Children, Bishops!' and 'Malawi is a One-Party State in the Name of the People.' All over the country, such demonstrations were being organized – it was rumoured by the government – to prove the lack of support for the 'confusionists' and the Catholic bishops. The two government-run newspapers – which were the only newspapers allowed – were giving these demonstrations front-page coverage, but were not reporting the riots.

'Once, I used to write articles and sell them to other countries,' said Elias, ignoring the women marching by. 'Sometimes to Zambia, sometimes to South Africa, sometimes overseas. But now – well, you know how it is.'

We could see how it was at Zomba Market. Men in the blue uniforms of the Malawi Young Pioneers stood at the gate, refusing entry to local people not carrying a membership card to Malawi's sole political party, and demanding money from them. The market was a reflection of lives spent struggling to make ends meet. Many stalls sold recycled goods: second hand clothes shipped from Europe, used nails, screws, hinges and locks, plastic shopping bags printed with last year's calendar, toy cars made from cardboard boxes, empty bottles of every description. Flour and oil were being sold from large drums imprinted with 'Donated by the USA'. Medicine men sat behind bottles filled with coloured liquids and bits of roots and animal parts. There was an indoor part of the market where fish was sold – smoked catfish curled around with their tails stuck into their mouths, piles of tiny, silvery usipa fish, whole fresh fish opened out, flattened and crawling with flies.

A third-class bus took us from Zomba to Nkopola, at the southern end of the lake. Despite a sign limiting the number of passengers to sixty-seven, there were over 150 of us squeezed on board, as well as all the usual sacks and boxes and bedrolls that I was coming to view as ubiquitous luggage in almost every country except my own. All the seats were taken by men; women stood in the aisle, with babies slung on their backs in papooses made from lengths of bright cotton. The air smelled of sweat, and stale milk. At every stop, there was pandemonium inside and outside the bus. In the doorway, disembarking passengers pushed against people trying to get on. Children swarmed at the windows selling bananas, bread, dried fish, pens, oranges, bags of chips and doughnuts. Young men vying for jobs as porters clambered up the ladders leading to the roof. Amid their skinny black legs would be Dag's large white ones, as he launched himself into this mêlée to check that no harm came to our red bags.

The bus driver had said he would take us down to the lake, but we were dropped off at the start of a track where a wooden sign pointed to 'Nkopola Lodge, 1km'. We sat on our baggage at the side of the road, wondering what to do. I flipped though our guidebook, a small, slim volume translated from German. We'd bought it in Canada, and Reg had told us that despite its kind remarks about the dictatorship, it apparently was banned in Malawi because of its 'misleading' photographs of people wearing ragged clothes.

'Nkopola Lodge is situated on the shore of Lake Malawi,' I read out. 'Prices start at one hundred and seventy kwatcha a night, but the luxury facilities justify such expense. Water sports facilities are excellent, unless you care about environmental pollution caused by motor boats.'

'You know what that means,' groaned Dag. 'A load of jerks getting pulled around on waterskis.'

A brand-new jeep, the trademark of foreign aid workers in Malawi, zoomed by. 'We could flag down the next one and ask for a lift to the lake,' Dag suggested.

'That track leads to the hotel,' I said. 'I bet we wouldn't be allowed to camp in the grounds.'

'We could hike down the beach.'

We were both silent for a while, pondering the idea of hiking anywhere with our baggage. 'I'm sick of heaving this kayak around,' grumbled Dag. 'It's wrecking my back.'

I was about to comment that it had all been his idea in the first place when a minibus emblazoned with 'Nkopola Lodge' pulled up next to us. Two smartly dressed Malawians hopped out, and one of them yanked open the back door for us. 'I hope you haven't been waiting too long!' he cried. 'Please get in and we'll look after the luggage.'

The track led past some stalls selling tourist souvenirs, and through high gates which closed behind us. This was a far cry from where we'd envisioned spending the night. Stone pathways ran through flower gardens fed by sprinklers; on manicured lawns white women sat under sun umbrellas drinking cocktails. No one was starving at the Nkopola Lodge; the evening buffet was being set out, platters of roast chicken and baked ham were carried past us, then jugs of cream and a sumptuous chocolate gateau.

Dag looked at me. He knew exactly which button to press 'We'll be eating dried fish for the next five or six weeks,' he said. Minutes later, we had checked in.

'It's never occurred to me before,' said Dag, over breakfast next day, 'that hunger is selective.'

He nodded towards the Malawian family sitting at a table close by. The parents were plump and expensively dressed, and their little girl was bedecked in ribbons, a flouncy dress and patent leather shoes, as if parodying a white American child on her way to a birthday party. 'Papa, I don't like my egg!' she wailed. 'It's hard!'

'Take it away,' her father curtly told the waiter. 'Bring her a softer one.'

'I used to think that when there was drought in a country, everyone suffered,' Dag continued. 'But it's not like that; no matter how bad things get in the village down the road, there will always be eggs and sausage for breakfast at Nkopola Lodge.'

We assembled the kayak on the beach, amid rented jetskis and under the gaze of two white South Africans who smelled of coconut-based suntan oil.

'What's all the muck in there?' one asked, peering into the front cockpit.

'It's mud from the River Ganges,' I told him, feeling a sharp pang of nostalgia.

He looked at me as if I was insane, and walked away.

19

A Secret House

We'd crossed the equator again, completing the third leg of our giant W around the world, and were now back in the southern hemisphere. Even though it was only two weeks since we'd been on the Ganges, the tropical heat made it difficult for us to get back into the rhythm of paddling. As we set off to kayak the length of Lake Malawi, the thought of the distance we had to cover – almost 450 miles – and the work it involved, was daunting.

The fishermen we met at our first night's campsite on Boadzulu Island thought we were crazy. 'You go all the way up the lake? In that boat? No engine? Only paddling? You like death?'

They warned us of crocodiles, hippos, storms and water spouts. More immediately alarming to us was the fact that our only map had a scale of 1:1,000,000. In Lilongwe and Zomba we'd executed the now familiar dance around libraries, book stores and government agencies, only to be told in no uncertain terms that detailed maps were unavailable for 'reasons of internal security'. Security of what, we wondered? The lake had no industry along it, no cities, no large towns, no hydro-electric or nuclear power stations, and only 17,000 inhabitants, most of whom lived in small villages. The government officials had shrugged; they didn't know, they said, because it was a matter of security.

Boadzulu Island lay over four miles offshore. It was steep, rocky and heavily forested. We'd already set up our tent on its only beach when the fishermen returned to their campsite. There were eight of them, ebony black and dressed in torn clothes, sitting on the gunnels of their long skinny dugouts and trailing lines baited with tiny fish.

'*Mzungu!*' we heard them say to each other. 'White people!' They hauled their heavy canoes ashore. Our kayak, although worn and faded now after eight months' hard use, looked incongruously modern among them. Shyly, the men accepted our apologies for having set up camp without first asking their permission. None of them had a tent: after talking to us for a while and cooking a few fish over the fire, they simply curled up on the smooth stones and went to sleep.

At dawn the fishermen set off again, telling us that there was a village in Nkhudzi Bay where we would be welcome. We reached there in early afternoon, and paddled cautiously towards the beach. Hippos abound in the southern end of Lake Malawi, especially in protected bays like Nkhudzi, with reeds growing from shallow water. I'd always thought of hippos as lumbering, placid creatures and the one that we saw a hundred yards away at first did nothing to contradict this. It lay in the water like a floating log, with only its tiny, twitching ears, its nostrils and the top of its huge oblong back above the surface. It looked so goofy and harmless that my first instinct was to go closer for a better look. Then it yawned, opening wide its cavernous mouth and revealing a pair of murderous yellow fangs. All the warnings we'd received about hippos came flooding back: that they are fiercely territorial, particularly when they have young, and that they can charge at high speed, both on land and in water. Already, we'd heard numerous accounts of them attacking humans. On Lake Malawi, their speciality was said to be overturning canoes and quickly putting paid to the unfortunate occupants.

'*Mzungu! Mzungu!*'

Children ran excitedly along the beach, doing somersaults and handstands. Some older boys waded into the water and helped us pull the kayak up the beach.

'You are tired,' said one, whose name was Edward.

He was right. After a four-hour paddle from Boadzulu Island we felt hammered by the heat. 'Please rest under this tree next to this old man. Then I show you the village.'

The tree was a leafy mango, and the old man, who studiously ignored us, was painstakingly mending a pink fishing net. The smaller children had gathered around our kayak, and were stroking its hull as if it were a furry animal. Lurching to his feet, the old man ran at them, yelling furiously. They scattered, and he returned to his fishing net without once looking in our direction. Confident that our boat and its contents would be safe close to this man, we followed Edward into the village.

Baobab trees with massive trunks and skinny branches towered from the red earth. Monkeys with powder blue testicles and scarlet penises scampered through bushes, scaring away bright yellow birds. Amid such a colourful setting, the village was drab and depressing. Its one-roomed mud huts had shaggy, overhanging thatch roofs like unruly heads of hair. A few scrawny, bald-necked chickens pecked around in vain for food.

'You want eggs?' asked Edward. 'Later I bring you eggs. You want learn Chicheŵa? I teach you.'

He'd stopped outside the village store, a shed with a corrugated iron roof. 'We drink Coke?' he asked hopefully.

We bought him a bottle, and Dag and I shared another. It was tepid, and tasted even worse than usual. We sat on the step of the store to drink it. Behind us, on the counter, a pop song blared from a radio, and the group of little boys who had been trailing along behind us starting dancing. They hopped about on the hard earth, with lots of rhythmic foot stamping and pelvic thrusting. When the song finished they gathered around us, holding out their hands for a reward. Some of them had red tinges in their hair, a sign of nutritional deficiency.

'I show you *mzungu* cottages!' announced Edward.

We walked out of the village, and through the fields of dried up maize. Edward told us that he was sixteen, and still in Standard Four class of elementary school. 'Sometimes my parents don't have kwatcha for my school fees, clothes and books. How can you help me?'

We'd reached the first of the *mzungu* cottages. It was a large, two-storey building looking over the lake. An operatic aria drifted from an open window. Parked in the driveway was a Mercedes with a trailer hooked on to it and a sleek motor boat on top. All along the road, the scene was the same: large houses, well-tended gardens, jeeps and sports cars and jetskis and sailboards. These were the holiday homes of rich Malawians, or of the white South Africans who had been welcomed by President Banda when other countries had closed their borders to them. We thanked Edward for showing us, and went back through the village to the beach. The old man was still there, and a boy hoping to sell some of his carvings and baskets. Edward soon followed with ten eggs. 'Fifty tambala each,' he said.

This was twice the price of eggs in Zomba Market, but we didn't have the heart to argue.

Just before I fell asleep, I heard a deep rumbling sound. 'Is that your stomach?' I muttered to Dag, but his breathing was slow and steady, and he didn't answer. Some hours later, my bladder woke me. I fumbled around to find my glasses, then unzipped the tent door.

'What are you doing?' muttered Dag.

'Going for a pee.'

'Wait, I need one too.'

As we headed off along the beach, I heard the rumbling again and realized that it came not from Dag's stomach but from the lake. We both stopped walking. 'There's a hippo out there,' I nervously whispered.

He gripped my hand. 'What's that up ahead?' he asked.

We peered through the gloom, and as our eyes adjusted to the dark we made out a huge, hulking form, with a smaller replica at its feet.

'Holy smokes!' whispered Dag. 'It's a mother and baby!'

We were so close that we could hear them munching on the scrub grass. 'Back – to – the – tent,' breathed Dag.

We were there in seconds, peering out through the screen at the three ton beast and its chunky little offspring.

'We're safe in here,' Dag reassured me.

'*Why?*'

'That's what everyone says. If you're camped on grass, they just graze right around the tent. What about needing to pee? Can you hang on?'

'For days,' I told him.

Further along the coast were two more bays lined with the private docks of fancy houses. Powerful motor boats zipped about, dragging people behind them on waterskis or dangling from parachutes, their wakes almost swamping fishermen's dugouts. We pushed on, having no desire to stop at any of these places. By sundown, we wanted to reach Monkey Bay, where we hoped to find some British friends of Reg Noble who worked for the Fisheries Department. But our map gave only the vaguest hint of its location. We paddled along a wild stretch of coastline with rocky headlands, steep cliffs and lush vegetation that rang with strange cries. When we asked fishermen where Monkey Bay was, they simply pointed ahead. Behind one headland was a cove where large boulders rose from the water. It would have been hard for a motorized boat to make its way through this maze, yet on the beach there was an imposing white mansion, long and elegant with high windows and colonnades.

'Surely this isn't Monkey Bay?' I mused.

'Maybe that's the Fisheries building,' said Dag doubtfully.

'Let's go closer and have a look.'

Some distance away, a fisherman was casting a line from his dugout. As we headed into the cove we waved at him, and cried '*Moni bambo!*' 'Good day, sir!'

His only response was to stare at us in astonishment.

Sunlight bounced off sand, water and white walls, and the mansion shimmered in the heat haze. As we paddled closer we saw that it was set amid lawns and gardens and surrounded by a high wire fence. There wasn't a soul in sight and the windows were shuttered, but I had the strong feeling that somewhere within that luxurious building, someone was monitoring our approach. Dag and I spoke at the same time.

'I think it's military—'

'This isn't a good idea—'

'*Come back!*' The fisherman's voice rang out across the water. '*Please come baaack!*'

We turned, and quickly retreated to his dugout. 'I couldn't believe it when I saw you going there.' He was whispering, even though we were out in the lake with no other boats around. 'It is one of His Excellency's secret houses.'

And had we stumbled on to its grounds, it's doubtful we would have got any further up the lake.

20

Troubled Thoughts

'Of course you can stay,' said Sharon Tweddle. 'Got a tent? Put it on the lower lawn. Carry the kayak up here, though, because the hippos sometimes come ashore to graze and they might stand on it. And don't leave anything lying around, otherwise the baboons will pinch it in the morning.'

We'd paddled up to Sharon's waterfront home on Monkey Bay to find her sitting at a picnic table making papier-mâché earrings. Next to her, Denis Tweddle was doing his daily twenty miles on an exercise bike. He had a fine view of the bay, the eagles floating on the air currents, the weaver birds flashing into their nests on the reeds. And on a table next to him was a large glass of gin and tonic, like a carrot on a stick.

The Tweddles had lived in Malawi for twenty-one years, and for much of that time Denis had been chief officer at the Department of Fisheries, which was a thirty-second walk from their house. 'That's why I need this exercise bike,' he grunted.

Denis was British; Sharon had been born and bred in Rhodesia. As whites, they and their two sons could not become Malawian citizens, and Sharon had never been allowed to work. 'I keep very busy though,' she said. 'I'm making this jewellery for a special recycling event my wildlife society is holding. And I've identified ninety-two species of birds, right here in this garden.'

Behind her, one of their houseboys was watering a flowerbed. The garden was immaculate, shaded by large trees and with lawns and rock pathways leading down to the beach. Inside the house, where we adjourned as the light faded and the mosquitos came out, things were less orderly. Every surface, including the floor, was heaped with piles of newspapers, magazines, books, toys, and recycled paper and plastic. Another houseboy was vainly attempting to tidy up, straightening the piles and dusting around them.

At the army base close by, someone was playing taps on a badly tuned trumpet. 'It's difficult to get a baby sitter because of the base,' grumbled Sharon. 'Local women are afraid to walk up this road at night because the incidence of rape is so high. I'm not prepared to put them at risk – rape's bad enough, and then they're likely to get AIDS as well.'

'If they haven't already got it,' commented Denis.

About a quarter of the population of Malawi, they told us, was HIV positive, and in the last two years 10 per cent of the Fisheries Staff had died of AIDS.

They call it Slims Disease,' said Sharon. 'Suddenly someone loses a lot of weight, and soon afterwards they die.'

Denis's workers were also beginning to feel the effects of the drought. 'I had five people come to me today to ask for hunger money,' he said. 'They want it to send to their relatives in the country, so that they can buy maize flour.'

The average monthly wage, he told us, was 50 kwatcha. A sack of maize flour cost 40 kwatcha, which left little for fish, soap, clothes or school and party fees. 'And a recent devaluation of fifteen per cent was matched only by a two to three per cent increase in wages,' Sharon added, 'so people are becoming progressively poorer.'

We sat in their living-room eating plates of bacon sandwiches and watching a video of *A Room with a View*. The armchairs were covered with throw rugs. English newspapers they'd recently received had headlines about Prince Andrew's marital problems. A bookcase was full of family photographs. Pieces of Lego lay on the carpet and their young son played with a Transformer toy. For a while I forgot I was in Malawi; I imagined myself somewhere like Surbiton, or Wolverhampton. Sharon soon broke the illusion. 'When you go to bed,' she said, 'take a flashlight with you and check there aren't any hippo on the lawn.'

At dawn, baboons crashed through the tree above our tent. They sat on the branches, chewing on long green pods and ignoring the Tweddles' dog, which was running around the base of the trunk, barking itself into a hopeless frenzy. While we breakfasted on the lawn, one of the houseboys chased a baboon out of the kitchen. It clambered up into the tree that was shading us, and sat as if in a yoga posture, its legs spread, its arms resting on the branch, its hands loosely hanging. It frowned at me, holding my gaze. 'How marvellous,' I enthused, 'to have baboons in your garden!'

Seconds later, a thick stream of urine poured down, narrowly missing my coffee cup.

Sharon invited us to stay for another night, so we walked into the settlement of Monkey Bay to change money and buy food for dinner. One of the two ferries that service the lake had just come into the port, disgorging a dozen young backpacker tourists. They'd been met by a minibus which would take them to a small resort on Cape Maclear, and they sat languishing inside it, waiting for the driver to emerge from the bottle shop. Carvers buzzed around the windows of the minibus, holding up ebony masks and salad servers, crying, 'Please buy! I have no food to eat!'

When we emerged from the PTC supermarket, one of a chain owned by President Banda, the carvers descended upon us. To escape them we stepped into the bottle shop. It was a square room with a concrete floor and a Wurlitzer jukebox that flashed coloured lights and played muffled South African reggae music.

'Hey!' shouted a man leaning against the bar. 'I saw you in your canoe in Manzinzi Bay! I was waterskiing.'

Paul was a young Malawian, smartly dressed in white shorts, a striped shirt and white shoes and socks. He had recently returned from Bradford, England, where he'd been awarded a Masters Degree in Law. Thrilled to learn that I hailed from Manchester, he insisted on buying us beer. We sat at a table with him, and when the barmaid brought the drinks she went down on her knees to serve us. 'This is our tradition,' said Paul, seeing my expression.

'Why is the women's hair shorn so close to their scalps?' I asked him.

'His Excellency encourages this style,' he replied.

Any further discussion of His Excellency, however, was neatly censored when Paul told us that his father was the British High Commissioner for Malawi.

'I have a brother at the Edinburgh School of Medicine, and another at Harvard. My father had many sons, but some have perished at the hands of magicians.'

'What did they die of?' asked Dag.

'There was no autopsy – everyone realized it was useless.'

'Why were they killed?'

'Jealousy. It is the biggest cause of bewitchment in Malawi. My family is rich and powerful and many people are jealous. We cannot escape this curse. You need not worry, the magicians cannot touch white people, only us with our dark skins.'

'Most Malawians believe in bewitchment,' said Sharon later. She was finishing the earrings and sticking pressed flowers on to cards for her recycling event. 'It doesn't matter how educated or well-travelled they are.'

I told her about the woman who had served us on her knees, and the woman ahead of me in the bank who had marked her receipt slip with a thumb print. 'Few women can read or write,' Sharon told me. 'Listen, families here are allowed to marry off their daughters when they're twelve years old or weigh ninety-eight pounds. Do you think anyone cares about educating women?'

She gave a long, exasperated sigh. The Tweddles got lots of visitors, many of them like us, who were in Malawi for the first time. I got the feeling she did a lot of this sort of explaining. 'Excuse me, but I've got to finish these cards for tomorrow,' she said, returning to her pressed flowers.

North of Monkey Bay was Cape Maclear, part of the Lake Malawi National Park. Steep slopes dropped to golden beaches and startlingly clear water teeming with colourful fish. We bypassed the Cape's resort, and headed for a couple of the off-shore islands that are also part of the National Park. On Mumbo and then Maleri Island we camped for several days without seeing another human being. The islands were benign places. Behind their pebbly coves and jumbles of white and grey boulders was luxuriant forest: creepers, vines and strangler figs wrapped around every tree, giving the effect of a cushioned greenery that you could fall on to from high and have a soft, safe landing. The water was warm, and had no lurking hippos or crocodiles, only the rainbow-coloured mbuna fish that nibbled on our toes. It should have been a place to escape the realities of Malawi's politics and poverty, but during the long hours of peaceful solitude, I found myself dwelling on these even more than I had during the past two weeks. They weighed me down, I became depressed about travelling in such a carefree way through a country whose people led such desperate lives. I was weary, I realized, of coming face to face with harsh inequities, and the confusions and guilt they trawled up in me.

One night, I lay on the beach with Dag, and shared my troubled thoughts. 'We've spent all our lives inside a bubble of privilege,' I said. 'And now we think we're travelling so roughly, having such an adventure. But we're still inside the bubble, it protects us even here.'

'At least you realize that,' he replied. 'Do you know how many people don't?'

We gazed up at the sky. It arched above us like some gigantic planetarium show, with the Milky Way its proud centrepiece. The air was so clear we could see galaxy upon galaxy, constellation after constellation. It was a dizzying, dazzling, humbling display. I let my thoughts spin up and, for a while at least, get lost in its infinite depths.

21

Clouds of Flies

There are several theories on how Lake Malawi got its name, but the one I like to believe is that a band of ancestral immigrants saw the lake shimmering 'like flames in the sunshine', and called it Maravi, or fire flames. I thought about those immigrants when we were heading north from Maleri Island, and could see ahead what seemed like hundreds of miles along the glittering lake. As this was the end of the rainy season, there were dramatic, ever-changing skyscapes. Puffy clouds bowled along like sprites, towering clouds rose from the horizon, phalanxes of dark, brooding clouds marched along, sometimes trailing the deadly tornados called water spouts. A southerly wind, the *mwera*, blew up, filling our sail and pushing us at a fast clip through 6ft waves. We were quickly soaked to the skin, but it was no matter, for the lake water was luxuriously warm.

It was late afternoon by the time we reached Sungu Point. According to our map this was a long, north-facing headland. In reality it was a series of marshy, reed-covered islets separated by stretches of shallow muddy water – the sort of country beloved by hippo.

'I don't like this,' I told Dag. 'I really, really don't like it.'

'I'm not thrilled myself,' he answered. 'But what do we do?'

'Let's head for Mbenje Island,' I suggested. We could see it on the horizon; it looked too steep to be the sort of place hippo hung out.

'It's ten miles away,' said Dag. 'We'd get there in the dark, and who knows what we'd find.'

Tentatively, we paddled on, keeping a keen lookout for twitching ears or large nostrils sticking above the surface of the water. 'OK,' said Dag finally, 'Mbenje it is. There's nowhere safe round here to camp.'

We followed the point to the last islet. On its far end there was a clearing in the reeds and a sandy beach where six men sat in a circle. They were small and sinewy, blue-black and almost naked. As we paddled towards them they stared at us fearfully. We were equally uneasy: stuck in hippo country, throwing ourselves on the mercy of a group of people with no idea of how they might react. As the bow of the boat hit the beach the men stood up. One of them walked towards us, and we fumbled around to find our Chicheŵa phrasebook. It proved unnecessary.

'My name is John James!' he cried. 'Where are you going in this strange boat?'

The men led us along a path through high reeds to their camp. Fish were drying on bamboo racks and being smoked over hot stones in fire pits. Several small huts had been built from the reeds, and John James told us we could set up our tent next to them. 'Hippo do not come here,' he assured me. 'But a crocodile walks across this beach every night.'

We bought a campango fish from John James, and fried it for supper. From the reeds came the clicking of frogs, like a wooden xylophone being struck. Soon, the cicadas joined in with their steady whirring, and a bird whooped and trilled. Then the fishermen began singing in strange harmonies and cadences, wordless songs made up of humming and sighing and twanging that seemed to come from the backs of their throats and the depths of their chests. On the horizon, the sky transmuted from pale blue to violet to gold to a deep glowing orange. Then darkness fell with startling haste. If the crocodile walked over the beach that night, I didn't hear it.

We awoke to a scene of arresting loveliness: reeds trembling in the breeze, rough-hewn dugouts lying on the yellow sand, the lake like green glass in the dawn light. As we dismantled the tent and packed the boat, the fishermen gathered around us making soft cooing sounds, like contented chickens. They had asked us for nothing; when we gave them gifts of stainless steel fish hooks their faces filled with delight. 'Sure?' asked John James. 'These are for us to keep?'

We assured them they were.

'So we will pray for you,' he said.

It took us just over two hours to sail through a steep chop to Mbenje, which turned out to be not one but three islands, all uninhabited. The first was merely an outcrop of rock, streaked with guano. The next two islands had rolling contours and were covered with scrub grass. At first they reminded me of the Scottish Isles, until we paddled closer and saw banana trees, a dugout anchored on the lee shore of the island and a tiny fishing camp. Two boys stood on the rocky shore beating something with a stick. They leaped back, then darted forward to start beating again.

'Must be a snake,' said Dag. 'I forgot to tell you – I saw a big one Boadzulu Island.'

'You *forgot* to tell me?'

'Well – I decided not to mention it.'

The boys looked up and saw us. '*Mzungu! Mzungu!*' they cried, and held aloft their trophy – a 5ft-long, and quite harmless, monitor lizard.

There was nowhere for us to camp on the three islands, and it was still early in the day, so we decided to head north towards Kirambu Point. It was a crossing of about thirteen miles, and we hoped that the *mwera* would push us there in a couple of hours. But the minute that we pulled up the sail, the wind dropped and soon the lake was mirror flat.

Languidly, we paddled for an hour, then stopped for a break. The sun was overhead, and unmercifully hot, so we clambered out of the kayak and went for a long, leisurely swim. Not having to worry about sharks was pure luxury, and we were too far from the shore for hippos or crocodiles to be a concern. It was still a novelty to be able to emerge from a swim feeling clean, instead of salt-encrusted, like in the Solomons, or muddy, like in the Ganges. And the lake water was mostly free of bilharzia, and potable. But we hadn't entirely escaped all discomforts of tropical paddling. I hadn't been quick enough with the tincture of iodine when I scraped my foot in Zomba, and the minor lesion had fast developed into a festering wound. A course of antibiotics had cleared it up but had also brought on an attack of thrush to complement the ringworm – not a worm at all but a fungal infection – spreading over my upper thighs. And Dag had developed painful ulcers inside his mouth and on his tongue. Letting the kayak drift, we pulled out the first-aid kit and set about treating our various ailments.

'Thank goodness we've got the EPIRB along,' I said, referring to our small emergency locator unit. 'Imagine if we were somewhere like Mbenje Island and one of us got bitten by a venomous snake. We'd never make it to the mainland in time.' I presumed Dag's silence was because he was smearing his mouth and tongue with ointment. I turned round. He'd finished treating his ulcers and had begun to paddle. And he was staring fixedly at the puffy clouds building above the mainland hills.

'We don't have it along,' he said.

'We don't have it along,' I repeated mindlessly, as the words sank in.

'I left it at the Tweddles. We'll pick it up on the way back. I figured – well – this is a freshwater lake . . .'

It's a *huge* lake, Dag. It has terrible storms! And hippos and crocs and snakes!'

'I know, I know. But who would interpret the message? Who would rescue us? Listen, if it's any consolation, you can write about this, I won't mind.' And with that he began cheerfully whistling

Three hours later, we reached Kirambu Point. The map showed it as marshy and uninhabited, but through the binoculars we could see a whole string of villages. A half a mile from shore we met fishermen out in their dugouts, collecting usipa from the nets they had set in the water.

'Not good today,' said one of the fishermen. 'Only three tins.'

Each 'tin' was a five-litre bucket, overflowing with the tiny silvery fish.

'Come to our village!' cried the men, and we followed them in.

Women and children had gathered on the beach to buy usipa. They stood with platefuls of the fish on their heads, staring at us as we got out of the boat. They were joined by men from the village who crowded around, watching us unpack and carry our bags to the spot where the fishermen had said we could camp. When it was time to haul up the kayak, one man came forward. 'I help you,' he said. 'For money.'

We blinked at him. It was a distance of a hundred feet.

'I am poverty man,' he said. 'My clothes are rags.'

This was true. His shirt hung off his shoulders, revealing skin covered with whorls of black hair. 'You help me? Give me shirt, trousers? Give me kwatcha?'

'I will give you kwatcha,' said Dag, 'if you give me something.'

While we were erecting the tent the man returned with his wife, whom he pushed forward as if offering to trade her. For a few seconds Dag's eyes filled with alarm, until she held out a cassava root.

'One kwatcha,' she said.

The deal was struck, and Kadzombe and Lilia settled down next to us. When I asked Lilia about where I could find the women's latrine area, she pointed into the reeds, next to a creek. 'What about hippo?' I asked.

'The hippo here are natural,' said Kadzombe. 'So they are safe. Only artificial hippo are dangerous.'

'Artificial hippo?'

'Those are the ones with a wizard inside them. They are bad hippo, they attack fishermen in their canoes, especially if a fisherman has a pregnant wife.' He turned to Dag. 'Is your wife pregnant?'

'I don't think so,' said Dag.

'Then you are safe from the artificial hippo.'

Kadzombe took us to meet the chief of the village. He led us through a grove of banana trees, and past an area where the red earth had been recently dug up and was sprouting with young green plants. I asked Kadzombe what these were.

'Cassava,' he said. 'This year we have no maize, so now we plant more cassava because it needs only a little water.'

'Why don't you always plant lots of cassava?' I asked.

'It is not traditional here,' he said.

The chief's house was built of bamboo and reed, with a round mud extension at one end. Sitting on the veranda was an old, half-blind man dressed in torn yellow overalls. He ran his fingers over the fish hooks we gave him, and nodded his approval. One of his daughters shuffled up to us on her knees with a plate of raw cassava slices. Through the door of the house, I could see a portrait of President Banda hanging on one wall. As a 'GVH' or Group Village Headman, the chief was responsible for several villages. Beneath him in each village was the 'VH' or Village Headman. Every month, Kadzombe told us, the GVH received 60 kwatcha and the VH 30 kwatcha each from the government in return for being its 'ears and eyes'. Each village also had its spies, members of the Young Pioneers who reported anyone who spoke or acted against the government. Even listening on the radio to the BBC World News could be viewed as an act of dissent; that night, we decided not to tune in, and I made my notes by flashlight, inside the tent.

There was a busy scene on the beach next morning. Men pushed their dugouts into the lake to start the day's fishing, and women bent over at the edge of the water, washing their pots. Roosters strutted about, vigorously crowing. Small boys ran down the beach, pulled off their shorts and dropped them in an untidy heap, then threw themselves head-first into the water and gambolled about like baby dolphins. Some older girls gathered around us, and watched us prepare our breakfast. Dag mixed flour, milk powder, sugar and water into a batter and made pancakes. We ate these with jam and shared a cup of black tea.

'*Mzungu* food,' the girls whispered, and held out their hands for a taste.

They squabbled over our rubbish – a tea bag, and last night's empty soup packet. The latter was a real prize, and they took turns in trying to read out the instructions to each other. We also had an empty milk powder tin, but we'd already promised this to Lilia, and I gave it to Kadzombe to pass on to her.

'Give me your sunglasses,' he said.

'I'm sorry,' I told him. 'I need them. I only have one pair.'

'When you go back to your country, you can buy more.'

'Yes, but I won't be back there for a long time.'

'Send me sunglasses from your country. Be my penpal. Give me your address.'

One of the little girls was stroking my feet. 'Give me tambala,' she said.

A woman came by. She was on her way to the lake, and she carried a bucketful of laundry on her head. 'Give me soap,' she said.

'Give me flour,' said Kadzombe. 'And sugar.'

Two days later, we needed to stop off in the town of Nkhotakota and restock our supplies.

They were two days of exhilarating sailing, with the *mwera* filling our spinnaker sail and 8ft high waves giving us high-speed
rides on their breaking crests.

'Yeeee haaah!' Dag would whoop behind me as the boat was
picked up by a noisy rush of foaming white water. Sometimes, I'd
register that the sail had gone suddenly limp, that I was staring
down into a deep blue trough, that a wall of moving water behind
us was lifting up the stern of the kayak, that at any second the
prow would bury in the bottom of the trough and we'd be flipped
over like a pancake.

'We're capsizing!' I'd fearfully yell, but before the words were
out we'd be up and over the wave and Dag would be shouting,
'Here comes another – *Yeeee haaah*!'

It was as tiring as it was exciting, and by the time we got to
Nkhotakota we were in need of a rest. The town lay behind a long
wide beach and a swamp. A pier ran out into the lake, but it was
in total disrepair, and whole sections of it had crumbled away.
Where the beach met the swamp there was a rice mill, and a
mountain of husks swarming with people in search of errant
grains. Next to this stood the District Rest House, which from 500
yards away looked rather grand. It was a long, low whitewashed
building with a large 'Restaurant' sign at one end, pillars around
its central entrance porch and a small second storey like a tier on
a wedding cake. Children had gathered around us on the beach;
we promised them 50 tambala each for the safekeeping of the
kayak, and walked up to the rest house. The closer we got, the
more tumbledown, and strange, we realized it was. Swamp grass
grew all around it. The restaurant was boarded up. A car radiator
was attached to the wall of the entrance porch, and a wheel hub
had been set into the concrete floor. The manager of the place
was a lugubrious character called Alex with a cataract over one
eye. We asked him if there were any free rooms.

'Plenty,' he said. 'You are the only guests.'

Beyond the porch was a large room with a semi-circular bar at
one end of it. The ceiling was caving in, and the walls were grey
and mottled. Off a long, dank corridor were several small airless
rooms with tiny windows opening on to the swamp. Green slime
was the main feature of the shower and toilet, and a tree frog sat
contentedly in the washbasin.

'I show you the best rooms,' promised Alex.

We followed him back through the bar and up to the second storey. At the top of a winding staircase, a complete car door had been built into the wall. 'Does it open?' I asked Alex.

'No, too dangerous, people would come up from the bar and fall into the swamp. But the window opens!' and obligingly he reached for the handle and wound it down.

Set into the railings of a large balcony were parts of a ship's engine, painted in bright but peeling silver paint. 'Who did all this?' I asked Alex.

'A District Commissioner, many years ago,' he said. 'Once this place was very fine, but now the government gives no money to Nhkotakota, and everything falls apart.'

He showed us the 'best' of the two rooms. Ripped mosquito nets hung over two narrow beds, large spiders' webs stretched over the corners and a wasps' nest festooned the window.

'You take it?' he asked hopefully.

We did.

The number of children guarding the kayak had mysteriously doubled in our absence, and all claimed to be the ones we had made the initial bargain with. After sorting this out and quelling the squabbles, we enlisted the help of three teenage boys to carry our boat up to the rest house. Alex told us to put it along one wall of the bar, assuring us that the door would be 'locked well' at night.

'You want to eat now?' he asked. 'I have only biscuits for sale, but there is a fine restaurant in town!' Town was half an hour's walk away along a path through the swamp. It was a ramshackle settlement, with a feeling of desertion and imminent despair. The main street was unpaved. An ancient petrol pump stood all alone, like a scene from a Hopper painting. Outside a bar called the Kaka Tavern, little boys kicked around a ball made of scrunched up paper tied with string. Women walked by from the market, clad in patched cotton dresses and carrying metal plates of okra on their heads. The bakery was closed for the day.

'It will open tomorrow,' said a man sitting outside it. 'But it will probably have no bread.'

We found the 'fine restaurant', a place called the Pick and Pay, and had a dreadful meal of burned rice and rancid meat. Someone had cut an article from the *Daily News* and tacked it to the wall. 'Nkhotakota is lagging behind in the party membership renewal exercise,' it read. 'Some areas of Nkhotakota have to date not remitted even a single tambala to the district party office.'

'We will not join the party, so the government leaves us to rot,' said Andrew.

He sported three gold earrings in one lobe, wore fashionable American-style jeans and baseball boots and smoked imported cigarettes. We were sitting with him at one end of the bar, straining to hear his words above the music blaring from the radio. Alex was at the other end of the bar, chatting with the rest house's two nightwatchmen who were in the process of getting drunk on the beer Andrew was buying for them. 'I heard on the BBC that Mr Chihana is preparing to come into the country from Zambia,' he told us.

Chihana was an exiled trade unionist and leader of the Alliance for Democracy, a blanket organization for groups opposed to Banda's dictatorship. 'A government minister fled the country today, and four hundred army troops went with him! We are on the verge of a revolution. If they stop Chihana coming into the country tomorrow, there will be bloodshed. I will go and fight!'

'You look more like a rock star than a revolutionary,' I said.

He took this as a compliment. 'I get my clothes from South Africa,' he boasted. 'I go down there a lot, for the music festivals.'

'What do you do for a living?'

He gave us a sly look. 'You know what I do.'

'We don't.'

'I saw you out there in your boat,' he said. 'I bet you paddle away from shore, light up a big spliff and re-lax!' He slipped a hand under his shirt and pulled out what looked like a large fat cigar wrapped in banana leaf and tied with string. 'Want to buy some Malawi Gold?' he asked.

We went down to the beach to try some of the marijuana. A warm breeze blew in from the lake, and the rest house looked romantic, silhouetted against a violet sky, a few of its windows glowing and the first star of the night twinkling above it. 'The police raid my house all the time,' confided Andrew. 'They know I am a big dealer but they never find anything because I'm cleverer than them. The police are all stupid, as stupid as Banda—'

'Ssssh,' I cautioned him, seeing the glow of a cigarette further along the beach.

'I don't care who hears me,' he said. 'The people of Malawi have been silent for too long!'

Back at the rest house one of the nightwatchmen was dancing in front of the kayak, as if trying to impress it. He danced like all Malawians we'd seen, with his backside thrust out, his arms held up and his hands hanging loosely, shuffling around in perfect time to the music. Dag bought another round of beer, and I, suddenly craving sugar, asked Alex for some biscuits.

'I only have lemon creams,' he apologized, 'and the top of this packet is ripped because a cockroach got in there. Don't worry, I put him away.'

As if induced by the thought of cockroaches, a crawling sensation started in my hair and on my neck and arms. Dag was scratching as well.

'I feel like I've got fleas all over me,' he said.

'I think it's an effect of the Malawi Gold,' I surmised. Then I noticed that under the dim lightbulb hanging from the ceiling were wisps of what looked like black smoke, with small bats flitting through them.

'*Nkhungu!*' cried Alex. 'Lake flies!'

So far we'd only seen these minute creatures from a distance, as they hatched from the beneath surface of the lake by the million and trillion and rose in billowing clouds up to 300 feet high. Fishermen had told us to avoid these dense clouds. Sometimes, they said, they were thick enough to suffocate a person.

'The wind must be blowing this lot onshore,' said Dag.

'Excuse me, but I close the bar, we go home!' cried Alex.

Within minutes he, Andrew and the two nightwatchmen were jogging away through the swamp, leaving Dag and me alone.

For hours, we vainly tried to sleep while the tiny flies crawled in our noses and ears, and mosquitos whined round our heads. Around two o'clock, thunder clapped directly above us and a dazzling flash of lightning heralded a torrential downpour. A strong wind blew up and whistled through the rest house. I kept hearing loud bangs, and imagined bats being thrown against window, and I half expected to have one fluttering maniacally around our room at any second. At three o'clock we went downstairs. The place was thick was flies, as if they were all taking refuge from the storm. It was easy to push open the door of the bar, which had been 'locked' by means of a stone placed against it. Water was dripping on to the kayak through the ceiling, and there was a sizable puddle on the floor. Frogs hopped along the corridor, a rat scurried by, and in the bathroom brown cockroaches scuttled over the walls. In the dead of night, and with rain lashing down outside, the District Rest House was like a set for a Hammer horror movie.

By morning, peace was restored. We sat on the balcony, drinking tea and eating lemon cream biscuits, watching another cloud of *nkhungu* rise up from the lake. When this one drifted to shore, some women were ready for it. They dipped winnowing baskets into the water, then waved them around in the advancing cloud. Contact with a wet surface immobilized the flies, which fell to the ground and soon formed sizable heaps. In a bookstore in Zomba, I'd copied down instructions for cooking the flies, and now I read these out to Dag. 'Clean the insects and remove any strangers. Press *nkhungu* together into small firm cakes. Wrap them in banana leaves and bake the cakes on both sides in burning grass. When cooked, remove the banana leaves, cool cakes and cut into slices. Dry in the sun and store until needed.'

Dag was busy trying to tune in our radio to the BBC, and was only half listening to me. 'Got it,' he said.

Between static crackles, we heard reports on Yugoslavia, on the upcoming election in Britain, on attacks against Turks in Germany. The final report was by Chris McGreal, a journalist who happened 'by chance' to be sitting next to Chihana when he flew into Lilongwe Airport that morning.

'Chihana stepped on to the tarmac and was immediately seized by several men in plain clothes. He tried to resist, and waved his speech in the air, but was pushed into a security car and driven away.'

I thought about Andrew listening to the same report. He'd promised to come to the rest house at ten to see us again before we left. When he didn't turn up, we went into town to look for him. Everyone there knew him. He'd left by bus this morning, they told us. He hadn't said when he'd be coming back.

22

A Curious Hippo

Fifty miles north of Nkhotakota was the British owned Dwangwa Estate, an enormous sugar cane plantation. Just beyond it there was a bay with a pretty white sand beach shaded by trees and lined with the weekend cottages of expatriate workers. As we paddled across the bay, a man sailed out in his hobie cat to chat to us. 'You sound English,' he said. 'Heard the election results? It looks like the Tories will get back in.'

It was midday. Surfboards were scattered over the beach, and people sat on loungers beneath sun umbrellas. In front of them, a houseboy in a red T-shirt walked up and down, dragging a rake behind him, making the sand neat for the afternoon activities.

We were now about halfway up the lake, and the soft, purple outlines of the Viphya Mountains had appeared. Along the beaches were temporary villages, with houses hastily erected from reeds and bamboo. The drought, and the pressure put on available land by an annual birth-rate of 4 per cent were forcing people to migrate from the interior of Malawi down to the lake, where at least they could catch fish to eat or trade for flour. Late one afternoon we stopped at one of these temporary settlements, in a tiny cove ringed by granite boulders. There were two small huts there, and we went to ask the occupants for permission to camp. Two men and a woman sat outside one of the huts, next to a rack of clay cooking pots. The woman wore a bra, a status symbol in these parts. She'd sewn on her own straps, and one of the cups stuck out through a rip in her cotton dress. The men's trousers had been so often patched they were more darns than material. They pointed to our clothes and then to themselves. This was a constant request, but we'd already given away most of our spare garments. And what was on our backs – my Fijian *sulu* and worn cotton shirt from India, and Dag's shorts and T-shirt were thin and faded from constant wearing, washing and exposure to the sun. We offered the people fish hooks, and with gestures and a few words of Chichewa managed to ask their permission to spend the night in the cove. The woman sat and watched us erect our tent, while the men tried out our paddles with their dugouts. On a flat-topped boulder we set up our 'kitchen', and started cooking a mixture of rice and dried tomato soup. From somewhere close by, I could hear a familiar deep chuckling and grunting sound.

'*Mvuwu?*' I asked the woman. 'Hippo?' She nodded, and called to the older of the two men, whose name was Jacob. He paddled ashore, then led us across the boulders to a point where we could look over to the next bay. It had a wide, flat beach, a stretch of dense reeds and, in the water, several wallowing hippos.

Twilight was closing in: on the horizon two huge clouds glowed orange and flashed with lightning. While we sat on the warm sand, spooning up our rice and soup, the 'hu hu hu' of the hippo seemed to come much closer. Nervously, I scanned the cove.

'Sound travels over water,' Dag reassured me. 'Besides, the hippo won't come up here. The beach is too steep, there are too many rocks and there's no grass for grazing.'

I was about to dip my spoon into the saucepan when, from right behind me in the lake, came a loud '*Phwoooosh!*' Without turning around, I made a pogo-like leap into the air, cleared the stove on top of the boulder, and fled towards the two huts. When I turned around, it was to see a hippo, head and shoulders above the water. It twitched its ears, opened its mouth in a fang-filled yawn and began lumbering towards the beach. Dag was waving his arms like a demented windmill and uttering what sounded like some primeval scream. '*Yaa yaaa yaaa!*'

Jacob had run down to join him and was chiming in with, '*Eeee! Eeee! Eeee!*' '*Run!*' I hollered. '*It's going to charge!*'

This seemed eminently sensible advice, but the men ignored it. By now they had each grabbed a paddle and were waving them at the slowly advancing hippo. I thought I was about to watch myself become a widow; I couldn't stand it. Opening my mouth as wide as it would go, and using every last vestige of breath, I shrieked, '*Get awaaaaaaay!*'

Although this had no effect on the men, the hippo seemed to take the hint. Snorting in derision, it slid away beneath the surface of the water, leaving only a trail of bubbles in its wake.

Trembling, I returned to the campsite.

'I've never seen you move so fast!' cried Dag admiringly. 'You shot off like a rocket!'

'That hippo could have killed you,' I remonstrated.

'Naah, it was just curious,' he said.

In no mood to argue, I zipped myself into the tent. The two men sat on the beach, laughing about the hippo, while the chuckles and grumbles continued to drift over the water.

Early next morning, Jacob crept up behind me and made loud hippo noises in my ear, then leaped over the nearby rock in mock imitation of my flight the previous evening. When he'd recovered from his mirth, he prepared for the day's fishing, going behind a boulder to change from his 'good' darned pants to his working clothes, a pair of shorts so ragged they were more holes than material. Before we left the cove I gave his wife thread, needles and a small pair of scissors. Considering the state of their clothes it seemed an ironic gift, but she was inordinately grateful. While we were packing up our breakfast things she pointed to the jar of peanut butter that we'd bought in Monkey Bay and finished off that morning. I took it to the lake, washed it out with sand and gave it to her clean and dry. She put the needles, thread and scissors inside the jar and clutched it to her chest. Then she curtseyed to me and hurried back to her hut.

Another long day – eight hours of paddling and sailing combined – brought us to Bandawe Point. We rounded it at four o'clock, and started looking for a place to spend the night. The shore was a series of cliffs, coves and hamlet sized villages. But the fishermen we stopped to talk to on the lake were adamant we should carry on.

'Chintheche,' they insisted, pointing up the lake. 'Where *nzungu* stay.' What they meant was the Chintheche Inn, a motel set on the beach, with an area for camping. Right next to it, beyond its boundary fences, was a village of shaggy houses with racks of fish spread out to dry in the sun. We would much rather have camped there, but the local people seemed to think this untenable, and pointed to the low, rather ugly building with the cars and camper vans parked outside it. While we were setting up our tent, a waiter came down from the motel carrying a menu on a tray. He wore a white jacket and shirt, a black bow-tie, yellow trousers, one shiny lace-up shoe and one red flip-flop.

'I have come to ask if you require dinner,' he shyly asked. We looked at the menu. 'Minestrone Soup, Beef Goulash, White Cake and Custard, Tea or Coffee.'

'White cake and custard sounds like English food,' commented Dag wryly.

'Yes sir, very English,' the waiter assured him.

'OK, we'll have dinner,' I said.

'Really?' asked the waiter, surprised by my willingness. 'Please do not come for half an hour. I will have to warn the cook.'

We were the only guests in the restaurant, and the meal was appalling.

'That was awfully brave of you,' said one of the two men at the bar, where we'd adjourned in the hope of washing away the taste of the white cake and custard.

'You sound like a fellow Mancunian,' I told him.

'Quite right,' he said, extending a hand. 'Name's Frank. And this is Simon from London.'

They told us they were teachers in Malawi, and were spending their Easter break here at Chintheche Inn. 'Come out and meet the rest of our group,' said Frank. 'We're having a barbecue on the beach.'

Sitting next to a fire pit beneath a baobab tree were their wives, Pat and Fay, a South African man called Andrew and his American wife, Lee. I asked them where they were teaching.

'At the Kamuzu Academy,' replied Andrew.

'You're not serious,' I said. 'At *Kamuzu*?'

'You've heard of it?' he asked.

Reg Noble had told us of the élitist school funded from President Banda's personal coffers. In contrast to the annual education budget of $8,000,000 a year, Banda had spent $15,000,000 to found the Kamuzu Academy, and forked out $2,000,000 a year to run it. This was money he could well afford, as he owned almost all the shares of Press Holdings, a corporate conglomerate controlling 30 per cent of the national economy. In Nhkotakota, we'd met some British volunteer teachers who had just returned from a visit to the academy. They'd described it as a fair imitation of a British public school, with an all-white staff, students decked out in uniforms and straw hats and facilities beyond the wildest dreams of any other Malawian school. From what they'd told me, I had imagined the teachers of such a place to be rather upper-crust, and not like Frank, who seemed like a grass-roots Labour man, or the others, who appeared by their dress and manner to be arty liberal types. When I voiced this, Frank took offence. 'I was educated at St Bede's,' he retorted.

'Not all the teachers are like us,' Fay chipped in.

'I understand there are forty-one teachers and four hundred students,' I said.

'You've certainly got all your facts in order,' snapped Frank.

'Doesn't that make you uncomfortable in a country where the class size is often up to a hundred and eighty? Where only four per cent of the population go to secondary school?'

'Listen,' said Frank, with the weary air of someone who had made this speech many times before, 'the bottom line is that we take a cross-section of kids on a scholarship basis, give them a first-class education and a fighting chance in the world. We teach a British curriculum and there are no restrictions on what we do or say in the classroom.'

'What about the current events in Malawi?' Dag asked. 'Can you discuss those?'

'It's difficult,' said Andrew. 'There was an occasion recently when someone wanted to publicly discuss the political situation and wasn't allowed to, but that's sorted out now.'

'You mean the chaplain,' I said.

This statement was greeted with stunned silence. 'How on earth do you know about that?' asked Frank eventually.

The volunteer teachers we'd met in Nhkotakota had told us about the academy's Scottish chaplain. After announcing that he was going to discuss the matter of the Catholic bishops' pastoral letter during the following Sunday's sermon, he was placed under immediate house arrest.

'He's been reinstated,' said Andrew defensively. 'He apologized to the school and now he's at work.'

'Actually, Andrew,' said Fay, 'he backed down.'

'We don't know that,' countered Simon, her husband. 'He never revealed the contents of his sermon.'

'And no one at the school read the letter,' added Frank.

'I find that hard to believe,' I told him. 'I wasn't in the country three days before I read it.'

'You have to remember that we're out in the bush.'

'But the chaplain must have had a copy.'

'Actually,' admitted Simon. 'I've seen it.'

'You have?' cried Frank.

'Me too,' added Andrew.

'Are you guys scared to talk to each other?' asked Dag incredulously. 'That letter's the most momentous thing to hit Malawi for years and you read it and don't talk about it?'

This time, the silence was an uncomfortable one. I asked what happened when the chaplain was arrested.

'Some police came,' said Lee. 'And a couple of cabinet ministers—'

'Cabinet ministers?'

'They're on the board of governors. They talked to the staff for a few hours, explained what was happening in the country and reassured the Catholic teachers that the bishops were safe.'

'Did anyone ask questions?' Dag enquired. 'Did anyone challenge the fact that the chaplain was locked up?'

'No . . .'

'The poor bastard,' said Dag.

'We went to talk to him,' Fay insisted. 'At least, some of us did. He said it was a matter between him and God.'

'But he was silenced,' I said.

'We're expecting another visit from journalists,' interjected Frank, looking suspiciously at me. 'The last one was from the *Guardian*. He posed as a tourist and asked to be shown around. It took me all of ten minutes to work out who he was.'

I could sense them all starting to close up. 'How do you feel,' I asked, 'about being paid a hefty salary by a dictator?'

'It's rather weird,' said Fay. 'Especially when you hear about some of the atrocities Banda is supposed to have sanctioned—'

'You have to remember,' her husband interrupted, 'how much Banda has done for this country. He carried it through independence. He created an infrastructure. There's peace.'

'And instead of running Kamuzu Academy,' Frank added, 'he could buy Mig jets.'

'Do you know how much it costs to run the place?' I asked.

'Honestly,' said Frank, who had taught there for twelve years, 'I have no idea.'

I quoted to him the figures Reg had told me.

'How very interesting,' he said, his voice heavy with sarcasm. 'Do you mind if we talk about something else now?'

There was heavy rain during the night, and we awoke to a blustery, cloudy morning and a grey and threatening lake. Parked close to our tent was a Volkswagen van, from which an elderly British couple emerged. They set up a picnic table, laid it with cups, saucers, plates and napkins, and fried up bacon and eggs over a camp stove. While the eggs cooked, the man scanned the horizon through binoculars. 'It's wild out there,' he called to us. 'I thought I could see trees but they're waves – like big bucking horses. Are you sure you'll be all right in that little boat?'

They were in Malawi for a holiday and to visit their daughter, who worked for the Save the Children Fund. For them, this was a return to Africa, as they'd lived in Tanzania thirty years before.

'Of course,' said the woman, 'those were colonial times, so everything was very different. But Malawi's a charming little country. There's law and order here, and the people aren't envious of the whites like in the surrounding countries. The only problem is this rule about having to wear skirts. I'm a trousers gal myself and I find it such a bother.'

I tuned into the BBC World News. In Britain the Tories had been re-elected, and in Malawi Chihana was chained up in prison, awaiting trial.

So far we'd been travelling fast up the lake, covering as much as thirty miles a day. But north of Chintheche, the coastal plain disappeared and the escarpment of the African Rift Valley rose sheer from the lake. For the next hundred miles, the nearest road access would be an eighteen-mile hike away through the bush. It was the sort of terrain we relished, far from towns and cars and tourists. Intending to meander along this section, we stopped at the small town of Nkhata Bay, and gathered enough provisions to last us two weeks.

Nkhata Bay had the atmosphere of a frontier settlement. Outside the bars along its winding red dirt streets, men gambled and prostitutes in flowered skirts and skimpy blouses slept on wooden benches. These girls looked vulnerable in sleep, the yellow soles of their feet turned out towards the street. Tacked to the walls above them were large signs, put up by the World Health Organization, warning of AIDS. The packs of condoms in the PTC supermarket cost the equivalent of a week's wage. The supermarket was a well-stocked place, catering mostly to the influx of backpacker tourists who came to camp on a nearby beach. By the doors, beggars sat with their hands outstretched. While we stocked up with dried foods, I was tempted by the rack of imported chocolate. The Cadbury's Flake I bought cost three times the original price and tasted as if it was ten years old. Feeling guilty at this waste of money, on the way out I gave the beggars handfuls of change.

No one was checking party membership cards at the market gates, and the vendors who sold us fruit and vegetables seemed cheerful and relaxed. But down at the fish-trading beach, when Dag pulled out his camera to take a picture of a dugout full of chambo, he was descended upon by a party official.

'Who are you?' demanded the man, a seedy character in an ill-fitting suit. 'Why are you taking these photos? Where are you having them developed?'

'I'm a tourist,' said Dag coolly, slipping the camera back into its box. 'I will develop them in Europe.'

'We don't allow pictures like these to be taken! Maybe you develop them in Zambia, and tell people that we Malawians all wear ragged clothes and live like monkeys!'

'We have no intention of going to Zambia,' Dag told the man. He snapped the lock on the camera box, and hurried me away to our kayak.

23

Dawdling North

The escarpment dropped to the lake in soft, forested folds. In the narrow bays, mud houses sprouted from the cleared red earth, and above them fields clung to the steep slopes. A narrow path ran the entire length of this part of the shore, connecting the numerous settlements. The people here set themselves apart from the lake shore-dwellers further south. They spoke a different language – Chitumbuka – and they were predominantly Catholic. Survival was a little easier for them, as there had been more rain in this area, and the traditional staple food was drought-resistant cassava. In Sanje village, four hours of paddling from Nkhata Bay, two young men called Herring and Blessco showed us their fields of groundnuts, potatoes and cassava, and their pawpaw, banana, grapefruit, orange and guava trees. None of the children that clustered around us had any telltale tinges of red in their hair. Many of the village houses had a latrine – called a 'long drop' – in a bamboo and thatch hut.

'Our problem,' said Herring, 'is that we have no money to buy jerseys or shorts for the village football team. How can you help us with this?'

The women in Sanje were less deferential than those we'd met further south. There was no kneeling and curtseying here. Old women marched up to me and shook me firmly by the hand, laughing merrily at my clumsy attempts to greet them in Chitumbuka. Herring's wife, also called Maria, invited me to her house, a square building made of mud bricks. Outside it, amid a tangle of orange and yellow poppies, there was a dove house and a chicken house, both on stilts to deter hyena, and a dog kennel built of straw. There were also some large earthenware pots filled with water and peeled, chopped cassava roots. When the cassava began to ferment and bubble, Maria would spread it on mats and let it dry in the sun, then pound it into flour in a hefty wooden mortar. To me it seemed a lot of effort to produce a tasteless porridge, but Maria was horrified to learn that I didn't eat *nsima* everyday. 'In your country, you do not have cassava food? How can this be?'

She insisted on cooking me some. Trying hard to smile, I forced down the lump of cassava porridge, and a 'relish' of horribly bitter usipa fish, which she had boiled whole. The meal had been prepared without salt; this was a luxury item few could afford.

During the night, a baby died in the village. Maria whispered the news to me at dawn, as she padded past our tent on her way to collect water. I followed her to the house of the bereaved family. On the veranda, a group of women sat singing hymns and swaying from side to side. From inside the house came the low, insistent wailing of the mother as she grieved over her dead infant. This was her seventh baby, and the third to die from malaria. Later in the day, the body would be buried beneath a mangrove tree with its siblings.

I returned to our tent, and sat staring out at the lake. Several children had followed me, bringing gifts of baobab tree nuts that were covered with a soft green fuzz. They broke them open, and taught me how to suck off the tart yellow sherbert coating the seeds. Then the boys showed off with handstands and somersaults, while the two girls stroked my hair and looked through it for nits. I thought of the bereaved woman, younger than myself, unable to stop having a baby each year, unable to stop the babies dying. These two little girls were destined for the same fate. My eyes filled with tears at the thought and I put my arms around them and hugged them hard. They squealed in alarm, struggled free and retreated to a safe distance, staring at me through wide, wondering eyes. The boys began jostling about, obviously daring each other to go close to the *mzungu* and risk being grabbed by her. It turned into a game, and soon I was pretending to be a snarling monster and chasing the children around the beach.

'You should take one of them back to your country,' said Herring.

He and Dag had just returned from fishing to find me sprawled on the beach, exhausted, while the excited children tugged at my hands and begged me to carry on with the game. I laughed – we'd heard the same comment in villages in the Solomon Islands and along the Ganges, made by parents who jokingly thrust their alarmed offspring towards us and exhorted us to make room for them in our kayak. But Herring wasn't joking.

'Why not?' he asked. 'You have no children. Take one of these, give him an education, a good life.'

'It's not possible—' I began.

'If you want, it is possible,' he interrupted.

I tried to explain to him that such adoptions were illegal in our countries, that we would not be able to get across the borders with one of these children. Herring simply shook his head. 'For *mzungu*,' he said, 'anything is possible.'

We dawdled up the coast, accepting every invitation to stop and camp along the way. People were excited to see us, and we were constantly told about the Germans who had hiked along the lake shore path four years previously. The lake was at its deepest here, and startlingly clear. It had also narrowed, and the steep mountains of Tanzania were only twenty-five miles away. At night, the full moon rose above them, casting a glittering path across the lake to where we camped, beneath a mango or a baobab tree, or next to boulders that still radiated the warmth of the day. Each sunrise brought lilac skies and mauve clouds. Our days of relaxed paddling were punctuated with bursts of natural dramas.

Rainstorms swept over us, leaving arching rainbows behind as if in apology for the disturbance. One day we watched in mesmerized horror as a deadly water spout dropped from a cloud like a skinny chimney and whirled across the lake towards us. At the last minute it seemed to change its mind about wanting to suck us up into its vortex, and veered away. When clouds of lake flies billowed up, we paddled like fury in the opposite direction. We escaped the insects, but they didn't escape us. At one of the villages, we were prevailed upon to eat fly cake, which was not the sweet sticky mess I'd envisaged it to be, but dry and crumbly and tasting like soil. It was served to us with *nsima* – a memorable meal, and not one I'd like to repeat.

There was no fly cake for sale at Usisya's general store; instead there were packets of chocolate cream biscuits and bottles of lukewarm Coca-Cola. Usisya was the largest village we'd visited, and the most prosperous. Its wide beach stretched the length of a long, curving bay, and was spread with hundreds of mats on which pieces of cassava and silvery usipa fish lay drying in the sun. The first cows we'd seen for weeks were drinking from the lake, and behind them in bamboo pens were goats, pigs and chickens. At the water's edge, women washed themselves, wearing only a length of cloth around their waists and not bothering to cover their breasts as we paddled up. The kayak was swamped by a series of three big waves as we landed on the steep beach, and some of the women ran up and helped us to haul it out of harm's way. Men watched from beneath bamboo and thatch shelters, where they lay around gossiping and smoking.

'I am a visitor here, too,' one of them told us. He was a dapper man in his mid-fifties and, judging from his nylon socks and leather shoes, wealthy by local standards. 'I was born in this village but now I live in Blantyre. Last year my wife died, and I have come here to get another one. I have been alone for months now and it is terrible, all this carrying water and sweeping the house and chopping wood. I need a helper. A letter came to me from here about a widow, an older woman, not expensive. I will pay two hundred kwatcha to her father. She has six children living and I have four. They are all grown. If God wills it, there will be more children yet.'

He reached into the small zip-up purse he was carrying and pulled out what I thought was going to he a photo of the woman. 'Look,' he said proudly. 'This is her shape.'

It was a piece of paper with her measurements written on it: 'Dress size 38, shoe size 6.'

I felt a strong pang of sympathy for the woman.

'Next week,' he said, 'we will marry and I will take her back to Blantyre.'

A man called Moses proudly showed us around his home. Moses was a big man in the village. By local standards he had had a glittering career: he had gone to Likomo Secondary School, studied Business and Personal Management at college, and worked in Tanzania as a store manager for a motor company. When he was twenty-nine he returned to Usisya to set up a fishing business. 'I have fifteen men working for me and six Tilly lamps! We fish when the moon is new and the nights are dark. The fish come to the lamps and we catch them in mosquito nets. I will bring one of my lamps to your tent tonight.'

In the yard there was a cooking hut, racks for drying pots and smoking fish, a long drop and a bath house. In the main room of the house, cracked china plates were proudly displayed on a wooden dresser, and taped on to the brick walls were fading magazine and calendar photos of blonde pin-up girls in revealing clothes and bikinis, circa 1960. A young, pouting Britt Ekland was there, running fingers with talon-like nails through her hair, and wearing an extremely short gold lamé dress, with a large keyhole in it to reveal her midriff.

The women of Usisya were more practically attired than Britt Ekland. They needed to be, for they worked like mules, smearing mud on the walls of their houses, harvesting ground nuts, pounding cassava, shelling beans, carrying water. Some of them looked up delightedly when we passed by and greeted us in Chitumbuka. Others were sombre, taken up with the serious business of mourning. There were two funerals in progress, one for a child, the other for a man who had drowned in the lake while out fishing.

'It was his time,' said Moses, who was showing us around the village. 'He was old.'

As this was Easter Sunday, for supper we treated ourselves to spaghetti noodles and a tin of tuna fish we'd bought in Nkhata Bay. Several boys sat with us, taking turns at stoking the small fire, and squabbling over the empty spaghetti packet and fish tin. They watched in horror as we sucked up the long white noodles, and refused the taste that we offered them. After the meal, they insisted on washing our two pots in the lake, then they ran home before the terrors of darkness could engulf them. We settled back against the giant trunk of a baobab. The fire's embers glowed, and an enormous yellow moon climbed the sky. It bathed us in light, and illuminated the dugouts lying on the pale sand.

'Have we got any moon screen?' joked Dag. 'We'll get burned in this bright light.'

Soon, it was even brighter. Moses came striding along the

beach, swinging a flaming Tilly lamp. 'Now you can see better!' he said, sitting it down next to us.

We may not have appreciated the lamp, but the local insect community did, and before long every bug on the beach was buzzing and crawling around. Impervious to this, Moses gave an impromptu seminar on business techniques. 'You must know how to handle people,' he said, 'how to recognize good workers and reward them. If I make six thousand kwatcha in two weeks, half is for wages, so each man gets two hundred kwatcha. But the men who use the Tilly lamps to drive the fish to shore, they get seventy-five kwatcha extra each, because without them we would have no usipa.'

Warming to his theme, he lectured us on personal management methods, on investments and returns, on striving for personal excellence. He drew diagrams and graphs in the sand to illustrate the points he was making, and he invited us to ask questions. Strange topics to be discussing in a remote village without road access, electricity or running water, but Moses was so authoritative and his message so clear I felt I should be taking notes in case I ever wanted to start a business.

Beyond Usisya there were few settlements. All the next day we sailed past tongues of land that fell from the escarpment and met the lake at narrow gravel beaches. The wind was strong and the lake choppy, and as we had a spinnaker sail up I couldn't see the horizon and soon began to feel nauseous. After twenty-five miles of this I was beginning to despair of us finding a place to spend the night. Then we rounded a rocky point and saw behind it a narrow river valley opening into a bay, fishermen mending their nets on the beach and children running up and down in excitement at the sight of us.

Shortly after we'd gone ashore at Chisanga beach, a teenage boy limped up to Dag with the usual 'How can you help me?' request. Some days before he had stood on a sharp splinter of wood, the wound had quickly festered and his foot was swollen to almost twice its normal size.

'My name is Mavuto. It means problem. I know I am a problem to you. Do you have aspirin for my pain?'

Better than aspirin, Dag had antibiotics for Mavuto. An appreciative crowd soon formed to watch him lance the wound, then clean, dress and bandage it. Nearby, some children played doctors and patients. The patients lay on the beach, and the doctors listened to their chests through pieces of straw, scribbled prescriptions in the sand and gave advice like, 'You must wash every morning and evening!'

There was no clinic in Chisanga. The next village had an 'African doctor' who used traditional methods, but for any other medical help people had to travel twenty-five miles by motor canoe.

'Sometimes,' said the young man next to me, 'this is too painful for them and too slow, and they die.' His name was Gift, and aptly so, for he was bright and well-spoken. 'Our problem here is transportation. We are so far from the road. But for the children this is good. Our village is like a nest, there is no bad influence, they do not know what stealing is.'

For us too, Chisanga felt like a nest, safe and welcoming, and we stayed there several days. Dag's prompt and effective treatment of Mavuto had immediately made us welcome. It also meant that there was a permanent queue of prospective patients, all men, next to our tent beneath a mango tree. Many of them had to be turned away.

'Sir, I am not well, I have gonorrhea.'

'I'm sorry, I have no medicine for gonorrhea.'

'Sir, I have hypertension. Can you give me Librium?'

'I'm sorry, we don't have Librium with us.'

'How about Valium, sir, can you help me with that?'

'Mr Dag, can you help me control my wife so we have no more children?'

'Sir,' said one rather ingenious character. 'I have no time. Can you help me with a watch?'

Dag spent hours trying to master the art of paddling one of the skinny, unstable dugout canoes, and delighted local people by constantly capsizing. I swam around him, revelling in the warm water, and the lack of hippos along this part of the lake. I didn't feel safe for long, however.

'Maria!' called Gift. 'Don't you mind that a crocodile sometimes swims there too?'

I did mind, and I was back on the beach as fast as my legs and arms could take me there.

'He is a visitor like you,' explained Gift. 'He moved into the river last week.'

The river was 200 yards from our tent.

'We saw him his morning,' Gift continued. 'Swimming just where you were.'

People kept arriving at our tent with food: an old man with oranges, boys with aubergines and cassava, the Catholic lay priest with fish. 'I do not want money,' they all said.

As we were nearing the end of our journey up the lake, we began giving away things we soon would no longer need: our kerosene lamp, radio, the rest of our trade items. But what everyone coveted was my small selection of photographs. These were snapshots of our families taken in and outside our Canadian home. It was nine months since we'd left there, and I found myself looking with almost as much wonder as the villagers at our house built of wood and glass, at our garden under snow. The most popular snapshot was one of my mother, taken when she had visited us from England the previous summer. She's standing outside in bright sunshine, and the picture is overexposed so that her grey hair and her skin look pure white.

'Beautiful!' cried the villagers. 'She is *soooo* beautiful!' They wanted to know everything about her: her age, how many living children and grandchildren she had. The news that my father had died two years before was greeted with much sympathetic clucking and cooing. When I told them she was a Roman Catholic, there was an eruption of joy. 'So you are Catholic too!' cried Petros, the lay priest.

'Well, no—' I began.

'Of course! You must come to see our church!' He led us to the top of the village, beyond the fields of groundnut and cassava and through a patch of head-high elephant grass. The church was a sad little building, with brick walls, an iron roof and a mud floor. Inside were several rough wooden benches, shiny from use, which faced a pulpit .

'The white missionaries used to come from Rumphi every month to consecrate the hosts, say Mass and hear confessions,' Petros told us. 'They would take a bus to Mlowe and then walk for five hours on the path. They were old men but strong, and they spoke better Chitumbuka than me. But now they are gone and we have African priests – men of my own blood! – and they are ignoring us. They will not walk here, they will only come by motor boat, and they say it is too expensive so they rarely come.'

We gave Petros a donation towards the upkeep of the church. 'God bless you for your generosity,' he said. 'I must record your gift.'

He took out a small book, in which the total of each Sunday's collection was recorded.

'Look at the past month,' he said. 'See how hard life is getting.' I peered at the list, neatly written in pencil.

	Kwatcha	Tambala
Week 1	1	20
Week 2	–	90
Week 3	–	84
Week 4	–	57

'Where does this money go to?' I asked.

'To the bishop. He says it is needed for parish work. So we are alone.'

I stopped him from recording our donation. 'Keep it for your own church,' I urged.

He pursed his lips, and shut the book.

'For your kindness I will bring some children to sing for you. I would like you to hear the full choir, how their voices work with the drums, but they are all in the fields.' The solemn little boys who filed into the church had an assortment of home-made instruments: goat-skin drums, rattles made of sticks and bottle tops, tin cans filled with dried beans. They sat in two rows, and played and sang in perfect harmony, their voices soft and reson-ating. As I listened, I kept thinking of their parents, scratching out an existence, and struggling each week to find a few pennies for the collection. When the children finished, Dag and I applauded them, and they beamed from ear to ear. As we were leaving the church, I was struck by a sudden thought.

'Was the bishops' pastoral letter read out here?' I asked Petros.

He pretended not to have heard. 'Please come back,' he said, 'with a machine to record the singing.'

No one in Chisanga wanted to discuss politics. Once, I teas-ingly asked Gift if he would like to be president of the country. 'His Excellency Gift!' I joked, and he looked nervously around to check that no one had heard. But under cover of darkness, he and his friends crept down to our tent to listen with us to the

BBC. There were no reports on Malawi. We heard instead that the Communist government in Afghanistan had fallen, that there was escalating violence in Serbia, that a man in California had been executed in the electric chair.

'Aaaaah,' said the boys as they listened. 'Oooooh.'

The news ended with a report on an AIDS benefit concert in London. There was a short blast of raucous music, and the boys began wriggling about in excitement. '*Mzungu* music!'

The lead singer of one of the bands was interviewed, and I wondered how many people like me were in remote corners of the world, listening to a crackling radio transmission of this young man saying, 'We're, like, the new spirit of youth, you know. We've got a new and fresh vibe, like, you know . . .'

On our last morning in Chisanga, Gift brought us two freshly laid eggs. 'So you will remember me,' he said.

While the eggs crackled in the pan, he and his friends plied us with questions. 'What foods do you grow in your village? Do you grow cassava?'

We described the cash economy, and how most people worked away from their houses and bought their food in stores. They quickly grasped these concepts, but the idea of unemployment benefits stumped them. 'Why do the families not help these people?' asked Gift.

'It's not our tradition,' we replied.

'I know about houses in Canada,' he boasted. 'Some are made from snow and ice, others from wood and insulation.'

'How do you know this?'

'I learned it at school. I learned too about your deciduous trees, and your cod and salmon fish.'

Gift was the only one of his friends who had managed to win a place at one of Malawi's handful of secondary schools. The Easter holidays were nearly over, and soon he would leave his friends in the village and return to the boarding school in Mzuzu.

'When you graduate,' I asked him, 'what will you do?'

He shrugged. 'What can I do? There are no jobs in Malawi. There is only fishing and farming.'

Fishing and farming – and, of course, foreign aid, huge amounts of it, as pay-offs for Banda's pro-Western foreign policy. There was evidence of such aid, and its non-existent impact on the lives of most Malawians, at Chilumba, a day's sail from

Chisanga. We travelled there fast, watching the coastline slip by, seeing headlands appear in the distance, enjoying the sense of our journey spreading out behind us and unrolling before us. The coastal plain widened and a road appeared, with the deep ravines of the Nyika Plateau towering above it. Towards late afternoon we sailed across Young's Bay to Luloma Peninsula. We were back in hippo country, with reeds growing from shallow water. But there were some rocky coves too, and it was from one of these that a young man beckoned us ashore. Behind him, on the beach, were two small straw huts. 'My father lives here' he said. 'I will bring him to you,' and he ducked into one of the low doorways.

After ten minutes of muttering from inside, the father emerged. He was a sombre man wearing a broad-brimmed straw hat. Behind him were his two wives, one his own age and one who looked young enough to be his daughter, dressed identically in blue cotton dresses and turbans. 'They are late because they put on fine clothes to meet you,' said McClean, the young man.

The older couple promptly returned to their house. McClean helped Dag to erect our tent, while the young wife sat with me. Thick, curly black hairs grew from her chin and I had to force myself not to stare at them as she talked. 'He is my second husband,' she said, nodding her head towards the house. I have five children by my first husband.'

'Five! How old are you?'

She shrugged. 'I can't remember.'

'What is his other wife's name?'

'I do not know. She is my sister.'

'Your sister?'

'Not my real sister. My friend sister. Our husband is ill. He is bewitched. He is trying to get well.'

Twilight closed in and she hurried back to her house before I could get clarification on these puzzling revelations. McClean also left us, saying that he lived somewhere else and would come back in the morning.

We awoke to the sounds of pestles thumping into mortars as women began pounding cassava, and paddles clacking on dugouts as fishermen signalled they were coming in with a catch. Outside our tent, McClean was sitting with a fish he had brought us for breakfast. With his clear, steady gaze, he watched Dag clean and cook it. 'I would like to try *mzungu* food,' he said, after the three of us had shared the fish.

Dag made some pancakes, and spread them with jam.

'Very good,' was McClean's verdict. 'But I feel sad for you *mzungu* because your food costs so much. We Malawians like cassava food, and it is easy to grow.'

He invited us to walk with him to the town of Chilumba, on the other side of the peninsula.

'It will take forty-five minutes,' he said. 'And there I will show you something wonderful indeed.'

After walking for ten minutes, we stopped by a large house with a tin roof. Next to it, an elderly man sat on a folding wooden chair beneath a shady tree. He was reading from a battered English history textbook about the spread of the British Empire. He wore a tattered cloth cap, and ripped shorts and shirt. 'This is my father,' said McClean, and disappeared inside the house.

The old man told us that he was a retired doctor.

'I do not like African medicine,' he said. 'It cannot be measured. White man's medicine has fine measurement, so I trust it. Some doctors also study African medicine but it is dangerous. To practise you must take on a spirit and I only took on the Christian spirit.'

McClean emerged from the house wearing white jeans, a zippered cream jacket and red flip-flops.

'*Very* smart!' I cried, and he covered his pleasure with a show of embarrassment.

As we carried on towards the town, we asked him about the man outside the house.

'He is my real father. The one on the beach is his brother.'

'Your uncle?'

'No, my father's sister is my aunt but the brother is my father.'

We shook our heads in confusion, but McClean carried on apace. 'Oh, I have many problems with these fathers. My father on the beach, he bewitched me with bad meat when I was a child. I was sick and grew too thin. We tried to chase him out of the house in the rains; there was a court judgement and we were forced to live with him. Then my father the doctor was bewitched and became malicious and had to retire. My mother left him and we built her a house. Because of all these problems I have not finished my schooling. If I had finished secondary school I would not be here now, I would be in the city or overseas. But soon I will take a wife to help me. She will take over my household duties, and I will return to my schooling.'

We had reached the house of his mother. She was sitting in the shade of the veranda next to a roguish looking character whose left hand and lower arm were amputated. As we approached, he stuck the stump into his trouser pocket.

'She is the mother who bore me ' said McClean. 'And he is my brother.'

'Is she his mother, too?'

'No, that is the wife of her brother.'

'Your aunt?'

'No, my mother.'

At the top of the hill was Chilumba Elementary School. It was break time, and we were swamped by excited children. They all wore blue and white uniforms, and carried exercise books and pencils in home-made plastic bags.

'Four times twelve?' McClean barked at them. 'Six times eight? Nine times seven?' and they chorused the correct answers. Their classrooms had tin roofs and dirt floors, and only the pupils of the top class sat at desks. Here, the questions from the last lesson were still on the blackboard:

HEALTH EDUCATION

1 Name two types of pit latrine
2 Give three reasons why people drink beer
3 State two ways in which river water can be made safe for drinking
4 Mention two types of heat exhaustion
5 Name the type of bacteria which cause the following diseases: a) syphilis
                  b) pneumonia
                  c) TB
6 Give two ways that you can treat a person with hysteria

'I'd fail Form Five,' I told McClean.

'*No!*' he cried, seeming genuinely shocked. 'You white people are wonderful. I do not understand all this knowledge that you have. Now I will show you the beautiful thing that white men have done!'

We dropped steeply down the far side of the peninsular. The rocky red path became a tarred road, which led to the source of McClean's awe. 'The *jetty*,' he announced, in hushed tones.

Along tracks on a new wharf was a massive structure of blue steel, all cogs and wheels and pulleys, a high-technology contraption for loading and off-loading container ships. Denis Tweddle had told us about Chilumba's container port. It had been built with European aid, by European contractors using European-made machinery. And it had never been used. In Monkey Bay, the container ship that went with it had lain idle, at anchor, for the past two years.

We carried on past the jetty and into the town, which was the usual depressing collection of dingy stores and food stalls along a dirt street. One of the stalls had a fridge, which didn't work, full of Coca-Cola. We bought three bottles and sat in the shade of a tree with McClean to drink it. 'You white people are wonderful, being able to build such things,' he said. 'This jetty will make Chilumba a very important place.'

We didn't tell him about the aid project to upgrade the road running from the Tanzanian border to the south of Malawi: a project that would render obsolete Chilumba's container port.

24

The Ants' Revenge

After weeks of basic camping, our room in Karonga's government rest house seemed full of wonder. I flicked a switch and a light came on in the ceiling. I turned a tap and hot water – albeit murky brown – flowed out. There were glass windows, a large mirror, a wardrobe with clothes hangers, a chair to sit on. We'd reached the end of our journey up the lake; we were back in the world of modern conveniences. That night, we wouldn't have to crouch over the camp stove and wash pots in the lake. We wouldn't have to eat fish or rice or *nsima*. We'd find a decent restaurant – Karonga was a fair-sized town by Malawian standards, there must be one about – and treat ourselves to a slap-up meal.

We seemed to be in luck. Not far from the rest house was a small resort called Club Marina. A couple of jeeps were parked outside it, and blinking coloured lights were strung around the entrance to the bar. But these were not the auspicious signs we'd hoped them to be. Even though it was past sundown, the tin roof radiated the heat of the day. Fuzzy reggae music played from a radio. A white couple threw darts. Several drunken and noisy Malawians played cards. A prostitute was asleep with her head on the table, and the girl next to her stared sullenly at Dag. After the first rush of alcohol-induced euphoria subsided, it was a scene that quickly depressed us.

The Club Marina restaurant did little to improve matters. Its tables were set with dark brown cloths and custard-yellow napkins. Ours had a centrepiece of several ketchup jars swarming with ants. Although, or perhaps because there were no other guests in the restaurant, our arrival seemed to infuriate the waiter. With bad grace he thrust menus at us. Hopefully, we scanned them.

> Nsima with fish
> Rice with fish
> Nsima with meat
> Rice with meat

Hope, fast ebbing away, was revived by the last line:

> Home made lasagne with pumpkin leaves

When we ordered this, the waiter frowned. 'It will take a long time because it is so cold,' he growled, and stalked off.

'He must mean it's in the freezer,' said Dag optimistically. For half an hour we listened to a symphony of crashes, bangs and oaths from the kitchen. We passed the time by killing the ants on the sauce bottles, heaping up the bodies and tallying our scores. Finally, the waiter kicked open the door from the kitchen, marched into the dining-room and set two plates of food before us. We stared in disbelief at what he'd brought. Lying on beds of stewed pumpkin leaves were what looked like pieces of charred wood. I rapped mine with a fork. The fork bounced off it, making a dull sound.

'We can't eat this,' I told the waiter.

'It is home-made,' he challenged me.

'I don't care. It's burnt.'

He grabbed the plates. 'We have meat, rice and *nsima*,' he said. 'So what do you want?'

After a terrible meal washed down by warm beer, we returned to the rest house. In its small courtyard, the nightwatchman was lying fast asleep against our kayak. His snores reverberated through the thin walls of our room, and the harsh light from a streetlamp flooded through the gap between our ill-fitting curtains. But the mosquito screens were effective, and the bed comfortable enough, and we managed to sleep for a couple of hours – until the friends and relations of the ants we'd murdered in the restaurant arrived to exact their revenge. They attacked on several fronts; we woke covered with ants. Flicking on the light, we discovered a multi-lane ant highway that stretched from beneath the door, over to bed, up the legs, and then fanned out to cover the mattress and the pillows. We shook the sheets, sprayed insect repellent about, stamped on the ground, but all to no avail, as reinforcements constantly arrived. There was only one thing to be done. Pushing aside the bed, we erected our tent in the middle of the room. As we lay inside it, hot and disgruntled, we remembered the warm winds and the insurpassable night skies of all our beach campsites, and wondered why we'd ever left them.

The people we'd met in the villages along the lake longed for what we took for granted. Most of them had never been in a car or seen television. It was unlikely that they would ever fly in an aeroplane or enjoy the comforts of running water and electricity. Lilongwe, the capital city, was to them a distant dream, a place where a new life was possible. Yet we dreaded returning there, and then having to go on to the hustle and bustle of Europe. We dreaded it so much that halfway through the three-day ferry trip from Karonga back down the lake, we disembarked at the tiny island of Likomo. The city and our flight to Germany, we decided, could wait.

The *Mtendere* was a singularly unpleasant ferry. It had only two classes, third and second. Third-class passengers spent the entire trip down in the bowels of the boat. The second-class deck was a cramped area, cluttered with lifeboats, wooden benches and our kayak. Smoke, soot and cinders constantly showered down from the funnels, piped music and bright lights were on day and night, and the smells drifting up from the toilets, just off the second-class lounge, were unspeakable. Venturing into these toilets required a strong stomach. Large shiny cockroaches sat smugly on the filthy seats; grey water with unpleasant bits and pieces floating in it sloshed about the floor. Things were marginally better in the small cafeteria, where a cheerful young Malawian with a fang-toothed grin served tea, coffee and meals. When we embarked, he had *nsima* and boiled fish, or eggs and chips to offer. Within a few hours, the *mzungu* on board had exhausted his supply of eggs and chips. In Karonga, I'd vowed never again to eat *nsima*; on the *Mtendere* I had no choice.

Most of the second-class passengers were unemployed university graduates from Britain and Australia. They were a genial bunch, in their twenties, 'doing' Africa over land. The women wore hiking boots and wraparound skirts, usually lengths of cloth they had bought on their way through Tanzania. The men's hair was cut above their ears – mandatory for getting into Malawi. They sprawled against their good-quality, well-worn backpacks, listening to Walkmans and reading. I was impressed by the reading material of the British travellers: books by Henry James, Robertson Davies, Ben Okri. The Australians favoured James Mitchener, Joseph Heller and John Irving. None of them seemed interested in Lake Malawi, and they hardly ever looked up to see the coastline slipping by. But Dag and I were agog. We'd spent five weeks kayaking up the lake, now we were steaming back down it in three days. Excitedly, we pointed out to each other headlands and coves we recognized, beaches and villages where we'd spent days and nights. Both of us were already nostalgic about the journey.

'It's too bad,' said Dag, 'that we can only do something for first time once.'

On the first evening we anchored for several hours at Chilumba Jetty, and on the second at Nhkata Bay. On both occasions, the *Mtendere* was turned into a nightclub for well-to-do Malawians. They streamed on to the deck, where beer was for sale, dressed in their finery. The men wore polished shoes, suits and large wristwatches, the women had straightened hair and were bedecked in bright dresses, high heels and make-up. Ignoring us tourists, and the third-class passengers who had sneaked upstairs to see the spectacle, they smoked, drank, flirted and danced to the piped music. As the evening wore on, we bedded down on the deck, and the party continued around us. Empty beer bottles rolled past our sleeping bag, cigarettes were stubbed out close to our heads and once I was stepped on by a woman in stilettos.

At six in the morning, the *Mtendere* anchored off Likomo Island, and our kayak was lowered over the side. It would be several days before another southbound ferry stopped again at Likomo. For once, we weren't going anywhere, we had no final destination pulling us on; and so it was with a wonderful sense of aimlessness that we paddled off towards the tiny island.

25

Wizards and a Witchdoctor

Mtembo came to our tent with three small fish that he'd caught in the lake. After frying them in a little oil and salt over our camp stove, we carefully picked through the bones for shreds of flesh while Mtembo chewed on the heads. The day before, when he'd invited us to camp on the beach near his village, he had been garrulous and cheerful. He'd drawn a map of the world in the sand, and asked us to mark the route of our journey on it. 'You do not go to South America?' he'd asked, and then proceeded to correctly name every country in that continent, and every capital city.

'Most North Americans couldn't do that,' I'd told him.

'Sure? I don't believe you!' he'd replied.

This morning, however, he was silent and brooding. I asked him if he had something on his mind. Closing his lips over his protruding teeth, he stared up into the branches of the mango tree we sat beneath. When he spoke again, it was with a forced air of indifference.

'People in the village have asked me about you. They say, Mtembo spent time with the *mzungu*, so he must know what it is they wear on their wrists.'

His gaze shifted to the strings that had been tied on to our wrists during *pujas* along the Ganges. 'African doctors wear beads on their wrists. I told the people in my village that Dag is an animal doctor. When the people saw you swimming there yesterday, they thought you had power over the crocodile.'

Dag and I exchanged a look. 'Swimming where?' we asked. Mtembo pointed to an uninhabited offshore islet, which was little more than a rocky outcrop, with a few trees clinging to it. The previous afternoon we had paddled out to it so that we could have a thorough wash in privacy.

'Two years ago, a *mzungu* went there in one of our canoes. He swam, like you, and a crocodile took him.'

Silently, we pondered this information. A yellow and blue striped lizard scuttled across my feet. Fifty feet away, small boys frolicked in the water, their black skins slick and gleaming in the sunlight.

'Early this morning,' Mtembo continued, 'an old woman went to the lake, near where the river flows into it. While she was washing, a crocodile took her.'

'This morning!' I gasped.

'Her grandchild was with her. He screamed and ran away. It's the same crocodile who took the *mzungu*.'

Dag gave a low whistle. 'How do you know it's the same crocodile?'

'It is a wizard in disguise. Every year he takes someone. The hunters cannot kill him. He will not die! Now, the people say our African doctor must sniff out the wizard and take away his power.'

'How will he do this?' asked Dag.

'I do not know, it is a secret.'

'Could we meet this doctor?'

Mtembo stared up into the branches. 'The people ask about the *mzungu* who is a doctor and who wears a strange bracelet . . .' His voice trailed off.

'We wear the bracelets only as mementos of our time in India,' said Dag. 'They have nothing to do with magic.'

This wasn't quite true – they'd been tied on as symbols of safe-keeping, and we were too superstitious to remove them. But it satisfied Mtembo. His lips slid back over his teeth and stretched into a wide smile. 'I will tell the people,' he said.

From Likomo Island, it was only a few miles across the lake to Mozambique. We'd originally planned to paddle there for the day, and return before nightfall. We'd met fishermen from Mozambique who regularly crossed to and fro in their dhows, and who assured us we would be welcome. But the headman of Mtembo's village had been adamant that we should not go. 'Listen to that shore,' he'd said, 'and you will understand.'

By day, we heard the crack of gunfire; at night, ominous drumming drifted across the water. Changing our plans, we decided instead to paddle a couple of miles north along Likomo to a beach where Mtembo had told us some *mzungu* were camped. 'All your friends go to that place,' he had said. 'They never come as far as here.'

A handful of tents were pitched amid a ring of giant baobab trees. On a boulder at the water's edge, a sign was painted in large white letters: PLEASE DO NOT USE THIS ROCK AS A TOILET. We pulled the kayak up the beach and walked over to the tents. Several people lay around on the sand, dozing or reading. A girl in a brief bikini looked up, regarded us for a second or two, and then returned to her book. 'Did a ferry just come in?' called out one of the men I had taken to be asleep.

'No,' I said.

He sat up and rubbed his eyes. 'I didn't think there was one due today. Where's your accent from?'

'Manchester.'

'I'm from Lowestoft. The name's Chris. Come and sit down.'

He was fairly tidy, but the man lying next to him looked as if he hadn't changed his clothes for several weeks. His hair stuck out like straw, and he snored through an unruly beard and moustache. A pair of spectacles lay on his chest. When Chris nudged him with a toe he growled, 'Fuck off,' without opening his eyes.

'Wake up, Grant,' Chris persisted. 'We've got company.'

Grant lifted his head, stuck the greasy spectacles on to his nose and squinted at us through them. 'When did the ferry get in?' he asked.

'It didn't,' I repeated. 'We came by kayak.'

'Huh.' He turned to Chris. 'What's for lunch old boy?'

'I just bought a fish from a kid. He's cleaning it for me and bringing it back. I'll fry it up. How much meths is left?'

'Two nips, about.'

'Spoken like a true degenerate.'

'Thanks, old boy.'

With that, Grant took off his glasses, laid them on his chest and went back to sleep.

'Have you heard anything new about what's happening in Malawi?' Dag asked Chris.

'Is something happening?'

'Well, you know, the bishops' pastoral letter, the riots, Chihana's arrest . . .'

'Oh, that,' said Chris. 'No idea. Someone told me that the Tories got re-elected in Britain, though.' He reached for a plastic bag. 'Fancy smoking some Malawi Gold?' he asked, as politely as if he was offering us a pot of Earl Grey tea.

'It's a bit early,' Dag declined. 'If we had some now we wouldn't get any further today than this beach.'

Chris sighed. 'I know what you mean. Me and Grant have been here for almost a month. Twice a week the ferry comes and every time we say, right, we'll pack up and catch this one, but we never manage it. We smoke a joint first thing in the morning and that's that. This is a bloody inconvenient place, as well. It's a forty-five minute walk to the town. Mind you, we're training the local kids. They go and do our shopping for us. We only have to pay them a few tambala. Some other people have had their money ripped off, but we've been lucky so far.'

Another man walked over to join us, and Chris made the introductions. Matt looked as if he had just stepped off a surfboard. He was blond, blue-eyed and suntanned, and spoke with a broad Australian accent.

'Haven't seen you around much the last two days,' remarked Chris.

'Been shitting myself silly, that's why,' explained Matt. 'I had a meal in that place near where the ferry comes in. Chicken and chips. Tasted all right, but it made me sick as a dog.'

'Did you take anything for it?' asked Dag.

'No, I don't believe in that stuff. Messes up your system.'

Chris, who was rolling up some Malawi Gold in a cigarette paper, vehemently agreed. 'I won't even touch aspirin,' he said. 'Pills are no good for you.' He lit the joint, inhaled deeply and passed it to Matt.

Within minutes, they were flat on their backs, keeping Grant company.

We paddled back to find Mtembo waiting for us by our tent. 'I told the people about your bracelets,' he said. 'And now I take you to meet the doctor.'

On the path that led up from the village, we passed women carrying water from the lake in metal buckets balanced on their heads. 'Come to my house,' one called to us.

Inside there was no furniture, only a couple of mats thrown over the cracked cement floor, a sack of maize flour and some hoes leaning against one wall. In a corner, a baby boy lay peacefully sleeping on a pile of rags. Flies crawled over his face, and chickens pecked at the ground around him. We sat on one of the mats, and the woman brought us tea in plastic cups.

'She is one of my uncle's wives,' said Mtembo. 'She lives here alone.'

'Your youngest?' I asked the woman, pointing to the baby. She nodded. A little boy had come in, and was clinging to her and staring fearfully at us. His bottom showed through a pair of ripped blue shorts which smelt powerfully of ammonia. The woman lifted him up and wiped the snot from around his nose. '*Mzungu!*' she whispered to him, but he hid his face against her breasts.

Outside the hut, a teenage girl swept the red dirt into regular striated patterns with a large palm leaf. 'My daughter,' said the woman.

'Does she go to school?' I asked.

'Class Three,' she replied, staring levelly at me. 'But she has no book. We have no money.'

I offered to buy her a book.

'No book in store,' the woman flatly informed me.

'It's true,' said Mtembo. 'For weeks now we are waiting for them to come. She cannot go to school without a book to write in.'

'Tomorrow you give me flour?' the woman asked. 'And soap? I have no soap to wash the clothes. And aspirin? I have much pain.'

We hiked for an hour across the low-lying, arid island. The path wound around gum trees and through flash-flood gullies. Reassured about our lack of magical powers, Mtembo was garrulous once more. 'This doctor is a famous man. The most famous African doctor in Malawi. He has much power. A man stole a bag from my house. I asked the doctor who the thief was and he told me. I went to the thief's garden and found him working there and he was so afraid! He gave me back the bag. Now, I have chosen a woman, and I will ask the doctor if she will be a good wife.'

'If he says yes, what then?' I asked.

'Then my friend will go to her father. They will kill a chicken and eat it together. The father will ask two hundred kwatcha for his daughter. My friend will offer one hundred and twenty. They will settle on this, because that is all she is worth.'

'What if she doesn't like you?'

'Oh yes, she likes. We met and talked.'

'Why do some men have more than one wife?'

'Sometimes a man has as many as five! But they do not live altogether. He has one here, one there. He has them for children. And for relaxing.'

'Relaxing?'

'The man goes to one of his wives, relaxes, and has another child.'

'How does he support them all?'

'The wives work in the fields for him. Then he gets his children, and later they look after him,' explained Mtembo. 'It is a good system.'

The path dropped down and the lake came back into view. By a large garden planted with cassava, Mtembo stopped abruptly. 'Soon we will come to the Misozi Hospital,' he said. 'You must behave in the correct way. First, each of you go into this garden and pick up a cassava stick in your left hand.' He watched carefully as we followed this instruction. 'When we reach the hospital, walk through the grounds with the stick. Do not look backwards as you go – this would be very unlucky. You will come to a tree where a boy stands. Give the stick to the boy. Return to the hospital the way you came. Do not look back!'

A split bamboo fence surrounded a compound of mud and thatch huts. Covering the doorways and windows of the huts were lengths of white cloth painted with red crosses; a few of these were pulled aside and we could see patients lying on mats spread over the dirt floors. Outside, on porches shaded by overhanging thatch, men and women sat and watched silently as we passed by. Chickens ran around between the huts, and mangy dogs scratched themselves. Mtembo led us through the hospital compound and out the far side, to a roped-off mango tree. At its base lay piles of cassava sticks, and watching over these was a small boy in ragged shorts. His eyes widened in alarm as we approached. Mtembo muttered something to him; reluctantly, he took our offerings and dropped them on one of the piles.

'Remember,' Mtembo warned us. 'Do not look back.'

In the heart of the compound was a long, rectangular house. From within it came a deep, oratorial voice, punctuated by soft, choral responses. 'It's Dr Kumpulota,' whispered Mtembo. 'He is speaking to his patients.'

He ushered us inside. At the far end of a bare room there were a lectern, a drum, an altar with a crucifix and, hanging on the wall above it, two photographs of President Banda. About thirty people sat on the dirt floor. Addressing them was a wiry man dressed in a white shirt and patched cotton trousers. He was leaning forward on the balls of his feet, like a cat about to spring. When we appeared in the room, he snapped his fingers at a man sitting close to him. A mat was brought in and spread out against the wall near the altar.

'We must go and sit there,' said Mtembo.

'I'd rather stay at the back,' I whispered.

But Dag was already nudging me forwards, and the doctor was pointing firmly at the mat.

A woman shuffled on her knees to the doctor. He handed her the Bible from the lectern, and she stood up and began to read from it. With one skinny hip stuck out, her head lolling and her back curved, her posture was one of submission and defeat.

'She is one of the doctor's wives,' Mtembo whispered.

'How many has he got?' I asked.

'At least three.'

She paused repeatedly to allow the doctor to elaborate on the text. He rocked to and fro, scanning the crowd with his fierce gaze and filling the room with his voice. His wife finished the reading, closed the Bible, and shuffled backwards on her knees to her place. The doctor grabbed a drum, held it between his knees and began beating on it and singing in a full-throated voice. The crowd joined in with him.

'He says they must open up the lungs,' said Mtembo, 'because it is good medicine.'

The singing grew louder and more insistent. Straddling the drum, the doctor hopped up and down the centre of the room, leading the people to a fervent crescendo, then gradually bringing them down again. Later, Dag told me he'd sensed an energy in the room that caused the hair on his neck to prickle. But I felt nothing – a fact not missed by the perceptive and charismatic doctor.

Putting the drum aside, he came over to us and sat down in a businesslike way. His patients clustered around, and small children reached out to pat my skin while the doctor spoke in rapid Chichewa. 'I welcome you white people,' Mtembo translated. 'As you can see, I am not a rich man. I ask no one for money. I live to serve and heal. Eighteen years ago, when my mother died, I became sick and crazed. I walked around the hills naked. I didn't eat. Then my mother's spirit came to me in my dreams. She told me to heal people. She taught me which herbs to use. She instructed me to take up this life.'

His bottom lip wobbled and fat tears began rolling down his cheeks. 'I cry because I see the spirit of my mother. When I heal, her spirit guides me. Because of her, I live like this, on dirt floors and beneath straw roofs. I could be rich, with cement floors and tin roofs, but I do not charge for this work.'

He pulled out a handkerchief and wiped away his tears.

'He wants to know if you have any questions,' said Mtembo.

Dag asked about the types of ailments he treated, and the medicines he used. Plunging into the crowd, the doctor yanked a young man to his feet. His ankles were bound with twine and he stood motionless, staring blankly ahead.

'He is suffering from madness,' Mtembo translated. 'He has been bewitched. He came here bound by the hands as well as the feet, snarling and biting like a dog. Now he is calmer.' The doctor pointed to a row of raised scars across the man's forehead. He had made these incisions with a knife, then rubbed into them a paste of ground up roots and water. A bowl of the paste was brought for Dag's inspection. It was thick and dark red, like henna.

'I also mixed it into his food,' said the doctor. 'Soon, we will be able to untie his feet. He will start to speak again.'

Next, a young girl was brought forward. She was about eight years old and one of her legs was plastered with a red mud that looked very similar to the one used to cure the previous patient's madness.

'Her leg was swollen,' said Mtembo. 'The white doctors could not help her so her parents brought her here. After a week of treatment, a magic bone began to come out of her leg. It stuck out right through her skin, here, where there is a scar!'

Mtembo poked at the girl's leg. She cringed, and her eyes filled with tears, but she made no sound. Someone pushed a rag into the doctor's hands. Carefully unwrapping it, he held out the contents for our inspection. It was a bone, about eight inches long, rotting away at either end. Dag picked it up.

'Is this the bone that came out of her leg?'

'Yes!' cried Mtembo. 'I saw it with my own eyes! A wizard put it there! Someone who was jealous of her family paid him to bewitch her.'

'It could be a fibula,' said Dag, 'and it's the right size for a child.'

He leaned forward and gently examined the girl's leg. 'The wound is badly infected. That's why she's in so much pain.'

'Are all her bones there?' I asked him.

'Of course they are.'

I turned to Mtembo. 'How many of the patients here are bewitched?'

'Ninety per cent.'

'Must they believe in magic for the medicines to work?'

'No. They must believe in God and the power of prayer.'

The doctor was now treating a small boy whose legs were covered in suppurating insect bites. With cotton wool soaked in water, he rubbed the scab off each bite and smeared it with red paste. I thought of the infected bite on my foot, for which I'd just started a course of antibiotics. And I remembered an Austrian we had met who was the first qualified doctor for fifteen years at Nkhotakota Hospital. He had no X-ray unit, a frighteningly short supply of drugs, and five patients to each available bed. He had told us of patients who were stricken with mysterious symptoms and ailments that would not respond to Western medicine. These patients he referred to William Kumpulota on Likomo Island.

In other countries and cultures, I'd been able to temporarily suspend all the carefully constructed rationales that I had brought with me from the West. I'd witnessed devils being cast out; I'd accepted that a river could be a goddess. But I couldn't reconcile myself to this belief in bewitchment, and the burdens of fear and suspicion it brought to a people already so weighed down by poverty and repression. Suddenly, the doctor jumped to his feet and began shouting. Mtembo's eyes widened as he translated.

'There is someone here who says she has no more questions but she is not speaking the truth. She does not accept, she does not understand our African medicine!'

The doctor sat down again, breathing heavily and glaring at me. Now I did feel the hair on my neck prickle.

'He wants you to ask more questions,' said Mtembo, a little nervously.

I decided to keep my mouth shut.

'What about the crocodile?' asked Dag. 'How will you sniff him out?'

'The doctor rolled his eyes. 'I have a magic stick. When I point it at the wizard it will reveal him. Then he must surrender himself, he must give up all his medicines and he must renounce Satan. If he refuses, he will die! Immediately! All the wizards are in fear of me. I have a room full of their evil potions. I can destroy them with lightning bolts!'

'I have seen him make lightning,' Mtembo excitedly added. 'It filled the sky, it hit a baobab tree and made it fall down.'

Without warning, the doctor flounced out of the room, followed by his patients.

'He says we must go now,' said Mtembo. 'But first he wants me to show you the donation box.'

We returned to the beach by a different route, which took us past St Peter's Church. This huge structure, styled on an English cathedral, was built in 1902 on the site where witches used to be burned. Rat droppings surrounded the baptismal font, the parquet floor of the chancel was cracked and buckling, and the stained glass windows showed the ravages of a terrible storm which had hit the island two years previously. The Dean came out to meet us. He was a dapper, earnest man. 'This was once a place of punishment, now it is a place of salvation,' he said, obviously repeating a well-rehearsed line.

Proudly, he showed us the vestry furniture that came from England, the signed photograph of the Archbishop of Canterbury, the cross that was sent by the people of Oberammergau. We sat with him on a sturdy wooden pew with a sign in red paint announcing that it was 'In Memory Of Chief Mkumpha (1)'. We told him that we'd just been to the Misozi Hospital.

'Did you meet Mr Kumpulota? He is a good man! And a brave

man! He has been imprisoned many times by the government.'

'Does the government want to stop his work?' I asked. The
Dean frowned, and shifted uneasily. 'I did not say that about the
government. But sometimes people get jealous, they make accu-
sations, they say he is causing death, so the government must
act. This is why the doctor must be brave. Now, the government
says he must move to Mzuzu because so many people there are
bewitched.'

'Do witches still exist?' I asked him.

'Oh yes,' he said. 'Satan is not yet defeated.'

Just beyond St Peter's Church there was a stretch of tarred
road and a 'Give Way' sign.

'How many cars are there on Likomo?' I asked Mtembo.

'No cars,' he replied.

'So why the sign?'

Furtively, he looked around and lowered his voice. 'It was put
there for Banda's visit in 1987. The government brought fifty
cars to the island, they built this road, they put up the sign. We all
had to be at the airstrip to welcome Banda, and people were
forced to come from Nhkata Bay to make the crowds bigger.
Thirteen planes flew in. The cars drove from the airstrip to the
church and back again. Then the planes left again, and the cars
were taken away by ship. Everyone on the island had to pay one
kwatcha each towards the cost of the visit. People with many children had no money left for food or school fees or clothes.' He
brought his voice right down to a whisper. 'It is only some of the
women who support Banda. All the men are against him, they
want multi-party democracy.'

It was mid-afternoon when we got back to our campsite, and a
storm was blowing in. The sky was slate-grey, the hills of
Mozambique a vibrant green, and wind scoured the surface of
the lake. Fishermen furiously paddled their dugouts to shore,
women gathered up their buckets of laundry and hurried past us
on their way back to the village. Lightning fizzed across the sky,
there was a loud thunderclap and rain hammered down.

'Let's wash the boat!' Dag cried.

We ran over to where it lay at the foot of a baobab tree, sprinkled it with laundry soap and scrubbed the *Mtendere* soot stains
off its deck. Soapsuds formed and washed away: we worked fast,
and we didn't notice Mtembo sitting by our tent beneath the

mango tree, worriedly sucking on his teeth. 'You know stories
about baobabs?' he asked, when we'd finished.

We had learned some along the way: that a solution made from
the seeds and the pith was used to treat fever and give protection
from crocodile attack, and that spirits are said to inhabit the trunk
and the flowers. Now, Mtembo had a new story for us. 'When
God planted the baobabs, he made a mistake and put them in the
earth upside down. So their branches look like roots and their
roots are small. That is why they often fall over in storms, particularly when the storm comes from an African doctor.'

I thought for a moment, while thunder rumbled across the sky.
'This storm came from Mozambique,' I told him.

'I go home now,' he said.

After dark, when the storm had passed, Mtembo returned to
our tent. 'We listen to the BBC?' he whispered.

From beneath his shirt he pulled out an ancient transistor
radio. The aerial was a long piece of wire, which he wrapped
around his head so that his tight curls held it firmly in place. 'We
must be careful,' he said. 'There are spies in the village.'

Huddling around the radio, we tuned in to the eight o'clock
world news. The measured tones of the announcer faded in and
out between layers of crackling and buzzing.

'Today in Malawi . . .' Excitedly, Mtembo and Dag pressed their
ears closely against the speaker, and Dag relayed the news to me.
'The government issued a statement to the world press. In it they
warned . . .'

Dag stopped, and his mouth fell open. Slowly, Mtembo lowered the radio from his ear, so that I could again hear the
announcer, who was now talking about South Africa.

'What did they warn?' I whispered.

'They must be kidding,' Dag said.

'They do worse things than that,' Mtembo told him. 'Terrible
things.'

'What did they say?'

'The people are much afraid,' Mtembo continued.

'*What!*'

'The government,' said Dag, 'announced that anyone else
caught attempting to oppose the one-party system will be . . .' he
paused, incredulously shaking his head, '. . . will be used as crocodile bait.'

*

Four days later we were back in Lilongwe. It was crawling with young men in green helmets. Chihana was still in prison, throughout the country there had been looting of Banda's PTC supermarkets, and in Blantyre police had shot forty people during a riot.

At the airport, porters hovered around us as we unloaded our baggage from the taxi. 'Sir, Madam, I'm broke, I'm hungry, I'm thirsty, let me carry.'

The two red bags were checked in, heaped on a trolley and wheeled away. We hurried through passport control, put our day sacks and camera gear through the X-ray machines, and walked through the metal detector without setting it off. Then a woman poked her head around the curtain of a tiny booth. 'Come in here please.'

I stepped inside. She sat on one side of a table, and motioned me to sit on the other side. 'Empty your bag,' she said.

I pulled out the sweater I'd brought to wear on the plane, the purse containing my documents, and my two thick notebooks. Notebooks full of two months of observations of the political situation in Malawi, with the names and addresses of everyone we'd befriended and enough of their dissident quotes to have them locked up indefinitely. My mouth went dry as the woman flicked through the pages of one of the books. Silently, I cursed myself for such mindless stupidity. I'd gone to ridiculous lengths to conceal my note-taking from prying eyes, only to let it come to this.

'What are these books?' asked the woman.

'My diaries,' I told her.

'About what?'

'My personal feelings.'

She put them down, and picked up my purse.

'It is not allowed to take kwatcha out of Malawi. Do you have any?'

'No.'

The hand went to the diaries again. She picked them up and put them back inside the bag. 'Where are you going?' she asked.

'Europe,' I replied.

'Ahhh,' she said softly. 'You are very lucky.'

We stood by the carousel of Munich's futuristic new airport, waiting for our baggage to appear. Around us people spoke German,

Italian, French. They were stylishly dressed in linen and fine cottons, and smelt of expensive perfumes and colognes. We were dressed in the clothes that a few days before I had washed in Lake Malawi and dried on a boulder. I began to wonder what we might smell of. The woman next to me was staring at my feet, one clad in a battered sandal, the other in a dirty sock covering the heavily bandaged tropical sore I'd brought with me from Africa. Her eyes ran up my body, met mine, and she started edging away. The carousel shuddered and began to move. First came leather suitcases, some with gilt initials and shiny locks. Then our red sacks appeared and slid down the shute. They looked more like punch bags than luggage. Aware of disparaging glances, we heaved them on to a trolley and wheeled it towards the Arrivals Lounge.

Behind sliding glass doors, our friends Olaf and Sabine stood clutching a bottle of champagne and scanning the crowd. I waved to them. I saw puzzlement, recognition and disbelief pass over their faces, and I realized that we'd been out in the bush for a little too long.

26

Portages and Pollution

The newly assembled kayak lay amid daffodils and daisies on the bank of the River Inn. Close by, beneath an old apple tree, five of us sprawled on the grass around a red picnic cloth. Dag, Olaf, Sabine and I had squeezed into Marcus's car along with the boat, baggage, two bikes, food and drink, and driven from Munich to Innsbruck. Dag and I were about to begin our 600-mile journey to Budapest along the Rivers Inn and Danube. Olaf, Sabine and Marcus were to accompany us by car and bike for the first four days. A champagne bottle popped.

'To old friends!'

'To new adventures!'

The toasts over, we began the serious business of the picnic. At first, I just sipped my wine, and watched the others reach for the food. Four kinds of cheeses, three different meats, salami, sausage, smoked salmon, pretzels, heavy bread, cream cheese, butter and fruit.

'Maria, I think that in Africa your appetite was stolen,' joked Olaf.

In a way he was quite right.

It was five days since we'd left Malawi and arrived in Germany. At first, we'd been shocked by the abundance and variety of food, by how clean and organized Munich seemed, and how privileged its inhabitants were. But we'd quickly begun to adapt. We'd gone to an expensive salon for haircuts, to a fashionable store for new clothes. We'd had afternoon coffee and cake at pavement cafés, and sat in beer gardens under the shade of flowering chestnut trees. And at our friends' apartment I'd washed up incessantly, struck by the novelty of hot water and suds, of being able to stand up and feel quite safe instead of crouching at the edge of a lake, worrying about crocodiles and hippos.

There was nothing to fear along the River Inn. After the harsh light and intense colours of Africa, we basked in the gentleness of a European spring. The sun was weak, the sky pale blue and the air smelled of newly mown grass. We heard the soft calls of thrushes, meadow larks and cuckoos. Twilight fell softly and slowly, and we could paddle until late into the evening. For those first four days, the Inn whisked us along beneath the gleaming snowcaps of the Austrian Alps, past fields with vine-covered barns, and horses that looked quizzically at us over hedges. We met up with our friends in villages where houses opened straight on to winding cobbled streets and flowers spilled out of window boxes. We sat outside pubs, drinking beer and eating bread, sausages and mustard. At night we camped in meadows of wild roses, poppies and irises. We walked barefoot on grass without worrying about poisonous snakes or centipedes.

The only obstacles along our way were the hydro-electric dams: sixteen of them between Innsbruck and Passau, where the River Inn joins the Danube, and twelve more along our route to Budapest. With Marcus's car and three extra pairs of hands, the first four dams were easily bypassed. But then our friends left us, returning to their jobs and apartments in the city, and we had about 500 miles and twenty-four more dams to negotiate alone.

We'd left the Alps behind, and on either side of the river were thick woods, with trees so full of leaves they formed a wall of gentle greenery. The sleepy villages we stopped at were unused to tourists.

'We're not really open,' a café-owner told us early one morning, 'but I'll serve you coffee as long as you don't sit outside and attract other customers.'

There was no other traffic on the river; we were alone, save for ducks, swans and their offspring.

'Stop paddling,' said Dag once. 'I want us to float towards these swans so I can get a shot of the cygnets.'

We were still thirty yards away when the male came at us, wings raised, neck back, head down and one foot extended behind him.

'Paddle slowly,' instructed Dag, twisting in his seat and clicking his camera. The swan came nearer, loudly hissing.

'OK, paddle fast!' shouted Dag.

Click click click went the camera – and the swan was in our wake, a yard behind the boat. Remembering stories about swans being able to break limbs and peck off fingers, I paddled as hard as I could.

'*Faster!*' yelled Dag, still clicking.

'*You paddle!*' I yelled back.

He did, and we pulled away from the swan. It flapped its wings so that it was slightly airborne and appeared to be running at us across the surface of the water.

'*Go back to your family!*' I screeched, waving my paddle in the air to fend it off. It paid no heed to me, and pursued us for almost a mile, right up to the next dam.

We worked out a system for portaging alone. We took the wide straps off the red sacks, looped them around our shoulders and under the kayak, and staggered the distance – usually 500 yards – around each dam. On some days there were three dams in our way; on others five. As well as carrying, this meant unpacking and repacking the boat, and carrying our baggage to and fro. My tiredness was compounded by hay fever – sometimes I sneezed so long and hard I couldn't paddle, and by another bladder infection.

By the time we reached the Simbach-Braunau dam, I was thoroughly wretched and unable to help Dag with the portage. Luck came in the form of a little shed containing three shiny, newly painted carts, left there specifically for transporting boats. The River Inn was the birthplace of kayaking in Europe, and before the dams were built it was a popular pastime. Although the carts and portage paths are little used these days, they are still maintained for tradition's sake. While Dag unpacked the boat I repeatedly nipped into the bushes, or sat miserably on the river bank, forcing down bottled water and dreaming of a comfortable bed and a bathroom. The dream came true far sooner than I expected. Within half an hour we'd passed the walled town of Braunau and were paddling along the bank of what looked like extensive parkland. We went ashore at a flower-filled meadow, ringed by trees. Peeking above these was part of a turreted roof.

'This could be someone's garden,' I said.

'No one will notice us here,' said Dag. 'Let's just set up the tent.'

But I didn't feel right about it – we'd never camped without permission in the Solomon Islands, India or Malawi, so why start here? Beyond the trees were long grasses, then a mown lawn leading up to a cobbled courtyard surrounded on three sides by high, ivy-covered walls, rows of arched windows, stables converted into living quarters and wooden gates big enough for horses and carriages to pass through.

'A *schloss*,' said Dag.

A castle – like the ones we'd seen from the river, and wondered who lived in them, and how they looked inside. Before we could creep away, a corgi raced out of one of the converted stables and began yapping around our ankles. It was called off by an elderly woman with cropped grey hair, who marched up to us with her hand outstretched. She wore army fatigue pants, a man's shirt, tweed jacket and boots, and was smoking a cigarette. She had a receding chin, sharp blue eyes and a bone-crushing handshake. She was, she told us, Baroness Colette von Handel, and Hagenau Castle was her ancestral home. We explained about our journey along the river and apologized for inadvertently stumbling into her courtyard.

'So, now you are you here, what do you want?' she demanded.

We asked if we could camp on her grounds. 'Of course! Where do you live? Canada? Do you know Vancouver Island?'

When we told her that we lived a mile and a half off its eastern shore, she was thrilled. 'It's my favourite place in the world! I know your little island; I've seen it from the ferry to Vancouver!'

She looked at me through narrowed eyes. 'You don't look well. Would you rather stay in a tent or a bed?' she asked.

I felt like kissing her feet.

'Bring your kayak round to the moat,' she told Dag. And to me: 'I will call my housekeeper, Anna, she will take you to your rooms.'

Anna led me to the guest suite in the fifteenth-century wing of Hagenau Castle. For three days I hardly budged from there. I lay in a large double bed, beneath an arched ceiling and a crystal chandelier. On the walls around me hung ink drawings of previous guests: Prince Maximus Schubatoff, Fred Wilhelm III, La

Comtess Guillaume de Wusttemburg, Erasmus Bernhard Reichsgraf von Derog. From time to time I'd get up and pad across the creaking parquet floor and the faded Persian silk rugs to the bathroom, where the pipes rattled and throbbed, and ivy clutched at the yellowed lace hanging over the open window. Or I'd wander into our drawing-room in the turret, where I could peer through the narrow windows and see our kayak floating in the still waters of the moat.

On our last evening in Hagenau Castle we were invited for supper with the Baroness. We followed Anna along a corridor stuffed with antiques: suits of armour, a wooden chest inscribed 'Maria Lehnerin 1790', a milk churn and an apple press, wooden crucifixes and statues, fencing swords and masks, and darkened oil paintings of fox hunts and solemn clerics. In an elegantly furnished sitting-room, platters of bread, cheese and sausage were laid on a low table. The Baroness sprawled over a sofa, still dressed in her army pants and tweed jacket, chain-smoking and drinking beer from a mug with an 'H' insignia. Hanging on the wall was an oil painting of a woman who bore a striking resemblance to the Baroness, except that she wore a long dress with a bustle and cinched waist. 'My grandmother,' said the Baroness, with a dismissive wave of her cigarette.

Silently I wondered what she'd make of her tough grand-daughter, who for two decades had been single-handedly running the family estate. 'My sister ran away to the States when she was twenty,' the Baroness told us. 'She hated aristocratic life. First, she worked as a cleaner in California; now is she rich. She cannot understand why I stayed here.'

Neither she nor her sister had children. 'This is old Austria,' she said, her blue eyes twinkling. 'Soon it will be gone.'

A few miles downstream from Hagenau there was a hydro-electric dam, and on the bank next to it a small castle in a state of total disrepair.

'It used to be lived in by Baron von Weinigen,' a fisherman told us. 'It's falling down because these days barons have to pay people to maintain their property, not like in the past, when they had slaves to do all their work. As soon as they have to pay they become stingy. You just have to look at what's happening to Hagenau down there.'

Without bothering to tell him where we'd spent the last three days, we carried on.

We spent that night camped in a wet field on the outskirts of Neuhaus. We'd come, it appeared, to the wrong side of the river, as the good restaurants and bars were in the old town on the opposite bank. The one pub we found looked fairly promising from the outside, with a blackboard menu offering various meaty dinners. Inside, a mirrored ball twirled from the ceiling and cast prismatic beams of light over men with shaven heads, scarred faces and tattooed arms who banged on game machines and bent over the pool table. At tables laden with mugs of beer and over-flowing ashtrays, other men with bad teeth, ruddy cheeks and big ears were playing cards. At our sudden appearance, all conversation stopped. The men turned round from their game machines, put down their cards and pool cues, and stared at us. Their eyes travelled up our thermal longjohns and shorts, roamed over our bright orange kayaking jackets, and finally came to rest on our faces. We tried to smile back, but any attempt at plain niceness dissolved in the face of such open hostility. From the corner of my mouth I muttered, 'Let's get out of here,' but the owners of the pub, who were just as ferocious-looking as their clients, had already descended on us. They pulled out chairs at an empty table and handed us menus. A sudden change was evinced when Dag spoke to them in German. They stepped back sharply, their faces filled with disbelief, and made no move to prevent our escape.

'What did you say?' I asked him when we were out on the street.

'I told them we didn't eat meat and asked to see the vegetarian menu.'

The humble Inn squeezed through a high, narrow canyon before finally surrendering to the Danube at the ancient city of Passau. And we left a quiet river and joined a busy waterway. Big tour boats with brass bands playing on the top deck churned up and down the river under Passau's two bridges and past its historic cathedral. Ostentatious motor yachts roared by. At the city limits, water skiers were towed by speedboats. Holidaymakers waved to us from their deckchairs on wooden houseboats. Cargo boats heaped with coal chugged by, tugboats pushed barges loaded with second-hand cars, often with mechanics busily working on the engines, on the way to be sold in Hungary and Czechoslovakia. And, for the first time on our trip around the world, we encountered other kayakers.

A day's paddle downstream of Passau, as we followed a winding stretch of the river through a steep, pretty valley, the rather elderly members of a kayak club began to overtake us.

'Good morning!' called their leader, a stout grey-haired man wearing a hat with a feather in the band.

'For fuck's sake,' Dag muttered behind me, 'there's a load of old fogeys catching up with us.'

I pointed out that, unlike us in our heavily loaded kayak on a 600-mile journey, they were in empty, lightweight racing boats, and only going as far as the next dam. This did nothing to assuage his ruffled ego.

'You haf a nice boat!' commented a septuagenarian as he paddled by.

'Thanks,' said Dag, rather grudgingly, 'but it's much slower than yours.'

'Ah not to worry,' the man cried over his shoulder. 'Remember that the vay is the goal!'

Infuriated by this remark, Dag began paddling as if being chased by a hippo. 'Faster, Maria!' he cried. 'There's a grey-haired granny right on our tail!'

'Good morning!' she greeted us as she cruised by. 'It's a fine morning for the river!'

'Her hair isn't grey,' I teased a seething Dag. 'It's blue-rinsed.'

The river became as regulated as a city suburb. In campsites along the banks, caravans were hung with potted geraniums and surrounded by picket fences, men fished from garden chairs and women hung out lines of washing. There were distance markers every hundred metres and every kilometre along both banks. There were 'Yield' signs where tributaries flowed into the main channel. A thousand yards before each dam, signs appeared warning of their presence, more signs told us on which side of the river we should portage, a '*Sportboot Umsetzanlage*' (sport boat system) sign told us exactly where we should pull out, where the carts were, where we should leave them when we'd finished and the route of the portage. There were signs pointing to telephones where the skippers of big boats could talk to the lock-keepers, and signs explaining how to use the telephones. Men in green overalls cleared the grass around these signs with scythes. Such orderliness was depressing; we were beginning to feel we were on a road rather than a river. But at least the valley was in a wilder state, heavily forested, dotted with churches and castles, and breathtakingly beautiful – until we got to Linz.

The river widened, the valley flattened out, and beyond the town of Linz were six miles of industrial horror: chemical factories, electric generating plants, mines, a forest of smoking chimneys – the air smelled foul and the river was unspeakably polluted. We wished we'd been less disparaging about the campsites further upstream, and stopped earlier in the day. At 9.00 pm, we went ashore at a motor boat marina. Dead fish floated belly-up in the river, and the ramp was covered with dark green mud.

'Don't step on that mud,' said Dag. 'It will rot your sandals.'

We set up our tent on scrubby, littered grass, with a panoramic view over the industrial spread on the far bank. It was a dispiriting end to a long day, during which we'd covered fifty miles and three done portages around hydro-electric dams. Despite darkness still being an hour away, by 9.30 we were in bed.

Although I'd regularly immersed my whole body in the River Ganges, I was now wary of even sticking my big toe into the Danube. Next morning, we eschewed our usual pot of tea boiled up from river water, and resolved to stop for a late breakfast at the next town. Our hoped-for breakfast turned into lunch, as there were two dams between our campsite and the town of Mauthausen. We reached there as the clouds that had been glowering at us all morning started lashing us with rain. Along the waterfront, touring cyclists hurriedly locked their bikes to railings and dashed for the cover of cafés and bars. We followed suit, and soon we were sitting amid a horde of well-toned forty- to fifty-year-olds in brand-new outfits of lycra tights and matching jackets, T-shirts, helmets and gloves. The men ran their fingers through neat, well-cut hair, the women took tiny mirrors out of their waist pouches and checked their smoothly tanned faces.

'How do they do it?' I whispered to Dag.

'Do what?'

He was busily scrutinizing the menu, which offered pork in various forms, potatoes in various forms and something which literally translated as 'old bread dumplings'.

'How do they manage to look so smart? I'm always such a mess.'

'You're not a mess,' he said, without raising his eyes from the menu.

'I am!' I insisted, looking despairingly at my dirty fingernails, my rumpled shorts and my longjohns bagging around the knees.

'I'm glad you'd don't look like them,' he said kindly. 'I prefer you kind of battered and rugged.'

Crushed by this remark, I stalked off to find a wash basin and mirror. Both were in the cupboard-sized toilet cubicle next to the kitchen. Although there was no plug in the basin, and no towel or soap, ten months of roughing it had left me adept at washing in such circumstances. I stripped off to my underwear and turned on the hot tap. An evil-looking purplish liquid flowed out. The cold tap proffered the same and so, I soon discovered, did the toilet cistern. I put my clothes back on, avoided looking at myself in the mirror and returned to roast pork and old bread dumplings.

Despite all the dams, we made fast progress, averaging thirty miles a day, until we hit the wine-growing area. Soon, the smoking chimneys of Linz, only two days upstream, seemed like a barely remembered nightmare. We sat outside fifteenth-century buildings, shaded by trellises of grape vines, drinking wine made on the premises. Dag introduced me to *griebenschmalz*, creamy lard dotted with lumps of crisp pork fat, which is traditionally eaten with heavy bread, and is said to line the stomach and facilitate more wine consumption. We tested this theory and found it worked.

'Is it possible to paddle on all fours?' Dag asked me during a four-hour lunch break we took in Wiebenkirchen-Wachau, 'because I think I might have to.'

Late one afternoon, with both of us nursing hangovers, we reached a dam where the '*Sportboot Umsetzanlage*' sign had another tacked beneath it: '*Ausser Betrieb*' – out of order. We paddled to the telephone, and Dag spoke briefly to the lock-keeper. 'He says we can go through.'

'Through what?'

'The lock. He's going to open it for us.'

'For *us?*'

The locks were massive structures, built for the river's long, narrow, multi-ton tourist and cargo boats.

'The portage route is blocked off. We have to stay here until the green light shows.'

The light on the river bank was red. As we waited, the bow of a barge slowly emerged above the lock gate. The gates opened, and a tug pushed the barge out into the river and past us. The light changed to green and we paddled forwards. When we were halfway along the lock a voice boomed from a loudspeaker, 'Drive no further!' We stopped next to an iron ladder that was flat against the concrete wall, and I had an irrational desire to tie up the kayak to one of the rungs. Behind us, with much dramatic chain-rattling and grinding, the gate closed, and we began to sink. The soupy green water sucked and gurgled, as if flowing down a giant plughole, then began to rush, boom and roar. Strong currents swirled around us and pulled us into the middle of the lock, and we had to paddle hard to keep the boat pointing ahead. I felt like Alice in Wonderland: the slimy brown walls stretched above me, the yellow lights at the top of them grew ever more tiny, the control buildings shrank away, the sky became a narrow slot. Then the water ceased to rush and gurgle, and stilled. Ahead, with more rattling and grinding, two huge black gates began to open; a crack of daylight appeared, then a heron winging by and behind it a wooded hillside. The green light flashed and we paddled forwards. For our sakes, to ease our journey to Budapest, millions of cubic feet of water had been displaced. High above us, a window opened in one of the control buildings. We waved and shouted our thanks to whoever it was who had just performed this miracle.

Twenty-seven portages, one lock and 450 miles from Innsbruck, we paddled into Vienna in the midst of a terrific thunderstorm. For several hours, fat drops of rain had bounced off the surface of the river, and worked their way down our collars and inside our spray skirts. Looking like a pair of drowned rats, we disembarked at some stone steps that led up to a long, low, wooden building. A large sign announced it to be the clubhouse of 'Friends of Nature, Paddlesports Division'.

We stepped through a side door, and into a hangar-like room, where rows and rows of kayaks and canoes of every description were stacked to the ceiling. Among them, brandishing a feather duster, was a diminutive woman wearing rubber boots, a blue cotton dress and a pink cardigan.

'Excuse me—'

'Waaaaahhh!' she screeched, scared out of her wits by our sudden appearance.

When she recovered from the fright, she told us that of course we could stay in the clubhouse, that usually people camped on the far bank, but the weather was so dreadful, and, besides, she could do with a spot of company. Frau Hansi, caretaker of the Vienna Friends of Nature clubhouse, led us between the rows of kayaks, and into a small locker-room where she said we could sleep. Next door was a cement-floored bathroom with two shower stalls and a washing machine. While we carried our kayak into the hangar and our baggage into the locker-room, Frau Hansi swabbed down the bathroom with a hosepipe and brush, and sang Edith Piaf songs in a warbling voice. Then she made us tea, fed us her home-made poppy cake and introduced us to her fifteen-year-old cat, Witch. She gave us maps and guidebooks of Vienna, two train tickets that she insisted we could repay her for later, an umbrella and a key so that we could get back into the clubhouse after she'd gone to bed.

In Vienna, we discovered, a glass of champagne was cheaper than a cup of coffee, and our three days there passed in a blur. Happily, we wandered along winding cobbled streets where double doors were thrown open on to imposing balconies, and the strains of oboes and pianos drifted out. In the main squares we stared at statues of winged horses and of plump women naked save for the veils drifting across their torsos. In old tea houses we sat at marble-topped tables and were served with exquisite cream cakes by waiters in tuxedos. We went to the opera, we wandered around art galleries. We ate vast quantities of sauerkraut and sausages. In the flea market we watched Eastern European refugees sort through piles of second-hand clothes. Outside a bar we saw swaggering neo-Fascist teenagers with bald heads and tattoos become thoroughly confused when three drunk Africans jovially gave them the Nazi salute.

Before we left Vienna, Frau Hansi scrubbed the stone steps that led from the clubhouse into the river. Then she stood in her rubber boots, holding Witch under one arm, waving goodbye until we paddled out of sight.

The Hungarian border post was a small wooden hut on the right bank of the river. Sitting outside it in the morning sunshine were three guards in brown uniforms. We paddled up to them and held our passports aloft, but they casually waved us on. Soon, the ugly brown and yellow high-rises of Bratislava appeared on the left bank, in Czechoslovakia. A pall of smog hung over the city, and stinking sewage gushed out of large pipes and into the river. We were low on food and needed to stop to buy more supplies, but couldn't face going ashore at such an unpleasant place. Unfortunately, there were no more villages further on, only miles of construction work for a new dam, and then an area where grassy dykes concealed any sign of life beyond the river. By midday, when we were peckish, thirsty and thoroughly fed up, the dykes on the left bank spread into a grassy area surrounded by trees. Some picnic tables were set on it, and a wooden kiosk with a Coca-Cola sign.

'Let's stop.'

'It's on the Czechoslovakian side.'

'So? The Hungarians didn't even try to stop us.'

'They might be stricter here.'

'It's only a little kiosk. There won't be any border guards around.'

'We don't have any Czechoslovakian money.'

'They're bound to take Hungarian.'

By the time we decided that we should stop, the current had taken us past the kiosk and we had to turn the kayak and paddle hard upstream. Two men were sitting on a picnic table, watching us approach. As we came nearer, one of them lifted a pair of binoculars to his eyes. It was only when we were alongside the shore, and the two men stood and advanced upon us, that I realized we'd paddled right into the arms of the Czechoslovakian police.

'Where are your entry stamps for Czechoslovakia? Where are your visas?' barked one of the policemen, flipping through our passports. We tried to explain, but he carried on firing questions at us.

'Where is this visa from? And this one? What country were you in last? Hungary? But you have no entry stamp! And before Hungary? Austria? But there is no stamp!'

Pulling out a notepad and pencil, he laboriously recorded our names, address, ages, professions and then our movements over the past ten months.

'Before Germany you were where?'

'Malawi.'

'Where is this?'

'Africa.'

'Spell this place!'

'And before then, where were you?' and so on.

Finally, he asked about the boat. 'What is its name?'

'Feathercraft.'

'Feetharcrift? What does this mean? Spell this!'

When the interrogation was complete, he opened up a green canvas bag, pulled out an old bush telephone and spoke into the receiver for several minutes. He rang off, slipped our passports into his top pocket, and smiled at us.

'We wait.'

'For what?'

'For a decision.'

'About what?'

'About you and your Feetharcrift. While you wait, please buy coffee.'

This caused further confusion. Our wallets yielded Hungarian forints, German marks, Austrian schillings, Malawian kwatcha, Indian rupees and Canadian dollars, but no Czechoslovakian koren. A dog snarled at me from beneath the kiosk, and the coffee we finally managed to purchase was too strong for me to drink. I offered it to one of the policemen, who suspiciously accepted it, as if he thought I was attempting to bribe him. After what seemed like an age, another policeman arrived, toting a sub-machine-gun. He pulled out a notebook and pencil.

'Your names?' he asked. 'The countries you have been?'

After another long laborious question-and-answer session, he scrutinized our passports for a full five minutes, then handed them back to us.

'You can go,' he regretfully told us. 'You do not need a stamp.'

There was no point tarrying along this part of the river. The small towns and villages we stopped at on the Hungarian side were grim and unfriendly, and the industrial wasteland continued along the Czechoslovakian bank. We covered sixty miles that day, and set up camp in the dark on a narrow strip of sand in front of a dense clump of trees. Clouds of mosquitos forced us into the tent to eat our lentil soup and bread. A barge, lit up like a birthday cake, slid by, and throughout the night the sound of heavy machinery and trucks drifted from the opposite shore.

Next day, just before we reached the city of Esztergom, a police motor launch zoomed upstream past us, did a U-turn and came alongside.

'What country?'

'Canada and England.'

'Where are your flags?'

This stumped us. We weren't using our sail on the river, and so didn't have a mast up. Even if we'd had flags along with us, we would have had nowhere to fly them from.

'It is law for vessels to fly the flag of their origin and the flag of Hungary!'

After extracting solemn promises from us that we would buy a Hungarian flag at the earliest opportunity, they let us go.

The campsite at Esztergom was clean, friendly, and extremely organized.

'Tonight's World Cup game is between England and Sweden,' an unseen person announced over a loudspeaker in Hungarian, German and English. 'You can watch it in the bar at eight pm.'

At eight o'clock sharp, the voice barked, 'The game has started! Come now if you intend to watch!'

Exactly twelve hours later, the voice was back. 'In ten minutes, helicopters will be spraying this area with insecticide as a precaution against mosquitos. You may wish to stay inside your caravans and tents.'

Men in dressing-gowns and women in nightdresses and pink slippers emerged from the shower houses and hurried along the concrete paths and into their caravans. Early risers, sitting at their plastic tables and enjoying breakfast in the sun, frantically started clearing away coffee cups and plates of toast. We clambered into our tent and peered through our flyscreen at the two choppers circling the town's huge domed basilica. They flew low over the remains of the Friendship Bridge, which until the last war had connected Hungary and Czechoslovakia. As their noise grew and they approached the campsite, we zipped up all the screens. The poisonous insecticide settled around us for half an hour before we emerged to complete our journey to Budapest.

What first struck me about Budapest, apart from the air pollution caused by its poorly tuned cars, was the preponderance of young, pretty girls walking large, hairy dogs. It was the third week of June, and hot; the girls bounced along wearing lacy off-the-shoulder blouses and tight mini-skirts. They paused to let their dogs pee against one of the old lamp posts on the Elizabeth Street embankment, and paid no heed to us or the kayak we were busily taking apart.

'They are the most beautiful girls in the world! I see on the television women in other countries, and against our Budapest girls they are nothing, nothing!'

Denes had been watching Sky Vision since we arrived in his third-storey apartment on the Pest side of the river.

'There is a concert for Paul McCartney in England!' he announced. 'Do you know Liverpool? Penny Lane, the Cavern?'

I told him I had been a student in Liverpool, that I used to shop on Penny Lane.

'Oh, you are so lucky to be from the West and to know Liverpool! It is my dream to go there.'

His apartment had high ceilings and long shuttered windows. Cream paint was flaking from the walls, which were hung with oil paintings of Denes's grandparents and great-grandparents. Above the television there was a framed map of Hungary showing its pre-Second World War boundaries.

'Ah! BBC news!' cried Denes. 'You want to see?'

There were depressing reports of the war in Yugoslavia, only a hundred miles or so away along the Danube. And there was an announcement that Czechoslovakia was dividing into two separate states.

'I do not blame the Czechs!' cried Denes. 'The Slovakians are ignorant sheep farmers!'

His wife Clara served us with tea, and a big bowl of cherries. Our connection with her family was tenuous: Dag's brother was a friend of Denes's brother, who lived in Germany. But they had made us instantly welcome. 'Tomorrow we go to the beach,' she said. 'Please come with us.'

We spent a morning racing around Budapest being tourists. The mediaeval town of Buda had delightful architecture, but was chock full of monster tour buses and crowds of Japanese and American tourists being led around by guides holding aloft rolled-up umbrellas. In Pest, the commercial and administrative heart of the city, Baroque statues erupted from the walls of buildings, ornate carvings curled around balconies and arched doorways, and shop windows had signs in German, Japanese and English. In courtyards, statues stood in niches, and old trees grew between flagstones. One such courtyard led into Denes's and Clara's apartment building .

'We will stop for lunch on the way to the beach,' announced Denes. 'We will eat real Hungarian food!'

We squeezed into a Trabant with Clara, Denes, his father and his father's girlfriend. The restaurant we drove to was shabby and smoky and packed with customers. 'I will translate the menu for you,' offered Denes. 'What is good is this: bone soup with lozenge, letter salad, swine stew with noodles, small strips of boiled paste strewn. All is prepared with goose fat, all is good.'

We took his word for it, and worked our way through a heavy, meaty lunch. The bill came, and was handed to Dag.

'How much?' asked Denes, looking over his shoulder. 'That's good,' he commented, but made no move to contribute.

The beach, an hour's drive from the city, was a grassy area next to a flooded quarry. It was like any public beach, crowded with red-skinned people smearing themselves with sun cream, harassed mothers trying to stop children wandering and bored fathers reading the newspaper. There were pedallos for rent and lots of food kiosks. Dag and I went for a swim in the cloudy water; when we returned, Denes and his family had settled themselves down on rugs.

'Would you like to drink something?' asked Denes. 'Yes? I will come with you to get.' He took everyone's orders. Clara wanted a Coca-Cola, Denes's father wanted beer, his girlfriend wanted beer and ice-cream. On hearing this Clara decided she wanted ice-cream too, and Denes's father announced he wanted sausages and bread.

'We buy beer, sausages, bread and ice-cream for everyone,' said Denes, the 'we' meaning Dag and me.

'You are so lucky in the West!' cried Denes as he accompanied us to the kiosks. 'Everyone is so rich!'

Soon, we all set off again to visit the historic town of Szentendre. Following a brief tour round its Baroque buildings and its Serbian religious memorials, we all trooped into a rather expensive-looking restaurant and sat in a courtyard shaded by vines. Again, Denes ordered for everyone: coffee, cake and schnapps. The schnapps came first, Denes made a toast to the two brave kayakers, we all downed the fiery liquid, and Denes's father ordered a second round. After the cream-laden cakes were consumed, a third round of schnapps was deemed necessary to help finish off the second pot of coffee. In due course the bill came, and was handed to us.

Back in Denes and Clara's apartment, we had another bowl of cherries and two hours of MTV. As soon as darkness fell, Denes announced it was time for dinner, and we all trooped back into the Trabant and off to yet another restaurant. I peeked into my wallet, and found it contained only six hundred florints, the equivalent of about three pounds. Dag had even less. He broke the news.

'Maria and I are almost out of cash.'

All around us in the car, faces dropped, and Denes slammed on the brakes. 'You have American Express cards?' he demanded.

We did. Faces brightened.

'I take you to machine which gives money!'

The machine was out of order. Gloom once again descended upon Denes and his family. They leaned out of the car windows to shake our hands.

'Goodbye,' they said. 'Good luck with the rest of your journey.'

And with that they drove off.

We took a bus back to our hotel. With the last of our change, I made a quick call to my mother in England.

'Aunt Madge has passed away,' she told me. 'The funeral's on Monday. Can you get here in time?'

27

More Pubs Than Paddling

'You vill haf to pay!'

'But we have round-the-world tickets!'

'These round-the-vorld tickets! Phah!'

An angry red flush was spreading up the neck of the British Airways duty officer in Munich Airport. 'Your tickets say Munich–London, and you come for the Manchester flight, and you come late and vith all this big luggage – vot do you expect?'

I'd been arguing with her for half an hour, and the flight left in twenty minutes. 'Mrs Foster in the city office said that—'

'Mrs Foster sits in her office and issues orders! She does not look at tickets! Ve do that!'

'Listen,' I said through gritted teeth, 'we have to get to a funeral.'

Behind tortoiseshell glasses, her eyes flickered to the computer screen and gleamed with triumph. 'The Manchester flight has closed!'

Dag came striding over from his negotiations with the airport manager. 'The bags are going through!' he said. 'Now we just need the ticket changed.'

'I vill not—!' began the duty officer.

She was interrupted by a woman with permed hair who pushed in ahead of us.

'Excuse me, love!' she shouted at the duty officer. 'I just got off the flight from London and I left me cardie on the plane, it's pink with bluebirds embroidered on it, can someone get it for me?'

The airport manager arrived and curtly asked the duty officer to hurry up with our ticket change.

'What about me cardie?' wailed the woman. 'I need it for me holidays!'

The duty officer looked about to explode. '*Vot is a cardie?*' she cried.

As if to teach us a lesson, the landing at Manchester Airport was terrifying. The plane bucketed down towards the runway, its wings waggling about and its fuselage vibrating so hard that the overhead lockers sprang open. With nervous smiles, the stewardesses scurried to close them, and an apprehensive silence fell over the cabin. Dinky cars streamed along a motorway, the fields of Cheshire zoomed up towards us, airport buildings jumped about, there was an almighty thump, the brakes screeched and the plane gave a final shake and decided not to disintegrate after all. Up and down the cabin, people broke into relieved guffaws and the man behind me said, 'Did you see the photos of that plane to Hawaii, when the front just sort of peeled off and everyone was sitting there all covered in blood?'

My mother took one look at us and set about borrowing clothes for us to wear at the funeral. Our pleas about the hot, muggy weather fell on deaf ears: Dag was stuffed into a suit, tie and shoes, and I into a black dress and high heels. The funeral was a drawn-out affair; during the eighty-one years of her life, Aunt Madge had never been known to hurry, so it was fitting that her send-off was conducted at a leisurely pace. There were two church services, the burial and a post-funeral reception in a restaurant. Finally, we all adjourned to my mother's house. The men sat in the garden, eating endless plates of meat sandwiches and drinking tea, beer and whisky. The women jockeyed for position in the kitchen, good-naturedly squabbling over who should wash up and make sandwiches and pour drinks for the men. I'd forgotten the rules of this game. After standing around for a while with a tea towel, trying to grab something from the drying rack, I gave up and went out to the garden. Accusing glares from the kitchen window reminded me that this was the wrong thing to do. Dag wasn't faring much better. He'd disgraced himself by dozing off during the Requiem Mass, and now his eyelids were drooping and his head nodding as one of my cousins gave him a detailed account of his children's academic progress. When Dag excused himself and went upstairs to bed, my relatives exchanged suspicious looks,

'It's only five o'clock,' said one.

'It's the heat,' I lamely explained, picking up a tea towel. 'And jet-lag.'

When the funeral was over, we hired a car and spent three days driving around northern England and visiting my old friends. Most of them were busy with careers and children, and had work schedules and time pressures that for us had become a distant memory. We found it hard to understand their annoyance when we turned up late for dinner; they were puzzled by our insouciance. We tried to adapt. Racing from Leeds to Sheffield in order to arrive in time for another dinner, we were involved in a motorway crash. Life by kayak, we decided, was far simpler, and preferable, to this.

Dag's sleepiness had persisted, and soon as we got back to my mother's house, he went straight to bed. After a couple of hours I went up to check on him. He was fully dressed, wrapped up in bedclothes, and shivering.

'What's wrong?' I asked.

'Nothing,' he replied through chattering teeth. 'I'm practising for Alaska.'

We both had blood and stool tests. The results showed that Dag had malaria and was mildly jaundiced, and that I had three intestinal parasites, two of which the doctor had never heard of before. Six days passed before Dag was in any shape to start travelling again. It was now the second week of July. At the beginning of August, we were due back in Canada. Going to Alaska, as we'd planned, would mean us extending our trip, and also running into the storm season there. We were both feeling jaded. Being jaded amid Alaska's storms, bears and freezing waters did not seem like a good idea. Being jaded in our beachfront house in southern British Columbia did.

'But what about the Jungle to Ice Expedition?' I asked Dag.

'I was thinking about that,' Dag said. 'If we go for a quick trip to the west coast of Ireland instead, we could white out the "Ice" on our letterheads and write in "Ireland".'

Two days later, the Jungle to Ireland Expedition set off from Manchester Bus Station, bound for Cork.

'Jasus, what's in this bag?' asked the taxi driver who took us from Kenmare out to the estuary.

'A kayak,' Dag told him.

'And what the fook would that be?'

'A canoe.'

'A canoo! Are ye off canooing? Well, ye have a fine soft day for it, thank God.'

The 'fine soft day' meant there was a steady, soaking drizzle. By the time we'd put the 'canoo' together I was shivering. We waded into what felt like bitterly cold water, carrying the boat clear of barnacle-covered rocks.

'The north Atlantic sure is different to the South Pacific,' Dag cheerfully commented.

I tried to ignore him as he chirped on.

'Isn't it good to smell seaweed and salt air again? Hey look, there's a seal! Maria? Maria? Are you all right?'

A stiff wind whipped up waves and threw cold spray in our faces. After what seemed like an age of paddling, I demanded we stop for a break.

'It's a bit early,' said Dag. 'We've only been going an hour.'

On either side of the estuary there were rolling green hills and a sprinkling of modern, characterless bungalows. At six o'clock, after a six-mile paddle, we pulled into a bay that had a beach at its far end. An old man in baggy pants and a sleeveless cardigan over his shirt was tramping through the reeds along the seashore, followed by a pack of nine sheepdogs.

'Ara, put the tent where ye like,' he said, when we asked him about camping. 'There'll be nobody to bother ye.'

Nobody except several bearded goats, two donkeys, a pony, eight cows and a massive bull, peering at us from the long grass and wild foxgloves behind the beach. The goats, donkeys and cows became skittish as we paddled up. But the bull was unperturbed, ruminating and continuing to regard us with a steady stare.

'He'll lumber off in a minute,' Dag assured me.

Without taking his eyes off us, the bull got to his feet. Between his legs hung the biggest pair of testicles I'd ever set eyes on. He snorted and took a step forward. The testicles swung about like church bells.

'Er, maybe we'll lumber off instead,' said Dag hastily, and started to back paddle.

It was eight o'clock before we had dinner; watery beef and barley soup that lacked both beef and barley, and some good swigs of Paddy's Whiskey. For once we had our radio with us, and we listened to the marine weather forecast. It was far from promising: heavy rain, strong coastal winds.

'Where's the EPIRB?' I asked Dag.

He looked vacant. 'I think,' he said slowly, 'that it's in your mother's house.'

From the perspective of our campsite on this gentle stretch of coastline, our plan to kayak around the Beara Peninsula seemed an easy jaunt. But our map told a different story. Contour lines veered together to show the steep cliffs and exposed headlands that awaited us. Our epic journey was nearly over, and in less than two weeks we'd be home. After all our experiences I should have been feeling stout-hearted and ready for anything; instead I was feeling decidedly wimpy. Dag's resolve, however, was strengthening by the minute.

'There's a village seven miles from here,' he said. 'It's bound to have a pub. Shall we hike over for a pint?'

A thick grey mist shrouded our world next morning. On opening the tent door I came face to face with a donkey. It raised its head from the grass it was munching and peered at me through the fog, blinking its long eyelashes.

'It's a ghost,' said Dag.

'I recognize it from last night,' I told him. 'It was with that bull.'

'It can't be the same one, we're half a mile away from that beach.'

From behind the tent came snapping sounds. I crawled out, and saw bearded goats breaking sapling trees with their front legs then chewing on them. A cow mooed. From somewhere deep in the fog came a derisive snorting.

'I think we should go,' said Dag, and we broke camp in record time.

Sun broke through the mist, the wind blew up and the clouds scudded away. The coastline became increasingly dramatic, rising into cliffs that met steep green fields. The clouds scampered back and playfully sprinkled us with rain. On the horizon a band of blue sky appeared above blue open ocean. Half an hour later, sky and ocean were grey, and the clouds above us had turned decidedly nasty. Rain lashed down, stinging our faces and hands. Around noon we reached Kilmakilloge Harbour, and sprinted into its shelter. We tied the kayak to a high stone pier that had a thick growth of seaweed. A jumble of lobster pots, nets, plastic buckets, gaff hooks and ropes lay strewn over the dock, and a man in a bright orange waterproof coat was picking through it.

'Where's Bunaw?' I asked him.

'Sure ye're here already!' he said, pointing to a small yellow building with a slate roof a hundred yards away.

The village of Bunaw was basically a pub and a resilient palm tree. We dashed past the tree, which was shuddering in the wind, and into the pub. On one side of a narrow hallway, raincoats hung from pegs. On the other side a broad-beamed woman in a full pinafore sat behind a counter heaped with bars of chocolate. This was the village store. It reminded me of a school tuck shop.

'If it's a drink you're wanting,' said the woman, pointing to a door next to the raincoats, 'it's through there in that room.'

'That room' had a bar just long enough for eight stools set close together. Its walls were gloss-painted in lime green and yellow. A sticky fly strip, thick with dead flies, hung from a fluorescent light. A shy barmaid with pale skin took our order for two hot whiskeys. As we warmed our hands on the glasses the man in the orange coat came in behind us. 'So you found your way?' he said. 'This girl here is Niamh, the postman's daughter. She pulls a foyn point.'

The girl blushed. Dag leaned over to me. 'What's a foyn point?' he whispered.

'A fine pint,' I translated.

'Make that three pints of Guinness as well,' said Dag, and the man beamed with pleasure.

'That's awful decent of you. What now are ye up to in that canoo?'

When I told him of our plan he shook his head. 'There's fierce seas out there. Once ye get out of this bay and along the way a bit ye'll feel them. There was a man, he had a foyn sailboat, been everywhere in it he had, he went down just south of here.'

The pinafored woman came into the bar.

'Hello there, Joan,' the man greeted her. 'I'm waiting here for the bread.'

'Ah well, usually he's here by ten,' she told him, 'but today, now, it could be two o'clock by the time he comes.'

The door of the bar was held open with a brick, as if the day was sweltering and we needed fresh air. Outside, a sign advertising ice-cream batted to and fro in the wind, rain fell horizontally, and a lane wound away between stone walls and disappeared in the low mist. Abruptly, the view was blocked by a large van which pulled up outside the pub.

'Here's your bread now!' Joan announced. 'Be quick and get what you want, they'll all be down on me soon enough.'

Within half an hour, the bar was full of men clutching loaves of sliced bread in waxed paper and drinking pints of Guinness. News of our plans spread quickly, and everyone had a story for us.

'An Irishman I know, he had a canoo like yours and he had a terrible time off the Blaskets.'

'Have ye been tossed out a' that canoo yet? Ah well, you will here.'

By three o'clock, hail was pelting down. Four soaked French cyclists squeezed into the pub and asked Joan, who was helping Niamh behind the bar, if she had any rooms for the night.

'You're lucky,' she said. 'I have two rooms left and with these people from the canoo I'm full up now.'

I leaned over to Dag to break the news that we were staying the night, but he was busy trying to follow what a ruddy-faced man was telling him.

'For fook's sake, there's thirty-knot winds forecast for tomorrow. It's the likes of me that'll have to go out there and rescue the pair of ye. We'll never forgive you if you go.'

An elbow dug into my back. 'Sorry for disturbing yees, I'm on a mission from God to get to the bar,' the owner of the elbow apologized. 'Five points of Guinness, when you're ready, Niamh.'

He looked at my glass. 'Jasus, what's that you're drinking?'

I'd reverted to Ballygowan sparkling water. The bottle boasted that it had been 'enjoyed for over 800 years'.

'Christ, that's terrible stuff,' he said. 'Niamh! Another point for this poor girl!'

Somewhere around late afternoon, Joan extracted us and the four cyclists from the bar. She led us across the hallway and into her living-room, sat us down at a large table and fed us with fish and dill soup, plates of cold salmon, tuna and mackerel with salad and fresh raspberries and cream. By the time we returned to the pub, the crowd had spilled out into the hallway, and a couple of musicians had arrived and were playing the fiddle and 'bones' – a percussion instrument made from smooth pieces of cow bones that were slapped together like spoons. Waves of Guinness were coming over the bar; pint glasses of it were passed over people's heads and handed to us, and then shot glasses of whiskey followed. A pall of smoke hung just below the ceiling; I noticed that the fly strip was gone.

'Christ, I'm out of moy head,' said a red-nosed fellow next to me. 'I had a skinful last noight, and I slept till eleven today, and I belted over to Kenmare for a bag o' plaster and I got there at ten past twelve and hadn't the fooking place closed for the day at twelve? So I thought, what'll I do with miself? I thought about it for a while and I decided to come to the pub.'

'Ow many sheeps 'ave you?' one of the cyclists was asking a farmer.

'Oh, mebbe a thousand.'

'So what is this work you do with sheep? You walk in the mountains and do what? Do you count them?'

'Now and then we do, aye.'

'And you 'ave to remove the wool, yes?'

'Hey, Dag!' shouted one of the musicians. 'How about a song from your country? Give us the one about the sheep-shagging kangaroo!'

'He's a Canadian, you fooking eejit!' his friend retorted. More and more customers crowded in; the pall of smoke became a cloud and hung around our ears; the musicians could barely be heard over the hubbub of voices. It looked like a party that could go on for hours, but just before midnight Joan shut the bar and started shooing people out of the door. 'Get up to bed now,' she told us. 'I've put hot water bottles in there for ye.'

What seemed like minutes later, Dag shook me awake.

'The weather's good! Let's get going!'

'What time is it?' I mumbled, burrowing down beneath the covers.

'It's seven o'clock already! I asked Joan for breakfast at seven-thirty. Get up!'

We sat in the O'Sullivans' living-room for half an hour. The table was laid for breakfast, but the house was as silent as if everyone had died in the night. At eight o'clock some hopeful sounds from upstairs presaged only the four cyclists, who joined us in the living-room, gazing dolefully out of the window. The wind was steadily picking up; there were white-capped waves in the harbour and fishing boats were scuttling in for shelter. No one said much; we were all nursing dreadful hangovers. At nine o'clock Niamh rushed through the living-room and into the large kitchen beyond it. After five minutes, the smell of frying bacon came drifting through to us.

'Pig,' grumbled one of the cyclists. 'Always pig. Bacon and sausages and 'am and, 'ow do they call it – gammon. I am sick of it.'

Niamh put her head round the doorway. 'There's bacon, sausage, eggs, black pudding, beans, tomato, toast. D'ye all want everything?'

'Of course!' cried the grumbler.

Breakfast improved everyone's mood, but the weather continued to deteriorate. By the time Niamh was clearing away the plates, rain was lashing at the window. ' 'Tis terrible out there,' she said. 'Sure, I hope ye're planning on staying here another night?'

Trying to leave Bunaw was one of the most difficult challenges we'd faced over the past eleven months. Our tiny, warm bedroom, to which we retreated after breakfast, felt like a nest; we snoozed and read all morning while the wind howled outside, and we were only roused when a fiddler started tuning up in the bar for a lunchtime session. The bar stayed open all afternoon; Joan whipped up another delicious dinner; people were jigging about to the fiddler's tunes until 11.00 pm. The next day brought no improvement in the weather, but the four French cyclists donned green waterproof capes and resolutely set off in the teeth of the wind. We were shamed into making a move. We packed up and wandered disconsolately to our boat.

'It's wild out there today,' warned a fisherman. 'If ye go, it'll be the last we see of ye.'

Hitch-hiking with a boat in our baggage down the Beara Peninsula proved remarkably easy. We stood by the side of the road in the pouring rain next to two sodden red sacks, and never waited for more than five minutes for a lift. The first was with an English girl who wore a Barbour jacket and green wellington boots, and who drove fast along the narrow lanes lined with stone walls and hedgerows of wild fuchsia. The second lift was with a toothless young farmer who talked non-stop to Dag all the way to Allihies without Dag understanding a single word. He drove us straight through Allihies village, which took about ten seconds, and to the bay where, if we'd been kayaking, we would have come ashore. We got out of the car and stood looking in awe and respect at the place where we'd been audacious enough to pre-sume we could land our boat. On either side of the bay were steep, forbidding cliffs; from the open ocean 20ft waves slowly rolled in and smashed against them, sending spray high into the air. There was a campsite in a field behind the beach; a lone tent was set up, and the wind was flattening the flysheet against its interior walls. 'Shall I take ye to the pub?' asked the young farmer. 'They pull a noyce point.'

The pub was larger than the one at Bunaw, more modern, but just as packed. Teenagers argued over whose turn it was on the pool table, while their young siblings sat on the floor drinking lemonade and eating crisps. Prim ladies clutched handbags on their laps and sipped at glasses of stout. Alternative types with pierced noses and Afghani hats gathered by the bar. Plump young women in tight jeans and frilly blouses leaned over the jukebox. Old men wearing crumpled hats and stained jackets played dominoes. Everyone drank steadily, and there was a lot of loud laughter. Presently the two musicians we'd met at Bunaw turned up. 'Be God, 'tis you agin. Did ye paddle here?'

They were members of a band called the Seven Kevins, and were on holiday, earning their drinks by playing in pubs. Neither of them was called Kevin. The fiddler, John, was tall and skinny with well-developed forearms, and was fashionably dressed in all black. His girlfriend Esther was on 'bones'. They were joined by an awful local guitarist, who insisted on drunkenly crooning romantic songs.

'I hope I don't fall in love with you,' he sang.

'Jasus, and I hope so too,' said the woman next to me. She told me she was from Cork City, and came to Allihies every year for her holidays. 'Me friends go off to Italy, Tunisia, Spain, but I'm not bothered with those places – there's always a great crack here.

I had me honeymoon here, and weren't all me kids conceived here, too.'

'How many have you got?'

'Three of them. Aged six, five and four.'

'You were busy for a while!'

'It was fooking hell. I felt like running off and sending them all a postcard.'

John started playing Hungarian rhapsodies; a man got up on a table and did a spot of flamenco dancing, sending glasses and bottles flying.

'Michael!' screeched the barmaid. 'Get down offa there! I've warned you before, you'll not be let in again. *Get down Michael!*'

At eleven o'clock the curtains were drawn and the front door locked. Anyone leaving had to go out the back way.

'We're fined five hundred punts if we're caught,' the barmaid confided. 'The *garda* nearly got us once, but we were too quick for them; when they came in the bar was clear. Twenty of us were hid up in the bedroom, but didn't one woman forget her baby down here and nearly give the game away?'

It was 2.00 am before we wove our way down the village street and into the bed and breakfast we'd booked into earlier in the day.

Dursey Island, at the tip of the Beara Peninsula, was blanketed in thick mist, and the cable car to it wasn't running because of the high winds.

'But, look, 'tis a beautiful place,' said the owner of a little café, showing us a postcard with a photo of the island taken on a clear, sunny day. Kayaking around the southern end of the peninsula was impossible, due to the inclement weather and sea conditions and our now chronic hangovers. We hitch-hiked over to Castletownbere, from where there was a protected stretch of water to Glengarrif. Fortified by Guinness that we drank in a bar at the back of a grocery shop, we reassembled the boat and set off.

Footsteps and voices awoke me from a deep sleep. Our campsite just outside Glengarrif was, it appeared, a meeting place for lovers. And the lovers who came across our tent and kayak were far from pleased.

'The fooking cheek o' them,' a girl said, 'putting up a fooking tent there.'

'And what the fook is that thing?' asked a male voice.

'It's a fooking canoo, you eejit!'

'Jasus, so it is, did ye ever see the like!'

Dag turned over, still half asleep. 'What language are they speaking?' he muttered. 'Where are we?'

28

Another Idea

Back in Vancouver, Doug and Larry stood in their Feathercraft workshop and regarded us with mild suspicion. We had turned up there wearing the fashionable clothes we'd bought in Europe, and looking the antithesis of a couple who claimed to have just returned from a year-long kayaking expedition. The boat was proof of our exploits. We pulled its various parts from the torn sack. The deck, once bright red, was now a faded pink. The hull was scratched, the mast was patched up, the rudder had been repaired, the sail was stained.

'Wow,' said Larry. 'We've never seen one in this condition.'

'Looks like it's been a long way,' Doug added.

A long way! That, I told him, was an understatement. Our kayak had been to five continents and fourteen countries; it had been transported by planes, buses, taxis, tractors, a luxury yacht, buffalo carts, dugout canoes, tricycle rickshaws and people's heads. It had been paddled on the Solomon Sea, down the Ganges, up Lake Malawi, along the Danube and to one of the best pubs in Ireland. It had been around the world.

But it wasn't home yet. From right outside the Feathercraft workshop, we paddled the kayak thirty miles across the Georgia Strait. People waved to us from the decks of ferries and sailing boats, surprised to see our little craft all alone in a big sea. A year before, this would have been a serious crossing for us; now it was a pleasant jaunt. There were no sharks, hippos or crocodiles to worry about; no bandits, no water spouts, no suffocating clouds of flies. All we had to do was maintain a steady rhythm, and the dramatic peaks of the mainland mountains shrank away behind us as the gentler contours of Vancouver Island rose up ahead. Familiar landmarks began to appear: Mount Benson, Nanaimo nestling at its feet, then the trees and bluffs of Protection Island, and finally the windows of our house, winking in the sunlight. Excitedly, I swivelled round in my seat and started to tell Dag how glad I was that we'd embarked on this marvellous journey together, how lucky we'd been along the way, how happy I was to be home. But he wasn't listening. He wasn't seeing me, either. His eyes had glazed over. It was an expression I knew well.

'I've just had an idea,' he said, 'about where we can go next.'

Index